BAD JULIET

BAD JULIET

GILES BLUNT

DUNDURN
PRESS

Publisher: Meghan Macdonald | Acquiring editor: Chris Houston | Editor: Jennifer Hale
Cover designer: Laura Boyle
Cover image: 123RF/andreyeremenko

Library and Archives Canada Cataloguing in Publication

Title: Bad Juliet / Giles Blunt.
Names: Blunt, Giles, author
Identifiers: Canadiana (print) 20250158965 | Canadiana (ebook) 20250159031 | ISBN
    9781459755727 (softcover) | ISBN 9781459755703 (EPUB) | ISBN 9781459755710 (PDF)
Subjects: LCGFT: Historical fiction. | LCGFT: Novels.
Classification: LCC PS8553.L867 B33 2025 | DDC C813/.54—dc23

We acknowledge the support of the Canada Council for the Arts and the Ontario Arts Council for our publishing program. We also acknowledge the financial support of the Government of Ontario, through the Ontario Book Publishing Tax Credit and Ontario Creates, and the Government of Canada.

Care has been taken to trace the ownership of copyright material used in this book. The author and the publisher welcome any information enabling them to rectify any references or credits in subsequent editions.

The publisher is not responsible for websites or their content unless they are owned by the publisher.

Dundurn Press
1382 Queen Street East
Toronto, Ontario, Canada M4L 1C9
dundurn.com, @dundurnpress

For Janna

Life can only be understood backwards; but it must be lived forwards.

— Kierkegaard

PREFACE

When a novelist has reached a certain age, the idea of writing an autobiography threatens to become irresistible. An author may feel the need to settle old scores, or "set the record straight," or perhaps unveil the scope and glory of an exciting life. The urge may reflect an ego inflated, needy, punctured, or otherwise damaged, so that the writing of a lengthy explanation of "why I did what I did" may seem not only seductive but downright medicinal. And compared to the invention of three hundred pages of fiction, the stenography of memories can appear easy. It is not.

Whatever my own impetus for writing an autobiography, however, I abandoned the project before I got as far as chapter two. The reason is simple: it had become clear that there was only one part of my life that I felt truly compelled to set down. The story takes place forty years ago in a transcendentally peculiar town surrounded by the mountains of upstate New York. In that town peopled by doctors and patients and haunted by deadly disease, I met two people who would teach me that everything I knew about love and trust and friendship was wrong. The love was real, the lessons painful, and although 1915 is a long way from 1954, the moments and scenes that follow remain forever vivid in my mind.

New York City, 1954

CHAPTER 1

"But April, Paul. April. You chose the worst possible time to play the prima donna. Every university in the country would have done their hiring for the fall. My best advice at this late date is to go back to Laurence and throw yourself on his mercy. Tell him you were under a strain. Get a neurologist to give you a diagnosis of some kind. I don't see what else you can do."

This was Simon Crawford, a former professor of mine and now a good friend. I hadn't seen him for a few months — when I am hurting I don't like to show my face — but when we bumped into each other in Central Park, he invited me to join him for dinner at Larson's Steakhouse on Broadway. It was now early autumn. I had spent the summer doing little more than reading endless newspaper accounts of the *Lusitania* disaster and the insane conflagration over in Europe. We crossed from the boat pond to the West Side, and the trees in their bright melancholy suited my mood.

Simon insisted on paying for dinner and that I order the roast beef, which was the best thing I'd tasted in months. He sat across from me offering sympathy and the kind attention of his gaze. Although not yet fifty, his hair had turned almost completely white, and his nose, long and prominent, was bracketed by parentheses that ran from bridge to jawline, giving him somewhat the look of a Roman senator.

"This is very good of you, Simon. Extremely good. Is it just a mission of mercy, or did you have something else on your mind?"

"Mission of friendship, not mercy."

Certainly, at this moment I was in need of both. It was 1915; I was twenty-two and had just thrown away a good job as lecturer in English Literature at Columbia University.

"There were five weeks left in the semester," Simon said. "Exams and papers looming on the horizon. Laurence had to scramble to fill the breach for you."

"He should have given me tenure. How many candidates have an MA at the age of twenty-two? What's the point of creating an English Literature department if you're going to hire a doddering Classics don to teach it?"

"That Classics don has a PhD from Yale. Besides, you were an employee under contract and you failed to honour it, Paul. Such things get around. It's unfortunate, but your chances of finding another position don't look good."

It had been Simon who had put in a word for me with Dean Laurence, which was essentially what got me the job I had forsaken in a ridiculous fit of pique. He was completely correct about my prospects. I had spent the rest of April and well into May writing letters of application to the few universities that were developing departments of English Literature. One or two invited me to apply again another year, but at present, they were sorry, there were no openings. By the fall the replies had ceased altogether. The fortress of academe had not only closed its doors against me but dropped the portcullis and pulled up the bridge.

"It must be a terrible blow," Simon said. "Especially coming so soon after Terrible Emily."

"Too cruel any time," I said, "but yes. I do feel pretty battered."

"Terrible Emily" was one of many epithets I had assigned to the sprightly blond Upper East Sider who had annihilated my spirit a little over a year previously. How could this diminutive creature, a blue-eyed vixen scarcely shoulder-high, inflict so much damage? One hears of people being jilted at the altar, but I always assumed such tales were exaggerations until it happened to me. Well, now I'm the one exaggerating. It wasn't right at the altar but two days before, by telegram.

Among the smells of whiskey and ale, sawdust and cigarettes, Simon talked about the exquisite pain of romantic reversals. He was surprisingly empathetic, considering that he and his wife, Caroline, were the happiest couple in my acquaintance. He waited until we had finished our main course; it was only over coffee and brandy that he finally broached what was really on his mind. "Have you ever heard," he asked me, "of a place called Saranac Lake?"

"Of course. The sanitarium is famous."

Simon nodded. "World famous."

A sudden fear gripped me. "Wait a minute. You're not saying you —"

"No, no — I'm not sick. God forbid." He rapped smartly on the wooden tabletop to ward off infection. "I have a friend up there — a physician named Alex Tissot, an old pal from Hopkins. He works at the sanitarium. It's funny, in a way. The North Country is a mighty comedown for him. He had a thriving practice on Park Avenue, treating wealthy neurasthenics, which I gather is the medical equivalent of striking oil. Anyway, one day he received the news that he had tuberculosis. Both lungs. Can you imagine?"

"Like getting a death sentence. It *is* a death sentence."

"Dire, indeed. He got a second opinion from a tuberculosis expert who wrote out a referral right then and there. He was admitted to the Adirondack Sanitarium, got treated, and much to his own surprise got well. He was so taken with what he called — still calls — the 'passion and expertise of the place' that he elected to stay. Just folded up his New York practice for good and has been up there ever since, treating patients and doing research."

"More power to him. Seems a grim line of work, though."

"One has to think not, otherwise a man of Tissot's calibre would never stay. I don't hear from him all that often, but the last time I did he was highly enthusiastic about a new program he was developing for the patients."

"I thought treatment consisted entirely of bedrest."

"Largely, not entirely. Tissot told me that one of the biggest problems they face is patient apathy. It's not much of a life lying in bed month after month, and it must begin to seem pointless after a while. To fight this malaise, he's developed a whole department devoted to patient enrichment — which is where you come in. They have various people teaching the patients languages, others teaching them practical skills from shorthand to telegraph operation to bookbinding, and they're expanding further still into Art History and English Literature."

"And he's hiring lecturers?"

"Lecturers, no. Tutors. The patients are mostly immobile, or practically so, and the teacher must go to the pupil, make his rounds like the doctors. It pays decently, considering meals and housing are covered. Anyway, he needs an English Literature teacher and the job is probably yours if you want it."

"First," I said, "thank you. Really, Simon, it's good of you to think of me. Especially —"

"Not at all. First person I thought of."

"Thank you. But you'll forgive me if I speak plainly?"

"Of course."

"You're suggesting I consider moving up into the Adirondack Mountains and live in what is essentially a leper colony."

He considered this a moment, swirling his brandy. He drank the last of it and set his glass down on the table.

"Yes," he said. "I suppose I am."

CHAPTER 2

Less than a week later, I was in Grand Central Station. The Montreal–Adirondack Express was scheduled to depart at 6:40 p.m. and arrive in Saranac Lake at 7:10 the next morning. The ticket clerk slid a form under the wicket. It informed passengers that, in the interests of public hygiene, all those travelling to or from Saranac Lake were required to check the appropriate answer to questions such as *Have you ever been diagnosed with tuberculosis? Have you experienced cough, fever, or chills within the past three weeks?*

"Very reassuring," I said, and slid it back.

"Not to worry, sir. Patients have a separate car or cars as needed. Not that there would be the slightest danger. The cars are thoroughly disinfected and fumigated at each end of each trip."

On the platform I counted five people in wheelchairs lined up to board the car just behind mine. None of them was coughing, but they could have been dosed up with opium to keep them quiet for the trip. I could understand their having chosen the cover of night for their journey; no one would want to be recognized by friends or associates as having tuberculosis. In my case, I just wanted a good spell of unconsciousness — a state to be prized when your entire emotional range has been reduced to anger and self-reproach. Once we were north of the Bronx, darkness enveloped the train as if a tarp had been thrown over it. Every few miles the sparse lights of a town or village appeared as pinholes in the fabric. Otherwise, the view consisted of little besides a translucent reflection of my own face, a rendering far more interesting than the bland physiognomy I encountered every morning in the mirror.

I settled into reading *Jude the Obscure* for a couple of hours but found that, although I sympathized with the protagonist's doomed passion for education, I did not much like him. I turned to the poems of Baudelaire. Critics called him a symbolist, but I saw him as Romanticism's dying breath. It was my artistic ambition to write the poems that would bring English verse firmly into the twentieth century, and I considered myself absolutely post-Romantic, thoroughly modern, possibly even avant-garde. Does that sound pompous? I was twenty-two; of course I was pompous.

I switched off my reading lamp and the night rushed by. A glow from the train windows slithered across the trees, and sudden ponds flashed between streaks of locomotive smoke. Beyond this, darkness gathered itself into pools deep and black.

I slept well and only woke when the conductor came through, announcing our imminent arrival; somehow I had missed the call for breakfast. I quickly washed my face and got dressed.

I checked my watch as we pulled into the depot at Saranac Lake: 7:10 exactly. The sun was not yet up. Simon had warned me about the winters — *they start early and last long* — so I was relieved to see no snow on the ground, just leaves blowing across the platform. When I stepped from the train, however, the October air hit my skin with the cool sting of December. My first thought was *I have made a colossal mistake.*

Taxis were parked in a neat row off to one side, some horse-drawn, two or three automobiles. I signalled to the driver of a particularly shiny Ford.

"Cab, sir?"

"Yes, indeed. Dear God, is it always this cold in October?"

"You'll need a warmer coat than that, sir." He opened the rear door of the car for me. "Luggage?"

I pointed to the baggage area, where porters were now lining up suitcases. "One large trunk, one tan valise, three cardboard cartons. Name's Gascoyne."

"I'll look after it. You get in and warm yourself up. You'll find a pig in there."

"You can't be serious."

He gave me a quizzical look. "A pig — you know, a hot water bottle."

I huddled in the back of the cab with my legs resting on the thing, its pink porcelain snout peeking out of a fur muffler. The car was new, and in pristine condition, not at all the rattletrap I had been expecting. My luggage duly strapped to the back, and three cartons of novels and poetry stacked beside me, my driver climbed into the front in a swirl of frigid air. I gave him the address on Main Street.

"Dr. Tissot's house," he said. "Would you be a doctor yourself, sir?"

"I don't know what I am."

"You look human to me."

"One appreciates the vote of confidence."

I rubbed the fog from my window, expecting to find trees and darkness but in no time at all we passed three hotels. The street itself was brightly lit.

"Is the entire town electrified?"

"Sure is — since oh-eight. This is Broadway we're on now. Not like the Broadway you've heard of."

Indeed it was not. But few small towns were fully electrified in 1915, so the place was dazzling in its own small way.

"And this is Main," my driver said, making a right. "High school across the street, and on your left, that's the famous Berkeley House."

"Place seems entirely composed of hotels."

"Eleven just within town lines, no kidding. It's the relatives — all the families visiting patients. Have to stay somewhere, right?"

He wheeled the car around and pulled up in front of a handsome house of brick and stone. The front door opened, and a stocky man was silhouetted against the light behind him. I had a quick impression of a beard and a limp as he came hurrying down the steps. I got out of the car to greet him.

"Mr. Gascoyne." He gripped my hand and shook it with both of his. "Alex Tissot. I'm delighted to see you but I'm needed up at the san." He turned to the driver. "Tony, can you take Mr. Gascoyne straight up to the Pryce cottage?"

"Sure thing, Doc." The driver touched his cap and got back into the car.

"Gascoyne, my apologies. Can you come round this evening for dinner? We'll eat at eight, but come early, say seven. We'll have a drop of something good and I'll explain what's what."

With that, he limped away toward his own car, and I was duly conveyed by a three-minute drive, mostly uphill, to what the sign outside called *Mrs. Ursula Pryce's Registered Cure Cottage and Boarding House.*

I had never heard the term "cure cottage" before I arrived in Saranac Lake. These unusual structures came into being because the Trudeau Sanitarium was always flooded with more applicants than it could take. Being a charitable organization, it took in only those who could not afford treatment elsewhere. Aside from patient care, the san was engaged in research aimed at developing new treatments and finding a cure. It may sound heartless, but it was for this reason that it admitted only those patients who were in the early stages of the disease — those who were most likely to get better. That meant thousands of patients needed to be treated elsewhere, and the cure cottages sprang up to serve that need. Unlike the small, purpose-designed buildings on the sanitarium grounds, these were not cottages at all. They were solid, middle-class houses, modified to meet the peculiar needs of their ailing residents. All of them had glassed-in porches, some had several such porches, still others were more porch than house. The windows tilted or opened casement-style so that patients could inhale the curative mountain air no matter how inclement the weather. In 1915, Saranac Lake had more than a hundred such houses. Mrs. Pryce's was a medium-sized example, but highly regarded owing to her excellent cooking.

By the time I stepped once more from the cab, the sun was up and the sky a brilliant continuum from rose to indigo. I experienced one of those woozy moments when time seems to expand; thoughts and impressions rush into one's mind with an almost physical sensation of overcrowding. Of course I had the usual impressions of the first-time traveller to the

Adirondacks — the bracing purity of the air, the cool authority of the mountains — but then there was the house itself.
Turreted, gabled, and verandaed, it could not have been less
like a cottage. The veranda swept around all three sides, and
above it glassed-in porches glittered and flashed in the still-low
sun. For a house full of sick people, the Pryce cottage looked
inexcusably cheerful.

CHAPTER 3

It is almost impossible now to describe the dread and revulsion the word *tuberculosis* evoked in the early part of the twentieth century. In the fiction of the 1800s, it made for a decorous ending to the life of a beloved child. In *fiction*. In the real world, particularly within literary coteries, it was imbued with the Romantic glow surrounding the death of John Keats at twenty-five. Such was the fate of sensitive genius at the hands of an ungrateful world "where youth grows pale, and spectre-thin, and dies." At twenty-two, I was not well versed in medical matters, but even I knew that TB was caused not by "noisome night air," but by a microbe called a tubercle, and the prospect of my new position had had me reading up on the subject.

Burgeoning research in social health problems had linked tuberculosis irrefutably to poverty, overcrowding, and hideous working conditions. So much for romance. In a matter of a few years, coming down with "consumption" had gone from making one "interesting" to rendering one a pariah. Physicians

in Saranac Lake were embarked on a quest for a cure, finding
none. This was a contagious disease of many symptoms, some
of them subtle and slow to worsen, but others — the growling
productive cough, the spectacular pulmonary hemorrhage —
were the ones everybody feared. By 1915, it was a leading cause
of death second only to heart disease and killed more than
ninety thousand Americans a year, which put paid to any sta-
tistical relationship to genius. Even cancer did not usually destroy a life so immediately and thoroughly. With TB, jobs were
lost, spouses abandoned, friends suddenly remote. Who wants
to live, work, or play in the presence of a contagious disease?

But Saranac Lake was known for other things as well. The
North Country, as it is called, was the last region of the nation
to be settled. It was dark and remote and therefore developed a
reputation for wildness and mystery; early reports suggested it
was inhabited mostly by bears. According to historians, the soil
was so inhospitable to crops that even the Mohawk tribes who
hunted there left no sign of permanent habitation. Wealthy
individuals purchased vast tracts of land, speculating that it
would reap them equally vast fortunes in iron or timber. A
man named William West Durant had made himself a fortune
by building rustic palaces for them, and there the Rockefellers
and Vanderbilts travelled with their champagne and servants
to experience the wilderness, Fifth Avenue edition. It became
famous as their playground. Tabloids and society magazines
were plump with pictures of Whitneys and Morgans in their
straw hats and summer jackets at their "great camps." This
turned out to be a lucky break for Saranac* because, although

---

* One of Saranac Lake's many peculiarities is that the natives often refer to it as simply
"Saranac." Not to be confused with an entirely separate town called Saranac, which
lies thirty-three miles to the northeast.

the tubercle thrived in poverty and overcrowding, it was no respecter of wealth or position, and when the wealthy got sick with it, they naturally preferred to go for their rest cure to a place they already knew and loved.

I mention all this because it accounts for the sheer weirdness of the place, that it should exist at all. Before the sanitarium, Saranac Lake was little more than a crossroads where you could purchase guns and fishing gear or hire a guide who could get you in and out of the deep woods without life-threatening injury, and with at least one ten-point buck to your credit. "Hotels" were few and rustic. But as my taxi driver had pointed out, if you bring in the patients, you have to bring in the doctors, the patients' relatives, and the people to care for them. And so, in this vast mountain wilderness with few villages boasting more than five hundred people, Saranac Lake housed some seven thousand souls.

I will spare you the details of my first year of northern exile. I refuse to describe the outrageous marrow-biting cold of the winter. Nor am I going to offer a tour of the Adirondack San, which by then comprised some forty-seven buildings on the hip of Mount Pisgah. Let me just say that I experienced certain … difficulties of adjustment. Yes, I may have been an academic, but in my fiction-stoked imagination, I was a rogue of hot blood and wild surmise. Furthermore, I had tasted the 100-proof whiskey of New York City, and a town of seven thousand seemed to the man of the world I wanted to be very small beer indeed.

My personal ivory tower was moated with prejudice. I refused to find the earnest and irony-free locals endearing, nor did I welcome the company of my tubercular housemates. I felt marooned by the town's isolation, by the lack of a university, and as the days grew shorter and colder my soul was transmuted into a miasma of loneliness, boredom, and a juvenile resentment at the injustice of my exile. Still, I managed to maintain an air of polite affability and, possibly out of desperation, slowly warmed to the patients who shared my new home. And, once I got used to their being nothing like college students, I even began to enjoy tutoring those patients who liked the idea of talking to someone who could expand their knowledge and appreciation of poetry and fiction. Despite their stark contrast to the literary critics I had worked with at Columbia, their simple love of literary entertainment eventually impressed me. One high moment came when an emaciated eighteen-year-old boy told me he found parts of *Paradise Lost* "as good as Jules Verne."

And Dr. Tissot turned out to be an invaluable lighthouse amid the darker days of my adjustment period.

I was at first appalled to see people behaving as if there were no danger of infection. How could they sit next to each other without fear? But Dr. Tissot calmed me down on that score. Saranac Lake, he assured me, had not had a single case of anyone — *anyone* — catching tuberculosis from a patient. Knowing, as they did, that the tubercle thrived in conditions of darkness, dirt, and poor ventilation the san's founders had set out to create conditions of the exact opposite, and thoroughly succeeded. Sunlight and fresh air were the patients' best friends, and they got more of it than anyone could have asked for. The cough was treated with pastilles, creosote inhalations, and sometimes opium. Signs admonishing *No Spitting — $50 Fine* were everywhere and rigorously enforced. Patient care and sanitary conditions were overseen by no fewer than three separate agencies. Tissot encouraged me to let the experts worry about infection and, without being foolish, to live as normal a social life as possible.

"It's a mistake," he told me, "to expect this place to offer the pleasures of Manhattan or the university. It's the same as visiting any new culture. You're going to be miserable if you don't take an interest in what it does offer." For a time I resisted the truth of this observation, but eventually, perhaps only to preserve my sanity, I followed his advice. I went so far as to hire tutors of my own who took me on tramps through the woods and showed me how to tell birch from aspen, egret from heron, and corrected my ideas on the homicidal predilections of the ubiquitous black bear. I learned to avoid fashion and simply opt for clothes that kept me warm and comfortable through January and February days that fairly stunned the senses. I learned it was possible to love the cold, the hush of a snowbound street, the sight of children skating on Lake Flower. On winter nights the hooting of the night train bound for New York told me it was time to turn off the light. I would open my window to let in just enough razor-sharp cold so that huddling under the covers felt like a return to the womb. Although still a callow sophomoric interloper, I came to love the taste of Adirondack air so rich with scents of loam and balsam and pine and the spicier notes of herbs and shrubs. I came to love the rounded, approachable Adirondack Mountains, stalwart, imperturbable guardians to the river, the lakes, the town. I could contemplate the massive sculptural clouds with the intensity of a fortune teller consulting his orb. Having abandoned the study carrel, I even learned to paddle a canoe, though I think my signature wobble was recognizable from the far shore.

In short, despite my resistance to the place and its people, Saranac Lake began to feel like something approaching home.

And so, one year later …

At two o'clock one afternoon in October 1916 — and it happened the same way every afternoon — Saranac Lake went quiet. The clatter of heels, the stutter of automobiles, the clop-clop of hooves ceased and a beneficent hush descended over the streets, the stores, the churches, and even the normally rambunctious high school at Main and Broadway. *Two p.m. to four p.m.: Rest in the reclining position. Reading but no talking is allowed.* So read the schedule in every building in the sanitarium, and in every private cure cottage. The silence was so dramatic, so sudden, it was like being instantly struck deaf. Visitors arriving in Saranac for the first time could find it unnerving, even sinister — this otherworldly hush in the house of death and disease. I certainly did. But now I had been there a year, and I had become used to it, and liked nothing better than to take a walk amid the eerie curative calm.

I had just come from lunch at Bosworth's Five & Dime. I couldn't always face the crowded table at the Pryce cottage, nor could I often afford the ostentatious austerity of the Berkeley Grill. Bosworth's boasted a second-story veranda that wrapped all the way round to the back where it overlooked the Saranac River. Despite its name, Saranac Lake is not actually located on any of the three Saranac Lakes. The river was narrow, at that point, elbowing its way right through the middle of town where it was mostly ignored. The aldermen kept meaning to do something to prettify it, but so far no decorative swans had been added, nor any secure pathway cleared alongside. A slender, often muddy, foot track ran along one side, but the river served mostly as a highway for sportsmen in their guide boats and canoes. In those afternoon silences, however, its unremarkable babble rose to the eloquence beloved by the poets, among whom I then counted myself. I would like to claim that as I gazed down at the rushing water I wrestled with the prosody of "Fra Lippo Lippi," or one of my own efforts, but far more likely I was pining for New York City and the chalky venues where nothing was more highly valued than poetry. Another advantage of the river's chatter: it muted the one noise that marred the enveloping serenity. Some of the cheaper cure cottages were located nearby, and there are few human expressions more unsettling to the soul than the crackling sodden roar of the tubercular cough.

I left the veranda and walked down mossy steps to the so-called footpath. The afternoon was overcast and under the trees it seemed evening. The previous day's rain had left the track slippery; I had to stare at my feet to evade the treachery of roots and wet leaves. It had become my habit to wander down here at least once a week, and I had never yet encountered a single soul. So I was surprised that day to catch sight of a figure, little more than a flash of white amid that toy jungle. It was only as I drew nearer that I realized it was a woman. That she was in trouble of some kind was immediately obvious; she seemed to stagger and lurch her way forward. Seeing me, she raised a pale hand to cover her face, a gesture of mortification, for she was soaking wet from head to foot — coat, boots, gloves — as if she had just washed up from a shipwreck.

Her words came out in a rush. "So stupid, so stupid — the edge was so slippery — a pretty leaf — I reached for it and — dear God, I'm just such a fool."

"Please," I said, offering my arm. "Allow me to help you."

She took my arm but kept on with her breathless self-indictment. "I knew it was stupid — obviously it was — I'm such a —"

"Now, now," I said, "the path is in a wicked state. I nearly fell in myself."

Her arm was shaking. I stopped and removed my coat, hanging it over her shoulders and cinching the belt tight.

"You're too kind. Really, you'll ruin your coat."

"It's nothing," I said. Few pleasures are keener than that afforded a young man handed the opportunity to help a young lady.

I asked where she lived. "I'll walk you there. You won't find a taxi at quiet time."

"It's not far," she said, still shivering. "I'm at the Pryce cottage on Clinton."

"How is that possible?" I said. "I'm at Mrs. Pryce's myself."

"I'm in her annex — 47-B."

"Good God, you're a patient? But that's —"

"I know, I know. I told you I was stupid."

As we trudged up the deserted street I tried to find something cheerful to say.

"At least there's no one around to see you in my ill-fitting coat."

To this she gave no reply, but simply tucked her chin deeper into my coat's collar and fixed her gaze downward. I wanted to ask her name, but it seemed an impertinence, given her embarrassment, and as we turned toward Helen Hill, her mood seemed only to darken.

CHAPTER 4

It may seem odd to a young man today, in the 1950s, that an aspiring poet would develop a close friendship with an older man, a medical man, but society was different in the early part of the century; people were different. Movies, while popular, had not yet attained the pinnacle they would one day reach in the jagged terrain of storytelling and thus the public consciousness. Books were the thing; everyone read books. Just as the knowledge of Latin allowed far-flung priests of all nationalities to talk to each other, the popularity of fiction and poetry meant that people of very different classes, backgrounds, and pursuits could converse easily. A university education, much like travel, was meant to be a broadening experience rather than the intellectual straitjacket it seems ever more intent on becoming today. And Dr. Alex Tissot was an unusual case.

I mentioned some pages back that he was my only contact in Saranac Lake, and the first person other than the taxi driver to welcome me. My recommendation from Simon Crawford had predisposed Tissot to find me acceptable, but there were deeper currents between us. He was in his late fifties, brisk and blustery, with greying hair and beard clipped short, but heavy eyebrows that were still jet black — a feature that, along with incipient jowls and a broad chest, gave him the look of a none-too-friendly bulldog. Despite this demeanour he was, in fact, thoughtful, generous, and supremely rational — sometimes annoyingly so.

He was easily the longest-serving doctor in the district and had only recently stepped down as director of the Trudeau Sanitarium, preferring as he put it to have more contact with patients and less with paperwork and fundraising. He was still revered, still invited to every conceivable social occasion, not least because whatever his other qualities, he had a charming way with gossip.

The doctor had long been a widower when he married his second wife, Margaret, a darting, birdlike woman whom I rarely saw (she was a nurse at the Reception Hospital and worked mad hours), and had a son named Daniel who had rashly joined the U.S. Army in hopes of one day destroying "the Hun." In 1916, despite the sinking of the *Lusitania* and other atrocities, Woodrow Wilson had still not declared war on Germany, but Tissot feared for his son and missed him terribly. From time to time, he would read me snippets from Daniel's letters, which were amusing at the expense of his fellow soldiers. I was not perceptive enough to realize it at the time, but clearly I fit into an aching gap in the doctor's life.

For my part, I find it difficult, even now, to admit how lonely I was and had been for some time. My parents had more or less dropped me like a Dickens orphan on the doorstep of New York University in 1910 and blithely sailed away to Egypt for a "year" that was now going on seven. My father was a professor of ancient history, and he and my mother were caught up in the Western world's growing mania for all things pharaoh. During my university studies, they had arranged for regularly timed deposits into my bank account. These were adjusted downward when I began earning my modest income at Columbia, and when I finally confessed that I had sabotaged that position my father went into a rage (via telegraph) and cut me off altogether. In other words, by the time I rolled up in Saranac Lake there was every reason for me to play understudy for someone else's son.

Over the past year, Tissot had become something of a mentor to me, and I had a standing invitation to join him in his den every Tuesday night after dinner. The two of us would sit in our angled armchairs, staring into the fire and enjoying a quiet conversation. He used the occasions to educate me about tuberculosis, about the philosophy behind the sanitarium, about treatments from creosote inhalations to pneumothorax, and the current state of research. These days he spent more time in the Church Street laboratory than with patients, hoping to duplicate Robert Koch's findings regarding tuberculin.

I saw him the day after my eventful river walk.

"And she was coming out of the water, you say? Out of the river?"

"She fell in — reaching for a leaf."

Dr. Tissot shook his head. "Ridiculous. She's just been given the all-clear, and now she may have set herself back weeks — months even. You informed Conway, I hope — or at least Mrs. Pryce."

Dr. Malcolm Conway attended to several of the patients at Mrs. Pryce's cottage, but he was a harried individual, bony and jittery, and always in a rush, always running late.

"Dr. Conway was not around, and it didn't seem my place to inform anyone. She was horribly embarrassed."

"Yes, yes, I do see. Still."

Dr. Tissot propelled himself out of his armchair and poked at the fire, sending a galaxy of sparks up the flue.

"You know her story, I suppose — Mrs. Ballard's?"

"I don't know anything about the woman."

"Ha," the doctor said, holding his brandy glass up to the firelight and swirling it. It flickered in his hand like an amber flame. "I thought everyone knew. She was quite the celebrity last fall when she arrived at the Reception Hospital. She was the class pet, teacher's favourite — everyone anxious to do things for her. It's a thing I've observed more than once, tragedy carrying its own kind of glamour."

I sipped my brandy in the meditative manner I copied from the doctor. "Tragedy?"

Tissot nodded. "Happened a year ago, year and a half. Nineteen years old, she falls in love with one Stephen Ballard, scion of the Rochester Ballards — you've heard of them?"

"The office furniture people?"

As a burgeoning poet I saw it as my solemn duty to take no interest whatsoever in industry, but even I could not miss the Ballard name. It appeared on little brass markers on every item of office furniture in the state, if not the country. Every desk, every filing cabinet, every credenza at Columbia had been labelled *Ballard Office Furniture and Devices Co., Rochester, N.Y.*

"Yes, those Ballards. Stephen Ballard is their only son and destined to be a very wealthy man when he meets and falls in love with our young princess. He was making a business trip of some sort, and no doubt to the horror of his parents and hers, he meets his true love on board and they decide to elope. They had

the captain marry them and crossed the Atlantic together ..."
Tissot paused for dramatic effect, stretching the moment out by
holding his brandy once more up to the light. "On the *Lusitania*."

"Dear God." I lowered my own glass to the side table. "The
poor woman."

"Poor woman, indeed. Mrs. Ballard managed to survive
but her husband was not so fortunate — although I suppose
one can hardly call a woman fortunate when she's no sooner
married than widowed."

"Dear God," I said again. As a self-important poet and
scholar, I felt that showing interest in current events was beneath me, but the *Lusitania* story had had me reading three
or four newspapers a day. It had come only three years after
the *Titanic*, and what with U-boats a constant threat in the
Atlantic, every human being on the planet was now alive to
the peculiar horror of dying at sea. And like the *Titanic*, the
Lusitania had represented the pinnacle of human engineering
combined with breathtaking glamour. But there the similarities
ended. The *Titanic* had been a tragedy of hubris and bad luck;
the *Lusitania* was deliberately sunk, and some twelve hundred
people murdered, by the captain of a German submarine. From
that moment on, those Americans who favoured entering the
war against Germany invoked the *Lusitania* at every opportunity; those who wanted no part of it pointed out that the
Germans had given fair warning and the ship was known to be
carrying munitions. But of all the *Lusitania* numbers thrown
about in the aftermath — from beam to tonnage to knots per
hour — the one fact that made people suck in their breath and
go silent was this: the *Titanic* had taken more than two hours
to sink; the *Lusitania* vanished beneath the waters of the south
Irish Sea in a matter of eighteen minutes.

"There is a happy side to the story," Tissot said. "Well, not *happy*, but somewhat redeeming of one's views on human nature and divine intentions etcetera. The Ballards — even though they had never met their new daughter-in-law — wired funds to cover the cost of her recovery in Ireland, and even invited her to come and stay with them as soon as she was well enough to travel."

"But she got sick, obviously."

"Yes — a mild case, at first. But the Ballards insisted she come back to America, and eventually Saranac, for treatment. I only saw her once or twice before she was placed with Mrs. Pryce — she was too wealthy for the San. According to Dr. Conway her progress has been slow owing to her dark moods, perhaps a case of morbid grief."

"I would have thought all grief was morbid — surely when a spouse has died."

"Not so, my young friend. Mourning is a natural response to the death of one's beloved, a healthy response. And one doesn't expect a full recovery for about two years — sometimes more, sometimes less — and certain milestones are passed along the way: the first smile, the first laugh, the first desire to seek out company, the first social occasion that has nothing to do with one's bereavement. But blackness, depression, endless misery, and tears — after a span of months these begin to smack of *morbid* grief, a species of obsession."

"Sounds like me," I said, the voice of Narcissus ever strong.

"Nonsense. You've expressed pain and bitterness over Dark Emily, as you call her, but I've not discerned anything like obsession. No, no, I'm talking about people who pore endlessly over old letters and photographs, constantly fondle a keepsake lock of hair. They haunt the place of parting, or the scenes of bygone happiness — they may even show up at functions to which they're uninvited in the hopes of catching a glimpse of their tormentor."

As he spoke I was seeing amid the flicker and sway of the flames sharp jagged snatches of my own emotional history. Darling Emily, with whom I had shared a leafy autumnal walk through Central Park, a Broadway play, a sudden kiss at the corner of Fifth Avenue and 59th Street. Emily, the Upper East Side sprite whom I now called Terrible Emily, Wicked Emily, Emily the Cruel. The memories still came unbidden: her small warm fingers when I held her hand, the sweet attractions of her shyness, her laughter, her teasing, and even her tears at the death of a beloved terrier named Watson. Especially those tears. She had allowed me to hold her close that day, for a moment anyway. But now I reminded myself that I was no longer Emily's slave — nor any woman's, by God — and sat up straight and willed myself back to the present.

"What you're describing," I said, "is the source of half the poetry in the world. Beneath the most powerful words ever written can only lie the world's most powerful feelings."

"Feelings remembered in tranquility — wasn't that how Wordsworth put it?"

Dr. Tissot could be annoyingly polymath — degrees in medicine, psychiatry, and possibly the widest knowledge of tuberculosis on the continent, yet capable of quoting Wordsworth, when he was not quoting Sigmund Freud, whom he read in German.

"One has to feel those feelings first," I said.

"My poor boy, you are a hopeless Romantic."

"God forbid," I said. "My goal in life is to write a poetry that is ruthlessly cool and detached. The Romantic vein is thoroughly mined. Dead and gone."

"Ha! You may think the Romantic Age is long gone, but I assure you we're still living it."

I shook my head. "Dead and gone. And besides, it doesn't suit my temperament. I believe I told you —"

"Yes, yes — you've learned your lesson etcetera. At the cruel hands of Miss Emily *sans merci*."

"I should probably thank her," I said, feeling my brandy. "Emily the Dread has cured me of any trace of the obsession you're talking about. I'm thoroughly inoculated. My mission in life — for the next few years at least — is to be a thoroughgoing cad."

"Not a cad, surely."

"Well, a heartbreaker of the first order. I'm going to enjoy as much female affection as possible while limiting my own emotional engagement to lofty amusement. It's no more than what Emily did to me."

"Ha. That's brandy talking."

"Why? I'm a poet, not a monk — I want and need female company but have neither a need nor a wish for a wife. What does one call such a person?"

"*Deluded* comes to mind."

"Clearly, you don't know me," I said grandly. "I'm the opposite of deluded. I see love and romance for exactly what it is and I want no part of it."

"Tread carefully, Gascoyne." Dr. Tissot put down his glass and levelled those stern eyebrows at me. "Revenge stories never end well."

CHAPTER 5

The cure cottages in Saranac Lake were divided into two types: "nursing" cottages for those patients who were confined to total bedrest, and "up" cottages for those who were well enough to venture out for walks. The Pryce cottage where I lived was an "up," and its annex — a four-square structure consisting almost entirely of porches — had been built to serve patients who were bedridden. It was from there that Sarah Ballard had been scheduled for transfer to the "up" side.

That word, *up*, brings me to another feature of Saranac reality. The sanitarium's founder had long ago initiated a requirement that staff and patients were at all times and in all places to exhibit an outlook of cheerful optimism. This attitude had seeped down from the san to infuse not just the cure cottages and hospitals, but virtually every corner of city life. Anyone who has experienced the often saw-toothed transactions of New York City could find this a welcome, even a curative, improvement. Shopkeepers, innkeepers, restaurant owners, and even the police were uniformly polite, patient, and upbeat. I have no doubt that Saranac Lake was the birthplace of the irritatingly cheery how-are-we-feeling-today stereotype of the nurse now common across the Western world. Most locals managed to find a happy tone and demeanour that seemed natural and that few could find irksome.

Ursula Pryce, matron and sole proprietor of her cottage, was a Scot by background and by nature direct, forthright, opinionated, challenging, outspoken, and stern — a female sergeant-major — but you wouldn't know this on first acquaintance. I only came to understand it after months of living in her demesnes, because her place in Saranac's treatment regime demanded a personality that was chipper, smiling, and see-no-evil, which could not have been more alien to her actual character. The layering of the saint on top of the sergeant could be disconcerting.

Now I am, generally speaking, a punctual person; I will go to great lengths to make sure I'm on time for anything important and try never to inconvenience anyone by making them wait. Ursula Pryce's cottage was widely acknowledged to serve the best food in town, so much so that other cottage proprietors contracted with her to provide meals for their own smaller homes. But Mrs. Pryce — perhaps owing to the misleading facade of her nature, or some contrary quirk in my own — brought out an uncharacteristic fecklessness in my character: I developed a terrible habit of being late for her storied breakfasts, lunches, and dinners.

I tried various tricks to remedy this. Rubber bands on the wrist proved useless, as did bits of string around the forefinger. Lately, I had resorted to placing my alarm clock and its urgent clattering assault on my nerves across the room, thus forcing me to

forsake my warm bed and cross the cold floor to silence it. To that
extent, and to that extent only, it was successful. But the moment
I strangled the alarm I would plunge back into the nerve-soothing
heat of my blankets and on the instant lose consciousness.

"Well, here he is!" she said one typical morning. "It's a
beautiful bright day to be sure but all the brighter for the arrival of Mr. Gascoyne — at any time."

"Good morning, Mrs. Pryce. Once again I must apologize
for my tardiness."

"Not at all. You're a poet, a teacher, an intellectual, Mr.
Gascoyne. You'll be burning the midnight oil with all your
multifarious researches and creations. It falls on ordinary mor-
tals to make allowances."

Surreptitious smirks appeared around the table, where my
four ailing housemates were finishing their oatmeal.

I sat down next to Leah Landers, an eighteen-year-old with
unruly hair and emotions who changed love interests every
other week. One often saw her sitting in the parlour scribbling
with fixed intensity into a diary.

"I try," I said, "but I find it almost impossible to face a cold
room first thing in the morning. That's why I sleep so late."

"You'll get used to it in no time," said Mrs. Pryce, despite
my having been resident for a year. A serving girl brought me
a plate of ham and eggs as she continued. "With a mind like
yours you'll understand that the rooms are cold for medical
reasons, germ-killing reasons. And your willingness to adapt
shows a deal of compassion we can only hope to emulate."

Broadway Ben gave me a cheery wave from across the table.
There were rumours that Mrs. Pryce was secretly sweet on him.

"Of course, if our climate truly troubles you, you could
take your pedagogical talents to Arizona or California. There

are plenty of sanitariums in the sunny climes, and they'd be overjoyed to have you."

"Couldn't even consider it," I said, digging in. "No one could serve meals that compare to yours."

"Oh, Mr. Gascoyne," Mrs. Pryce said. "You make my heart glow." And to the table at large: "Isn't it wonderful how a generous remark never goes amiss — especially from a man like Mr. Gascoyne."

Toward the end of my student days, and certainly throughout my minuscule career as a professor of English Literature, I had come to take considerable pride in the ascetic nature of my existence, especially the sparseness of my table. But I will tell you something about the tubercular patients of Saranac Lake: they ate like lumberjacks. At breakfast they ate oatmeal, they ate bacon and ham and eggs and toast, and along with coffee or tea they drank gallons of milk. When I first arrived, I thought it must be a result of the mountain air, but I was soon put right by Dr. Tissot. "Tuberculosis is a wasting disease," he told me. "This we counteract by feeding our patients the highest quality food available — in large quantities."

Leah, the girl sitting next to me, was certainly testimony to this principle. She could not have been more than five foot four and a hundred pounds but she could demolish a steak twice the size of anything I could handle. As I was finishing my cereal, she leaned confidentially toward Madeleine Barr, the soft-spoken woman sitting on her other side, and murmured a series of numbers: "99.2, 99.4, 99.2, but today 99.8!"

A year previously I would have wondered if they were involved in a gambling ring rather than confessing body temperatures. Mrs. Pryce entered the room just then and witnessed the whole thing. "Miss Landers," she said, "what is the number one rule of mealtimes?"

"Patients do not discuss their illness at the table."

"Such a sharp young thing. I wish I had your memory."

"I don't see the point," Leah protested. "Illness is the most important fact of our existence. It's the one thing we all have in common."

Several heads nodded around the table, though no one spoke up to defend her.

"Dear girl," Mrs. Pryce said, "I can only agree with you that yours is a frustrating disease. But if you remind yourself that you have the good fortune to be curing in the foremost treatment centre in the world, you'll find the clouds will part and the sun will shine through. This is not just my opinion, but the firm prescription of our brilliant doctors: optimism and good cheer at all times."

Even Dr. Tissot, hardly a purveyor of treacly platitudes, had said much the same thing when I queried him on the practice. "I've seen it time and time again," he told me. "Patients start dwelling on their weight and their temperatures and next thing you know they're spiking a fever. They simply must trust in their doctors, that they know what's best, and they're on the best path to renewed health. Anything less is a guarantee of despair."

After a brief silence, the conversation resumed. There was talk of an upcoming performance at the Pontiac Theatre, discussion of a "Klondike" serial being shot just outside town, comments on the latest issue of *The Saturday Evening Post*, and reflections on the terrible war in Europe and whether the States would ever enter the fray. Broadway Ben, a successful composer and fifty years old if a day, offered a song on the spot. *"If ever you see Leah, Please tell her that I need her, whenever I am near her my heart goes boom-boom-boom!"*

Well, it could not replace the literary discussions I had revelled in at Columbia, but it was civilized, friendly, and undeniably cheerful. I had been terrified, back when I arrived, to sit in the same room as these patients, let alone at the same table, but the Pryce cottage was situated directly across the street from the cemetery — a fact often noted with dark humour when Mrs. P was not around.

CHAPTER 6

Because the patients were strictly regimented as to their eating hours (and pretty much everything else) I had mornings free to write. This I did faithfully, putting together the stray notes I made in tiny pocket-size notebooks and trying to hook them together into poems. Whenever my poetic craft failed me, I turned to fiction, developing a couple of short stories — vignettes meant to be revealing of our time and culture. Frankly, they were intended to excoriate society's elaborate mechanisms for hiding the need for sexual fulfillment and to prevent it from ever coming about. I was annoyed, at least in my fiction, by hypocrisy, though I certainly practised it in reality.

Saranac Lake, being a treatment centre, was graced with a prodigious array of nurses. When I was not writing, or tutoring my growing list of patient-pupils, much of my thinking was devoted to nurses. It was not difficult to meet members of this secular sisterhood. My job took me not just to the sanitarium up on the hill, but to several of the cure cottages in town. What more could these medical maidens desire from life than the company of an impoverished poet? The company of not-impoverished physicians is the quick answer — they were forever marrying doctors — but I did not allow this to dissuade me.

They were a tough bunch, these nurses. They had to be, what with looking after people who were extremely — often mortally — ill. Life, they knew, could be all too short, and was therefore too precious to spend with an impecunious litterateur with nefarious intentions. They were constantly declining even my most innocent invitations. This was especially disappointing because, contrary to my expectation, Saranac offered a first-class menu of entertainment, for it was home to a prodigious number of vaudevillians, actors, writers, and musicians. This was largely owing to the philanthropy of talent agent and impresario William Morris, who often covered medical expenses for his entertainers, actors, and theatre folk. The loyalty of their fellow troupers resulted in local productions and headliners that no comparably sized town could even dream of. The Pontiac Theatre on Saranac's Broadway became virtually a northern branch of that grander Broadway three hundred miles to the south.

A month or two before my riverside encounter with Sarah Ballard, I had managed to interest a nurse named Bella Troy in attending some of these productions, and over time my siege of Troy came to resemble the mythic one — in duration and desperation if not in heroism or loss of life. Bella was taller than I, and her face had the bony carved nobility of a figure on a totem pole. She was not a creature to be toyed with, Nurse Troy, which made me all the more determined to win her over — a silly notion, because she was already won over to the extent that she was willing to accompany me to a play, a movie, or even to the dining room of the Riverside Inn. But that was as far as her interest went.

My immediate objective was to win a kiss. To that end, I took Nurse Troy to the Pontiac to see *Married or Not*, a comedy by Jasper Keene that turned out to be well worth the price of admission. As one farcical scene piled onto another Miss Troy laughed harder and longer. I took immense pleasure in this — not just because she had a pretty laugh, but because I've always found something a little erotic in female laughter, perhaps because it is spontaneous, sincere, and to a good extent beyond their control. Of course, it was not I but Jasper Keene who was tickling this breathy music out of Nurse Troy, but to see those noble cheekbones and knowing eyes transformed into expressions of girlish delight gave me hope that before the night was over Nurse Arabella Troy would be in a highly kissable mood.

"Well, that was truly wonderful," she said when we were outside under the lights of the marquee.

"I enjoyed it too," I said. "I could happily sit through that one a second time."

"Me too," she said, and squeezed my hand in both of hers. "Thank you so much for taking me."

I seized the moment by suggesting a glass of wine at the Riverside — few places offered a finer view than their windows overlooking Lake Flower — and she readily accepted.

Ha. More territory won. In addition to its first-class theatre, Saranac as a whole, and the Riverside in particular, stocked a wine cellar flush with elegant Bordeaux and Burgundies. We enjoyed a glass of claret on the inn's enclosed veranda and watched the moonlight rippling on the water. She told me a little about her housemates, and about the doctors she worked with. I told her about some of my pupils, how heartening it was to see one or two of them develop a deeper love for stories and poems. I quoted Shelley, I quoted Blake, I was utterly shameless in my efforts to impress her. I recommended novels Bella might enjoy, but the conversation veered into her work and tuberculosis itself. Being deeply familiar with Milne's biography of Keats, I was able to quote the poet's last words, harrowing and heroic as they were: "Severn — I — lift me up — I am dying — I shall die easy — don't be frightened — be firm, and thank God it has come!"

I know, I know; my behaviour was unbecoming, even a little snaky, adding a pinch of "death" to the moonlight and wine to make myself seem profound.

"*Easily*," she said, infusing a wealth of skepticism into that single word. "Most patients don't go *easily*. Far from it."

"No. No, of course not," I said, trying to recover. "Nor did Keats. I mean, he suffered horribly right up to that last point."

She looked away; I had nothing to teach her about tuberculosis.

After a quiet interval, the conversation got back to Saranac-approved happier subjects. She chatted about some of her colleagues, noting that one of them had been chastised by Dr. Tissot for carrying cheerfulness to unhealthy lengths. I told her about my fruitless efforts to appease Mrs. Pryce, of whom she'd heard a thing or two, and even managed to make her laugh.

The night was cool, and fragrant with fallen leaves and the smell of balsam as I saw her home. She lived in a compact red brick house she shared with two other women on Olive Street. The porch light glowed softly as we said goodnight at the bottom of the steps. She thanked me again, but when I moved to kiss her she stepped back and raised a warning finger schoolmarm fashion.

"Forgive me," I said, with what I hoped was a winning note of dejection, "I'm an oaf."

"You are not an oaf," she said, as she turned and mounted the steps, "but I'm not a fool."

"You must know I adore you."

"I know no such thing. We simply enjoy each other's company."

"So you feel nothing at all for me?"

By now she had the door open. She turned to face me one last time and said again, "We enjoy each other's company."

CHAPTER 7

Nurse Troy's sober comment on the cruelty of death by tuberculosis stayed with me as I met with my pupils, most of whom were confined to bed and cure chair. One could never become wholly inured to a patient's sudden need to cough that ragged wet tubercular cough, or how they might, with an apologetic expression, turn away to use the disposable sputum cup that was always nearby. But Dr. Tissot had said my function was to keep their minds engaged on matters other than their illness, and to help prepare them for their eventual return to the world of family and employment. I had to accept the fact that, with few exceptions, I was merely a distraction from their fears; I was entertainment. It wouldn't have occurred to me at that stage of my life that all art, however rarified, might be entertainment.

About two weeks after my riverwalk encounter with Sarah Ballard, Dr. Tissot told me to pay her a visit. "Conway tells me she seems none the worse for her ill-advised swim, and he's worried that boredom or perhaps the morbid grief we discussed will succeed where tuberculosis has failed."

"Has she asked for me in particular?"

"Why — because you snatched her from the jaws of death? Don't flatter yourself. She simply selected poetry and fiction from our limited menu. It's a good sign. Until now she's shown no interest in any of our offerings."

And so I found myself on a sunny autumn morning making the grand trek from 47 Clinton Avenue all the way to 47-B. I was not usually nervous when meeting a new pupil, but I was heading up to Mrs. Ballard knowing that she had been through the horror of the *Lusitania* and the loss of her husband. The *Lusitania* had been a highly public disaster, but the knowledge that this woman had also lost the man she had just married was deeply intimate, and I approached with a guilty anxiety, which I dealt with by assuming an air of invincible pedagogical self-confidence.

I found Mrs. Ballard on her private porch on the second floor — private in the sense that the only access was through the wide door that opened from her room, but it was between two other similar porches that were separated not by walls but windows, so the privacy was limited. It is perhaps needless to add that when a male tutor was visiting a female patient the door to her room remained wide open at all times.

The windows, too, were wide open and a wash of disinfecting sunlight streamed in from the south. In my previous encounter with her, she had been deathly pale and downcast, but now she was seated in her cure chair at the regulation 30-degree angle, as pink-cheeked and hale as any farmer's daughter. But you couldn't trust such appearances. All the cure cottages hewed to Saranac's prescribed fattening regime that, combined with the hectic flush of fever, could give even the severely stricken a deceptive look of health, and I can say with no hesitation whatsoever that, until that moment, I had never once felt attracted to any female patient. Here they were, many of them my age, many of them smart, pretty, lively, and all the other things that draw one human being to another, but the fear of tuberculosis was a powerful inhibitor.

Until that morning.

At the time of which I write, if you were to believe the movies and the magazines, the ideal female face was, at minimum, a solid oval and sometimes approached a solid square. The Gibson Girl had masses of hair but a jaw and shoulders that would not be out of place in the boxing ring. I suppose it was the female equivalent of the men's top hats and high collars and moustaches, in that it made women appear far older, and tougher, than their years. But I was immediately drawn to the fetching details of Sarah Ballard's face — grey-eyed, heart-shaped, and with an expression, at rest, of regret. Her gaze was often directed downward, not in humility but in apparent reflection. Small, delicately formed ears and a chin that was pointed, though not severely so, gave her a look that was not exactly fragile, but vulnerable, mild, and as I say, something of an air of regret. I felt immediately drawn.

Dr. Tissot had mentioned the glamour of tragedy. This woman, who was more or less my own age, had visited Hell and come back alive and I suddenly sensed — without thinking it, exactly — that her fall into the river had been no accident, and the knowledge opened a crack in my heart.

"Hello again," I said, and that jaunty *again* should give some idea of how obtuse I was — she could hardly enjoy a reminder of our earlier meeting and its soggy circumstances — but the grey eyes lit up.

"It's you," she said brightly. "How perfectly mortifying."

"You didn't know?"

"That the English tutor had a sideline in rescuing young ladies? No, I didn't, but I'm perfectly content now that I do."

Her porch overlooked Pine Ridge Cemetery across the street, and on her lap was a large pad on which she was making a sketch of it.

"Isn't it a bit gloomy, looking out on all that?"

"Lots of things are gloomy till you make something out of them — a photograph or a painting. This is just a sketch of my colleagues."

"Colleagues?"

"Enforced bedrest. Theirs is even stricter than mine. I'm sure they want to break out of there as much as I do. You'd think they'd at least try." She slid the sketch pad into a rack attached to her cure chair and gestured toward the visitor's chair. "By all means proceed, Mr. Gascoyne. Speak some literature at me."

I began by telling her about my own studies and pursuits, and about the various "courses" I could offer.

"If you're interested in Classics, we could do *The Iliad* or *The Odyssey* — in translation. If early novels strike your fancy we could read *Don Quixote* — again, in translation."

"Aren't these rather long texts?"

"Well, we could meet, say, twice a week — or however often you like — and discuss a chapter at a time. I guarantee there'll be much to discuss, much to enjoy. But if lyric poetry is more to your liking I have a particular expertise in the Romantics."

"Romantics — those would be love poems?"

"No, no. Well, not necessarily. They address themselves to the wonders of nature, to the essential questions of being alive, being an individual, questions about the nature of man. Time, eternity, transience."

"It sounds far too profound — for me, at least."

She turned her gaze to the window, the long shadows of pines and gravestones.

"My education was inconsistent and interrupted at various times. I could always draw, so I did learn a bit about art. But my literary education was mostly confined to Shakespeare. I don't mean I read a *lot* of Shakespeare. Just what we had in school: *Romeo and Juliet*, *Macbeth*, *Othello*. They terrified me. All these emotions ..." Although still under doctor's orders to lie still for much of the day, Sarah Ballard had an engaging, almost entrancing way of moving one hand as she talked. Now her right hand inscribed circles in the air as if the emotions she spoke of were closing in at any moment. "So out of control — everyone so passionate, so *ardent*. It's as if they're transformed almost into demons, their feelings catch fire so. I can't imagine seeing those plays on stage. I think I'd faint from sheer ..."

"Well, *Macbeth*, certainly. Even Keats said he wouldn't want to read it late at night."

"Those characters. They somehow become more real than humans. It shouldn't be possible. And yet, there they are — there *we* are right there on the stage: more than human and yet still human. Goodness, you see what I mean. Poetry, deep questions, make my head spin — I start to blither."

"Far from it. You've just articulated a sensitive response to three masterpieces. We could explore some other Shakespeare, if you like."

"Clearly, you have a kind nature, Mr. Gascoyne — you give me far too much credit. I just meant I tend to be rather excitable. And Dr. Conway has forbidden me to read anything that gets my blood galloping. Perhaps you could choose a more tranquil text."

"George Herbert's Latin poems?"

"Ha. Now you're teasing me. You look serious in the extreme, but I detect an impish side to your character."

"I have no sides whatsoever. I'm thoroughly one-dimensional."

I asked if she'd read any Henry James.

She shook her head.

"Thomas Hardy?"

"*Tess of the d'Urbervilles*," she said, not looking at me. "But it was so sad. So cruel. As if he lined up his characters only to torment them. I couldn't bear it."

"You blame Hardy? Not fate? Society?"

"I couldn't bear it."

Her features had gone from sunlight to shadow. The blankets that kept her warm in these autumn temperatures were wrapped envelope-neat, envelope-tight. Her passage on the *Lusitania* would have been in my mind anyway, but the Saranac cure chairs held their patients recumbent in exactly the posture of passengers on an ocean liner. And through the side windows that separated her "private" porch, I could see other patients similarly seated in a line all along the length of the building. Except that we were overlooking a sunny graveyard, the resemblance to the deck of a Cunard could hardly have been more complete.

A nurse entered with a glass of milk and waited while her patient drank it.

When she was gone, Sarah made a face. "Six glasses a day they make us drink. And eggs, eggs, eggs. I feel fat as a pig. But if your weight goes down even half a pound, they force you to eat even more."

I decided on a change of tack. Over the past year, I had come to realize that my pupils sometimes were less interested in reading than in writing — writing being one of the few things they could do while curing. They desperately wanted to keep in touch with their distant families, but the nature of the cure meant that they had little to tell them in their letters. Most resorted to sending postcards — often postcards from Lake Placid so as to spare the family the stigma of communicable disease. They would speak with envy of friends (those that remained loyal) whose letters were lively entertainment, or of columnists and short story writers whose work they found memorable. Being yet an apprentice myself, I could not presume to teach them the art of fiction or poetry, but I had lately come up with an idea that seemed to get some of them pretty excited. I asked Sarah if she might care to join the Memoir Club.

She gave me a look — a narrowed gaze, an all-but-imperceptible curl to the lips, with head canted slightly toward one shoulder; I couldn't tell if it was quizzical, curious, or pitying. It was somewhat the look of a cat.

"Memoir Club? Is there such a thing?"

"It's just something some of my pupils like to do. Each week you write a short piece — a memory of some kind. It can be as short as a single page or as long as five. You like to sketch, well, these would be literary sketches of people or events that you remember."

"But real people. True events."

"Well, yes. But it's not history — you're allowed to exaggerate or even to add invented material if you want. You can merge characters, or change dates and locations as needed. It's not court testimony. The primary aim is to entertain. My role is simply to help you make them more so, to be a sort of editor.

At the same time, I can recommend books to read that may illuminate any literary issues that come up."

"How perfectly mad. I could never do something like that."

"Yes, you could. I know, because you speak so well."

"But to write of oneself like that, I could never ..."

"No need to be indiscreet. You merely put down something that happened to you or something you observed, perhaps concerning some particularly vivid personality — a teacher, a relative, or friend. Even a pet."

She shook her head. "I couldn't."

"Did you ever keep a diary?"

"You do ask a lot of questions — are all professors so inquisitive?"

"Sorry. It was just a suggestion."

"I did have a diary. For a time. But I didn't keep it up."

"Why was that? Just lost interest?"

"Quite the opposite. I enjoyed it too much. It was like having a secret friend — one to whom I could confide anything. But it also felt ... wrong, in some way. Duplicitous. What I recorded about my life — about my parents and friends and so on — and what my life was actually *like* were so utterly different. Even though I was writing down the truth, it didn't feel like the truth. Perhaps I'm given to nervous ailments of one type or another, but I began to feel under a peculiar strain. It was as if ..."

She held her hands open, facing each other, as if holding an invisible, and infinitely fragile, orb.

"As if? Go on."

"As if my existence was becoming fictional and what I wrote was becoming true. Well, that doesn't make sense — let me try again. When I started keeping the diary, I resolved to fill it full of complaints, those excruciating woes the adolescent female is prone to. My motives were of the highest, I assure you. I hoped by writing them out to myself I would stifle any urge to express such self-indulgent, woe-is-me self-pity in public (not that I was often *in* public). I wanted to be pleasant company, and no one enjoys the litany of a complainer. But then no one enjoys the diary of a complainer either — not even the author — and *that* I think, is why I abandoned the enterprise."

Her right arm made unconscious movements as she spoke: hand now open, now closed; now at a flag-like angle to her wrist, now fanned open as if to stop an oncoming cyclist. The motions were small, yet highly expressive, and while she seemed unconscious of them, her slim pale fingers drew my gaze again and again. If I had not known that Sarah Ballard had recently been deathly ill, nothing in her appearance or manner would have given the slightest hint.

CHAPTER 8

After lunch I ventured into the kitchen to inform Mrs. Pryce that I would not be in for supper. To miss a meal without warning her risked one of her jolly rebukes.

"Very well, Mr. Gascoyne. But you'll surely not want to miss Madeleine Barr's send-off. It's the kind of happy event that cheers one's soul. Four thirty sharp. Not that you need reminding, you're far too considerate to be late."

I spent the early part of the afternoon at the cramped little desk in my room. I was three hundred lines into a monologue à la Robert Browning, although it was not dramatic in the way of his great works. A tide of melancholy rose and ebbed inside me, rose and ebbed, and sometimes settled into a swampy numbness. The subjects of these moods were no mystery: I thought of my long-lost Emily, and the things I *should* have said when she rejected me; and I thought of my flight from Columbia, and my rejection by the entire realm of academia. These in turn gave way to self-annihilating reflections on my future, which looked to be penniless and solitary. Whether these were the actual *cause* of my sadness is another question. Young men, particularly those with poetic pretensions, will often try on melancholy as a style, imagining that the more sensitive type of female will find it attractive. It pains me to admit I was one of them.

I thought I was making progress — with the poem, I mean. My plan, once the verses were complete, was to smash it up, to create sharp-edged fragments of observation that would pierce hearts and make the literary tastemakers sit up and take notice. Theatrical scenes took shape. Unencumbered by a Catholic education, I felt free to write a section called "Missa brevis," replete with introit, Kyrie, and so on. I was hacking away at my "Gloria," when it was time to head over to the train station.

These send-offs were a Saranac tradition. Whenever a patient from a cure cottage got well enough to go home, his or her (ambulatory) housemates gathered at the train station to see them off. By the time I got there, all the patients and several of the staff from the "up" side of Mrs. Pryce's institution were there. Miss Barr, an elementary school teacher from Connecticut, was not one of my pupils; I only knew her from mealtimes, and she was quiet even then. I hurried through the station just in time to see her boarding the train and waving to the little crowd. I waved to her along with the others.

"Well done," Mrs. Pryce observed. "Nicely on time."

"Good to see a patient recover," I said. "Although Miss Barr seemed quite happy here."

"An example to us all. She made every effort to lift the spirits of everyone else."

"Could be in for a little rain later," I said, pointing at the clouds massing around Baker Mountain. Then, realizing my remark could be construed as negative and therefore unhygienic: "Mind you, few things are more exhilarating than an Adirondack thunderstorm."

Mrs. Pryce gave a little cluck, and bustled her way closer to the train, apparently delighted with everyone except myself. I wanted to believe she was good-hearted at bottom, but she terrified me.

The train whistle shrieked. Its daytime call had none of the night train's baritone melancholy. It shrieked again, and as the train began to move we all waved again at Madeleine Barr's gloved hand flickering in the Pullman car window.

My meeting with Sarah had put me in an excellent mood. The clouds held off, and I took a slow walk down one side of Main Street and back up the other, killing time before my appointment with a Wordsworth-loving pupil named Ronnie Barstowe, but when I arrived at his cure cottage it turned out he was far too sick. Unless you have seen tuberculosis up close, it is impossible to describe how *transformed* someone who suffers from it can be. Apparently, Ronnie had experienced a bad hemorrhage in the night, and now this cheerful young man of eighteen or nineteen lay propped in his cure chair on the porch paler than it should be possible for any living human to be. A man seated beside him — a man in well-tailored chalk-stripe — looked up at me.

"He ain't talkin a lot today, poor kid."

"Shame," I said. "I was looking forward to our chat."

"Oh, say, you the poetry teacher?"

"Yes, I suppose I am."

The man got up and shook my hand. He was shorter than I by a couple of inches, but broad in the shoulders like a boxer, and his suit, being perfectly cut for his build, completed his look of easy power.

"I have to thank you," he said. "Kid loves what you're doin. Won't shut up about it. Talks my ear off."

"Ronnie's a terrific student. He has a naturally inquiring mind — open to new things."

"Ha. Never thought of it that way myself. Always thought of him more like a puppy. Always bouncin around, always up to somethin."

"I take it you're his …"

"I'm his brother. Ronnie's a lot smarter than me in some ways, but kind of a dreamer with it. He don't deserve to be sick like this. I can't understand a world where a guy like Ronnie gets sick and I don't. I mean, I look at him now, I'd never know it was the same kid I grew up with. He don't deserve it."

"It may not be as bad as it seems," I said. "I've only been here a year, but I've seen patients get up and around after the most terrible setbacks."

"Yeah? I dunno. All I know is I'd take a bullet for this kid. He don't deserve this."

"No. Far from it."

"Far from it is right."

"I'll leave the two of you alone," I said, and made for the door.

"Okay. Stay outta trouble, Professor."

Sarah Ballard was sketching on her porch the next time we talked. She would always be sketching — sometimes a still life, sometimes mountain and cloud, sometimes a face from memory. Today she was finishing Mrs. Pryce, a head-and-shoulders portrait that captured not just cheerfulness, but a hint of desperation.

Her initial entries for the Memoir Club were three little vignettes. In contrast to her lively manner of speech, and the freedom of her pencil, her first attempts at writing were stilted. She wrote of a favourite teacher, a dog she had had for a time, and her mother, who apparently had died when Sarah was barely thirteen. She spent much time on physical description, but little on action or incident. Clearly, there was something getting in the way of freer expression.

"It's true," she said, when I put this to her. "My head is always somewhere else. I seem always to be thinking about, well, anything except what is right in front of me. It's the same with reading. I have to reread a paragraph several times because I see the words but not what they're meant to evoke. All I see is ..."

She stopped, her gaze fixed on some middle distance between us.

Very gently, I said, "The *Lusitania*?"

She remained still for a moment, as if she had not heard. Then she nodded silently, and looked away. The weather was colder now, and she was tightly enveloped in many blankets; I was in my raccoon coat. These were common in hunting paradise Saranac Lake long before they became all the rage elsewhere. Curing patients sat out on their porches no matter what the temperature might be and were swaddled accordingly, but visitors such as myself had to remain dressed for the outdoors.

"Can you tell me a little about it?" I said. "If you write about it — maybe it will stop insisting that you dwell on it."

"The *Lusitania* is the last thing — the last thing in this sad, sorry world I want to write about."

Through the glass partition, I could see three other patients in their cure chairs, once more lined up like transatlantic passengers. Sarah was in some ways still trapped on the *Lusitania*, as if the behemoth had not yet concluded the business of drowning her.

"I know that your husband died," I said. "And I'm sorry you had to go through such a ..."

"My father too."

She said it so quietly I had to ask her to repeat it.

"My father also died."

"I'm sorry. What a terrible thing."

She looked up, her face brighter. "I could write about him — my father. I mean, if that would interest you."

"Of course. It's the Memoir Club — you can write about anything you want. And talking about it first might make the process easier. Prime the pump, so to speak."

Sarah's eyes softened and her shoulders relaxed, and then began the revelations that would fill my thoughts and days for the coming year.

"You would have liked my father," she began. "Aside from anything else — and he was many things — he was a *manly* man — big. Imposing, you could say. On the street, if we were walking together, or perhaps at a playground, other children would drift toward us — especially little boys. His voice was deep, and he spoke in an authoritative manner, but also softly, and children couldn't resist him. He didn't like to sit still, either, if he was not working. He was always in motion. When I was small — at a playground, for example — he would never just sit and watch. He would have a ball to throw, or he'd get me going on the swings, or spinning the merry-go-round so hard you'd half expect children to come flying off like spindrift."

"He sounds a lot more entertaining than *my* father," I said. "But when writing, it's best to recall specific stories, specific scenes, rather than trying to give a general picture."

Sarah nodded, the expression on her face almost comically solemn.

I prompted her. "How did the two of you come to be on the *Lusitania*?"

"My father was a photographer. Lionel Redmond?"

I shook my head. "My knowledge of such things is limited."

"He was much in demand as a portrait photographer. But he was really an artist, and only took these commissions because we needed the money. If his life had been different, growing up, I'm sure he would have been a painter. What he loved to do was invent stories about people — imaginary people — and then take a photograph of a scene from her life, or his life. 'One doesn't *take* photographs,' he liked to say. 'One *makes* photographs.'"

A gust of wind blew through the porch; it had started to rain. Across the street a cemetery worker draped a tarp over a freshly dug grave. As the rain rattled on the tilted windows it washed away all other sounds, and I heard only Sarah's voice and the distant cawing of a crow.

"He made many trips to London, sometimes twice a year. He had several commissions from various worthies over there — he was even proud of one or two. I don't remember the names, but they must have been wealthy people because they had to pay the expense of his journey across the Atlantic and back."

"And the sums must have been considerable for him to brave the U-boats. Was he not at least fearful for *your* safety, if not his own?"

"I'm not sure he gave it much thought. My father was oblivious to many things."

She paused, watching the rivulets of rain chasing each other down the windows, and in the silence I thought about her voice. It was deep for a young woman, a soothing alto, a voice for offering sympathy, sharing confidences, and was in perfect accord with the serious grey eyes.

"It was my idea. I mean, I could tell he wanted me to come but he was too mindful of the danger to suggest it. What you have to understand is that my father was a complicated man — despite his bluff exterior — a lonely man. My mother died when I was thirteen and he missed her terribly and talked of her all the time. He'd be showing me his latest photographs and suddenly he'd go silent, and then he'd say, 'Your mother would have liked this one.' I missed her too, of course, but it broke my heart whenever he said something like that because his pain was obvious, so *naked*.

"In addition to that, here we were living in a tiny New Jersey village called Angelique. My father was a man of the world, and New Jersey must have seemed utterly provincial to a man who has seen Paris and London. There was not another artist of any stripe, let alone a photographer, anywhere nearby."

"You weren't terribly far from New York, though. Surely ..."

"It's not far geographically, but first you have to get to Hoboken, then the ferry, then a taxi, and all the time carrying bulky equipment. He had a gallery there, but he never enjoyed going, I think because his photographs were not so *esteemed*, as he put it, in New York as in London and Paris. There's a dreaminess to my father's work that was at odds with the documentary and abstract modes that were generating all the excitement in Manhattan. Perhaps it's even at odds with photography itself, but in any case he felt he had to travel, and yet travelling just seemed to make him all the lonelier."

"Did you have someone to help look after him — after your mother died? Or did all that fall to you?"

Sarah smiled and shook her head.

"We looked after each other. So when he announced that he was going to London, I asked if I could go with him. He said no, it was too dangerous, and if anything ever happened to me, he'd never forgive himself. It didn't seem to bother him that *he* might be killed, and I could tell he was gratified, even touched, that I wanted to go with him."

Her expression dared me to castigate her dead father for putting her in danger, but all I said was, "And so ... the *Lusitania*?"

"Oh, no. My father would never have booked passage on such a grand ship. He booked us on the *Cameronia*."

I had forgotten about this. One heard many breathless tales of people who had narrowly escaped death by cancelling their bookings on the *Lusitania* or the *Titanic* at the last minute, but few accounts of passengers who blithely chose the opposite.

"The *Cameronia* may not have been Cunard or White Star but it was perfectly comfortable. We had only just settled in when they told us we had to disembark because the British government had commandeered the ship for a troop transport. We were *so* disappointed. We thought at first we would have to scramble to find a hotel and book another ship etcetera but no, they were putting us on the *Lusitania*. We were absolutely thrilled."

"Where was your husband in all this?"

"I hadn't met him yet."

"You met on board ship?" Even as I said it, I suddenly remembered that Dr. Tissot had told me as much.

She gave a rueful smile, and — perhaps responding to my expression — added, "I know. It's the kind of thing you read about in magazines. Getting off the *Cameronia* was chaotic. They had to round up a fleet of taxis and trucks to move everyone and their luggage — the *Lusitania* was docked a dozen blocks south of our pier — but somehow they did it and we all got on board. Have you ever been on one of the great liners?"

I had not.

"Well, it must've been ten times the size of the other ship — absolutely massive — and it was like the grandest of grand hotels, or maybe even palaces. Everything you touched, everything you saw, seemed to be of the very best — so many gleaming surfaces, so much comfort on offer everywhere you looked. And with the sea breezes and the wash of sunlight it was like being transported into some glorious dream."

Her face darkened. The rain had eased to a steady patter on the angled windows, and the porch was rich with mountain air and the smells of wet loam and autumn leaves.

"I don't think I can talk about …"

"Your husband. Of course. That's the beauty of writing — you can pick and choose what to write about. And when."

Considering her initial reticence, I was amazed at how much she had already told me. It was as if she had been yearning to tell her story but no one had wanted to hear, yet I could hardly believe that to be the case. I would even go further: there was, in her tone and in the way her eyes glittered as she spoke, an element of compulsion.

"Let me just say I took to Stephen immediately," she said. "Even my father liked him, and he normally could not abide young men. 'They're so noisy,' he would say. 'So full of themselves.'"

"Do you agree with him — am I that way?"

"Well, you're not *noisy*."

"High praise indeed."

"Stephen had a keen interest in photography, so he got chatting to my father about exposures and so on. Normally, my father could not tolerate amateurs, but Stephen had an irrepressible quality that charmed him out of his usual coolness. He had one of the latest Kodaks strapped around his neck and was constantly snapping pictures." She laughed at the memory. "That, too, would normally annoy my father. Maybe it's true of all photographers, but he couldn't bear having his own picture taken unless he took it himself. He was like a cat having its fur rubbed the wrong way. But Stephen had a gift for finding people's soft spots. With my father, it was his hat. He had this preposterous Stetson that he wore everywhere — not the cowboy kind. It was black felt, and a bit floppy, and had a very large brim. I believe they were fashionable forty years ago. We were all on deck waiting to cast off, and my father made a striking figure in his black coat and his magnificent hat. Stephen came up and said, 'Excuse me, sir. I am thoroughly entranced with your Stetson and would very much like to photograph you.' I thought my father would shoo him away but being transported to the *Lusitania* had put him in a rare mood."

"Is that your husband on the dresser in your room?" I had noticed the silver-framed photograph, and thought the subject, while handsome enough, looked a solemn, serious type, and not the lively creature she was describing.

"Mrs. Ballard gave it me. She and Mr. Ballard have both been so kind. They had absolutely no responsibility to take me into their lives — why should they take in someone they'd never met? — but their generosity has been boundless. And completely undeserved."

"They had no idea you existed?"

"None. Well, not *quite* none," Sarah corrected herself. "They told me later when I first met them that Stephen on that very first day sent a postcard telling them he had met the love of his life and hoped to marry her on board ship — isn't that extraordinary? I wouldn't have thought it possible, but apparently the pilot boat took on mail before it went back to shore. I remembered Stephen joining us at the dinner table and telling everyone who would listen that he had posted a letter home. He was extraordinarily pleased with himself but, as I say, he was an irrepressible sort of person."

She bowed her head, and I waited. Two or three porches over, a horror was taking place. A thin man I recognized as Dr. Conway was attending to a woman patient, and her blankets were covered in blood of bright crimson. So was the lower part of her face, making it look as if her lower jaw had been shot away. I was seated in Sarah's line of sight, so she saw nothing of this.

"Well," I said, trying to hide my shock, "he was clearly very taken with you."

"And I with him. I don't mean I was in love at that point, I was just … well, I don't know what I'm trying to say. You see, I would make a terrible writer. I can't even tell the story of the most important thing that ever happened to me."

"I disagree," I told her. "And I look forward to reading more."

It is appropriate to note here that Sarah wrote many entries for the Memoir Club, but recounted just as many, or even more, in person. For reasons that will later become clear, I no longer have access to her writing, and forty years on I can no longer distinguish what she put down on paper from what she told me face to face. But I do remember the order in which her stories came, and my only aim is to present them as clearly as possible.

"A memoir sounds such a grand thing," Sarah said. "The prospect seems terribly pretentious for someone like me."

"Not at all. All sorts of people write memoirs: sailors, bee-keepers, opium eaters. It's not the same as an autobiography. Just think of it as a letter."

"Oh, could I?" A slim hand reached out toward me but I was seated too far away.

"Of course." The smile that broke those pensive features felt to me like winning a prize.

"Excellent. I actually enjoy writing letters. I even look forward to it."

"Then I'll look forward to receiving them," I said.

A nurse appeared bearing a glass of milk. A glance to the left told me that the drama I had witnessed earlier had now been cleared away, and a short while later I took my leave.

CHAPTER 9

I felt like a walk — a long walk — so I set off along Pine Street and covered a circuit that took me around the town, past the general hospital and Lake Flower, and all the way back to Main Street and the Berkeley Hotel. If anything qualified as the centre of town, it was the Berkeley, but it wasn't the hotel that interested me, only the Berkeley Grill on the ground floor. Mrs. Pryce, as I have mentioned, was an excellent cook, and I never had the slightest reason to carp about my suppers there. But sometimes I couldn't face the table full of invalids and the excessive servings of good cheer. I had told her that morning that I would not require supper.

"Of course," she had said. "Don't you bother about us. A man of your gifts must be out in the world. You'll be needing company that can appreciate your intellectual abilities." While some might construe Mrs. Pryce's words as harmless, I sensed an ill-suppressed wish that I be hospitalized with a case of ptomaine.

The Grill was really too expensive for me. Although it was informal, the place was all dark wood — oak tables and chairs, nothing plush in the place at all — and a massive stone fireplace at one end. It offered some of the pleasures of a railroad station, in that one could observe people from all over the world on their way to somewhere else. Mostly, it catered to the "sports," as they were known, who were not wealthy enough to own their own camp, but could easily afford to hire a guide for a couple of weeks' hunting and fishing amid the darker networks of the Adirondack wilderness.

Of course, not every denizen of the Berkeley Grill was a hunter. The smaller tables were often occupied by solitary men, in town to visit their bedridden wives or sons or daughters. Their faces were drawn and haggard — even a little stunned — the faces of men who had had every reason to expect the world to treat them well, only to find their lives upended, their loved ones torn from them by a microscopic shark called a tubercle. More often, parties of three or four men talked excitedly of adventures about to begin or just concluded.

Somehow, the law of supply and demand never reached the Berkeley Hotel. Venison was readily available everywhere in the Adirondacks, but here it was always priced out of my range. I ordered a modest pork chop. Moderation clearly did not apply to the noisy table to my right. Two of the men joked and laughed with the waiter as they ordered the most expensive items on the menu, and let out a whoop when the gravel-voiced older man ordered three bottles of Chateau Latour.

One of them launched into a diatribe about the deterioration of Saranac Lake into one giant hospital.

"Jasper, here, is the perfect example of what I'm sayin. You get 'em out in the woods, in among nature, and they get *better*, damn it. Those lungs clear right out. But no, *my doctor says I have to lie still.* D'you realize they got a lady up in the san been lying there fifteen years? Fifteen *years* — and you never see the woman. I wouldn't give two hoots if it wasn't destroyin my damn business, but it is. They've turned a huntin and fishin paradise into a place any healthy person would avoid at all costs."

It was a chronic lament of the local guides, who felt that the TB "industry" had turned their glory days into a distant memory. An animated debate ensued.

I had chosen to eat out hoping to indulge my pensive mood. But it was difficult to think, with the next table becoming more boisterous with every swallow of Bordeaux. All thoughts of poetry past, present, or to come deserted my head. I finished my pork chop and sat there picking my teeth and thinking melancholy thoughts of Dark Emily, more detached and curious thoughts of Sarah Ballard, and lascivious thoughts of Nurse Troy.

I was determined to win Nurse Troy at least to the extent of a physical dalliance, without hurting either her or myself. This was not as callous as it sounds, because Saranac Lake was imbued with a uniquely free sexual ethos. The town was teeming with young people staring death in the face and many patients, knowing life might end at any moment, were determined to live it to the full. The disease was communicated in the air — anyone with an active cough, the local lore went, was to be avoided at all costs — but kissing, paradoxically, was said to be safe. Patients fell in love with each other all the time, and sometimes married. But an illness-free man had to think twice about getting involved with a female patient. I focused the less-than-chivalrous part of my mind on how to disarm Nurse

Troy so that she might consent to free me — and I assumed herself — from the tiresome burden of virginity.

The guffaws from the next table became impossible. I signalled for the cheque and paid it. As I stood up and reached for my coat that gravel voice accosted me.

"Young man?" he said. "Young man, I'd very much like it if you would join us for a drink."

I was surprised to be asked. I had considered these men little short of louts, and for a moment I was offended at the assumption that I was of their stripe. But the dark-haired, dark-bearded man who accosted me was courtesy incarnate. He stood up and hoisted a chair from a nearby table and placed it beside his own.

"Thank you," I stammered, "but I really should be —"

"Now, now," he said. "We've disturbed your peace and quiet with our rowdiness. I well know the irritations of dining alone in a crowd — please allow us to make it up to you."

He was much younger than I had thought from the sound of his voice, which was remarkable. Gravelly, as I have said, but it also had a liquid, chewy quality — every vowel and consonant given its full weight, so that the result made each word sound thoroughly considered. These qualities lent a sonorous authority to every sentence he uttered, even the briefest anecdote. If this makes him sound rather a bore, it did not make him one, because his questions, statements, and observations were all delivered with homely qualifiers or calming notes, such as the *now, now* I just mentioned, or *oh my* or *heavens, yes* — expressions redolent of the Victorian patriarch. He sounded like a friendly bear who has just consumed a satisfying quantity of honey. He was also a curious person who looked you straight in the eye as he spoke, and as you spoke, so that you felt valued and important. I apologize for the cliché, but a certain physiognomy around his eyes, which were astonishingly blue, made them "twinkle" in a way that made him seem always to be on the verge of saying, *by God, you're right* and clapping you on the back. Yet despite this manner and speech of a much older man, he was not more than thirty-five or thirty-six. I might have taken him for a captain of industry — a great oilman or railway tycoon — but no. This was playwright Jasper H. Keene.

When he said his name, I felt a quiver of excitement. In addition to the play I had just seen, Keene had written an earlier Broadway hit, a drama so successful that more than one critic wondered if America had found its own Somerset Maugham. I told him I had seen *Married or Not* and admired it tremendously, but once he had introduced his table mates (Charlie Sands was his guide, and Joel Abrams his agent), he wanted to know all about me.

"Come and sit, my boy, and tell us all about Paul Gascoyne." The moment I sat, he poured me a glass of wine.

"Now, how does a young man of — what, twenty-four?"

"Twenty-three."

"How does a young man of twenty-three come to be on his own in Saranac Lake, New York, in the Year of Our Lord 1916? I don't see a wedding ring, but have you a relative or family member here for the cure?"

An intrusive question from anyone else, but Jasper had a way of implying long friendship even on first meeting — he insisted that I call him by his first name — so that I took no offence. I told him about my position as tutor, and he asked me endless questions so that his companions grew silent and no doubt bored.

"Poetry," he said. "Queen of all the arts. And if I'm not mistaken, you'll be writing it yourself. Come now, you can tell us."

"Well, yes, I am. Trying to."

He slapped his hand on the table. "Come on, then. Let us have a Gascoyne poem. Our ears grow dull with too much blather — not least of all my own."

I resisted the entreaty, but I could see my resistance was only irritating the company so I gave in.

"It's not really finished," I told them. "It's part of a Mass. A broken Mass. It's called, uh, 'Sanctus.'"

"Don't be shy, son, don't be shy. You wrote it, you took a risk, if it's terrible that's just too damn bad and you'll go on to write another."

I had to look up toward the ceiling to consult memory. Then,

> All through the night I dreamed
> Of Mary's shimmering face
> Pale, almost proud
> Or so it seemed
> An earthly face
> I felt with each warm breath
> As if she had contrived
> A physical faith — a death
> I could learn from
> Having survived.

"Well, now," Keene said. "That's just fine. That's splendid. 'A death I could learn from.'" He looked around at the others. "Gentlemen, the man's a poet."

I was blushing furiously but deeply pleased; I took several gulps of wine.

The other two men rose and made their goodbyes — I don't *think* it was strictly as a result of my poem — and thanked Jasper for the sumptuous dinner. When they were gone, he ordered another bottle of wine and for the next two hours questioned me closely about poetry, about my upbringing, about my hopes and dreams. He asked in particular about my father, and I told him about the granite-faced man who presided over the household when I was growing up — a professor of Ancient History, a lover of the Classics, a translator of Virgil, and a man whose affections, if he had any for the living, were thoroughly mummified and entombed.

"Oh, my, yes. Fathers are difficult. My own pappy would reach across the table and —" Here, he swung his hand across the table, stopping so close to my cheek that I felt the wind of it. It was a highly theatrical move, and in that moment I could see the actor Jasper had briefly been before taking up his pen. "Didn't like 'smart talk,' as he called it. Oh, heavens, yes. But surely the old man must have been impressed with your writing?"

It had never at any time occurred to me to express my literary aspirations to Professor Reginald Gascoyne. The idea made me laugh.

"But he loved the Classics," Jasper said. "He must have recognized a touch of Catullus in your lines? I surely believe I did — despite your looting of Catholicism?"

The notion that my work should bear any resemblance to the Roman poet of love and lust was so unexpected that I found it impossible to respond. Instead, I took up the mantle of interrogator and fired questions at Jasper that he answered with more consideration than they deserved. Eventually, I came up with the most obvious question of all: what was Broadway's hottest playwright doing in Saranac Lake? *Married or Not* had been running for several weeks.

"Came up here originally as a 'lunger,'" he told me. "Spent some excruciating time in the Reception Hospital and then just quit. Charlie Sands hauled me out into the woods and I swear the man cured me — oh my, yes — or at least the Great Outdoors did. These days, I'm just here for the peace and quiet while I write the next play. Mountain air does wonders for the old grey matter, don't you find? Plan is to get the thing mounted by next spring, at which point it promises to earn me unconscionable sums of money. Tell you what," he said, pulling out his wallet, "let me give you two more tickets to *Married*. Just give them away if you don't care to use 'em. You'd be doing me a favour, keeping attendance up. You could bring your Nurse Troy again, if you think it might further your cause in that quarter."

Yes, I had told him about Nurse Troy. Why a famous playwright should have cared, let alone remembered her name, was a mystery to me — a delightful one — and I readily accepted his offer.

I don't want to burden the reader with too much medical detail, but it is perhaps well to note here the thinking behind the stern bedrest regime that tuberculosis patients were required to follow. When the lungs are infected with the bacillus, it eats away at any tissue surrounding it. This causes irritation in the chest, which in turn causes a persistent cough. Eventually, the damage is enough to cause internal bleeding; the cough will become flecked with blood and the bacillus now has entry to the bloodstream. Although its reproduction rate is slow, as microbes go, new bacilli will take up residence in other spots in the lungs, where they, too, begin to consume surrounding tissue. The lungs may now have several bleeding cavities, breathing becomes more and more difficult, and without treatment the prognosis is grim. Complete bedrest, if mandated early enough, allows the body's natural healing mechanisms to form scar tissue around the internal wounds and prevent them from bleeding. In this way a mild to moderate case could be "arrested." Such patients could eventually return home, though only in exceptional cases would they be able to work — the curtailed breathing made for constant weakness and fatigue.

When I first met Sarah, she had only just achieved the near-arrested stage. The disease no longer appeared to be advancing, there was no hemorrhaging, and her fevers were slight and brief. Should she continue this well for three months, her case would be deemed to be arrested and she could return home. For now she could take short walks, but any physical exertion greater than this could cause the scar tissue to tear, provoking a hemorrhage that — if it didn't kill her — could add months, or even years, to her recovery. In short, she was living on a cliff edge and, despite her attempts at optimism, the possibility of sudden death was always with her. I believe it was this, and not any natural charm or teaching skill on my part, that provoked her to overcome her initial reluctance to write her fragments of memoir and even discuss them with me. As she would later put it: "I want at least one person to know me before I die."

She wrote of her first few days at sea. On May 1, 1915, the transfer of some forty unexpected passengers from the *Cameronia* to the *Lusitania* caused much confusion. New arrivals passed each other in the long corridors clutching their tickets and peering at the numbers on every door they passed. Just finding one's way to the appropriate deck presented a challenge.

Sarah and her father were lucky. They were assigned cabins in second class on the starboard side. "My cabin had four slim beds," she told me, "an upper and lower on either side, all covered in blankets of the richest scarlet. At night, or whenever you wanted privacy, you could draw a heavy gold curtain that hung all the way round."

Her father in a cabin down the corridor very quickly developed a ferocious case of seasickness that would keep him in bed and within reach of a toilet or bucket for most of the voyage.

"It was astonishing," she said, "because he was such a seasoned traveller. But apparently, this happened to him every time at sea. You'd think he would've learned to stay home."

She missed his company as she explored the ship that first day, because Lionel Redmond was the sort of man who *knows things*. Had he been up and around he would have been explaining how the ship's massive turbines worked, how much coal she was likely to consume, and what they could expect for their average mileage per day. He would have been naming the wheeling sea birds. But by the morning of the second day, he was all but immobilized with nausea and could not leave his cabin.

Why her father should have suffered so and she herself feel perfectly fine Sarah could not fathom; for the entire crossing, the seas could not have been more gentle. But whatever the reason, it gave her complete freedom to wander the ship and, not coincidentally, spend a good deal of time in the company of Stephen Ballard.

"The Ballards are wealthy," I said to her at some point. "Why was he not comfortably ensconced in First Class?"

"I wondered the same thing. He told me that his father had come from humble beginnings and didn't like anything that smacked of 'pretension.' And the idea of spending the money he'd worked so hard to earn made him quite irritable. I saw it myself eventually. He'll spend money on good quality, but not on what he calls 'needless luxury.' So when he packed him off for a business trip to London there was apparently no discussion of First Class."

Diners in second class ate at long tables, and even though Sarah would seat herself shyly at one end, Stephen always contrived to be nearby with a smile on his face and a camera around his neck.

"I've learned," he said, "that to be a good photographer you have to be aggressive. You have to go up and speak to people who might very well prefer you keep your distance. You have to break social conventions again and again if you're going to get any decent photographs at all. I mean, you just have to acknowledge that photography is really a kind of *staring* — that it's rude by nature — and carry on anyway."

Sarah told him that her father would disagree — vigorously — and that far from a form of aggression he saw photography, at least as he practised it, as a kind of courtship. You had to win your subjects' trust, get them to relax and be completely comfortable in your presence. Lionel Redmond would spend days getting a photograph just right.

"Ah, but it's not as if he's going to marry his subjects," Stephen said slyly. "So wouldn't it be more accurate to call it not courtship but seduction?"

Sarah was offended by the term.

"I mean it in the broadest sense," Stephen assured her. "You know, persuading your subject, perhaps by means not always subtle, to co-operate in the project at hand."

Sarah's father, responding to Stephen's heartfelt enthusiasm, had showed him a portfolio of his own work shortly after they left New York Harbor. They were old-fashioned, fanciful scenes for the most part, recreating a moment of drama or its aftermath — young ladies in grief, young men suffering remorse, "poets" struggling with their latest ode. There were sleeping children, farmers' daughters, and tragic figures out of Shakespeare.

"Yes," Sarah allowed, "it did take a good deal of persuasion sometimes to get his subjects to co-operate, to dress up in odd costumes and lose an afternoon posing for this eccentric man in the funny hat. But it was a benign business, even affectionate. Nothing feigned or insincere."

Stephen Ballard for his part was delighted to find a young woman who was so knowledgeable; Sarah had been her father's assistant from a young age, helping him with lights and backdrops and costumes. Her amorous new friend had been fearing he would bore her to death the way he bored everyone else with his talk of f-stops and shutter speeds and focal planes. She reflected later that it was *his* enthusiasm for *her* that made him so irresistible. Stephen was handsome, but not (as she put it) in the way that makes a girl weak in the knees. He was neither tall nor broad-shouldered nor graceful nor athletic; rather he was a bundle of energy and enthusiasms, and his biggest enthusiasm as of May 2, 1915, was Sarah Redmond.

Although he claimed to be laconic by nature, Sarah's questioning eyes — not to mention her knowledge of photography — turned him into a hopeless chatterbox. The two of them wandered the length and breadth of the ship, talking about anything and everything that came to mind: their fellow passengers, the immense size of the crew, the unfathomable sublimity of the Atlantic, predestination and free will, the afterlife, the difficulty of living with parents (or parent, in Sarah's case), the obvious fakery of the Spiritualists, the horrific insanity unfolding in Flanders and France, and their favourite books.

U-boats, not generally considered a topic conducive to romance, were also a recurring topic — with Stephen, at least. The Germans had placed a warning in all the New York papers the morning of her departure. Without mentioning the *Lusitania* specifically, it claimed an unlimited right to attack "any vessels flying the flag of the United Kingdom or any of her allies" anywhere in the war zone, which included the waters surrounding Great Britain. Sarah had heard nothing of this until Stephen brought it up.

"Not that I think a U-boat attack is likely," he told her, "but I plan to buy one of those personalized life jackets from the purser. They put your name in big letters. After the *Titanic* there was a lot of confusion about who was dead and who was missing."

Sarah confronted her father about the German warning, and he groaned something about not wanting to frighten her unnecessarily and turned his green-tinged face back toward the cabin bulkhead.

"You mustn't blame him," Stephen said to her on deck. "He was only trying to protect you. I wouldn't have brought it up myself except I assumed you already knew."

"I don't need protecting," Sarah said hotly. "Do I look like I need protecting?"

"Well, no, I —"

"I don't."

Stephen, a little taken aback by her vehemence, made a little bow and adopted the tone of a courtier. "Milady, I apologize. I meant no offence. 'Tis just the way the male of the species is trained."

"And anyway what is the supposed 'protective' value of keeping a woman in the dark about a potential danger?"

Stephen conceded she had a point. "But I shouldn't worry," he added. "This ship can outrun any submarine."

"Maybe so. But it's not the submarine itself one worries about, is it?"

"You're a fierce young woman, Miss Redmond."

"I certainly hope so — if by fierce you mean I prefer to live in the real world and not a made-up one."

Their conversation wandered into other byways: what it must be like to live underwater, the nature of war, the pomposity of nations, and the silliness of human nature generally. Sarah had never encountered anyone so easy to talk to. Unlike most men — except for his one "protective" lapse — Stephen did not talk to her as if she were a child or defective in some way. He chatted with her as with an equal, asked for her thoughts and opinions on everything, and seemed to give them at least as much weight as his own.

Nothing interested him more than Sarah's opinion on whatever was under discussion, and just when you thought there couldn't be anything more to say about a subject, Stephen's mind would take a dogleg into something quite different that, once enunciated, seemed inevitable. Suppose, for example, you were talking about the remarkable Teddy Roosevelt, who aside from having been president, was a war hero, a mountain climber, a big game hunter, and the author of dozens of books. Sarah had read his recent autobiography, and had often thought how wonderful to be a creature of such prodigious energy, such catholic interests, such high ambition — and the wherewithal to make things most of us cannot even dream come true.

"Your father is certainly a remarkable man," Stephen observed. "Is he like that?"

They were waiting for a table at the Verandah Café on B deck. Aromas of fresh coffee and pastries combined with the sea air caused Sarah's belly to squeeze itself into a pang that she was sure would be audible even over the ship's great engines. Teddy Roosevelt? She thought of her father, face jade-green and slick with sweat, lying in his narrow bed in sheets stamped with the famous Cunard crest. And yet she didn't laugh, didn't protest.

"My father surely has a rich imagination. And he is a deep student of the rules of art and beauty. The books on art that line our parlour must be worth a fortune. He studies painting too, you see, because there aren't enough tomes on the art of photography — not for his taste, anyway. So he has several books on composition, for example, and more on perspective, and line, and colour and who knows what. And he reads them all the time."

She had to stifle a giggle before continuing.

"I sketched him once, lying propped up in bed with a huge book — something he had imported from England called *Netherlandish Masters*. He was wearing his night cap, of course, and the tiniest reading glasses. And he looked like a character out of Charles Dickens. He was not at all charmed by my drawing. Far too vain."

"He has a lot of ambition, I think."

"Oh, yes. Lionel Redmond is not a man to keep his art hidden away. God forbid. No, he's always been out in the world with it."

A table finally opened up and they continued their conversation over coffee and croissants, the first Sarah had ever tasted. Stephen noticed that the waiters ferried the coffee across the café floor with the spoons angled out from each cup. Naturally, he had to ask the waiter why this was so, and was told it was to keep the liquid stabilized through any pitch or yaw of the ship. They shared a comfortable pause in their conversation. Sarah looked out at sky and cloud, and listened to the snap of the awnings overhead.

"No art can match this," she said, and inhaled deeply, filling her lungs to their capacity with sea air before letting it slowly out again with a sigh. "It's simply not possible."

"Exactly what I was thinking," Stephen said. After a moment he added, "Matching the world, though. Do you think that's really what the artists are vying for?"

And off they went again.

CHAPTER 10

My being drawn to Sarah Ballard in some yet undefined
way did nothing to slow my pursuit of Nurse Troy.
Despite my attempts to appear thoroughly rational and modern, I think I saw Sarah as an untouchably ethereal creature,
and not one likely to be attracted to me. Nurse Troy was another matter, and far from ethereal.

Well, this is going very well, I thought, as Bella and I were
seated at the perfect table with the perfect view over Lake
Flower. Jasper Keene's play had turned out to be easily worth
a second viewing, and Bella had said so too. By giving me the
two tickets, I felt Keene was my fairy godmother, perhaps my
Pandarus. Bella even allowed herself a second glass of wine over
dinner. Promising, indeed.

In truth she was less impressed with the play than with
the fact that I had met Jasper. She asked more than once
why he had taken such an interest in me, and I had to admit
I was equally mystified. But gratuitous kindness is a rare

and precious commodity and one shouldn't question it too
closely.

As I walked her home, the moon was high and bright so
that the pavement beneath our feet seemed lit from within.
We reached her little house and when she did not turn to bid
me goodnight at the gate nor even at the foot of the porch I
thought this was it — Gascoyne, you've got it made. She would
invite me in, her housemates would retire to a discreet distance,
and this would be the big night.

She sat down on a glider beneath the front window and
patted the seat beside her.

"Come and sit for a minute," she said.

The glider looked a good deal off-kilter but I took my place
beside her with unwholesome eagerness.

"That was really a most enjoyable evening," she said.
"Thank you."

"It's *still* a lovely evening," I said. "You look beautiful in
this light."

"Ha. What a line."

"It's true. You look beautiful in all lights."

She just shook her head and looked at her hands folded in
her lap. I placed a light grip on her far shoulder and leaned in
for a kiss. She turned her face to the side so that it became a kiss
on her cool cheek. At first. But then she adjusted her position
so that our lips met. This was the most exciting moment for me
since the departure of Dark Emily who, before deciding to rip
my heart out, had vouchsafed me more than a few kisses. Every
nerve in my body lit up.

When I leaned in again, Bella's hand came up between us
and gently pushed me back.

"That's enough of that," she said mildly.

"Not for me."

"In that case, Mr. Gascoyne, you don't know what's good for you."

"*Mr. Gascoyne?* Really?"

She stood, took my hand, and pulled me to my feet, and I refuse to recount my protestations, my shameless testicular whining, which only strengthened and could not change her adamantine will.

As I walked away, the molecules of humiliation, frustration, and most of the other negative emotions smashed into each other within my chest and formed a throbbing ball of anger — partly at Bella but mostly at the curse of male lust. I dimly recall gesticulating and muttering to myself as I stomped along. Instead of turning left onto Main and heading back to Ursula Pryce's unloving home, I continued back toward the Riverside and along the edge of Lake Flower, then up and down darker streets whose names I did not know. Somewhere in the distance, a train whistle screamed and a harsh bell clanged. I passed a house from whose open window issued the faint sounds of a piano and a woman singing.

I chose the hillier walks, hoping they would tire me out, and eventually they did. I resolved, huffing and puffing now, to quit Miss Bella Troy and pursue erotic success elsewhere. But where? I had no other possibilities lined up. Since, as I say, physical gratification and childish "vengeance" on Emily were my chief motivations, the idea of pursuing Sarah Ballard did not even occur to me. She had lost both husband and father, and taking advantage of personal grief was a line that even my amoral desires would not permit me to cross.

I had reached the edge of the town where the forest threatens to overrun it and turned back. Avoiding Helen Street, which would take me back to my tragically lonely room, I veered off again and found myself on the long driveway of the Reception Hospital. This was where patients were assessed upon arrival for admission either to the sanitarium or to one of the privately run cure cottages. It was also a dreaded place for the severely ill, because it was the infirmary to which they were consigned if their disease progressed beyond a level such "lay" institutions could manage. The building windows were brightly lit but the grounds were dark. I found a bench toward the back, right up against the surrounding woods, and sat myself down. Gradually, the crisp night air and the stillness of the streets had their calming effect on my agitated soul.

A clattering shook me out of my thoughts. A truck drove through the hospital gate and around to the back. Doors slammed open and shut, and rough voices snapped instructions to one another. I couldn't imagine what their noisy work was all about, but I got up and resumed my restless walk. At some point I must have crossed Main Street again and somehow found myself at the train station.

The locomotive clanged its bell and let off blasts of steam. I walked the length of the platform where half a dozen passengers waited under the lights. They looked strangely orderly and obedient as they boarded their respective cars. As I reached the end of the platform, another clattering sound took me out of my reverie and the mysterious truck I had seen at the hospital pulled in. Two men climbed out and set about opening the back of their vehicle as a conductor came over to give them instructions. Their voices were quieter now, but perhaps that was only an effect of the steaming locomotive. In the spill of light, I could now read the lettering on the side of the van: Fortune & Co. The irony of the name was far too overt for my literary sensibilities. Fortune manufactured and sold the thousands of cure chairs that Saranac's main industry demanded. And when a patient passed beyond reach of all sickness and suffering, well, Fortune provided furniture for that too.

The men slid a long plain box from the back of the truck and placed it on a waiting dolly. They repeated the action with another box, followed by a third and a fourth. When all four were neatly stacked, they were trundled down to the far end of the train. This was the famous 10:20, the night train for New York, and these four passengers had not been as lucky as Madeleine Barr. I watched from the platform until it rounded a curve and hooted once more as the last of its tail lights vanished.

I believe I have mentioned that the rules concerning visitors of the opposite sex were stringent — even for people such as myself who were paid to visit. So I was surprised when I knocked on the open door to Sarah's room and heard a man's voice. It was with even more surprise that I recognized the rich theatrical tones of Jasper Keene. He had his back to me, seated in the visitor's chair beside Sarah's, but he was pointing to something beyond the window. I knocked on the frame of the porch door, and they both looked around and up at me.

"Well, as I live and breathe," Jasper said, "it's the poet himself. How are you, Gascoyne?"

"Very well, indeed. And I must tell you I enjoyed the play even more the second time. So thank you."

"Not at all, my boy. Glad you could use the ticket. Good of you to sit through it again."

Thus began my career as literary and psychological ana-
lyst of anything Jasper Keene ever said. Two things to parse
here. First, he used the singular "ticket," not tickets. This
seemed tremendously discreet, considering his frank appraisal of my Nurse Troy campaign the other night. Second,
the use of "my boy," though he was only some twelve or
thirteen years older than I — a considerable difference in
age, but hardly generational. I was not in the least put out
by this. I found his paternal manner charming, cordial, all
the more so because of his manly voice — mahogany and
whiskey combined.

Sarah was finishing a sketch of him, turning it now so that
he could see.

"Oh, now that is *fine*," he said. "Truly fine. But you're flattering me."

"It's perfectly accurate," Sarah said. Then to me: "Jasper is
my cousin. I wasn't expecting him. But here he is as a wonderful surprise."

And here I must explain the phenomenon of "cousining,"
as they called it in Saranac. Yes, *cousining* had become a verb,
but not in the Renaissance sense of *cozen*, as in to cheat or
hoodwink. To *cousin* in the Saranac sense was to take on a
person of the opposite sex as a — let's call it a regular visitor
— under the guise of their being a family member. It was the
only way members of the opposite sex could visit each other.
If two people were deemed *cousins*, that could mean anything
from their sharing a common interest in stamp collecting to
their carrying on a raging adulterous affair that was bound to
end in heartbreak for one, two, three, or even more people.
Sarah's use of the term unsettled me; I would have to revise
my understanding of her, preliminary as it still was.

"Sarah has been telling me you're a wonderful teacher," Jasper said, "and I quote, 'he finds just the right note between encouragement and criticism. It makes me want to do better and better.'"

"Stop it," Sarah said. "You're embarrassing me."

"How so? I'm handing him a bouquet of compliments. What can possibly be embarrassing about that?" He winked at me. "Frankly, I'm jealous. The girl won't show me a single line she's written."

"Certainly not," Sarah said. "You're a professional."

"I understand she's telling you all about the *Lusitania*."

"And writing about it, yes."

"And oh my, isn't that something. I tell you, Paul, I don't want to talk politics, but I don't know what is wrong with Wilson. The minute he declares war on those barbarians, I'm there. Just point me in the right direction, I'm there. Put me in a trench, put me on a destroyer, I'm there."

"I'm not mad keen on soldiering," I said. "I don't think I'd be very good at it."

"It's war! Of course you'd be good at it! It's a simple matter. You get up in the morning and kill as many Germans as you can. It's life and death, my boy, life and death. What could possibly make life sweeter than thousands of bullets screaming round your head? Everywhere around you, lives winking out. By God, it gets my blood up. What could possibly be more exciting?"

"A good line of poetry," I said.

"Well answered, son, well answered."

I suggested that perhaps we should skip today's session, so as not to spoil Mr. Keene's visit.

"It's Jasper, boy, Jasper. Let's have none of this 'Mister' stuff or I'll have to start calling you 'Professor.'"

"Please, no — I'm not a professor."

"Good. Never understood the concept of English Literature professors, myself. It's not possible to *teach* Shakespeare. Or Milton, or Shelley. What in God's name is there to *teach* about a Keats ode? It's all right there on the page."

I have answers to such charges. But Jasper Keene could be an intimidating force. There he was, at least a foot taller than I, dressed in a jet-black coat that hung about him like a theatrical cape, and essentially accusing me of being a fraud.

"Perhaps you imagine such things are manufactured out of iambic pentameter," he went on.

"Well, often — among other —"

"Please don't." He covered his eyes and held out a restraining hand. "I couldn't stand it. Tell him to stop, Sarah, he's hurting me. He's destroying the magic of poetry, he must be stopped. He's damaging the atmosphere."

"He is not," Sarah said. "You told me yourself he's a good poet."

"Did I, now. But that was before I knew the nature of your intercourse. Before I knew you were sharing the intimate details of your encounter with the ultimate seducer."

He was saying this with a smile, a smile that made his eyes all the brighter. I thought he could only be joking and forced a little laugh. But he went on.

"I suppose you're telling him the story — that all-too-brief tragedy — of your shipboard romance. She won't tell me, you know. And the loss of your munificently talented father."

"Well." I turned to Sarah. "I'll leave you to it. I'll see you at our next scheduled time."

"Oh, please don't go," Sarah said, and reached out a pale arm toward me.

Jasper twiddled his fingers at me. "Ciao, *Professor.*"

"Good day," I said. "And good luck with the next play."

"Thank you, my boy. Appreciate the sentiment, but it's never a matter of luck. It's a matter of courting the muse. Courting the muse."

I stepped back from the porch and made my exit through Sarah's room.

I went out and headed up Helen Hill, changed my mind halfway up, and headed back down I knew not where. My feelings, to say the least, were confused. I understood why Sarah found Jasper attractive. He was the sort of handsome that people used to call "dashing," and he had an air of imperturbable authority that could carry one away if it didn't cow you altogether. And of course he was famous. But his drastic change of tone — warm and fatherly one night, and ... well, I didn't know what it was now. I couldn't tell if he was angry at me, or at Sarah, or at both of us. Would he have been so hostile to *any* male visitor? Or had he misconstrued my flirtation with Bella Troy as a general campaign to seduce all womankind at once? I couldn't imagine I would fit *that* bill.

CHAPTER 11

These days I was seeing Sarah at meal times, but we did not talk much. In contrast to her liveliness during our tutorials, she barely spoke at all, keeping her gaze mostly on her plate as the cheery exchanges of the others flew by. Even Broadway Ben's show business anecdotes couldn't animate her. She seemed to shrink into herself amid this group, as if she preferred not to be noticed. Once I saw her out on Main Street with Mrs. Pryce and young Leah Landers, but that seemed to be the extent of her socializing.

"Jasper Keene," I said at our next session, "is a most unusual man."

The temperature was hovering around freezing and fat snowflakes drifted down past the porch windows. Even in my coat and hat I was cold, though Sarah, like all the patients, was unfazed. She usually wore a pair of fingerless gloves to facilitate her sketching, but today a fur hat framed her face in a most becoming way, and she had a muffler on her lap.

"But you did like him, didn't you?"

"He seems … changeable. And perhaps unpredictable?" A generous understatement, in my view.

"Ah, but that's part of his charm. I admire him tremendously. He has a courageous quality that I lack — that most people lack. Did you know he was a patient?"

"Yes. Quite surprising, he seems so robust."

She smiled. "We met in the reception hospital. He had already been there for some time, as they couldn't quite figure out his case. But he drove the staff absolutely wild — he would do song-and-dance numbers in the halls and put on ridiculous hats to make people laugh. Essentially, he behaved as if tuberculosis were strictly for *other* people and not Jasper Keene. They put him under the care of Dr. Fenwick, which was a frightful error — Fenwick is the strictest of the strict."

"Yes, I've heard the rumours."

"Jasper stood it for about a week before he hired himself a guide to smuggle him out to the woods. He stayed out there on his own for about a month and came back completely cured."

"Surely not. That would make headlines."

"Well, not cured. Arrested. Anyway, don't judge him too harshly — I know the two of you could be the best of friends."

I was not sure of this at all, and I wondered for the first time if her being drawn to Jasper was entirely healthy. I changed the subject and asked about her memoir writing; I had received no further installment.

"I simply can't do it," Sarah said. "The words won't come. I sit and stare at pen and paper and nothing comes out."

"You don't have to write about the sinking," I said. "Obviously such a traumatic event …"

"No, it's not that it's painful. Somehow it's the actual writing that stops me. I can talk about it — with you, anyway. I trust you, for some reason."

No doubt she only meant that I seemed harmless, but still it cheered my heart. I suggested she just tell me some of the happy bits and perhaps write them down later. What follows is an amalgam of both, augmented by my own memories of newspaper accounts.

"What can I tell you?" she said. "We were on a magnificent ship. There was wine and moonlight, the ocean breeze and the crash of the sea. And below it all the constant throb of the engines. We did nothing but talk and talk day after day. And I think it was on day four we saw the captain taking a stroll on the deck and Stephen said, 'Let's ask him to marry us.' Just like that. He hadn't even proposed to me at that point, so I thought he was joking and said so. He promptly got down on one knee and asked me to marry him and when it finally got through to me that he meant it I said yes. It seems mad, when I tell it. But it also seemed ..."

"Inevitable?" I suggested.

"Inevitable. So I said yes. And we went running along the deck and caught up to the captain and asked him to marry us.

"He was quite a gruff personage, Captain Turner. But some people appear gruff when really they are only shy. I believe there was a tenderness in him that his bearish demeanour was meant to protect. In any case, he said he would be happy to perform the ceremony, provided we understood certain things.

"He asked where we were from. And when we told him New York and New Jersey he said, 'You realize New York does not recognize a marriage at sea unless the couple has already taken out state marriage licenses.'"

"Really?" I said. "I thought it was a special power captains have, like a priest's."

"So did I," Sarah said. "And that's what makes it all the more remarkable that the Ballards have taken me under their wing. Anyway, we assured Captain Turner that we didn't care. We were far too caught up in the excitement of the moment, the storybook aspect.

"He also informed us that there would be no reassignment of cabins to accommodate what he called our 'connubial status.' I was hideously embarrassed, but Stephen assured him that we perfectly understood, and the matter was settled. We were married the next day."

"Your father must've been thrown for a loop."

"I was petrified at the thought of telling him, but it turned out to be worry for nothing. The weather had continued calm and sunny, and he was beginning to feel like himself for the first time since leaving New York. He was feeling so good that he joined us in the Admirals' Lounge the following morning — neither of us wanted a chapel — and he gave me away."

Sarah went quiet, and her expression took on an inward cast.

"I don't remember much about the rest of that day. Stephen went out of his way to charm Father and succeeded brilliantly. I remember a lot of laughter. I was thoroughly giddy — astounded by my own happiness — and even my usually-too-serious father could not resist it. And then …"

I gave her a moment.

One of the most striking things about the morning of May 7 — and I remembered this myself from the newspaper accounts — was that the day broke with a preternatural stillness. The mist that clung to the waters in the early hours soon melted away, revealing a surface as unruffled as any Adirondack pond. A dozen miles off the port side, the Irish coastline glowed iridescent green.

"Two details I do remember," Sarah said. "They were things Stephen noticed. The first was that there were no warships in sight; he had expected one or two to escort us up the channel to Liverpool.

"The other was that we were going so slowly. I wouldn't have noticed myself, but Cunard had this silly betting pool every night where you wagered on the number of miles we might have travelled in the past twenty-four hours. Stephen entered every time, and he was always within five or ten miles — it was over five hundred miles on the first day. But this morning they had posted the mileage and it was only four hundred sixty or so. Which he found disturbing. I mean, you would think, now that we were in what the Germans called 'war zone waters,' we'd be making full use of the ship's magnificent engines but apparently not. Anyway, it didn't bother me. When your world is perfect, you can't imagine it's about to be blown to nothing."

The day was so welcoming that even her father was up and about, quite recovered from his nausea, though still unsteady on his feet. The three of them had an early lunch together, and afterward he asked his new son-in-law to take a turn with him about the promenade deck. Sarah went off to the library to write postcards.

"Surely having your father around for his honeymoon must have put your husband off to some degree?"

Sarah shook her head. "The two of them took to each other quite readily. Stephen's interest in photography stood him in good stead there."

So the two men headed off on their promenade, and Sarah settled into the library and spent the next half-hour writing postcards. She sat for a while afterward reading her book, and then took her own little promenade along the port side. The deck was crowded with passengers, and there was excitement in the air that soon they would once again be on dry land. Suddenly, people were talking with strangers they had ignored for the entire preceding voyage.

Sarah was watching the green jewel of Ireland glide by in the distance when she heard what she called a *clunk*. "Like someone dropping a heavy object — maybe a sledgehammer — on a metal floor. It wasn't all that loud really." But the ship made an unnatural movement, a kind of jerk or lurch that everyone felt, and this was followed by a tremendous explosion that tore upward through the deck well forward of where Sarah was standing. A white pillar of water shot high up into the sky, and then cinders and black smoke and debris, well above the smokestacks and the Marconi wires. It seemed to hang for a moment in the air, and then it all came raining back down onto the decks.

"I heard people saying 'torpedo,' 'torpedo,'" Sarah said, "but I wasn't taking anything in. I couldn't comprehend it. I was standing there with my mouth open, my mind a complete blank. And then there was a second explosion — from somewhere deep inside the ship. It didn't sound at all like the first — more like a boiler blowing up."

Her first thought was to look for Stephen and her father, but she had no idea where they were. She gripped the railing and took a few deep breaths. When she turned back, a steward was telling people they could put on life jackets if they wanted but there was absolutely no chance the *Lusitania* was going to sink, no chance at all. Crew members were under orders to *not* lower the lifeboats. The order was soon reversed, because in a matter of minutes the ship was listing sharply starboard and the bow was nearly down to the water.

The disaster of the *Titanic* three years earlier had taught the shipping companies a few things; the *Lusitania* had more than enough lifeboats and life jackets. And the safety pamphlet in every cabin explained how to strap on the life jacket and which lifeboat you were assigned to. But other lessons had not been learned. There had been no emergency drills for the passengers, which meant that they were not practised at putting on their life preservers. And because so many seamen had been absorbed into the British Navy, the crew was largely inexperienced. To make matters worse, portholes on the upper decks were left open, allowing water to pour into the ship at hundreds of tons per minute.

Sarah decided to retrieve life jackets from her cabin and check her father's at the same time. She would meet Stephen at a lifeboat near their respective cabins. The list of the ship made getting down the steps difficult. She clung to the rail but by the time she made the corridor the lighting failed.

"The darkness was terrifying. I could hear the water pouring into the corridor at the far end — the bow end — and I couldn't see a thing at first. Then I realized there was a bit of light from the portholes at the end of the cross passages, but the ship was tilted so badly it was only the light reflected off the surface. I tried to get to my cabin but the water was rushing in and the list was so sharp I had to put one foot on the wall, one foot on the floor. There was no way I could get to my cabin, let alone my father's. I turned to go back, got to the stairs, and then it was like a hallucination — there was Stephen at the top."

The two lovers held each other in a fleeting moment of relief. Stephen had already been to his cabin to retrieve life jackets. He was wearing one that said *Mrs. Stephen Ballard*; his own had now gone missing. Apparently, in a burst of romantic hubris he had gone ahead and ordered *two* personalized jackets, one for himself and one for his wife-to-be. This he now took off and placed over Sarah's shoulders and pulled the straps tight. She told him not to, that she could use one of the lifebelts on deck, but he wouldn't hear of it.

The lifeboats were designed to hold forty passengers comfortably, as many as seventy in a crisis. They were heavy craft, each equipped with a sail and multiple sets of oars. But now the list to starboard had rendered all the lifeboats on the port side useless; they hung inward above the deck, pressing all their weight against the structures of the ship, making it impossible to lower them over the side. Sarah and her new husband made their way to starboard.

"I can't begin to describe the chaos," she told me. She stared into a nether distance, her voice now a numb monotone. "People running this way and that, fumbling with their life preservers. People screaming each other's names. It was madness."

On the starboard side, the lifeboats presented the opposite problem from port; they were hanging too far out over the water to reach. Seamen had to stretch from the railing with boat hooks to pull them in, but they were extremely heavy. Had the German U-boat captain, assisted by God or fate or luck, tried consciously to engineer the greatest possible panic he could hardly have done better. The law of inertia meant the ship, although slowed by the waters soon to close over its bow, was still going about 18 knots, even though the engines had now quit. These factors caused secondary tragedies on top of the all-enveloping disaster.

A lifeboat filled with women and children was lowered, but it hit the water with so much forward momentum that people were hurled over the front and into the water. A second lifeboat snapped its forward rope, spilling everyone — again mostly women and children — into the sea. As if planned by a satanic *farceur*, a third lifeboat crashed down on top of the poor souls already thrashing in the water, killing many at a stroke. The screams were terrible.

"I looked around for Stephen but he had climbed into a lifeboat that was stuck. He was trying to free the stern rope, when the forward end came loose, and everyone …"

Sarah stopped, grey eyes staring straight ahead, mouth open a little. The snow had turned to rain that pattered gently on the windows. I doubt if she was seeing the rain-blurred cemetery, or the shadowy hulk of Baker Mountain, but I cursed myself for having prodded her to recall her nightmare. I also felt a tremendous desire to throw my arms around her, unthinkable in 1916, and the first tender stirrings of love, or at least the urge to protect. I suggested we stop for the day.

"No, I want to continue. I just … I want to continue."

She spoke with surprising urgency, even an element of compulsion, and I was reminded of Coleridge's ancient mariner condemned endlessly to recount his own catastrophe at sea.

"A steward helped me into one of the collapsible life rafts," Sarah resumed in her monotone, "along with too many other people."

It proved to be defective. Key parts were rusted or broken, which meant that the seats, which were supposed to hold up the sides, could not be fitted into their slots. It sank beneath them and all aboard were dispersed into the water, which was now a cold hellish cauldron of capsized lifeboats, chairs, ropes, wires, planks, dead bodies, and people screaming.

"One woman was in the throes of childbirth," Sarah said, "screaming and crying, and all around her there were dead children bobbing in their little life jackets."

Many of the dead floated face down in the water, having put their unfamiliar life jackets on backwards so that they were tipped forward rather than back. Some were badly injured and drifted in clouds of blood.

By now the angle of the ship was steep. As it descended nose down into the depths, the stern was canted high in the air. One man dangled from a rope off the rear railings. As the ship sank deeper it twisted suddenly to port and he was swung into a still-turning propeller that sliced off a leg. Sarah found herself clinging to an upturned dog kennel, trying to kick her way toward one of the lifeboats that was still upright. Beside her, a woman was hanging on to a dead man, the buoyancy of his life jacket enough to keep her afloat.

Survivors reported that the ship made a terrible noise in its last moments — an "unearthly wail," a "dying howl" that they would never forget. Sarah turned to look and saw the four massive smokestacks slamming down to the water.

"After that," Sarah said. "Nothing. Blackness. The next four or five hours was cut from my life, and I woke up to whatever was left."

I have a vivid memory of reading this part of her memoir. I had a good fire going in my room, and was seated in my armchair with a blanket over my lap. A squall had kicked up outside, flinging fat snowflakes that clung to the window and slid downward as they melted. The night train was hooting its departure.

I knew from newspaper accounts that the British Admiralty maintained a hard-nosed policy regarding U-boat attacks: naval vessels were strictly forbidden to go to the aid of a stricken ship

— a cruelty that reflected the lesson of earlier encounters where rescue ships had themselves been sunk by submarines just waiting for them to show. For passengers on the *Lusitania*, it meant anywhere from four to ten hours in fifty-five-degree water until fishing boats and other small craft could come to their aid.

"When I first woke up, I didn't remember anything at all — about the explosion, I mean. And the sinking. I woke up soaking wet and unable to move. I thought I was still aboard the *Lusitania*. A very odd-looking man was staring down at me. He was wearing a watch cap, and he had a pipe between his teeth, and he was calling over to someone else, 'Mary, love, bring us some tea. This one's not dead.' They had put me among the bodies that were laid out along the dock.

"When they tried to move me, I was violently ill. My skull felt as if it had been cleaved open. Later, somebody told me I had been hit by a board of some kind, but it may just as well have been an axe. I had no memory of anything. I thought I was still aboard ship and couldn't imagine why I was being addressed by an Irish fisherman."

Soon the fisherman's wife was helping her out of her life jacket and calling her Mrs. Ballard. When asked why, she showed her the bold print on the jacket: Mrs. Stephen Ballard, New York. The jacket had a pocket for valuables, and from this the Irishwoman plucked a ring and slipped it on Sarah's finger.

"I still have it," Sarah said, holding up a pale hand. "I suppose I should stop wearing it sometime soon." She slipped it off and handed it to me. "What do you think?"

I examined the ring in the window light, the metal still warm from her finger. It was a simple gold band with what they call a "nickel" edge. The name "Stephen" was engraved on the inside, nothing else.

"I think you should wear it as long as you want."

I handed it back and she put it on.

"It was the most awful feeling, on that dock. I was suspended in the most dizzying way. Imagine not remembering if you were married or not. I didn't even recognize my own name. They could've told me I was Queen of Sweden. I certainly wasn't convinced I had married someone named Stephen Ballard, but I tried to let on that I was fine, aside from my head wound. I was in shock. You couldn't not be, after going through that experience. And I was overwhelmed by the sight of all the dead, especially the children, and the weeping mothers and fathers; it was like witnessing the Last Judgment. But I wasn't really grieving — not for my personal loss, because I — it was as if none of it ever happened. I didn't remember what had happened to Stephen. Not then. Or to my father."

Her Irish rescuers wrapped Sarah in a warm blanket. Hot tea was brought and a jam tart, and then she was loaded into an ambulance and taken to Queen's Hospital. As she recalled the kindness and care of the Irish doctors and nurses, her voice became livelier and we ended on a cheerful note. Sarah told me that Mr. and Mrs. Ballard were coming to visit again, and she very much wanted me to meet them.

"Surely they won't want to waste any time on an ink-stained wretch like me."

"Mrs. B. will completely adore you. Mr. Ballard can be a little brusque, but he has a heart of pure gold and I've insisted they meet my personal professor. Now don't contradict me. This is a tenured position I'm offering and you have it for life."

I don't know if Cyrus Ballard was a millionaire or not. He was certainly not in the Carnegie-Rockefeller-Whitney range of robber barons, but he had a house on Fifth Avenue a block or two above Washington Square, and another in Rochester, where his furniture business was centred. And he and his wife were planning to build or purchase another right in Saranac Lake so that they could visit Sarah for longer periods of time.

He was easily rich enough to impress Mrs. Pryce. Even though this was their third or fourth visit, it was the only time I ever saw her genuinely excited about anything. She rarely spoke to me outside of mealtimes, but a few days before the big event she asked me to follow her through a heavy oak door at the back of the front hall, which led to the private part of the house. She closed the door softly behind us.

"Mr. Gascoyne, Mrs. Ballard has asked for you to join us for a private dinner on the night her parents-in-law arrive. Mr. Ballard, as you may know, is a highly successful industrialist. Now, anyone can tell you've been well brought up, so I've no doubt you'll overcome your habitual lateness."

"Set your mind at rest, Mrs. Pryce. I'm very much looking forward to meeting them."

"I've thought about serving roast duck but it may make for rather too rich a meal, and the servings, if I'm honest, would not be the largest. I'm of a mind now that a roast of beef would be more appropriate for a man of affairs like Mr. Ballard, even though I've served it to them before. What do you think?"

I was astonished that she would seek my opinion but I agreed that a roast of beef could scarcely go amiss.

"Good. Now I'll take this opportunity to broach another matter, if you don't mind. And please know that I don't intend the slightest criticism."

She opened the glass doors of a side parlour and motioned me inside. It was a pretty little room and, unlike the curative part of the house, decorated in the manner of Victorian clutter; light spilled in from a large window and winked off picture frames, mirrors, and bevelled glass.

"First, I want to caution you against raising literary matters at table. Mr. Ballard is one of nature's truly self-made men, which is to say, despite his great success, he is not a highly educated man like yourself and would not be comfortable discussing William Shakespeare and Dr. Johnson."

"I think I can manage standard levels of politeness."

"With your lofty education, you'll know that the well-mannered seek only to make *everyone* comfortable."

"I'll try my best, Mrs. Pryce. If you have some reading material on the finer points of office furniture, I could prepare myself properly."

"You're giving an excellent impression of an imbecile, Mr. Gascoyne. You could be an actor."

"Who says I'm acting?"

At this, she folded her arms in front of her chest and gave a smiling though bull-like snort.

"As I was saying. It was Sarah Ballard who asked that you join us, and I want to address you on a related matter. I have been in this business for a good long while now, and I know the signs. When you look at her — and you look at her a lot —"

"Mrs. Pryce."

"Allow me to finish. When you look at her, it's with a particular *warmth* — I think I may use that word — I am not the only one who's noticed."

I admire the woman, I started to say, but she cut me off again.

"People are talking — not harshly, mind, but talking — and if I've seen it once I've seen it a thousand times. Young people alone and far from home? No proper employment? Missing spouses or parents or children? Facing an early death or lifelong debility? Hearts get broken, Mr. Gascoyne. The poor girl is already in the sights of Mr. Jasper Keene, and I don't know which of you is the more dangerous. Hearts get broken, Mr. Gascoyne, and I do not want to see it. The doctors tell us that our every effort must be toward maintaining an atmosphere of optimism and good cheer."

"And any admiration between the sexes must make happiness impossible?"

"How has it worked out for you so far? I'm well aware of your pursuit of Nurse Troy."

"Pursuit!"

"Did you imagine your mission clandestine? We're a city of nurses, Mr. Gascoyne, and nurses talk. As to Nurse Troy, while I wish you happiness in romance as in all things, you won't be the first to come to grief on that quest, nor do I fancy you'll be the last. But it's not you I'm worried about. If you break Sarah Ballard's heart — after what she's been through? That barbarous Teutonic atrocity? The murder of husband and father? And then to be stricken with tuberculosis? She's vulnerable, Mr. Gascoyne, she's vulnerable. And I know you share my hope that she come to no further harm — whether at your hands or anybody else's."

Mrs. Pryce had perfected a mode of attack clearly modelled on the U-boat captains she deplored: launch torpedoes and retire at once. Before I could manage to form a coherent reply, she had opened the glass doors and cruised off down the hall.

The night of the Ballards' arrival found me once more (and punctually!) in that parlour. I should perhaps clarify that separating the Ballards in this way from the rest of the household was not an act of snobbery on Mrs. Pryce's part. Most visitors preferred to keep a hygienic distance from their tubercular kin, not to mention their ailing housemates. Mr. Ballard was ensconced in a wingback chair, bouncing one knee up and down as if he had urgently to be somewhere else, and occasionally holding up his sherry glass to examine the fire through it. That motion, and his own glinting spectacles, gave him somewhat the look of a jeweller. He said very little, but every once in a while emitted a sort of bulletin: *terrible train service coming down; damned if I'll pay for first class. Wilson? Not an admirer. In for a bit of snow, they say.*

Mrs. Ballard, a diminutive woman with the rosy cheeks of a Meissen figurine, stood beside Sarah, who was seated near the fire, and rested a protective hand on her shoulder. Now and again Sarah would raise her own hand and place it over her mother-in-law's, grey eyes shining with the firelight. Every so often the two of them would lapse into a brief *tête-à-tête*, sharing quiet exchanges before remembering they were in company. Together, the bereaved mother and the motherless young woman seemed united in a world of two, exuding a familial warmth I could only envy, given the frostbitten bookishness of my own upbringing.

In an effort to burnish my credentials as a man of culture (without mentioning Shakespeare or Dr. Johnson), I asked Ballard if he and his wife had seen the plays of Jasper Keene. Despite not being at all certain that I *liked* Jasper, I had no hesitation in enjoying the reflected limelight in knowing him.

"Dunno," said Ballard. And turning to his wife: "Have we?"

"Of course we did — on Broadway last year. We saw *The Lady's Man*. We should've got box seats — then you'd remember."

"Box seats. What nonsense."

"I haven't seen that one," I said. "But I did just recently see *Married or Not*."

Before I could casually mention that the playwright himself had given me the tickets, Sarah spoke of how delighted she was with her room in the "up" cottage.

"It has an even better view of Baker Mountain." She didn't mention her "colleagues" in the graveyard across the street.

"You keep a fine house, Mrs. Pryce." Ballard raised his sherry glass in salute and took a sip.

"To Mrs. Pryce," I said, raising my own glass in a pathetic attempt to curry favour.

"Oh, it's nothing grand," Mrs. Pryce said, clearly glowing under the compliment, "but heaven knows I do my best."

A serving maid came around with a plate of elegant hors d'oeuvres.

"It astonishes me," Mrs. Ballard said, "how you get hold of such delicacies out here in the wilderness."

"No mystery there," I said. "The first visitors to the area were extremely wealthy, and ensured they could live in the manner they were used to. I, for one, am grateful."

I noted Mr. Ballard's skeptical silence. At the same time, I was observing within myself that it is with the wealthy as it is with the famous; one hopes for their approval without even knowing them. Despite his taciturnity, or perhaps because of it, Ballard gave the undeniable impression that he inhabited a world wider than my own. All my studies, all my reading and writing, would never measure up to his empire of bricks and mortar, his command of a labour force, his discernment of supply and demand; they seemed not as real. There was no question as to who was the useful member of society.

Sarah apparently did not share Mrs. Pryce's aversion to discussing literature in her father-in-law's company.

"Mr. Gascoyne has me reading the most wonderful books," she said to Mrs. Ballard. "Have you ever read *Middlemarch*?"

"No, my dear. Is it good?"

"It's the most perfect novel ever. I think you would enjoy it immensely. It's about a woman who marries a scholarly man she admires, but along the way comes to realize that he doesn't respect her in the least, or even love her. It's written by a woman and I think she must be one of the most brilliant women who ever lived."

"It sounds lovely," Mrs. Ballard said. "I'm so glad you have such stories to take your mind off things."

"It's not just that. It puts my mind *into* things — things I never thought about before. Or at least never thought about in quite the same way."

"George Eliot is truly one of the greats," I said grandly. "An anatomist not just of society, but of the human heart."

Mrs. Ballard looked at her daughter-in-law. "I thought you said it was a woman."

I started to explain that it was common for female novelists of the Victorian era to take a male pen name but Mrs. Pryce diverted the conversation with a question for Mr. Ballard concerning the latest restrictions on logging in the Adirondacks. Was it not problematic for a manufacturer of desks and chairs? It was a good question — so good that I wished I'd thought of it myself — but he seemed preoccupied with other matters and transmitted the briefest of bulletins from his wingback chair.

"We're doing fine," he said. "Plenty of wood around." He looked as if he wanted to say something quite different, but he lapsed back into his preoccupation.

"You must forgive my husband," Mrs. Ballard said. "Mr. Ballard feels it's his duty to do nothing but work, work, work every minute of every day, even though I beg him not to. Even as we got off the train, he felt it necessary to stop into Western Union and check for any messages. Couldn't leave it alone for even so much as a day. And I'm afraid whatever crisis he uncovered there has darkened his mood ever since."

The silence that followed was broken by the maid, who informed Mrs. Pryce that supper was ready. Mrs. Pryce led us into her private dining room, which was laden with eye-catching crystal and silverware. For some of the cure cottages, looking after the sick was a matter of one or two patients, which would earn them a bit of extra income, but Mrs. Pryce's operation was clearly raking in a sizeable profit. She sat Mr. Ballard at the head of the table and myself at the other end. Sarah, on my immediate left, looked resplendent in a blue satin dress, and when she smiled at me I felt a flood of warmth in my chest, and I wondered if Mrs. Pryce might be wrong about who was vulnerable and who was not.

The roast did Mrs. Pryce proud. And somewhere in her highland Presbyterian background she had learned about wine, because she served a Bordeaux that even I with my unsophisticated palate could tell was good. Mr. Ballard stirred himself to emit a gruff compliment with which I readily concurred, but my attention was really fixed on Sarah and the elder Mrs. Ballard.

Sarah's mother-in-law was one of those people who are adept at small talk, swift with the light remark or pleasant observation that no one could find objectionable. In contrast to the grudging manner of her husband, she seemed aglow with an innate kindness, brimming with goodwill to all. She looked at me with an appreciative if misguided gaze that seemed to say she'd never encountered such a splendid example of the American male. It was no wonder Sarah adored her.

"How did you come about your own fine education, Mr. Gascoyne?"

I told her briefly about my father, archaeologist and professor of Classics, and my mother, the translator.

"Oh, I didn't know ladies undertook such work."

"My mother has a natural gift — for the Romance languages at least."

"And they're in New York did you say?"

"In Egypt, actually. Digging up pharaohs and whatnot."

"Goodness me, such an educated family. And here you are, carrying on the tradition."

I was dreading the usual question about my aborted professorial career, but I suspected Sarah may have warned her off the topic because neither she nor her husband raised it.

Mrs. Pryce sailed right into it.

"Mr. Gascoyne was a lecturer at Columbia University before he decided to grace us with his presence."

"And I feel ever so lucky that he did," Sarah said.

"Seconded," said Mrs. Ballard stoutly.

She and Sarah were as at ease with each other as if they had spent their entire lives together instead of a matter of months. If anything, Mrs. Ballard seemed *too* affectionate, *too* protective, and I realized that her daughter-in-law must, to the extent such a thing was possible, fill the emptiness left by her son, who, along with some nine hundred other *Lusitania* passengers, including Sarah's father, had been counted among the missing.

When the dessert things were cleared away, Mrs. Pryce proposed that the men retire to the parlour with a brandy. The idea appealed to me because I was curious about this man who had taken Sarah under his wing, despite never having met her, and despite her having been wife to his son for little more than twenty-four hours. Also, I found myself for the first time interested in a man of industry, as Mrs. Pryce had put it. Perhaps this was the first stirrings of a novelist's curiosity, and no doubt I was overestimating my conversational skill, but I welcomed the challenge of getting this brooding, saturnine man to talk about himself and his business and his "adoption" of Sarah.

He cleared his throat. "Can't stay for brandy, I'm afraid."

Mrs. Ballard turned to him with a look of astonishment.

"Mrs. Pryce," he continued. "I want to thank you for a splendid meal. You are an elegant hostess, and my wife and I are grateful. And — something I should have expressed the minute we arrived — we're also grateful to you for providing such excellent care for this young woman. A young woman who has done absolutely nothing to deserve it."

Our expectant smiles vanished in an instant. The colour drained from Sarah's face. Mrs. Ballard looked ready to faint.

"You see," he pressed on, "my wife and I were under the impression that Miss Redmond had married our son, Stephen, on board the *Lusitania* and was now our daughter-in-law — or at least we treated her as such even though we had never met her and even though shipboard marriages are not recognized in the state of New York. We were under no obligation to this woman — we did not *have* to pay for her transport back to this country, we did not *have* to welcome her into our home, we did not *have* to pay for her medical care. So it is with the deepest shock that I have learned, via a message waiting for me at Western Union, that she is not and never has been married to our son."

"Cyrus," his wife said in a panic. "Cyrus, what are you doing? What are you saying?"

"She has lied to us, my dear. She has lied to you, Mrs. Pryce. She has lied to everyone. Here we were, broken-hearted at the loss of our son, presented with the chance of a new daughter — a fragile creature apparently orphaned, marooned in a strange country, and deathly ill. A winsome creature to be sure, with a sweet face and a manner suitably demure, and yet a complete and utter fraud, I tell you, a complete and utter fraud. It's quite a joke on me personally. I pride myself on a certain acumen — an eye for the good deal, able to judge between the honest and the sly, but I fell right into her trap. Stephen's death had clouded my vaunted judgment and, oh yes, she was ready to take advantage, poised to spring. She has stolen our affection under false pretenses. She has abused our trust as she has abused yours, Mrs. Pryce, and you may do with her what you will, because she is no longer — and never has been — in any way related to us."

The revelation was clearly news to Mrs. Ballard. She moved to pick up her water glass but her hand trembled too violently and she set it back down. Mrs. Pryce remained silent, the only time I had seen her so. I finally found my tongue.

"Sir, this is an outrageous charge. How can you possibly back it up?"

"Simple. The wonder is that I waited months before acting on my natural skepticism. I have a business contact in Liverpool. I had him track down Captain Turner himself. On the *Lusitania*'s last voyage, the captain performed exactly one marriage ceremony — and it did not involve our son. Such was the telegram I just received."

"But Stephen sent you a postcard. He'd met the woman of his dreams and he was going to marry her."

"I see she has taken you in as well. There was, indeed, another marriage scheduled to take place at four o'clock Greenwich Mean Time on the afternoon of May 7."

"But she has the ring," I said. "And she was wearing a life jacket saying Mrs. Stephen Ballard."

"You may be interested in her explanation for those circumstances; I am not. My own guess is simple theft. At four o'clock of May 7, Stephen was to marry a woman named Evelyn Howard. Captain Turner remembered because he has a cousin of the same name, though the middle names are different and his cousin is decades older. By 2:33 the *Lusitania* was at the bottom of the sea. Captain Turner showed my contact his pocket watch; it had stopped at 2:36. The marriage did not take place, Stephen's body was never recovered, and neither was Evelyn Howard's."

Mrs. Ballard was now sobbing into her dinner napkin.

I turned to Sarah. "Is this true? You never married him?"

She nodded tightly, not looking at me. She was struggling with the ring.

"It's true."

She pulled the ring from her finger and placed it on the tablecloth in front of Mrs. Ballard. "I'm sorry. I won't even ask you to forgive me."

"Good," Ballard said as she rushed from the room. "Because we do not and will not."

CHAPTER 12

Sarah did not come down for breakfast the next morning. She wasn't in her room either. I heard Mrs. Pryce knocking on her door and calling her name. When later in the morning Sarah returned, Mrs. Pryce trudged up the stairs after her and banged on her door again. Apparently, it was not opened, because I heard every word, at least from Mrs. Pryce's side.

"Miss Redmond, you cannot stay here. I will not have it."

More knocking, and a muffled reply.

"What's that? I want you out of here. Taking advantage of people like the Ballards? It's a disgrace. I'm surprised Mr. Ballard hasn't dragged you into court. He'd be well within his rights."

More knocking.

"No one can believe you anymore, Miss Redmond. Making up stories to stir up sympathy? And in a treatment centre? I want you out, do you hear? No doubt some other cottages will give you a bed, but I will not have the reputation of this establishment undermined. Do I make myself clear?"

I heard the door open and Sarah's mild voice but could not make out the words.

"Good," Mrs. Pryce said. "The sooner the better."

A short time later, a taxi arrived and Sarah was taken away. I could not fault Mrs. Pryce's reaction. Sarah's deceiving of the Ballards was inexcusable on its face. Even more shocking to me was her coolly handing me a pack of lies. If I felt stung by this, and I did, I couldn't imagine how the Ballards must have felt. In wilder moments I wondered if she'd even been *on* the *Lusitania*. Perhaps even her tuberculosis was a lie. In calmer moments I just shook my head and thought what a tawdry little episode the whole thing had been, and ultimately how sad. I would miss my illusory fragile castaway, but was relieved to have learned the truth before becoming any more entangled.

In the days following, I threw myself into my own work, sketching story ideas about innocent young men ardent for and deceived by the most duplicitous of sirens. But I did not write them. I focused instead on my poems of urban despair and made the fundamental mistake of thinking that because I worked so hard on them they must therefore be of the first rank. I submitted them to Harriet Monroe's *Poetry* in Chicago and was certain she would fall for my artfully broken sentences, my sighing ellipses, the Parisian grace notes that hinted at the submerged incalculable agony of twentieth-century man. She did not. At night I read novels until the wolf howl of the night train told me it was time for bed. I could not hear it now without seeing coffins.

Sarah kept intruding on my thoughts, even though I considered our association at an end. I had no wish to see her — an extreme response, considering my previous budding tendrils of affection. But those were now quite torn out. They had been for a different woman than the one I now knew (so I told myself), an honest victim of war and disease, brought to the edge of breakdown by loss of husband and father, not the conniving fraud who had insinuated herself into the Ballards' grieving arms. Wishing only to forget her, I stayed cocooned in my little room and my work, venturing out only to serve my other pupils.

I visited Ronnie Barstowe, and found him radiating such febrile intensity I could almost feel the heat coming off his face. This is one of the more unsettling features of tuberculosis; even the severely ill can suddenly find it impossible to do what they most need to do: lie still. Tubercular fevers are not high, as fevers go, yet they are sometimes accompanied by near mania; it takes a powerful will to resist this high-voltage current of energy and ideas.

Ronnie chattered on, wide-eyed and fever-flushed, politely turning aside every now and then to cough into a cheesecloth, or to make use of his sputum cup. I sat in a chair a safe six feet from the bed in which he was propped at the regulation 30-degree angle. It gave him the look of a young country lord, albeit an ailing one. He talked nonstop.

"I don't want to upset you, Professor, but I'm afraid I won't have time for poetry in the next few months. My sights are now firmly set on the fields of industry — power generation, to be specific, and as a side study Mr. Furbeck is teaching me all about radio. Did you know he built his own transmitter and receiver? Powerful. And — what'll probably be even more useful for an immediate job — he's teaching me telegraphy and Morse code. There's still lots of jobs for those skills.

"See, what I need to do, I need to stay ahead of developments. Marconi's a phenomenal genius and radio's the coming thing. Already you can build a spark transmitter in your own home, and pretty soon even ordinary people will be talking to each other all over the world, person to person. It'll be a vast community. I'm so excited about this.

"Soon as I get out of here I'm headed for Union College, Schenectady — they've got a whole wireless department and a two-hundred-foot antenna. And I got a friend in Syracuse, his pop works at Mohawk Power, have you heard of them?"

I had not, but he wasn't waiting for a reply.

"They're going to be expanding all across the state. Thanks to Mr. Furbeck, I feel like I'm actually looking into the future, and nothing's going to stop me being a part of it — for sure not this stupid disease."

He barrelled along on this gung-ho flight of fancy. I sat there nodding and smiling where it seemed appropriate and didn't even try to interrupt. He only settled down when a nurse came in and stuck a thermometer in his mouth.

The second she took it out she turned to me and said, "This young man needs to rest."

Later that day I stopped into the humidor, not for tobacco but for the vast array of newspapers and magazines on display. There was a familiar-looking man at the counter when I went to pay; his chalk-stripe suit would have done credit to a banker.

"Whaddaya know," he said. "It's the professor."

He turned to the tobacconist before I could correct him and said, "Lemme pay for the professor's magazine, and add a couple more coronas."

"No, no," I said. "It's very kind of you, but really …"

He finished his transaction and tucked two fat cigars into my breast pocket.

"You're Ronnie's friend," he said. "Now you're my friend."

"Actually, I think Ronnie's far more keen on radio than poetry these days."

"He's a dreamer, all right. Doctors in this place, I got nothin but respect for 'em, but my kid brother ain't lookin long for this world. You stay outta trouble, Professor."

And with that he left the store.

"Quite a pal you've made," the tobacconist said. "Who'd've thought we'd see a guy like that in Saranac Lake."

"A guy like what?"

"You don't recognize Benny Barstowe?"

"Benny Barstowe?"

"The gangster. Gun running? Extortion? Guy's unkillable — been shot more times than Norma Talmadge."

I stared out the window after him. He was striking up a conversation with Madame Lupu, the local fortune teller. She was pointing out the symbols on the huge Tarot card that decorated her sandwich board and laughing at something he said.

One snowy afternoon I received a note from Sarah.

> *I will be at St. Bernard's Church tomorrow*
> *afternoon at 3:00. I hope you will come.*
> *Sarah*
> *P.S. Please don't despise me!*

It had been two weeks since I had seen her. During this time Bella Troy had decided to play hard to get — at least to me. One Friday evening I observed her out with another man and promptly stepped into a stationer's to avoid them. I purchased the latest issue of the *Atlantic* and resolved in future to deprive Saranac's own ice princess of my company, which I obviously valued more highly than she did. But I don't believe that was why I had begun to miss Sarah. Once my initial shock at Mr. Ballard's revelation had begun to wear off, she filtered once more into my thoughts. Surely she must have some explanation for her actions. I found I missed not just *her*, but how I had felt in her company, even though I could not have said exactly what those feelings were. But now, perversely, I was feeling an insistent pull that was only intensified by the receipt of her note; I was drifting toward her like a leaf on a stream.

I was lying in bed when this thought reminded me of the leaf she had reached for by the Saranac River — the possibly fictitious leaf that had provoked our first meeting. I got up and stumbled shivering to my desk to make a note of the leaf and its echo for possible use in a story or novel. I remembered how she had looked under Mr. Ballard's verbal assault, her head bowed as she struggled to pull the ring from her finger, her voice husky as she answered my question. *It's true.*

I began to doubt my own response. All right, so she did not marry Stephen Ballard. But it now seemed preposterous to me that Sarah — Sarah as I had known before this dark turn of events — could have purposely set out to take advantage of the Ballards' grief. Either my judgment of fellow human beings had been madly off-kilter, or there was more to the story. I couldn't get the images out of my head: grey eyes, blue dress, and the angle of her exposed neck. It reminded me of a painting I had seen somewhere of Isaac, head bowed to receive his father's blade.

It was still snowing the following afternoon when I left my after-lunch appointment and walked to the church. Sarah was seated in the last pew. She turned to me at the sound of my footsteps and stood, putting a shushing finger to her lips. There were two or three solitary worshippers spread out among the pews.

"I didn't realize you were religious," I said when we were in the vestibule.

"Please," she said, indicating the door. "Voices echo in here."

I began to point out that it was snowing, but she was already pushing at the door. I held it for her, and she opened an umbrella as we stepped outside.

"I suppose I should give it back to the Ballards. I *will* give it back to them. Virtually everything I own rightly belongs to them — except what I bought with Cunard money. Even that only came through because Mr. Ballard put the fear of God into them."

She was hurrying along in front of me, as if afraid to look me in the face.

"Slow down, for God's sake. You've only just got well."

"You've no idea how good it feels to walk, even in the snow, when you've been locked in bed for a year."

I took hold of her elbow and forced her to slow down.

"Sorry," I said. "I don't want you to get sick again."

"I'm sure you'd be quite relieved if I died. But I wanted to tell you — I *must* tell you — what really happened. I can't bear the idea of your hating me."

No one could hate you, I thought, though I was far from certain on Mr. Ballard's account.

"Let's go over there."

A miniature park occupied a triangle of grass where Church merged into River Street. Its small stone gazebo offered some shelter and a view of Lake Flower. We sat side by side on a bench but it felt too close, too "cousining," and I got up almost instantly, ostensibly to admire the view.

"See, you do hate me — you're just too much of a gentleman to say it."

"You told me you were married to Stephen Ballard. Told me in vivid detail. You wrote it out — the date, the place, and who performed the service. That is hardly a lapse of memory. It's not a slip of the tongue. But worse than that, you told the Ballards. You took advantage of their grief over their son and allowed them to treat you as if you were someone you're not. Someone their son had loved. What possible excuse could you have?"

"I know, Paul. Please. Allow me to tell you what happened, and then you can flee from me as fast as you like."

"Very well."

I remained standing, leaning back against a stone pillar of the gazebo with my arms folded in front of me.

Sarah let out a heavy sigh. "When my father and I were shifted from the *Cameronia* to the *Lusitania*, I was put in a second-class cabin with a woman named Evelyn Howard, a lovely person with the most beautiful English accent. We were strangers, but she was polite, considerate, and easy to like. She was also tremendously excited because she and Stephen Ballard were eloping. They were planning to get married in England, but then couldn't even wait for that; they were going to get married on board. We were friendly right from the first. We both felt lucky that we had this four-person cabin to ourselves. It allowed us to spread out a little.

"So she was the reason I met Stephen Ballard. She's probably the reason I'm alive. Stephen was just as I described him: charming, friendly, even a little eccentric — but in an adorable way, with his camera and his various enthusiasms. He was absolutely besotted with Evelyn. His eyes just lit up when she was around or when he spoke of her."

"Why wasn't he in First Class?"

"I told you. Mr. Ballard does not condone extravagance. You've met him. Does he strike you as a spendthrift?"

"What about the life jacket? How did you come to be wearing one labelled 'Mrs. Stephen Ballard'?"

"I didn't steal it, if that's what you're thinking. As I told you, Stephen was obsessed with the *Titanic*, and knew that the authorities had had a terrible time identifying people in the aftermath — so he went to the purser and bought these two special life jackets with 'Mr. Stephen Ballard' written on one and 'Mrs. Stephen Ballard' on the other. I thought it was terribly romantic.

"Of course, Evelyn and Stephen devoted most of their time to each other, but I did see them at mealtimes and occasionally for a game of cards. We all got along so well it was as if we were old friends."

"What about all those wonderful conversations you had — with Ballard? Did those happen?"

"Yes, that's true — mostly. We did have wonderful conversations, but it was with the two of them, or between Evelyn and me alone."

"Still. Extremely misleading, you must see that."

"Oh, Paul. I just — yes. I mean, you did tell me it was a memoir, not autobiography, not history. It was okay to make things up."

"It's not the same. You know it's not the same."

"I've already admitted I've been living in a fictional world for quite some time. It seemed impossible to step out of it for one person and not for others who had much greater claim to know the truth about me."

"Go on, then."

I turned away coolly as if momentarily interested in the traffic clattering along River Street. I can't defend my attitude, except to say that once you imagine yourself on a moral high horse it can be difficult to dismount.

"Then — after the explosion — it wasn't *exactly* as I wrote it, but almost. I tried to get to my cabin to get my life jacket but the corridor was too flooded. When I came back up the steps Stephen was there, carrying a life jacket. I asked him where was Evelyn but he was in shock, stunned — not weeping — just stunned, blank. He told me she had been waiting for him on the port side — some crew members had almost succeeded in getting one of the lifeboats over the railing. Somehow they lost hold of it and it came crashing back and she was crushed against the deck wall. She was dead."

Sarah spoke softly, with no particular emphasis on the horror she was describing.

"Stephen didn't know what to do — in terms of Evelyn, I mean — no one was going to help load a dead person into a lifeboat. He put the life jacket on me. He had intended it for Evelyn, obviously, and someone had stolen the other one. I tried to stop him. I told him I would take one of the lifebelts on deck, but he wouldn't have it. He put it on over my head and tightened the straps. He came with me over toward the starboard lifeboats but he wouldn't stay. The last I saw of him he was helping a little boy with his life jacket."

She broke down in tears then, dabbing at her eyes. "Sorry."

"Where was your father in all this?"

"I don't know. Stephen didn't know. It was all such confusion, such chaos. We had been in port cabins but the lifeboats on that side were unusable, the ship was listing too far the other way. Which meant we were not exactly first in line for a starboard lifeboat. The ship was sinking so fast the bow was already under water. People say this or that was 'like a nightmare,' but I've never had a nightmare that compared to this. Suddenly, the world was ending. The sea, which just minutes ago had been placid and welcoming, had turned into this monster, this ferocity incarnate, boiling up the decks intent on devouring us, swallowing the entire ship. I did manage to get into a boat, but the ship was levelling out by then — I suppose from all the water in the lower decks and so on — so the lifeboat practically lowered *itself* to the water. Or rather, the *ship* lowered it as it sank. But they couldn't cut the rope — a man was hacking at it with an axe — and the ship was coming down right beside us. I don't have words to describe the sheer size, the immensity of it. And then one of the hooked things — the poles they hang the lifeboats from?"

"The davits?"

"One of the davits. Again, worse than any nightmare. This inanimate object suddenly becomes this hideous malevolent *thing* that wants nothing more than your immediate extinction. You could see it coming and nothing could stop it. It hooked itself over the side of the lifeboat and flipped us over, threw everyone into the sea. When I came up, the screams were unbearable — probably some of them were my own, but the screaming was almost worse than the rest of it. I started to swim but it was impossible in a long dress. If it hadn't been for Stephen's life jacket, I would have drowned right then. But I found something to cling to, a little doghouse that must have come from the hold or somewhere. And then ...

"And then?"

"And then I don't remember anything."

"You woke up on a wharf in Queenstown."

"Yes. Just as I told you. They thought I was dead and had laid me out among the corpses. At that point, I didn't remember *anything* — Stephen, Evelyn, who I was — nothing. It was all utterly blank. They started fussing about me, bringing me hot tea, and a woman took my life jacket off and started calling me Mrs. Ballard. Because of the life jacket. I didn't think she could be talking to me. There was a little pocket on the jacket — for valuables, I suppose — and she found a wedding ring and put it on my finger."

I became aware that I must've looked a high-toned skeptical prosecutor standing at the pillar looking down at her, firing questions. Around us the snow was easing off but the day remained gloomy and cold — or perhaps her story made it feel that way. I went to the bench and sat beside her.

"They wrapped a bandage around my head. I had a bad wound on the back, just above my neck. The pain became absolutely blinding and I think I fainted because the next thing I remember I was in hospital. The doctors, the nurses — the Irish people — were so generous, so kind."

"And so you became Mrs. Stephen Ballard."

"*I* didn't know *who* I was — but everybody else seemed to know. And that's the story that got out. I was far from convinced myself. It seemed impossible I could have got married and not remember it, but I was in no position to argue because I couldn't remember anything else either — my name, my father, nothing. Then Mr. and Mrs. Ballard showed up."

"Just like that."

"I didn't *summon* them, if that's what you mean. I was out of the hospital by then. They showed up in the hotel lobby wanting to meet me. A pair of benign apparitions. I didn't know them; they didn't know me. I told them right away my memory was gone and the doctors couldn't say when it would come back and I didn't know much of anything about myself. I told them I had no memory whatsoever of even meeting Stephen, let alone marrying him. At that point, I didn't even remember his putting the life jacket on me. Far from trying to put a story over on them, I found it extremely odd that these strangers were telling *me* such a story. Think of it, Paul. Imagine if an older man and woman came over here right now and told you you were married to their daughter and you had no idea if it was true or not. You couldn't be sure that it was *not* true, but you had no memory of it at all. Aside from the unreality of that particular situation, just losing your memory — even for a short time — is devastating. To not know if you are married or single, or where you live, where you come from or who your family might be. I was profoundly lost. I felt I had no choice but to trust these two kindly people. The first thing they showed me was a photograph of Stephen. He didn't look in the least familiar, and I told them so. They showed me the postcard he'd sent — a *Lusitania* postcard he'd sent before the pilot boat went back. 'I've met the woman of my dreams and we're eloping to England to get married — maybe even on board ship! Don't be angry with me — she's an angel, and I'm madly in love!'

"They stayed on in Queenstown, taking me out for walks and dinners, and Mr. Ballard took up my cause with the Cunard company. They were not speedy at working out compensation.

They had to work out who I was by a process of elimination; my accent was American, there were very few female passengers in their twenties. All the Ballards knew was that Stephen *intended* to marry — it didn't occur to them or to me that he would have got married on board. Or at least not until much later. Don't forget, they were still hoping he might turn up by some miracle and it would all be straightened out. In some ways I suppose I was a welcome distraction. Mrs. Ballard took me shopping and bought me a couple of pretty dresses. Do you imagine I didn't protest? Of course I did. I kept telling them they shouldn't put themselves out like this, but they insisted."

"Why *would* they do that, though? Why so quickly? So eagerly?"

"You have to remember the main reason they were there. They were praying their son was going to turn up safe and sound. The chances were slim, almost nonexistent — they didn't arrive until a week after the sinking — but they thought he might be injured somewhere, lying in a coma or, like me, without a memory. They put ads in the Irish papers with his picture, they put up posters — there were a lot of those on the streets and in the post office and so on.

"All the bodies, even the unidentified ones, had been buried before they got there, but they had been photographed, and relatives were urged to go over the photographs at the Cunard office to see if they recognized anyone."

"Your father was missing. You must have had to look too."

"Yes, once Cunard were sure who I was. I told the Ballards I wanted to go with them. They didn't want me to. They worried it would cause me irreparable harm — the horror of it — and Mr. Ballard pointed out that it could serve no purpose if I had no memory. But I thought it might bring my memory back

— the jolt of it — I might suddenly know for sure, for myself, whether I was married to Stephen or not. The doctors agreed with me, and so I went with them to the Cunard offices. The sight of those photographs …"

I could imagine. The bodies that came in after a day or two would be horribly mangled and disfigured — by gulls and other sea creatures — if not from the explosion and nature's general postmortem indignities.

"There were so many babies. They looked like dolls in their little bonnets. Their tiny faces. Each with a number tag — that was the saddest thing. The poor Ballards had to look especially hard at the photos of the dead young men. And here was I beside them as they were dealing with this terrible loss. I suppose I represented something salvaged from the wreckage — a bright spot, the woman their son had fallen in love with. From their point of view, especially Mrs. Ballard's, it was as if a part of their son had survived, and she started to cling to me. And I to her. But there was no picture of Stephen."

Sarah turned to look at me, grey eyes inquiring. "Does that answer your question?"

I nodded silently. I had forgotten my question.

"And your father?"

"Eventually, Cunard got hold of a portrait of my father and determined that he was also among the missing."

We sat quietly for a few minutes. It was snowing heavily now. Sarah went to the gazebo railing and removed her gloves. She extended a hand out into the falling snow, turning it this way and that till it was quite wet, then she turned toward me, rubbing her hands together as if washing them.

"I know what you must be thinking. How is it possible, over a year later, I still haven't told the Ballards the truth? I wonder at it myself, Paul. When they were ready to return to the States, they insisted I come with them, and live with them at least until I was fully myself again. I suppose a stronger woman would have said, 'No I can't impose on you this way — not under these circumstances,' but I am not a strong person, I never have been. And what alternative did I have? So, yes, I came back to the States with them.

"Mrs. Ballard became more and more motherly toward me, always making sure I ate enough, and ate the right kind of foods — they're both very taken with the ideas of Mr. Kellogg. She had me eating every source of iron known to man — and B vitamins, my goodness, the B vitamins are her cure-all for everything, even grief.

"They put me in a lovely guest room overlooking their gardens, but even so, Mrs. B embarked on decorating another — even larger — room for me. She consulted me on everything from curtains to rugs to furniture and all the time I didn't know how to say stop, she was taking such pleasure in it. And she told me all about Stephen. I don't think I've ever sensed such a deep capacity for love in another person as when she showed me his things. This is his lacrosse racquet, she would say, and hand it to me while she told me about his many other interests: history, for example. There were stacks of books on Roman History on the shelves in his room, and on astronomy, on insects — especially bees — and several books by Teddy Roosevelt. And, of course, there were photographs he'd taken, mostly landscapes and pictures of the Great Lakes and Niagara Falls. She told me so much I began to feel as if I *had* known him, though I still could not believe I'd married him. Of course, she cried when she first began talking about Stephen, but gradually I saw that it was soothing for her, in some way, to talk of her son with another woman who had loved him. She was developing a strong affection toward me, and I for her — and I could see it meant a lot to her, mothering me. And, yes, I admit it felt good to be cared for, to be cosseted. I *mattered* to her, whether or not I deserved it, Paul. I *mattered* to her.

"She soon took it for granted that I was Stephen's beloved wife. She put a picture of him in my room — you've seen it — but they stopped asking if I remembered him. It just became a living fact that I was their daughter-in-law. And even *without* having the right memories, or any memories, it became a happy time — or rather, a sad time with a few rays of sunshine. Throughout all this I was not deceiving them in any way — not consciously.

"Mr. B was more restrained in his affection, but he was kind to me, gentle. He spoke to me almost in a whisper, as if I might shatter at the least disturbance. And he could see that my presence was making his wife — who truly *was* fragile — that I was bringing her comfort in her sorrow; it wasn't just a matter of cheering her up. We became the embodiment of the old wedding cliché: *you've lost a son but gained a daughter.* Unfortunately, in our case it was not through marriage."

Sarah came back to the bench and sat beside me. She spoke straight ahead, as if to some unseen other, so that I was able to steal glances at her in profile, the curves of brow and cheekbone complicated by her facial expression of sorrow and regret.

"About six weeks after our return, I had my first stirrings of memory. And it wasn't over anything I saw or heard, it was through something I *smelled*, odd as that may seem. Mrs. B took me to a tea shop — a very British little place with the Union Jack and pictures of King George everywhere. And the place was suffused with the smell of crumpet — these small, chewy griddle cakes that they cover with butter or jam and clotted cream. The *Lusitania* served them for breakfast every morning and the aroma was all throughout that wonderful dining room. The smell brought the memory back. Vividly.

"I must have looked transfixed because Mrs. B asked me what was wrong. The sensation was like trying to remember a dream but you just can't quite capture it, like clutching at smoke. I was inhaling this wonderful aroma and I was seeing faces. 'It's Stephen,' I said. 'I'm remembering Stephen,' and I told her about the *Lusitania*'s dining room and how, when we had breakfast there, it smelled just like this tea shop. Mrs. B smiled at me and placed her hand over mine and gave it a squeeze.

"By then I had been seeing Stephen's picture every day for weeks, so when this memory of him arrived in my head I was immediately able to put a name to it. I wasn't remembering that we were married, just his name and his face and the setting. I was also seeing Evelyn's face — Evelyn Howard — but I didn't know who she was or why I remembered her so I didn't mention it.

"That was how it started. And then, at night, more memories would come — not of the ship, necessarily, but of everything, anything, random scenes all out of order. I began to remember my mother, my father; I saw images of the house where we had lived, a beautiful garden. And I remembered more about Stephen. I remembered him taking pictures of everything and everyone on board. Mr. and Mrs. Ballard loved that, it was so in character. Mrs. B had tears in her eyes as I told her. 'I'm so happy you're here,' she said to me. 'So happy you're here with us, my darling girl.'

"But gradually I remembered more about Evelyn, that she was getting married, and yes — eventually — that it was

Stephen she was going to marry. They weren't going to wait for England, they wanted the captain to marry them. And I remembered Stephen telling me about buying their special life jackets. Evelyn thought it a bit macabre, at first, until he showed her the wedding ring he'd hidden in the pocket. It was all terribly sweet — he doted on her, you see, the way his mother was now doting on me.

"And I remembered the sinking itself. It had all been a blessed blank to me until then, and suddenly there it was. I can't tell you what a shock this was. Once again my whole world was coming apart. I was utterly undone. I did nothing but cry for three days straight. The Ballards were so good to me, looking after me through this — I must have been such a burden, so tiresome — but they just gave me … everything. I can't blame them for feeling betrayed. They have every reason."

Sarah fiddled with the umbrella, partially opening and closing it, sometimes tapping it on the ground.

"I wanted to tell them the truth — please believe me when I say that. I wanted to tell them that it wasn't me, that Stephen had been planning to marry someone else. But then I would see Mrs. B's face — so loving, so kind. She clearly felt closer to me than ever, she was slowly recovering from her grief, and I just couldn't bring myself to rupture the fragile beginnings of peace.

"At night I would think, *I must tell them*, but then I couldn't. Mrs. B and I would be having a quiet afternoon in the park or the botanical garden and I would think, *Now. I'll tell her now*, but I couldn't. I couldn't, Paul. I know it was wrong — I *knew* it was wrong to keep the truth from them, but I couldn't make myself do it. One day I screwed up my courage and resolved to tell her, only to find her in Stephen's room, in tears — it was his birthday, he would have been twenty-five — and once again I couldn't do it.

"I don't blame you if you don't believe me — but *I* know I would have told them, only then I got sick. I developed a fever that came and went, came and went, and a persistent cough and I was hideously tired all the time, and then one day I coughed and the handkerchief ... came away bloody."

Sarah was describing TB's scarlet herald, Keats's "death warrant," that instant when she realized death was reaching for her a second time. Surely this was the moment to offer her some gesture of affection, some ember of the love she had just forfeited. In the weeks and months to come, I would sometimes wonder if, had I been man enough to put my arms around her, had I held her close and assured her that she would not have to face her predicament alone, things — her future and mine — might have turned out differently. But I did not. I could plead the reticent propriety of the age, or admit to a misplaced sense of male *gravitas* that demanded I behave as if *I* were the injured party. Or I could — almost plausibly — claim that, while I had abjured my goatish pursuit of Bella Troy, I had not yet forsworn my avowed immunity to love. More likely, I was simply frightened by the surge of emotion brought on by Sarah's sorrowful eyes. Whatever the reason, however obvious it might be to others or however obscure to me, I mumbled a thoroughly inadequate apology for having doubted her, which Sarah, for her part, insisted was entirely unwarranted.

CHAPTER 13

For well over a year now, I had been visiting patients and saying chirpy things about the pleasures of reading and writing. But the truth was, although I had written quite a few good *lines* of poetry, I had never completed anything one could call a truly great poem, nor had I managed enough first-rate verses to fill even the slimmest of volumes. My former pleasure in the craft was definitely in decline. Indeed, I had not renewed my subscription to *Poetry*, which I had used to study with the avidity of a general surveying his maps. But the Saranac Lake Free Public Library was a good one, and eventually I came across the June 1915 issue, which contained "The Love Song of J. Alfred Prufrock."

At first, I read it with a feeling of kinship, recognizing at once Eliot's debt to LaForgue. But rereading it laid me low. Whereas I had tried to bring only certain of the French poet's attitudes to bear on my work, Eliot had imported far more. The work could have almost been a translation, and yet I knew it wasn't; it was new. There was a philosophical depth to his work that I could never have mustered. With the world-weary tone and the all-encompassing *angst*, not to mention the implied life experiences of the narrator, Eliot's voice was that of a much older man, but he was only a few years my senior. His deployment of urban imagery, of city grit, his glimpses of lives at a spiritual dead end, all gave a sense that the entire urban enterprise was unwholesome, lost, and destined for failure. The man was inventing Modern English Poetry before my eyes. I was enough of a poet to see it, and enough of a critic to know I could not compete.

I never did get used to the early bedtimes of the cure cottage. The intent was to ensure every patient got their needed rest, but for me it made the hours of darkness seem all the longer. The rule of enforced cheerfulness gave way at such times, and it was not unusual to be awakened by the cries of a patient in the throes of nightmare, if not waking despair. Not being a patient, I was allowed to keep my own hours, but Mrs. Pryce had made it clear she did not welcome anyone coming or going after nine.

I would have had a troubled night anyway, after my long afternoon with Sarah, but in addition I had now to accept that I was not and never would be a poet. In between berating myself for abject failure, I was seeing images from Sarah's story. Hearing the fate of the *Lusitania* told in her newfound honest voice made the catastrophe much more real. I viewed her now with a degree of awe, as if she had actually died and come back to tell the tale. And her heartbreak over the loss of the Ballards' affections now aroused in me a belated yearning to help. As I lay there in the interminable dark, I saw her slim hand reaching out to catch the snow, her enquiring eyes as she asked me, *Does that answer your question?*

The night grew colder. I fell into a restless sleep, and at one point thought I heard footsteps on the front porch. I drifted in and out of a dream: I was on board the *Lusitania*, clinging to the stern railing as the waters churned toward me.

In the morning I was grumpy and barely noticed that young Leah Landers was not at breakfast until someone else pointed it out. Mrs. Pryce was not there either, and the staff had clearly been instructed to tell us nothing. The other patients assumed she had thrown a hemorrhage and had been carted off to hospital, but later in the day I learned from Dr. Tissot that the girl had been seen wandering alone along Cedar and Margaret Streets where the two railroad lines merged. She had found a dark area just beyond a curve — the engineer could not have seen her until it was too late — and had lain herself down across the track and waited for her sojourn in Saranac Lake to end, courtesy of the night train.

Sarah had paid me in advance for more tutorials, and the next time I met with her it was on the cure porch of her new residence. We were reading works of Saranac's most famous former resident, Robert Louis Stevenson. The lively tale of *Kidnapped*, not to mention the hideous Mr. Hyde, managed to take Sarah's mind, at least briefly, away from present circumstances. She was now living in a small boarding house on Neil Street, a bungalow with none of the charm of Mrs. Pryce's cottage. I had no knowledge of her financial affairs, except that she was now cut off from the Ballards. She had mentioned the settlement from the Cunard company, but I had no idea how much that might be. Her father had apparently been a well-known photographer, so perhaps there was a legacy from that quarter? Insurance money? And what about the house in New Jersey she had mentioned? Surely she could live there, if she chose? Back there she would not be known as the fraudulent Mrs. Ballard but only as Sarah Redmond, the photographer's daughter. My suspicion was that she had selected the depressing new location as a form of penance.

I learned that Mrs. Pryce was not the only local resident to consider Sarah an outcast. Sarah told me she had been refused service at a milliner's, and even one of the librarians had been reluctant to lend her books.

At this time when I was frustrated with my own artistic pursuits, I began to wonder if Sarah might be able to earn some income with hers. I wanted to know how she had come to it, and at what point she might have felt that she would always be drawing or painting, no matter what else was going on in her life. Although she claimed she had never intended it to be anything other than an amusement, I felt that she brought more seriousness to it than that. She kept little of what she made, but when one of her drawings did manage to please her, it pleased her enormously, with the kind of egoless delight one takes in the art of others and never in one's own. "Look," she would say, "isn't that good? Look how her white dress is echoed in that tiny speck of cloud. A complete accident, but I'm so happy with it." Or: "The hands actually turned out right. I can't believe it. I love hands — they're so eloquent — but I always ruin them."

When I asked her to tell me about her development as an artist, she wrote several pages about her father.

"My father disappeared when I was eight years old. My mother told me he was travelling for work and would be gone for some time. I missed him terribly. There were letters at first

— from France, from Spain, from England — and I wrote back to him, including drawings I thought would please him. But the letters slowed and by the time I was ten they had stopped.

"He would come to me in dreams — nothing special about them — usually we were just talking. I painted portraits of him from memory. My mother would say, 'Draw something else, Sarah. You mustn't dwell on your father so.' I resisted her advice, but after a few years I knew my portraits would be all wrong, so I stopped.

"It was my first experience of heartbreak. To get up in the morning and not have him whistling and making silly jokes, to never have him read to me, or talk to me about drawing and painting or whatever I was reading left a vast emptiness. But the real pain came when the letters stopped. My mother's attempts to excuse him — *he's terribly busy, you know how forgetful he is, he loves you more than anything on earth* — could not disguise his desertion. I was desolate. His absence became a *presence*, a dark shapeless entity that invaded my thoughts and dreams with a feeling of suffocation. I would wake struggling to breathe, as if a crushing weight had been placed on my chest, pressing the air from my lungs.

"It must have been terribly difficult for my mother. I was too wrapped up in myself to notice, but here she was, thirty-five or so, with a child and no husband and yet not unmarried. She worked twelve-hour days at Bell Telephone in a basement full of women at their switchboards. It kept food on our table but left little time for what you might call a family life and none for a social life. We were lucky in one thing: the people who lived next door to us. The Gartners were a childless couple, just naturally kind, generous people, always helping others. They took an interest in my welfare right from a young age. I don't know how we would have survived otherwise. My mother arranged for me to stop at their place after school and have dinner with them. She would pick me up when she got back from work. This went on until I was twelve or so and old enough to look after myself.

"Shortly after my thirteenth birthday, my mother died. It was quick, compared to tuberculosis. A diagnosis of cancer, a surgery, and then another surgery, and then watching her eaten alive from the inside. In her final days, she told me there was some chance my father would return but, should he not, the Gartners had offered to look after me. Such good people. They told me several times they would love to have me live with them.

"They were at my side on the day of my mother's funeral. Almost no one else attended — two women from Bell, two or three neighbours, and that was it. She had done nothing but work in a company basement for the past seven years, and her only living relative — my Aunt Isabel — lived in England. No one knew her. Imagine that — to be on this earth thirty-five years and nobody knows you. Then at the burial, a rugged handsome man with a full beard and something foreign in his bearing appeared on the other side of the grave. I might not have recognized him, had he not been wearing his signature wide-brimmed hat.

"My mother had never suggested he was dead, but the idea that my father was alive, enjoying his life while expressing no interest in mine, was so painful that it was easier for me to think him dead. I was never fully successful at it. I had been haunted by gauzy imaginings — the two of us bumping into each other, strangers in a famous museum, or in an art supply shop, or on a crowded train. The shock of mutual recognition would be swallowed up in joyful hugs and kisses, in breathless summaries of our missed years. But my life was not designed by Charles Dickens, and there was no such joyful reunion.

"I remember his first words. The tears in his eyes as he spoke them: 'To see you again after all this time — it's so overwhelming I can't speak.'

"It was only then that Mr. and Mrs. Gartner recognized him. The two of them stood there open-mouthed. My own reaction was muted. He had arrived on a day of intense grief. I was nowhere near coming to terms with my mother's death.

"'It's you,' I said, 'you're alive,' or some such nothing. That was all I could manage before my tongue dried in my mouth.

"It was only a short walk from the church to my home, but it felt deeply strange to walk back with my father. Eerie. This man was someone I knew intimately, someone I loved, but at the same time he was a stranger. A layer of numbness sealed itself around me. Shock? I can't say. I was adrift, carried along through no will of my own, unmoored. Part of me was watching the two of us walking home from a vantage point a little behind and above, as if I were up on a balcony, looking down. It reminded me of sketching, that distanced feeling just before you set pencil to paper.

"It's astounding, how thoroughly anger can hide. Had anyone asked me a month previously if I was angry at my father I would have thought you mad. Of course I wasn't. But anger soon made itself known, and my father was in for a stormy time of it. *How could you abandon us? How could you do that to Mother? How could you break her heart — she, who never did anything but love you? Did you despise me so much that you couldn't be bothered to write?* He tried to defend himself but I could not hear him. My feelings were an ocean's roar in my

ears. I veered between searing rage one day and Arctic silence
the next. How he bore it I don't know. His life in Europe,
whatever it may have been, could only have been tranquil in
comparison.

"He insisted I was wrong. He *did* write to me.

"'I wrote to you from London,' he said. 'I wrote to you
from Paris. I wrote to you from Montpellier, from Toulouse. I
wrote you from Denmark. When you stopped replying, I knew
your mother was intercepting my letters. She denied it. She said
you had given up on me, that it was too painful even to think
about me. I couldn't believe that, Sarah. You were always such
a loving little girl. But two years without a response? Three?
Yes — eventually — I gave up writing to you.'

"Who to believe? Either my mother had been deceiving me
year after year, or my father had forgotten his own daughter.
Our arguments were bitter. Bitter on my side. I told him how
Mother had sunk into melancholy over the years, a melancholy
that she tried to disguise with cheerfulness. But cheerfulness is
not happiness. Cheerfulness is a pretty mask you put on for the
benefit of others, to make *them* feel better, to protect *them* from
a disagreeable truth. To a degree it works. I am familiar with
it now, from both sides. Others will be fooled — my mother
certainly fooled me for a time — but the cost is high. You remain a stranger to everyone. And become one even to yourself.

"With his thirteen-year-old daughter constantly making
him a present of her anger, my father could no longer deny
how his dereliction had destroyed my mother. He could see his
wife's anguish in his daughter's. And I will say this to his credit:
he was overcome with remorse. Slowly, my anger spent, I got
used to his being back in the house. It eased the pain of losing
my mother. All during her illness, I had admonished myself,

'Sarah, you must be an adult now. You may still be a schoolgirl but you cannot afford to be "girlish." No wallowing in moods and disappointments.'

"My father sank into a miasma of self-recrimination. His first few months home he did no photographic work at all. He would rouse himself to sort through my mother's things, trying to decide what to keep, what to discard, but he made little progress. I would come home and find him sitting limply on the sofa, staring into space.

"'It is truly astounding,' he said from this supine position one day. 'I go through life imagining myself to be a good man. Not necessarily outstanding. Perhaps not even remarkable. But more or less a decent, law-abiding person who, whether or not he always succeeds, always *tries* to do what is right. Always *intends* to do what is right — to be kind, reasonable, generous. So it comes as a profound shock to realize that I am, in fact, vain. Selfish. Greedy and unreliable. I'm what a banker might call *not sound*. How devastating to discover that, in every way that matters, I am a distinctly inferior man.'

"'That's not true,' I told him. His remorse was doing much to soften my anger and arouse my sympathy. 'You are very far from those things.' I reeled off his accomplishments, his stature in photography circles, his talent as storyteller and portrait artist. I listed his warmth and passion and, yes, his generosity. His imagination, his devotion to art, his early fatherhood to me — even how well he had looked after Mother and me, before he left.

"'Before I abandoned you.'

"'I'm sorry, Father, but you can't undo the good you've done.'

"'Nor the bad,' he insisted. 'And there's a lot more of that.'

"My words did nothing to cheer him up. Self-blame destroyed his nights and then he would sleep late into the next day, only to wake with a sense of futility and time wasted. He began to be tormented with headaches that enflamed his senses so that curtains had to be drawn. It became my role to comfort him. I would sit on the sofa and he would lie with his head on my lap, sometimes weeping silently, sometimes just sighing and shaking his head as one does over regrets.

"I tried to distract him by asking about his life in Europe. He had many funny stories. He met peculiar characters over there, especially in England. 'Charles Dickens,' he would say, 'has been unfairly accused of exaggeration. My researches confirm that he is merely accurate. Dickens is to the English what Audubon is to birds.' And then he would relate an unlikely anecdote concerning a 'silly Englishman' whose photograph he had been commissioned to take.

"One time he fell asleep in my lap and started to dream. He repeated my mother's name in the saddest voice, and clutched at me as if I were my mother. His nightmares grew worse. I would wake in the dark and hear him cry out. In the morning he would be bleary and exhausted. I became more and more afraid that he would kill himself or disappear again. Something had to be done, but he refused to see a doctor. One night his cries were so heart-wrenching that I left my bed and went to his room. I sat beside him on the bed and took his hand and spoke softly, soothingly — I was afraid to wake him too suddenly. His thrashing subsided but the murmuring continued. I held his hand until I could no longer keep my eyes open and then I stumbled back to my own bed.

"In the daytime he appeared to have no memory of it. And I wasn't about to embarrass him by bringing it up. My calming presence seemed to have eased him into a comfortable sleep; he didn't look so haggard and woebegone. And so it continued. When his cries woke me in the dark, I no longer waited. I went to his room and said my soothing words and waited for him to settle. It was as if I were his wife, or even his mother. As if he were four instead of forty. Frankly, it felt unsettling and unfair, but I was thirteen years old and couldn't think what else to do. My schoolwork suffered. In the classroom I would find myself fighting off sleep. The teacher would ask a question and I would be at a loss. The principal asked me if I was ill — what else could account for my plummeting grades?

"I came to feel that it was not my soothing words that eased my father's mind but my mere presence. So, to preserve my own nights from complete ruin, I would simply touch his hand as he lay there moaning, and say, 'It's all right, Father. You're all right. I'm right here.' Then after a few minutes, I would lie beside him, on top of the covers, and close my eyes and fall asleep. I was always first to wake. I would be finishing my breakfast by the time he emerged, and we would exchange a few sunny sentences. As if everything were normal. If he was aware of what happened at night, he gave no sign of it.

"Gradually, his nights grew calmer, and his daytime self was once again the artistic dynamo I loved and admired and wanted to emulate. That's why I'm telling you all this. It was at this time that I saw what peace and joy one could find in artistic pursuits — even as tormented a man as my father. Once again he was full of photographic projects, and I worked with him whenever I could — as set designer, as costumer, and countless times as a subject. He lined up a whole series of Shakespeare characters, transforming me by turns into Ariel, Puck, and Juliet.

"We had a bit of a disagreement about Juliet. Father wanted the scene where Juliet kills herself with the dagger. I didn't want to do it. It was childish of me, but I hated the idea that she kills herself over this boy who destroys their whole lives because he can't keep his temper. I wanted to do the balcony scene — the moment where she recognizes Romeo and is filled with joy. Father wouldn't hear of it. So we constructed a crypt, and I made myself a beautiful dress. But I was not a good Juliet. No matter how many exposures we took, I never managed to look convincing. I did try, but neither of us was happy with the finished product.

"Father turned to characters out of myth next. Iphigenia first.

"'I hope you're not going to kill me again,' I said.

"My father laughed. He had a wonderful laugh — a clattering cascade of masculine notes, and his face suddenly all black beard and white teeth. It was a joy to hear it again.

"'No, we won't kill you this time,' he told me. 'We'll be capturing the moments just before the girl is sacrificed. She is dancing for Achilles and the assembled soldiers. They fall silent before her beauty, knowing they are going to kill her. In that silence she sees for the first time that she is beautiful. For one fleeting second she feels her power. And then she notices the tears in her father's eyes. And then in the soldiers' eyes. And the truth dawns on her.'

"'You'll need to hire another model,' I told him. 'I'm not old enough or pretty enough.' I was still skinny as a boy.

"'No false modesty, Sarah — I won't have it. You're perfect, and that's that.'

"He had purchased muslin for my dress, and showed me photographs of dancers. He fussed endlessly over the costume.

"'Too many layers,' he said. 'It has to be diaphanous.'

"'We can't,' I told him. 'It will be immodest.'

"'This is not a photograph of a twentieth-century *bourgeoise*. It's a picture of a Greek princess roughly 1200 BC. A girl about to be sacrificed. Sarah Redmond has nothing to do with it.'

"We made the photograph together and he was delighted with the result.

"'No gallery will show that,' I said. 'It's too revealing.'

"'Let me worry about the galleries.'

"Honestly, Paul, my feelings about that photograph were mixed. Evenly mixed. I was ashamed of my immodesty but at the same time pleased.

"The photographs that followed required much manual labour. They involved water. We already had an outdoor studio behind the house, but now with shovel and sledgehammer and pickaxe he excavated a small pool and constructed a high fence around it. I shivered in that pool first as a perfectly ridiculous mermaid lacking a bosom and covered in goosebumps. Then it was back to Shakespeare — Ophelia drowning in her nightclothes. Father had constantly to rearrange my hair just so, and my hands just so, the fronds just so. Even the water just so. I panicked when the water turned my nightdress translucent. I would cover myself with my hands and he would get angry.

"'You're not Sarah,' he would insist, 'you're Ophelia. You're killing yourself. You are singing as you die. You are not remotely thinking about your appearance. Now be a proper model and stop fussing.'

"Gradually, my father's total lack of concern over my near nakedness put me at ease. He had me look again at his art books with the photos of classical sculpture. I came to accept that certain subjects could not be covered in clothing, and I was soon posing in the meagerest strips of fabric.

"Making a photograph with him never felt like work. He was now content to fulfill portrait commissions on his own, but I was essential to his project of illuminating mythic women. As my body became more womanly, the subjects changed. I was Susannah now, no longer Ariel, no longer Puck. I was Helen, I was Circe, I was Pandora. 'Surely you must want other models for some of these,' I would say, but he never did. 'That would destroy the very concept,' he would answer. 'You are *all* women — all women manifested in one. That's the whole point.' He allowed me time for my own drawing and painting, and taught me a lot about composition and point-of-view, but still we created countless scenarios together over the next few years.

"Of all the images in that series, my favourite was the simplest. It was not based on a story, it was just called *Drowned Girl*. We redecorated our pool to resemble a shingle beach, with seaweed, clamshells, gull feathers, and the like. Father even installed a paddle contraption that could generate ripples. In the photograph I am washed up on our imaginary shore, naked, bruised, the water lapping at my legs. The first attempts were not persuasive. No matter how pale my skin, how exhausted my posture, how motionless I might lie, I was never dead enough. The remedy lay not in me but in our 'shore.' Father scooped out the outline of my body, so that when I next lay down the figure achieved the collapsed, defeated look of the dead. Later, I watched in the morbid red of the darkroom, as the image of my drowned self materialized beneath my father's hand.

"'Why does she have to be naked?' I asked him.

"'Because it's more interesting. More mysterious.' Such was my father's answer. I pointed out that there was no rape, no faerie realm to justify my nakedness. His answer to that was *as far as we know*. A person of depraved mind might say he simply wanted to pose my naked body for his own illicit pleasure. But no one would say this who knew him."

Well, this was like nothing I had ever read — in fiction or non — and that remains the case forty years later. Father and daughter were engulfed in the emotional maelstrom of her mother's death, and they were both artists; their home was bound to be something of a hothouse. But her midnight visits to her father's bedroom made me deeply uneasy. Nor was I convinced that Lionel Redmond's "mythic" series demanded that Sarah's costumes dwindle from vestigial to transparent to nonexistent.

Aside from scattered allusions to incest in the Bible, or observations of the poverty-blighted regions of my own country, incest was never mentioned in my bookish world or in the world of anyone I knew or had even heard about. Yes, incest loomed in Classical writings now and again, but with no more realism to me than sea god or cyclops. It came up in Roman histories — but one couldn't help suspecting the original sources of being motivated by (no doubt well-deserved) political bias against the accused despots and spider women. So, no, I did not think the worst.

Part of me wanted to dismiss the account as pure fiction. Sarah had, after all, managed to maintain a false chronicle for a period of months with the Ballards. But I believed her explanation of how and why that occurred. What did she have to gain by inventing such a lurid account of her childhood? To shock me? This seemed unlikely; she had several times addressed me directly in those pages, and the overall tone was that of a letter rather than a narrative designed for literary effect. If Sarah did indeed shock me, it was not just at the related events themselves, but at her willingness to put them down on paper.

For the next day or two, I entertained the notion that Sarah might even be mentally unstable, or suffer from a "nervous ailment" brought on by her experience on the *Lusitania*. But then, with a kind of shrug, I decided that in writing her memoir, she had merely done what I had asked her to do and had done it in a manner that certainly got one's attention. In any case, I did not raise any misgivings about Sarah's mental health at my next Tuesday night visit with Dr. Tissot; I wanted only to discuss her financial circumstances.

"Well, she's cooked her own goose, that one," he said. "I mean, taking Ballard's money under false pretenses — the woman's lucky she isn't in jail."

"That is certainly the general perception," I said. "But it is far from the full story."

I told him in as much detail as I could recall what Sarah had told me about the *Lusitania* and after. The doctor harrumphed a few times and rubbed his chin, his demeanour softening as I spoke.

"A sad tale," he said, when I was finished. "A sad tale, indeed. I suppose one can see how it might happen."

"Mrs. Ballard absolutely dotes on her — *doted* on her — I saw it for myself before Mr. Ballard laid the whole thing waste."

"One can hardly blame the man."

"He didn't have to publicly humiliate her. Even his poor wife had no idea what was coming. She turned white as a sheet. Sarah isn't lying about the affection between herself and Mrs. Ballard — I saw it for myself. He's done both of them an injustice."

"You mustn't allow yourself to get worked up over it. If we concern ourselves with the lives patients leave behind when they come here, there'd be no end to it. It's not talked of, nor should it be, but do you have any idea of the divorce rate among our patients? Some spouses sue for divorce the minute their partner is diagnosed; it's abominable, but there you are. We can't go getting embroiled in all that."

"But you're a qualified psychiatrist," I said. "I would've thought you'd have more sympathy."

"Sympathy is one thing. We can't go getting embroiled."

"I've no intention of getting *embroiled* ..."

"Are you so sure of that? You seem quite fervent."

"I'm worried about her. How is she to survive?"

Dr. Tissot let out a sigh and drank the last of his brandy. He pointed out the same things that had occurred to me — Cunard, her father's house, and what about her father's work? His photographs must be worth something.

"Clearly, she should be consulting a lawyer — an estate agent, or an expert of some sort. But in the short term, I was wondering if you might consider taking her on in the Craft and Study Guild. She makes beautiful sketches — portraits, landscapes — in pencil, in ink, pastel. I think she'd make an excellent instructor."

"Oh, dear."

"Oh, dear what?"

"You're as bad as she — reaching after pretty leaves and tumbling into ice-cold rivers. And yet you seemed such a rational young man."

I attempted to dispute with him but he wasn't having it. As far as the doctor was concerned I'd gone and done exactly the opposite of what he'd recommended back when I first arrived.

"You've got it bad, Gascoyne. The would-be cad has gone and fallen for the girl. Ha!" He slapped his knee and the bulldog face lit up. So the eyes of the gods must have shone as they watched their mortal playthings come to grief.

Some days I liked to work in the public library, particularly when the weather got cold. Sarah had not told me *which* librarian had been rude to her, and I didn't think my eschewing the place would improve anyone's manners. I was now writing the first few chapters of a novel. Of course, I had not abandoned my aspirations toward high art, and hoped somehow to achieve that aim while at the same time writing a story that would have readers breathless to turn each page. My raw material was my personal humiliation at being jilted by Terrible Emily, and while my first attempts naturally played up my "innocence" in the matter, I soon realized that Emily's predicament was the more interesting. That meant starting over, but it also freed me from merely transcribing my own miseries and allowed my imagination to slowly build characters quite different from the real people who had inspired them. The most surprising thing, once I had made this change, was the ease with which I could turn out many pages of this compared to the agonies of squeezing out even a single stanza of verse.

The day after I spoke to Dr. Tissot, I was just coming from the library when I bumped into Jasper Keene in front of the Berkeley. I must have been still deeply involved in my story, because if I'd seen him first I might well have crossed the street to avoid him. How I could have missed his trademark black hat, I don't know.

"My boy, I'm very glad to run into you." He gripped both my arms and peered intently into my eyes as if searching the back of my skull. "My behaviour on our last encounter was inexcusable. Please forgive me."

"It was nothing," I said. "Please don't worry yourself."

"No, it was not nothing," he said firmly. "I don't know why I behaved that way. I'm a perfect child sometimes, a perfect child. Now let me make it up to you by buying us both a drink. In fact, let me buy you dinner at the Grill."

"Can't, I'm afraid. Mrs. Pryce will beat me senseless if I miss another meal."

"All right then, my boy. A drink it is."

He draped an avuncular arm on my shoulder and steered me toward the Arlington. We sat at the bar and he introduced me to the bartender, a handsome goateed sharp-faced man he called Billy.

"You'll want to remember that name, Billy. Gascoyne's the coming thing."

Billy served us a couple of whiskeys on the rocks, and then we immediately started talking about Sarah. Jasper had heard all about her humiliation first from Billy, Saranac being an absolutely rabid gossip mill, and then from Sarah herself. As with me, she had begged Jasper to let her explain.

"Girl didn't have to explain anything, far as I was concerned. She was drowning, the Ballards were a life raft — who are we to sit in judgment?"

"So you believe her? That she wanted to tell them the truth?"

"Oh, my, yes. Of course I do. Although …"

He went quiet for a moment, staring into his drink. He picked it up and took a sip and put it back on the bar.

"Although I'll admit I'm somewhat chagrined she felt the need to tell you everything she told me."

"Why, Jasper? She just — she knew we must be thinking the worst and wanted to tell us the way it was. She sees me regularly to talk about books — she couldn't very well ignore the subject."

"Well, here's a little confession of my own. I have a jealous nature, my boy. No, I don't want to say *nature* — it's not my whole being — but I have this flaw, this weakness. I don't like it in myself. It is certainly not a pleasant thing to have, Lord knows it isn't, but I have it and I wish I did not. So there you have it, my boy, you are forewarned. No, not fore. Not warned. I'm explaining. There. I am explained. But let us talk of other things — shoes, ships, sealing wax — what are you writing?"

I told him about my fall from poetry and my venture into novel writing.

"Show me at once," he said, gripping my arm again. I swear, I never saw Jasper without coming away *marked* in some manner — with fingerprints, if nothing else.

"But you don't even know the story."

"What is the story?"

I told him the basic premise: over the course of one night, a young woman must choose what kind of life she wants to live.

"Now, that's exciting. Truly. You must let me read it."

"Of course. The minute it's done."

"No, now. Let me see your beginnings. I'll tell you if I think you're veering off track. I can't tell you how many times I've wished I could have shown my first pages to a mentor of some kind. Would have saved me so many false starts, oh my yes, so many."

"You may be sorry you asked."

"Piffle. No false modesty, boy. No false modesty."

"What if it's perfectly appropriate modesty? Or insufficient modesty?" I said these things but I was digging in my satchel for my first forty pages. "And really, there's no reason you should be my editor."

"It's a token of my apology, my boy, a token of my apology. Now hand 'em over."

I received a handwritten note from Jasper.

> *Mr. Jasper Keene and Miss Sarah Redmond request the pleasure of your company at dinner on Friday, 8 PM, Riverside Inn — and don't be too damned formal!*

My happiness at the invitation was tempered by its being in both their names, as if they were a married couple. Someone more alert to the subtleties of male friendship might have considered that Jasper was trying to remind me: *Hands off, pal — she's taken.* He had warned me he was prone to jealousy, but it was hard to take seriously because I was not aware of anything he could possibly be jealous *of.* If he thought I was in love with Sarah, he would hardly have invited me along. Or perhaps he would have. In some ways Jasper was and has remained a deeper mystery to me than Sarah. In any case I showed up at the Riverside Inn a good ten minutes early.

The manager, Jack Parsons, was a nervous, affable, squat little man with rather the shape of a bowling pin. He greeted me (not by name) at his podium-like outpost near the door.

"I believe there's a reservation," I said, adding with great pleasure, "probably under Keene?"

"There's no reservation under that name," he answered, "but it's no matter — there's plenty of room. We've just emptied out."

"Ah, yes — everyone's gone to the theatre."

He sat me at a good table, placed three menus on it, and asked if I would like something to drink.

"Thank you. I'll wait till the others arrive."

I sat there, excited and nervous, tapping my finger on a corner of the menu. Only three other tables were occupied; I recognized one of my pupils, and we exchanged a cheery wave. After I'd perused the menu three or four times and glanced at my reflection (hideously formal) in the wide expanse of window, I checked my watch. Five past eight. When I looked up again, Sarah had come in and was walking across the dining room toward me without waiting for the manager.

"How nice to see you," I said, rising. "May I take your coat?"

"I believe I'll hang on to it for the moment. I've been cold all day."

"Where's Jasper? I assumed he was escorting you."

"Jasper," she said, and let the name hang between us for a moment. "Jasper is a man of many virtues, but reliability is not among them. He sent me a message saying he's unavoidably detained and not to wait for him."

"Oh, that's disappointing."

"It's typical, I'm afraid."

"Well, I've got some good news in the meantime. I think we should drink to it."

I signalled for the waiter, and we each ordered a glass of white wine.

"Come on, now. Tell me," Sarah said, setting her coat on the chair beside her. She was wearing a dress of grey silk that matched her eyes and, with it, a slim black choker with a tiny blue stone. It called attention to her throat — pale, sculpted, with a tracery of tiny lilac veins.

"It turns out the Craft and Study Guild can use another art instructor," I told her, "and I have recommended you."

"Paul, that's so kind. But I can't teach anybody anything. I'm not nearly qualified. I'm simply not good enough."

"Yes you are, I've seen your work. Just show Dr. Tissot a selection of your drawings and I'm sure the job's yours."

Our wine arrived and we toasted her job prospect, despite Sarah's reluctance. Conversation was awkward at first. Our meetings had heretofore been built around a purpose — we would discuss what she had written, or talk about what she was reading; small talk was kept to a minimum. She hadn't shown me any writing since her move, and I didn't want to raise books as a topic because it was Jasper who had set up the evening and I didn't want to behave as if it was another tutorial.

Sarah asked about my family background, which made me feel no less awkward. Professor Reginald Gascoyne was still mightily angry with his only son, which in turn caused my mother anguish that she tacked on to their archaeological reports in sorrowful addenda. It pained me to talk about them, but Sarah had been so brave and honest in our last meeting that I could hardly refuse. Her grey eyes expressed a worried

sympathy as I told her about my father and his constant scold-
ings for my "botched" academic career.

As I spoke I noticed over Sarah's shoulder that diners at two
other tables were staring at us. I thought I had noticed it earlier,
when Sarah had arrived.

"I think fathers may be harsher with sons than they are
with their daughters," she said. "They expect so little of us.
My father praised my drawing and painting far beyond their
merits, and involved me in his own work without expecting me
to make a career of it. And after my mother died, we became
very close. I was all he had."

Her voice faltered, and she paused for a moment before
continuing.

"If anything, he became *too* dependent on me. Well, it's
easy enough to understand — my mother had looked after
everything in our household. My father was allowed to do
whatever he needed to do, travel wherever he wanted, spend
hours in his darkroom, vanish into Manhattan to haunt the art
galleries — anything to pursue his photography. Sometimes he
would just lie on the floor staring at the ceiling, just daydreaming — *working*, he called it, and I actually believe he was."

She looked around for any sign of Jasper. "Shouldn't we
order? It appears we're on our own for the evening."

The manager was attending to another table, but I got the
attention of our waiter, who came over promptly, pencil at the
ready. I ordered for Sarah, and was about to order for myself
when the manager came over and interrupted. In the few times
I'd eaten at his establishment, Jack Parsons had always been
cheerful and gracious. But now he plucked the waiter's pad
and pencil from his hand and said, "I'm afraid I must ask you
to leave."

"What?" I said. "You can't be serious."

"I am completely serious."

"This must be some joke of Jasper's," Sarah said. "He has an unfortunate taste for practical jokes."

"No joke."

"But why?" I said. "What possible reason can you have?"

"Certain people have certain friends," he said darkly.

"What people? What friends? What are you talking about?"

"It's all right," Sarah said to me. "I know what this is."

"No, I want him to explain."

"Very well. If I *must* spell it out for you. Certain of my customers — patrons — are good friends with Mr. Cyrus Ballard, and they know all too well how his kindness and generosity have been abused. And to use the tragedy of the *Lusitania* for personal gain? There are certain lines, sir, certain lines a civilized person does not cross."

He picked up Sarah's coat and handed it to me.

"Please go. For the comfort of *all* our patrons. I won't charge you for the wine."

"Very big of you," I muttered, but Sarah was already heading for the door.

"Sarah, wait!"

I hurried to catch up and helped her with her coat. The waiter, looking sheepish, retrieved mine from the coat check.

We buttoned and wrapped ourselves up outside and I suggested that we head over to the Berkeley Grill. Sarah adamantly refused.

"Somewhere else, then," I offered. "You won't have any supper waiting for you at the boarding house."

"It doesn't matter. They're right to despise me — I despise myself."

"You mustn't," I said. She was in such distress that I put my arms around her before I knew what I was doing. "You mustn't, Sarah. You've explained very clearly how things happened. You didn't mean to hurt anyone."

Her shoulders shook as she wept silently. I stood there holding her, inhaling the scent of her hair, her neck, and experiencing some trembling myself.

"Come on, now," I said, forcing myself to pull away. "We'll have a pleasant walk, some fresh air, and then we'll sit down to a lovely dinner at the Berkeley — or the St. Regis, if you prefer. Come on, now."

I went ahead a few steps, walking backward so I could coax her along as if she were a kitten.

A voice from behind called out, "Do my eyes deceive me? Or do I spy two landlubbers abandoning ship?"

"Jasper!" The change in Sarah's demeanour was instantaneous — despair to joy. "You came!"

"Abject apologies to both of you. I've no excuse, I was just so caught up in my work. First nothing comes, I pace the room, I tear my hair, nothing. Then, just as it's nearly time to leave I manage to actually have an idea. It's obvious! A completely obvious solution to the scene! Why it takes me four hours to see it, I'll never know, but that's the kind of day it's been. What's going on? Why are you adrift on the street like a couple of orphans?"

Sarah looked away as I told Jasper what had transpired.

"You don't say," Jasper said, tugging on his moustache. "The man threw you out. Just like that."

"Well, he didn't throw us out, exactly. He asked us to leave but he didn't make us pay for our drinks."

"Come with me," Jasper said, taking me by the elbow. "You too, Sarah," now taking *her* elbow.

Sarah protested. "No, Jasper. I don't want to go back in there. I couldn't."

"Oh, but you can, my dear. You must. No, by God, you're both coming with me."

I was in no more hurry to re-enter the Riverside than Sarah, but Jasper wouldn't hear of it. He towed us both inside the front door, and called across the dining room. "Jack Parsons? Jack Parsons, a word with you, if you please!"

I have already mentioned Jasper's theatrical voice, and he was putting it to good use. The manager was chatting with a couple at one of the window tables, and he whirled around at the sound of his name. Seeing Jasper, he smiled tentatively and bustled toward us. Diners at the other table turned in their seats to see. One lady pointed toward us, and I could read her lips as she spoke to her husband. *That's Jasper Keene.*

"Mr. Keene, how good to see you."

"Please, Jack — it's Jasper. We're old friends at this point, are we not?"

"Well, yes, the entire staff is always —"

"Oh my, yes. It's a good deal of your champagne I've drunk, have I not? Indeed I have. Now, Jack, I had hoped to discuss with you arrangements for a gala affair. I have a new play coming, and we're going to be officially opening it here in the spring, rather than Broadway — I know, isn't it stupendous? Charles Frohman desperately wanted it but as you know he died in the *Lusitania* atrocity, which this young lady" — placing a hand on Sarah's shoulder — "managed to survive. And by God I am grateful for that mercy — oh my, yes — not only because she has captured my heart, but because she is a prodigiously gifted artist, one who will be sharing her gifts with the unfortunate patients at the san among others."

He leaned forward a little and spoke *sotto voce.*

"Now, I don't want to mislead you — the contract isn't signed yet — but John Barrymore can't wait to sink his perfect teeth into the part I'm writing for him — juicy is not the *word*. And Mary Young will be more than a match for him. I get goosebumps just thinking about it, don't you?"

Parsons managed a complicated smile and started to speak but Jasper barrelled right over him.

"I don't mind admitting to you that this play is putting a strain on the old cranium. It turns out writing a play does not get easier after you've had a success or two — oh my, no. This one is giving me trouble, this one is giving me fits of despair. Luckily, I have the editorial assistance of a literary scholar and a promising poet, Mr. Paul Gascoyne — perhaps you recognize the name — if not, you soon will, because Mr. Gascoyne, besides being an invaluable friend, is a man of penetrating intelligence, exquisite taste, and absolute Olympian dedication to his art, which is why he abandoned a comfortable position at Columbia University to pursue his calling in the curative yet intoxicating air of the Adirondacks. You ask Dr. Tissot what he thinks of this man. Ask Robbie Stevenson. For that matter, ask Miss Sarah Redmond, who will be more than happy to tell you the literary joy Professor Gascoyne brought her when she was suffering from the dread disease that seems demonically attracted to the young, the passionate, the gifted.

"Yes, Miss Redmond not only survived the *Lusitania* despite being given up for dead, she went toe to toe with the cruel disease we all fear more than death itself. Why, the girl is the very embodiment of Western civilization, she's confronted barbarism and plague and come back from the front lines to aid others in the fight. There's really nothing any of us can say in

the face of such courage and grace except … thank you —
that's all — just: thank you."

"But some of my patrons," Parsons said. "They're friends of
the Ballards. They're upset about the —"

"The rumours, the innuendo. You're not alone is mis-
reading the situation, my friend. Why, Cyrus Ballard has it
exactly wrong himself. Far from *taking* anything from the
good man, Miss Redmond — despite her own reservations,
mind you, despite her own misgivings — stayed on with
them out of *kindness to Mrs. Ballard* who, as even the most
hard-hearted can agree, was devastated by the loss of young
Stevie. Now, I don't wish to go into the details of how this
tragic misunderstanding occurred, but I guarantee you, when
Mr. and Mrs. B have had a chance to reflect, they'll realize just what they've lost and they'll come looking for Miss
Sarah Redmond. Courage and grace, Jack, courage and grace.
When such qualities appear at our doorstep, who among us
would turn them away?"

"Well, nobody — of course. I've often said as much."

"'Course you have! You're a gracious man — a very genius
of hospitality. Now for God's sake, Jack, bring us your best
and we'll forget your earlier misunderstanding. How could you
know? You couldn't. Now feed us and we'll drink to the dam-
nation of germs and Germans."

"Of course, Mr. Keene. Come this way."

"It's Jasper, Jack — Jasper. We're all friends here, are we
not? Oh my, yes."

It is perhaps needless to add that our service for the rest of
the night was impeccable.

"It must be wonderful to be famous," I said. "You get treated with such deference."

"I'm not truly famous. Barrymore is famous, Chaplin is famous. Those two are treated like royalty — with awe, even — which they richly deserve. I'm just somewhat *known*, that's all. When people recognize my name, I get treated with a smidgeon of extra care, as one might fuss over a blind person."

Sarah asked him if Barrymore would really be appearing in his play.

"That, my dear, is a question for his agent. May it come to pass."

I raised my glass to Barrymore, and we all toasted.

"Listen, you," Jasper said, poking me on the forearm, "that was a fine thing you did, arranging a place for Sarah with the Craft Guild. Mighty fine."

"Oh, it was nothing. I just put a word in with Dr. Tissot, and ..."

"Don't pooh-pooh it. You've done a service for the woman I adore. I appreciate chivalry wherever I find it."

"And so do I," Sarah said, and raised her glass and the three of us drank to "Sir Paul Gascoyne," one of us blushing to the tips of his ears.

"I tried to do her a service myself, you know, but she denied me that happiness. Wouldn't have it." He turned to Sarah tenderly. "Really, my dear, there's no need to stay in that igloo. I could still get you a room by the month at the St. Regis or the Berkeley."

"Never. Chivalry is one thing, but my days as a charity case are over."

"Oh my," Jasper said. "I surely didn't mean to insult you." He took hold of her hand and folded it into an elegant fist. "Punch me now. Give me a good one, I deserve it."

"Nonsense. But I'm not going to take money from you or any man."

She wondered aloud about her teaching prospects and how exciting it would be to be out and about and meet new people. She had visited the Craft Guild studio some time ago, and found the director of the art program a very talented watercolourist. She sat back, looking pensive a moment, then added, "But maybe they'll change their minds about me. It's not as if there's anything in writing."

"I'll tell you what *is* in writing," Jasper said. "Forty pages of an excellent new novel by one Paul Gascoyne."

"You're writing a novel?" Sarah said. "That's wonderful news. I know you would write a beautiful novel. Will you tell me what it's about?"

"I think I'd rather just wait until it's finished. I only showed Jasper because he threatened to call in the authorities if I didn't."

"I offered to give him the benefit of my experience," Jasper said. "And I have absolutely none to offer. The boy is a natural. No, no, Paul, it's true. You have an instinct for setting a scene, you know when to come in, when to withhold, when to sit back and let your characters do all the work, oh my, yes. Really, I'm the one who should be getting his help with *my* work."

Is it any wonder that the disgraced son of Professor Reginald P. Gascoyne was giddy with an intoxicant more powerful than any wine? It struck me all but dumb for the rest of the night. Jasper filled the gaps to overflowing with anecdotes of opening night disasters, technical snafus, and recalcitrant actors who *would* insist on changing dialogue on the fly.

"You know people wondered why Jimmy Hackett delivered so many lines of *Hamlet* lying on his back? Up in the flies, they had set up a massive roller with his big speeches printed on them in huge letters. Some poor little gaffer had to roll the thing so he could say his lines!"

"But I saw that reviewed as a brilliant manoeuvre — the lying down, I mean."

"Oh my, yes. And so it was — under the circumstances."

He became serious, and talked about his own work. Sarah asked him questions about his beginnings as an actor, and then as an actor-manager competing with theatrical machines like the Shuberts. A look of pain would cross his face, and then a funny story, but it couldn't quite mask the pain. I found myself watching not just Jasper but Sarah's reactions to Jasper. Watching with an ache. He made her laugh in a way I did not; his stagey speech interspersed with homely phrases clearly delighted her. She reached often for his arm to give it a squeeze, awarding these little trophies whenever he said something particularly striking. He won more and more of these as the night wore on, and I none. It was this, and not her generous response to my novelistic aspirations that hit home. Without intending to, she was making clear what Jasper's invitation had only hinted at: she was his. And upon the instant of my seeing this, the god of irony decided to shatter my imaginary shield of immunity, and I realized that I had fallen — helplessly, fatally — in love with Sarah Redmond.

CHAPTER 14

By now, my list of pupils was substantial. This did not pay enough to put aside anything for savings, but if I kept to a not-too-draconian budget, I could live comfortably. My biggest expense was books. Saranac had a couple of decent bookstores, reading being the main occupation of most patients, and I've already mentioned the library, but I often had to ask the booksellers to "special order" books for me. It was always a bright moment when I picked up such an order and hustled it back to my room to snip the twine and unwrap the brown paper.

I was finding that writing fiction was changing my perception of my favourite novelists. George Eliot and Henry James were giving way to Stephen Crane, Joseph Conrad, and the old master of Saranac himself, Robert Louis Stevenson. As I worked and reworked my own burgeoning novel, I studied Crane for his imagery and observation, Conrad for his vice-like plotting, and Stevenson for his imagination and sheer storytelling power. In short, I was a student again, and once more in love with my subject. My general attitude took a distinct turn toward the optimistic, so much so that even Mrs. Pryce could not upset me. I could now meet her Panglossian observations with an exorbitant cheeriness of my own.

"Good morning, Mr. Gascoyne. Is it not a beautiful day?"

"I would go further, Mrs. Pryce. I would call it a *perfect* day, a *sublime* day."

In fact it was dark as evening, thunder growling over lake and mountain.

"Nothing like a good storm to blow away your troubles and clear the mind."

"Nothing like a good *Adirondack* storm."

"You're very chipper these days, Mr. Gascoyne. It does my heart good to see it."

But whether stormy or snowy, whether bright or gloomy, my days — even crowded as they were with patient-pupils — felt solitary. Waves of happiness were definitely lapping at the Gascoyne shore, but I was never truly content unless I had some prospect of seeing Sarah.

Over the next couple of weeks, Jasper, Sarah, and I fell into an easy friendship *à trois*. I had my scheduled sessions with Sarah, but as her strength increased, she and Jasper also invited me to join them on snowy walks, or for afternoon tea at the Arlington. Jasper even invited me to join him for another drink at the Berkeley, where he pressed me to give him more pages to read. Most novelists — or successful writers of any kind, I imagine — will have a special person in their background

who rekindled their creative fire even when the whole enterprise seemed doomed to failure. For me, that person was Jasper
Keene, and it is perhaps not surprising that his generous attention bred in me a near-canine loyalty. This, and his prior claim
on Sarah precluded any prospect of my courting her. Except for
our tutorials, I never saw her alone until one winter day, when
I found myself sitting opposite her on a bench in Pine Ridge
Cemetery. Sarah unfolded a portable stool she had scrounged
up from the Craft and Study Guild and took out her sketch
pad. We were not scheduled for a tutorial; she had simply sent
me a request to sit for her, to which I immediately agreed.

It was December now, and although the day was far from
harsh few people would choose to remain seated outside for
any length of time in a temperature of thirty-five degrees
Fahrenheit. But Saranac's population of patients, former patients, and those who cared for them had to accept it as a normal, even enjoyable, part of life or quickly go mad. Anyway,
thirty-five degrees was nothing compared to the minus thirty
or worse attacks of January and February. The balsam-scented
air, raucously punctuated by jays and ravens, made sitting outside a richer experience than the uninitiated might suppose.
Sarah, given her intimate experience with death, could have
been expected to avoid a setting that most would consider morbid even in the brightest days of summer, but she was perfectly
happy to sit among her "colleagues." It didn't hurt that the
cemetery, with its stone terraces and gates, with its company of
conifers and broadleaf greens, was the prettiest place in town.

I was flattered Sarah had chosen me as her subject; I had not
yet learned that artists don't necessarily view the person sitting
for them with any more admiration than they might hold for
the dead rabbits of still life. The urge began to swell within

me to tell Sarah how I felt about her. We were alone, I had her sustained attention, I could make my case. I would understate things; I wouldn't even hint at any thought of "stealing her away" from Jasper. Aside from the moral question of declaring love behind his back, which I was struggling to settle in my favour — I wasn't interested in stealing. My devoutest wish was the same as any lover's: to be wanted, no theft required.

Sarah took pains to arrange me on my bench at what she considered a good angle. This done, she sat down and began to draw, her arm making wide sweeping gestures so that I couldn't imagine what aspect of my physiognomy she could be capturing. Now and again, other people would come along the path, but Sarah could not be distracted. Her intensity in the project unsettled me. Though she glanced at me, her glances were not the casual ones of conversation; they were clinical, devoid of emotion, and of a duration no longer than the click of a shutter. Her concentration was so complete I couldn't bring myself to interrupt, and the courtly phrases I was rehearsing in my head — shy yet amorous, unassuming yet compelling (or so I imagined) — refused to escape my throat. A downy woodpecker attacked a spindly pine, accompanied by the *chut-chut-chut* of a crossbill that eyed me warily from a low branch.

"It's all right," Sarah said, eyes on sketch pad. "You're allowed to talk to me."

"I know, I just — self-conscious, I suppose."

"You should try being swaddled in a cure chair if you want to know about feeling self-conscious."

She glanced up at me, then back at her sketch pad, glanced up, then back, and so it went on. I took advantage of the opportunity to study her fragile beauty, the gracile bones of her face, the slightly sorrowful cast of her expression when silent. Her grey eyes looked blue today, reflecting the clear sky overhead. That prehensile gaze. It should have been clear that affection played little or no part in the way Sarah looked at me, but my heart responded as if it might. This, frankly, was peculiar because Sarah was nothing like my "type," which tended to be the energetic, no-nonsense blond. Two of my previous romantic interests had been merciless tennis players, and Emily — equally merciless with my emotions — was a powerful swimmer. None had been particularly creative; despite my admiration for the great women novelists, I had never looked for this in a woman. But now, here I was, hostage of a wounded, diminutive, grey-eyed creature like none I had ever met.

"It's getting colder," I said. "We'd better get you indoors."

"This is nothing. I'm used to far worse."

"I'm not."

"All right. I'm making a hash of your portrait anyway. I know where we can go."

We transferred ourselves to the "conservatory" at the back of the Arlington Hotel, where one could sit for an hour or two for the price of tea and cakes. It was dazzlingly bright after the cemetery, and the light streaming in through the glass quickly warmed us up. No acceptable conversational material entered my head, which was filled with off-limits phrases such as, "You're so pretty I can't breathe."

"Paul," Sarah said when our tea arrived, "I want to ask your advice about something."

"If it's about the stock market, I urge you to go elsewhere."

She paused a moment, pale slim hand hovering over her drawing. "I want to ask you about Jasper."

"You know the man better than I do."

She shook her head. "He's a complete enigma to me. I feel it requires a man to explain him."

"Well, he's devoted to you, obviously."

"Is he? Sometimes I believe that he is. But just when I feel we are getting really close, he disappears. He vanishes back to New York or off to his hideaway in the woods or God knows where."

"He does have a tendency to slip away," I conceded. Except for one accidental encounter, my meetings with Jasper were always at his instigation. But if I called for him or sent a message … nothing.

"I never see him for more than an evening or an afternoon. It's as if I'm a flower and he's a hummingbird — stops for a moment, then darts away. I don't know where he is right now, for example, do you?"

"Haven't the foggiest."

"Not that I need to know his daily itinerary. But how can he be so affectionate, so loving, one minute and just disappear without a word the next? Sometimes he's gone for a week, two — I hadn't seen him for a month when you first turned up." She smiled at me. "When you turned up so delightfully."

Her smile was belied by a distinct quaver in her voice. If I had previously surmised that her near-drowning in the Saranac River had been intentional, this was the first time I suspected it might have a connection to Jasper. If so, their entwinement was deeper and of longer standing than I had so far guessed. She put her pencil down.

"What I want to ask," she said. "It's embarrassing to confess such ignorance — but what I want to ask is, is this usual? Is this what men do? Is that what you do? To someone like Nurse Troy, perhaps?"

My tongue chose that moment to develop a stammer worthy of royalty.

"Do you flatter them, Paul? Do you caress them with beautiful words and phrases and then vanish?"

"I believe I've told you the woman I was going to marry called it off two days before the wedding. And as for Nurse Troy," I added righteously, "I saw her walking out arm-in-arm with some fellow I knew nothing about."

"But was that beyond the bounds of your acquaintance with her? Perhaps she was unaware of your feelings. Or too conscious of your lack of feeling?"

"That's putting it harshly."

"I'm just asking, not accusing. I don't *know* anything, Paul."

I was afraid of the answer, but I asked anyway: "Is it hurting you terribly much — Jasper's vanishing?"

"*Hurt* is not the right word. I feel … crushed. Vanquished. Extinguished. Or maybe like a dead person who only suddenly, belatedly, realizes she doesn't exist."

"Sarah," I said. "I'm sorry to hear this. I had no idea you were so …"

"Do you think he's doing it on purpose?"

"Why would he do that? He clearly adores you. Do you mean as in absence making the heart grow fonder?"

"That old saw refers to *unavoidable* absence. *Unwanted* separation. But I think Jasper *wants* to be away from me and I don't know why. I don't know what I've done. I sense that he's doing it on purpose — I don't know why it feels that way, it just does. He tells me he has business in Saratoga Springs, or in New York, and I believe him, but I don't understand why *he* doesn't seem to understand … that it crushes my spirit so."

The anguish in her voice was unmistakable, and she sagged a little on the stool. If you were mine, I wanted to say, I would never cause you such pain. But I tried to be soothing.

"I don't think it can be on purpose. That just doesn't make sense. What man in their right mind would want to be apart from you?"

"Oh, Paul. You're sweet to say that. You're always sweet. But you do have a tendency to literary exaggeration."

"Not in this case."

"But what can I do about it? How do I get him to not keep … disappearing? It's pathetic to say, Paul, but it's killing me."

I'll stay with you, I wanted to say, but of course I did no such thing. I reiterated my belief that Jasper was devoted to her, that his "disappearances" meant no harm. All writers need vast tracts of time alone, I told her. Other than that: "I'm sure Jasper has no idea how this is upsetting you. Maybe you should just tell him."

"I could never do that. It would make me pathetic in his eyes, weak, and he can't abide weakness — in himself or anyone else."

"But he does understand passion. He won't see *that* as weakness."

"I don't want to be … I don't want to *burden* him."

"If that's the case, maybe you should part."

She drew her head back and frowned at me as if I had questioned the existence of gravity.

"Part from Jasper? I couldn't. I wouldn't. Anyone can see we're drawn to one another, that we fit together like two puzzle pieces. Never, Paul. Jasper has me, body and soul."

That *body and soul* stung — or at least put me in my place. I apologized for my limited menu of advice, but suggested that if she wouldn't raise the issue with Jasper, she could hardly expect it to change. *Body and soul.* Really? Today it seemed Jasper brought her anguish, not joy. But perhaps the same could be said of my affections for the two of them.

"Will *you* talk to him, Paul? Oh, please — will you? I know he wouldn't resent it coming from you."

There may be men — men composed of sterner stuff than I — who can resist an importunate female, but I have never been one of them. Pleading her case with Jasper was the last damn thing I wanted to do and I wanted to say it aloud — wanted to shout it — but I could not, and when we parted that day, I limped home as battered as any outmatched featherweight.

Before dinner I went round to the Berkeley to see if I could roust Jasper, but was told he was out of town. The front desk could not say when he was expected to return. I left a note asking him to get in touch when he got back. I realized, even as I did so, that I hoped he would stay away long enough that Sarah would get over him. I would be the stalwart comforter and confidante, the messenger of good cheer, her granite-solid indispensable man.

But later as I lay in bed listening to the night train, I told myself that I was bigger than that, that Jasper was my friend, and that if I *truly* loved Sarah I would want only what was best for her happiness. I had to accept her words at face value: she was Jasper's, body and soul. And so I drifted into a honeyed sleep, congratulating Paul Gascoyne on his devout chivalric selflessness.

Despite my newfound ambition toward achieving glory in the novel, I was still so steeped in poetry that I sometimes dreamed in iambs and dactyls — or rather, my dreams might be accompanied by a whispering voice trying to narrate the fantastic events unfolding in my head. It usually spoke when I was in a semi-wakeful state, adrift along the foggy shores of memory, dream, and sleep.

Consequently, when I dreamed the image of a large talking raven at my window and heard the urgent whisper of Edgar Allan Poe — *suddenly there came a tapping, as of some one gently rapping, rapping at my chamber door* — it was nothing unusual for me. I slumbered on for a few moments to Edgar's throaty dactyls. And then I was awake — sitting upright, stunned, blinking — because someone actually *was* rapping at my chamber door. Far from "gentle," it rattled the thing at latch and hinge.

"Paul? Wake up, Paul — it's your conscience calling. Open the door, my boy, open the door."

I put on my robe and went to the door and opened it. Jasper stepped in, a rime of snow on Stetson and shoulders.

"Jasper, what on earth—"

"Sit down, my boy, sit down. And don't speak."

I sat on the edge of the bed.

"I believe you're acquainted with the bartender at the Arlington — don't answer, I know you are. But you don't know him nearly as well as I do. Bill and I go back a long way, oh my, yes. He's much more than a bartender. So I go in there for a drink after my sojourn in the woods with Charlie Sands — I'm ready for fun, ready to squire my lady, ready to carouse with my friend, ready to talk books and plays and poems and all manner of thing. Oh, how I was looking forward to seeing not just Sarah, but you *and* Sarah. I thought we made a delightful unit of three — oh my, yes — a delightful unit of three.

"You see, Paul, although I have achieved some modicum of success and you have not yet published so much as a *haiku*, my admiration for you has been sincere — why? Partly because I saw in you a fellow traveller on the road of art — I saw myself as a young man starting out — but also because I thought you had the *sine qua non* not just of the artist, but of a man intent on living the best and most profound kind of life. I thought that, like me, you were seeking not just the *fruits* of experience but experience itself — the rage, the sorrow, the ecstasy itself — that you sought to burn always with that hard, gemlike flame, to maintain this ecstasy, that that would be your absolute unwavering aim ..."

Jasper did not pause here, but I want to convey his attitude. He spoke with urgency, with intensity, but it was not what he was saying that made the hair on my neck raise itself. You have to picture his eyes — always dark, often passionate, but now his gaze was unblinking, the jet-black eyes of the snake that mesmerizes the bird, the eyes of the demon-boy who decides he *will* crush that spider — the final gaze beheld by murdered men.

"Jasper, please. You have to calm yourself."

He didn't even slow down.

"Such men," he raged on, "love *truly* when they love, such men regard the bonds of friendship as sacred — no less sacred than the bond between a man and his beloved. A man's friends are his brothers-in-arms, always to be heard, to be helped, and never to hurt, never betray. So imagine my surprise, *Professor*, imagine my dismay, and the sense of swinish betrayal, when I find that you have been courting Sarah behind my sleeping back."

"Jasper! What are you — I did not! I would not!"

He fixed a hand at my throat and toppled me backward on the bed.

"Lie again and I will break your neck. Now sit up and shut up."

I slowly raised myself, rubbing my throat.

"For God's sake, Jasper."

"You were with Sarah at Pine Ridge Cemetery, for an hour or two, according to my sources. And then, I have it on excellent authority, you spent another hour with her in a loving *tête-à-tête* over tea at the Arlington. Oh yes, *boy*, tears were shed, comfort was offered, touches exchanged. You *touched my beloved*, you treacherous thieving swine. You *touched my beloved*. I suppose you read poems to her. *As if she had contrived a physical faith — a death I could learn from, having survived.* Well, that's Sarah if I ever heard Sarah. Was it just luck, or were you already onto her when you scribbled that little ditty? Is that why you wormed your way into my confidence? To close in on the woman I loved? Insinuate your reed-thin body between us, you mewling, puking *infant*. Oh, I'll wager you were subtle, as chatty and sweet as a serpent selling apples, I suppose you explained to her — deftly, subtly, in the guise of *protection* — that Jasper Keene, far from being the man of her dreams, is a creation of Queen Mab, a lizard of a Lothario, a depraved Don Juan bent on dragging her hellward down the honeyed highway of seduction. Admit it, you conniving little cuntmonger. Admit it, and take your punishment like a man."

He pulled a pistol from his coat pocket and clouted me with it.

"Speak, you spider."

"Jasper, she loves you! She came to me for advice!"

He levelled the gun at my chest.

"Oh, and I'll wager you gave it. *No, no, not Jasper, Sarah — that way madness lies. The man is a joker, a wild card, never to be trusted. He whispers of love, but comes to you armed with*

Casanova caresses, the killing kiss, whereas I ... I, Professor
Goody-good, will love and protect you all your days. The man
is a fever, he comes and goes, comes and goes. You're a con man's
castaway — just when you need him he leaves you marooned,
whereas I ... I am always with you, I am the air you breathe, I
am cool water when your mind is on fire, and for your wounds
a snow-white bandage. No, no, bring to me your broken heart,
I am love's hospital and crisp clean sheets."

"Jasper, listen to me. Everything you're saying is wrong. It's
just completely, utterly wrong."

I felt the cold circle of iron as he pressed the barrel of the
gun against my forehead.

"Wrong, is it? That must be why the dear girl spent hours
sketching you. The way one sketches a lawyer when seeking
legal advice. The way one sketches a surgeon while he cuts your
husband open."

"She was upset about your being gone. She loves you. She
wants you *here*. But you stir up her emotions and then you take
off into the woods, or Manhattan, or wherever the hell you go.
It devastates her every time. If you could've seen the expression
on her face, you wouldn't doubt any of this. She worries that
you don't love her, that you don't even *like* her. She thinks you
may despise her, that you're using these sudden disappearances
to manipulate her in some way."

"I ... I manipulate *her*."

"Yes. Because you get her all worked up. She's left here
yearning for you and wondering why you disappear and say
nothing, and what the hell is she supposed to think, Jasper?
Now get that stinking gun out of my face."

I think he had forgotten about the gun. He peered at it
a moment and put it on my desk as if it were no more than

an ashtray. His eyes seemed suddenly to clear, a sleepwalker waking on the edge of the cliff.

I touched my head where he had clouted me and checked for blood. There was none, but a small lump was already beginning to form.

"For God's sake, Jasper. I tried to tell her that you were not doing anything on purpose to hurt her, that you were just a man who needs to be able to go where he wants *when* he wants, and that other people don't much enter into it."

"Really? That's *good*, that's *good* — true too. *Ha.* Too true. You know, I believe I will sit down."

He pulled off his coat and hung it up as if he had just arrived and had not been threatening my life. He sat down heavily and leaned forward on his knees, head bowed. He'd kept his hat on, so all I could see of him was the dark circle of its brim.

"Jesus Christ, Jasper." I couldn't think of any other response. "You damn near murdered me. I'll have to tell the police."

I picked up the revolver and put it in a desk drawer. Then I thought about it and turned on the desk lamp and opened the drawer again and took it out. It was far too light to contain any lead. I broke out the cylinder. Nothing. Not even blanks. I held it under the light and read *Broadway Stage Armory* etched along the barrel.

"Perfect," I said. "I should have known."

Jasper's shoulders were quaking. I watched until I couldn't stand it anymore. I found a handkerchief for him, which he took without a word. He wiped his eyes and blew his nose. I tossed the gun on the bed and sat beside it.

"Well, isn't that a thing," he said. "Grown man crying his eyes out. Isn't that a thing."

I just huffed.

He got up and went to his coat and reached into his pocket and I thought surely not again but he pulled out a flask.

"You must try this. It's Mackinlay's — a very superior whiskey. Chaplin sent me a case after *Married* opened."

"Charlie Chaplin."

Jasper found a glass and poured me a double. He handed it to me and took a drink from the flask.

"Man's a comic genius. *There's* passion for you. Man like that."

"Did he give you the gun too?"

"Gun?" Jasper looked puzzled. "Oh. No."

We drank in silence for several minutes. The whiskey was good. It burned away some of the fear and a little of the anger, but there was still a trembling in my knees.

"How strange," Jasper said, "to still make discoveries about yourself at the age of thirty-six. If you had told me a year ago that I had a jealous nature, why, I would have thought you a profoundly *un*observant man. I imagine some men discover hidden *strengths* in themselves, hidden *virtues*, but I ..."

"Well, there *is* such a thing as *rational* jealousy."

"Oh my, yes."

"Not that this is a case of that."

"Ha. You wound me, sir."

"For example, a man who is unlucky enough to be married to a woman who is ... less than faithful. No one would fault him for jealousy."

"No."

"But Sarah loves you and misses you and when you are gone she uses *me* to talk about *you*. This does exactly nothing for my self-confidence. I admit I am supremely attracted to her, but —"

"She's taken, Paul. She's taken."

"I know that. And I would never try to win her away from you." I emitted the words with a certainty they were far from deserving.

He looked at me with mournful eyes and I thought once more of sad-eyed Poe. "You're telling me the truth now, aren't you — yes, I can see you are."

"I am, yes."

"Dear God, I've been an idiot. Worse than an idiot. I'm sorry for it, Paul — truly. I'm sorry for it, and I hope you'll come to forgive me. You've a large soul and I believe you will — though perhaps not immediately."

"Not immediately. I'll have to stop shaking first."

"I'm not a good man, Paul — not really. Not ultimately. But you, well, I believe you might be."

"Oh my, yes," I said, mimicking him. "Dear me, yes. My boy, you have spoken an undoubted truth."

"Ha. Well, we must do everything we can to further your literary career, because clearly you have no future on the stage."

CHAPTER 15

I stayed away from both Jasper and Sarah for a while after that, and spent as much of my free time reading as writing. I finished all of Stevenson, a writer who would have been on no university curriculum anywhere, and even ventured into H. Rider Haggard, an author who would have given my Columbia colleagues a severe case of nausea. I picked up an order from the bookstore, without even remembering what it was. When I opened it back in my room, I was a little disappointed that it was a copy of Jasper's first play, *The Lady's Man*. The lump on my head had soon gone down, but I had not yet recovered from Jasper's fit of jealousy, and at this point I wanted to read only novels. But later that night, I opened up the little paperback (it was more like a folder, really), intending just to glance at a page or two.

It had me right from act 1, scene 1. The dialogue had such wit that I thought at first he had intended a comedy, but the self-loving protagonist, who addresses the audience about his every plan à la *Richard III*, soon gets himself into ever more tense situations and inflicts grievous harm on all who know him. He comes to a much-deserved bad end, but the mordant dialogue and vivid characterizations make it a far from depressing story. My esteem for Jasper's abilities, already high, rose to something like literary adoration, if you can call it adoration when the feeling is tainted with envy. More than anything, I hoped that I could bring a comparable dramatic authority to my novel or to anything else I might write.

During this time I visited Dr. Tissot more frequently, and stopped in to say hello to my pupils even when I had no session scheduled. Ronnie Barstowe was not doing at all well. His skin was waxy, his voice reedy, but he tried mightily to keep up his energetic optimism. He was sitting up in bed, tapping on a dummy Morse code key to practise sending messages.

"Mr. Wilkins wheeled me over to the Craft Guild the other day and I sent a message to a fellow in Louisbourg — and he sent me one back. Isn't that amazing? I didn't even know where Louisbourg was."

"I don't know where it is, either."

"Nova Scotia, Canada. They have a Marconi tower there."

Radio telegraphy had made the front pages of newspapers back when the *Titanic* sank, its frantic distress signals having become the stuff of legend. Those signals had saved the lives of hundreds of passengers, who were scooped up by the *Carpathia* within two hours.

Ronnie tapped at the key, which made a pleasing *nick, nick, nick* sound.

"There. Do you know what that was?"

"Not a clue."

"I said, *How good to see Mr. Gascoyne.* At least I think I did. I'll have to check the marks against the manual. I can't wait till we're able to transmit speech. That's coming, Mr. Gascoyne. That's coming real soon."

Judging by the rawness in his voice, the poor kid probably shouldn't have been speaking at all. He tore off a slip of paper and set it aside on the bed where it curled back into a roll.

"When I finally get rid of this stupid disease, I'm going to live somewhere that has a Marconi tower and talk to people all over the world. Think what it will mean for world peace — if people from all over the world can talk to each other? This stupid war would never have started! Everyone will see that we're not so different — we all want health and love and a decent job — and there's no reason why we can't get along. It's lack of communication, Mr. Gascoyne, lack of communication's where the problem is."

His eyes filled with tears — not of sorrow but of physical pain. He lurched for his sputum cup and coughed horribly into a handkerchief before using it and closing the lid. He lay back, exhausted, and as I left he seemed reduced to nothing but a pair of enormous desolate eyes.

"I'll come again," I said, but I learned next day that he had been removed to the infirmary at the reception hospital.

As the days passed, the stack of pages on my desk steadily grew. Now that the muse of poetry had departed, my novel was enjoying a spurt of growth. I wanted to see it in print; I *yearned* for it. But that was my bad angel speaking. The angel on my other shoulder, whose voice was suspiciously like Sarah's, urged caution. My plan was to finish a first draft, and then hone and polish it until it was worthy not just of publication but of the term *art.* I went through gallons of ink.

I was scratching away at my book one day when there was a shuffling outside my door, followed by a thump, which was followed by knocking. I opened it, and a messenger stood there proffering pen and receipt pad.

"What is it?" I said, indicating the cube-shaped parcel on the floor.

"Search me, sir. I just deliver 'em."

The parcel was heavy and my desk cluttered. I carried the thing to my bed and found a pair of scissors to cut the multiple windings of string that held it together. Inside was a battered case with faded lettering that said *Royal*. I had to undo several latches in order to lift the lid off, and there it was: a typewriter with the muscular matte-black look of a locomotive. The smell of ink and metal was intoxicating, and a word typed itself out in my mind: *professional*.

A handwritten note was rolled around the platen. I tugged, and it came away with a satisfying *thrrrrip*.

> *This magnificent machine belonged to Charlie Klein of* Music Master *fame, but I got it off David Belasco, who was sick and tired of it cluttering up his theatre. Presumably,* The Music Master *passed round its platen at least once. It wrote* Married or Not *for me, and promises that if you treat it as one would a woman, buying it plentiful ribbons, it will type your masterpieces for you. Now that you are embarked on fiction, it's supremely important that you not be in love with your own hand-writing — a syndrome that is the only explan-ation for many contemporary doorstops. I hope*

you may use it in happiness, and from time to
time remember how deeply sorry I am for my
behaviour the other night.

Your unworthy friend,
Jasper

I had not seen *The Music Master*, but I knew that it had
been a massive hit and highly regarded and that the typewriter
must have meant a lot to Jasper. I cleared off my desk and rolled
a piece of paper into the works. It was harder to use than one
might suppose; my fingers plunged into the keys and slid off, or
I would hit two at once, or spend ages seeking the semicolon.
I decided right then and there to sign up for the Craft Guild's
typing course, and so I did.

Even the briefest foray into producing fiction will demonstrate
that what they say about happiness is true: it is supremely difficult to write. Narrative, after all, thrives on conflict, and a
stretch of happiness provides none. So I'll be brief. Despite
the torch I was carrying for Sarah, not to mention her own
for Jasper, the five or six weeks that followed Jasper's gift of
the typewriter were, for me, supremely happy. Jasper stayed
in town for a longer stretch than ever, and he and Sarah delighted in each other's company. They generously invited me
along on numerous outings — such outings as are afforded
by an Adirondack winter. There were skating parties, parades
in support of war bonds, parades in support of tuberculosis
research, a macabre misadventure when Jasper tried to teach

me how to ski, and one sunny day when he proposed a walk up Baker Mountain.

My willingness to pal around with a man who had threatened me with a gun, even if a fake gun, demands some explanation. It had more to do with Jasper's character than my own. His bluff, brash exterior, his wide smile and ready handshake, his exuberant attitude, had initially drawn me in, the same as it drew everybody in. And I was not immune to the cachet of merely knowing the man. Yes, he had frightened me half to death, and he stood between me and Sarah, but against all this he had given me his faith (now, concretely in the form of a typewriter in addition to his praise) and most compelling of all, his vulnerability. It was a mighty heady drug to have seen him weeping. To an admiring young writer, it was as if Zeus himself had appeared and sobbed, *I'm just not up to the job of being Zeus.*

He broached the idea of "a walk" up Baker Mountain with me, first, before bringing it to Sarah.

"I know the girl," he said. "She won't do it unless you come along. She'll think it's too risky."

"Jasper, she has TB. It's a mountain. It's covered in snow."

"My boy, it's covered in trees. The ground gets less snow than Main Street. And we'll be going up on the sunny side, where most of it's melted."

"I'll go up with you, if you like, but it's far too much for Sarah. It's not so long ago she was bedridden. She didn't cure out in a cave or wherever it is Charlie Sands takes you."

"Fine. Just the two of us."

A few days later, he showed up at my door, along with an extra set of cleats and a packed lunch. And Sarah.

I told her I didn't think it was a good idea. The doctors were adamant about too much exertion, too much excitement.

She stood there in the foyer with Jasper, happy and bright-eyed.

"You don't know how *good* I feel, Paul. I feel stronger than ever. I can walk miles now."

"But not up a mountain. Jasper, this isn't right. You told me it would be just us two."

"It's twenty-four hundred feet, Paul, and it's practically in the middle of town. Hardly Mount Everest. Come on, my boy, we deserve a bit of fun."

Well, they talked me into it.

The day was one of pure boundless sun — so much so that the light bouncing off the snow required the three of us to wear sunglasses. Breezes caromed off the surrounding hills, but the temperature hovered in the kinder regions of a Saranac winter and, despite my earlier reluctance, I set out with my friends in a fine mood.

Jasper was correct that Baker was no Everest. Of the three mountains surrounding Saranac Lake, it was by far the lowest. But — something he neglected to mention — it was a lot steeper than one might want for a Sunday walk. Jasper had been up many times, and he was determined to show us a certain craggy overlook that he claimed as his "special place." We were still on the lower quarter when I asked him what he meant by the term.

"Everyone has a special place," he said. "Oh my, yes. When you arrive at your special place, you are all but overwhelmed with the sense of *rightness*, with the sense that, *yes, this is where I was always meant to be.* For me, it's the place where I feel most myself, most free, expansive, brave, ambitious, generous, and full and all words meaning some combination of plenitude, amplitude, and energy."

"I don't think I've found mine," I said, but wondered if a *person* could be that special place.

"There were days," Sarah said, "when I went out with my father — he with his camera and me with my sketch pad — and the two of us would work away, not saying a word until it was time for lunch or time to go home. There were cliffs near where we lived in New Jersey, and if the light was right, you could see faces in them — and the faces changed moods with the changing light."

I seemed to remember Sarah telling me that her father didn't care for landscapes, that he only photographed people, and I made a comment to this effect.

"For his public work, that's true. But he liked to take the odd landscape just for pleasure."

"Branch!" Jasper had taken the lead to find the safest way around the fallen trees, the hidden roots, and rock piles. He held the branch aside until Sarah could take hold of it.

Snow on the ground obscured the trail and made the footing treacherous. My breath began to be laboured before we were even halfway up the slope, and I displaced my own discomfort by asking Sarah if she was all right.

"Of course she's all right. Girl's strong as a horse, fit as a fiddle, aren't you, my dear?"

"The fiddle maybe," she said. "Not sure about the horse."

She sounded winded.

"Jasper, maybe we should stop here. I don't think it's fair to Sarah."

"Sarah?" he said without slowing. "Are you exhausted, my dear? Do you require coddling? Need to be tucked in?"

"No, no, I'm fine. Just — maybe a *little* slower."

"Of course. No need to rush on such a fine day."

He stopped, hands on hips, looking magnificent in his black hat and sunglasses, a forbidding aura about him, so that I was reminded of a photograph I had once seen of a jaguar. All three of us paused and absorbed the forest *hush*. There is nothing like the quiet of an Adirondack forest, especially in winter. It isn't silence. Indeed, the sweetest part of it may be the sound of wind through the trees, punctuated by the soft *whump* as a clump of snow drops from a branch and hits the ground. Upward, one could see little, but downhill the town was laid out like a set of miniatures on a table.

Jasper marched on. Neither Sarah nor I was used to walking up mountainsides, and as I felt Jasper's "slower" pace was illusory, my mood began to dim. And yet I resolved to say nothing; I would admit to no weakness of my own, and would protest only if Sarah became distressed. Jasper tramped onward like some kind of black-hatted Moses, stopping every now and again to wait for Sarah and me.

"A little slower, please," Sarah breathed.

"In God's name, why? My dear, we are practically crawling."

"Jasper," I said, puffing in an unmanly way, "we're doing this for *enjoyment*, aren't we? We're not here to be tortured."

"My boy," he said grandly, "any endeavour that doesn't drive you to the edge of suicide isn't worth doing."

"You mean like eating? Reading? Admiring a work of art?"

But Jasper was already off, and we stumbled after him. Another twenty minutes of this and I was on the edge of calling it quits and staggering back down the mountain on my own. We reached a slope where it was necessary to "scramble," clutching for roots, rocks, or branches to get us up the sudden steepness. A Danger sign — bright red and lettered in stern typography — did nothing to slow Jasper down. *Keep to the Path*, it said, but Jasper veered off to the right and over more treacherous ground. I was about to complain again when the trees opened up to a fantastic panorama of white and blue. Even in sunglasses, I had to shield my eyes.

"Ladies and gentlemen," Jasper said, scarf flapping in the mountain wind, "I give you Jasper's Sublime."

"Magnificent," I said, my grumpiness instantly blown away. "Truly magnificent."

Sarah took a few steps onto the little plateau before us. To one side lay a massive erratic. Erratics were common amid the Adirondack forest; you'd be walking along a loamy foothill and suddenly come across a huge rock, unlike any other nearby, carried there by a glacier thousands of years ago and miles from wherever it was formed. This one was easily six feet tall and nine feet wide, and must have weighed many tons.

Sarah stood there scanning the other mountains that, to my eyes, presented now a far more godly aspect than they had mere hours ago. "Jasper, darling, thank you for bringing us here. For sharing your special place."

"Yes, thank you," I said, though I was smarting from that *darling*.

"My dear, you went toe to toe with this pompous old mountain and you whupped him. If you weren't thoroughly cured before this moment, you surely are now. Come now, you have to see this. It'll show you the true measure of your triumph."

He took her by the hand and led her around the erratic to a ledge that was hidden behind it. The high winds up here had cleared it of snow. The ledge was granite and bare, except for a single young birch, hardly more than a sapling.

"Jasper, no," I said. "It's too dangerous. Sarah, come back — the view's perfectly astounding from here. There's no need to do anything—"

"It's fine, Paul. I'm going to cling to this tree, don't you worry."

Jasper was paying no attention to me whatsoever; he was issuing instructions to Sarah.

"Just you hold on to that for the moment," he said, "while I step behind you."

"I don't think there's room, is there?"

"There's plenty of room."

"Jasper, why are you doing this?" I said. "It's so unnecessary. You're taking risks for no reason."

"Not much risk. Plenty of reason."

He unclipped the canvas strap from his satchel and tossed the bag to one side, instructing Sarah to remain absolutely still. He stepped aside so that the birch was between him and Sarah, and passed one end of the strap around her waist, before looping each end around his wrists and clasping them tight.

"Now," he said, "for the experience of a lifetime, I want you to lean out over the edge while I hold you tight."

"Oh, I can't," she said. "Really, Jasper, I can't do that. I'm already terrified even clinging to the tree."

"Jasper," I pleaded, "do not do this. It isn't fair and it isn't right and you're terrifying Sarah — and me — for no reason."

He spoke to Sarah. "Charlie Sands did this for me in one of our first ventures together. The reason, he told me, was so that I would learn to trust him. Because if I didn't trust him, he did not want to lead me into the Adirondack forest. I'm not ashamed to admit I was frightened. I don't ask you to be fearless, only to be brave. Now, I am fully braced around this tree, and I have you strong and true with the belt. Ignore your fear and simply lean out a foot or two and you will have the experience of a lifetime."

"No," Sarah said. "I can't do it, Jasper. It's too much."

The tremor in her voice tore at me. I could not conceive how Jasper could not hear it or, if hearing, how he could ignore it.

"Jasper," I said with an attempt at firmness. "This is not right. This is not the behaviour of a gentleman."

"I strive only to be a man, Paul — a full man — and *gentlemen* can go hang. Come, come, Sarah — you're not a coward, are you? Not a timid wee mousey? You're the girl who wants to live life to the full, are you not? You told me so yourself — you want to burn with that hard gemlike flame we talked about, oh my, yes. Truly, my dear, I'd rather see you dead than have you shirk this little test."

"But I don't want to, Jasper. That counts for something, doesn't it? That I don't *want* to?"

"Indeed it does, my dear. That is the very point. The point is not the stunning view — the point and the power lie precisely in doing this thing that *you do not want to do*. In overcoming your own fear. Do that, and you can do anything. Absolutely anything."

There wasn't an inch of room on the ledge for me to step in, even had I the courage to do so. I dared not even speak, lest it distract him and cause disaster. Around us, the brisk winds and the smells of snow and balsam took on a threatening cast. For this is the truth about the Adirondacks: it doesn't take much to go wrong for them to kill you.

"You're sure you have me?" Sarah said.

"My dear, I have you. Lean out now. You're completely safe."

"You're sure."

"Completely, utterly certain."

"Oh, my God," she said, leaning out over the drop. "Oh, dear God."

"No need to clutch the belt, dear. Let your hands free, as if you're flying."

"Oh, my God," she said again. "Oh, Jasper. Oh, dear God."

Her hands unclenched from the belt and she raised them as if in surrender, pale fingers vivid against blue sky. Her sunglasses dropped from her face and plummeted out of sight.

Jasper leaned back, pulling her upright again and she caught hold first of the birch tree and then of Jasper as he stepped around it and took her in his arms. She broke into tears, her whole body shuddering as she wept. He stroked her hair, and gradually the jagged sobs turned into laughter.

"Oh, my God," she said. "I'm completely insane. I've gone utterly, fatally mad."

"That's my girl," Jasper said. "Isn't she wonderful? A little madness is a fine thing in a woman, a fine thing. Oh, I adore you, Sarah. Truly, I adore you."

"You're the one who's mad," I said, and set off downhill.

"Wouldn't have it any other way," he called after me. "My boy? I wouldn't have it any other way."

CHAPTER 16

At our next literary tutorial, Sarah insisted on talking first about Jasper — the last thing I wished to discuss. It wasn't only that I was angry at him, and hurt at his disdainful remarks toward me; I was disappointed in myself, dismayed that I had been unable to turn our mountain pilgrimage into an experience if not joyful then at least less fraught. Sarah wanted to mollify me by pointing out all Jasper's good points, including his admiration for me as a writer, but I'm afraid I wasn't having it and let my anger spill over into my appraisal of Sarah's writing.

"How is it," I inquired, "that every episode you record about your childhood is so sunny? Your father vanished for a long time, you told me, and only came back when your mother died when you were twelve."

"Thirteen."

"Thirteen. And yet everything you write — and everything you say — about your growing up is summer and sunshine."

"Well, those are my memories, Paul. I was fortunate to grow up in a household full of books and art, in a pretty neighbourhood, with never a worry as to how we would put food on our plates or pay for our little house. Why is that a problem?"

"That is, indeed, a fortunate way to grow up. But for the purposes of writing, it has no conflict, no drama. If you truly can't recall any such times or incidents you may have to invent some, or at least exaggerate. Without them, a story has no life."

"It seems an awfully one-sided proposition — that I write such things about myself while you remain more or less a stranger."

"Well, you are the pupil, after all. I'll show you some of my work if you think that would be helpful. But for now let's concentrate on you. Conflict. Drama."

Sarah furrowed her brow and looked down at her lap.

"Come on, now, Sarah. Tell me something about that idyllic New Jersey home of yours that *hurt*," I said, "something that *stung*, something you've never *forgotten* — precisely because it was *not* the idyllic home we'd all love to grow up in but never do."

"Why, Paul? What's to gain by recalling such things? How is this not just idle curiosity?"

"You won't know till you write them out, will you. Come on, now — surely you must have had *one* such moment. Your family *was* human, was it not? And yes, of course I'm curious. I want to know you."

"Do you?" She looked away from me, brow furrowed, perhaps hurt by my bullying. But then she spoke up.

"Well," she said, "I suppose I could tell you about David."

"Write about it," I said. "Put it on paper."

Over the next few days, while I pecked away at Charlie Klein's
typewriter, Sarah put down the following story in her elegant
handwriting. As in other sections concerning Sarah's past, what
follows is partly what I remember from those pages and partly
from our talk about them. If the result reads more like a letter,
well, that captures the conversational tone of her writing.

"The day of my mother's funeral," Sarah told me, "my father
came home from his travels. He seemed strange, foreign, as
you can imagine after seven or eight years, and he was dishev-
elled and unkempt — but naturally still wearing his signature
black hat. Within that dark time, his reappearance was clearly
a stroke of luck for me — I don't know what I would have done
otherwise. I would have had to leave school to go to work as a
domestic or something. And it was lucky for him too, I think.
He said many times that he was tired from all his travels. The
kind of camera equipment he used was complicated and heavy
— difficult to manage without an assistant, especially with the
work my father did, you know, reconstructing scenes from stories and getting people to pose as the various characters. All that
took time and energy that other photographers could devote to
the perfect aperture, the perfect focal length.

"But it wasn't just that. Every now and again, he would reach
across the dinner table and take hold of my wrist and say something like 'I'm the luckiest man alive, to have a daughter like you.
You look after me in a way that I haven't had since — well, since
your mother and I parted.' He blamed himself bitterly for their
breakup, admitted he'd been selfish and inattentive, and not the
kind of husband my mother had deserved. He was truly regretful.

"I looked after him — cooked his meals, did his laundry, mended his clothes, and so on. But if he had been selfish in our earlier existence together, he was now generous and kind. He was constantly fixing things around the house. He told me he learned such skills on a farm in the English Midlands. I can't imagine a less likely farmer than Lionel Redmond, so they must have taught him an awful lot. He made me a beautiful set of bookshelves, and a quite extraordinary easel for my drawing and painting hobby. So we truly did look after each other and you can be as cynical as you like, Paul Gascoyne, but it was a blessed existence — for both of us, but especially for me.

"When my father first came back, I was decidedly horrible to live with. My mother's death had devastated me. I was moody and impatient and inexplicably angry all the time — at myself, at the world, at God for taking my mother away. But my father always seemed to know when to try to coax me out of it and when to just let me be. He even cooked a few times — another thing he seemed to have learned on his travels — how many men would do that for a thirteen-year-old harpy? And slowly, we grew into the happy existence you're so tired of hearing about.

"Anyway, being an adolescent girl, I naturally became interested in boys. I was comparatively late to this. My classmates were developing crushes long before I ever did, and it rather strained one or two friendships because I got sick of hearing about the 'wonderful' Joe or Frank or Charlie of the moment, and they got sick of me being sick of it. I caught up, eventually, but I was never as tremulous as they were over their various Adonises — though I realize just as I'm telling you this that I'm tremulous over Jasper. I don't think it's the same, though. I'm passionately *in love* with Jasper — the real thing, the thing the poets write about (though not you, I notice). Jasper is not a matter of an adolescent crush. I had a few boys I liked to talk to, and one I tried to accidentally bump into at the school or the library or wherever. And then there was David.

"I won't describe him because it's beside the point. Let's just say, I loved the way he looked — I mean, I was *taken* by his looks. My friends admitted he was attractive but none of them found him particularly exciting. I liked him because he *spoke* well; he talked like a rational adult. His father was a pharmacist, and David was avidly interested in medicine. I'd be very surprised if he hasn't become a doctor by now. Unlike most of the boys I knew, David actually learned things in school and out, read books we didn't have to read and thought about them and talked about them. I loved the way he always asked my opinion about such things as if my opinion might matter. So it was a selfish love in some ways; he reflected back at me the things I thought were best about myself. He made the most flattering comments about my drawings — not that he was sophisticated in such things — but he was terribly excited by this odd talent of mine. 'How do you *do* that?!' he would cry. 'It's like magic! How can you make a few lines on a piece of paper look so much like something *out there*,' meaning the real world. I didn't deserve such praise, but he made me feel valued in a way no one else did, except my father when he said those things about being lucky to have me to come home to, and an occasional approving *harrumph* about a sketch.

"Oh, did I tell you about *Calico Lane*? It was a children's book — or rather a series of books — that my mother read to me as a child. Very British, and madly popular in England. My mother even had a small set of dishes and glasses with the characters on them. They had titles like *Down the Calico*

Lane, The Magician of Calico Lane, The Invasion of Calico Lane, etcetera. I think there were about eight of them. Mother and Father both used to read them to me. The characters were all animals — a pipe-smoking badger named Snuff, a totally undependable robin named Rita, a squirrel named Russell who's always getting into trouble. My mother had adored them when she was a child and I adored them too. My father used to read them so well, doing funny voices for all the characters. Those books were why I took up drawing — it wasn't because of my father's photography — it was because the Calico Lane books were so delightfully illustrated — simple ink-and-watercolour panels that conveyed both humour and affection not just for the characters but for the real animals *behind* the characters. They were why I first wanted to draw. I copied them endlessly.

"To get back to David. I don't know how it started, but he and I used to exchange little notes — surreptitiously in class at first, and later we would hide them in each other's books or notebooks. *Russell wants to walk Rita home*, he might say. *What is Rita daydreaming about?* Sweet little notes like that. He had a British mother too, it turned out, so those books had been part of his upbringing and we just fell into calling each other by these pet names.

"We were not 'kissy' at all, although I'm sure we would have worked up to that, but we did become fond of holding hands. It is amazing to me how powerful such a simple gesture can be — it warms my heart, physically, just now speaking of it. We held hands in the library, we held hands at sporting events, we held hands walking home, though we still often tried to hide it, I'm not sure why. I was certainly proud to be seen with him. And yet — I don't know — some reticence on my part, some

nervousness or apprehension kept me from ever mentioning
David to my father.

"Father did ask me occasionally about boys, in a jokey, paternal way. 'Any heartbreakers catch your fancy these days? No
Achilles of the track meet?' And I would always say no, and
when he asked why, I would say because the boys were all silly
or only interested in baseball, which he seemed to find highly
amusing. I *wanted* to tell him about David, but something kept
me back. I would have had no hesitation in telling my mother,
and probably that's the way it is with most girls. *All* girls. You
talk to your mother about such things, never your father. So
I would tell myself to wait a while, wait for just the right moment, but it never seemed to come, and the prospect made me
so uncomfortable that I actually stopped thinking about it at all.

"And then one day I came home from school. I yelled hello
and went straight to my room, as always, to put my school
things on my desk. And I remember noticing that my father
hadn't answered, which was odd, because he was always home
at that time of day unless he had to travel somewhere for a commission — but I always knew his schedule and he had nothing
to call him away that day. I called out again and still no answer.
The house was dead quiet — and that in itself was unusual
because the floors were outrageously creaky. You always knew
when someone else was home — honestly, you could hear a
cat walking around on those floors. So I thought he must have
gone out for a stroll or to pick up a parcel from the post office.

"Anyway, I walked into the kitchen and let out a cry — I
nearly fainted, it scared me so much. Father was just standing
there, absolutely still, arms folded across his chest and staring
at the floor. He looked up when I came in and said, 'I know
what you've been up to.' I couldn't imagine what he had in

mind — my grades were good, my teachers had no complaints. I asked him what he meant and he said, 'You know exactly what I mean.' Truly, I had no idea and I told him so. But his tone — even though he had not said anything harsh — his tone was like nothing I'd ever heard from him. Not just that it was cold, but there was a tremor beneath it. It was rage.

"He picked up a scrap of paper from the counter behind him and read from it: *Russell is looking forward to holding your paw.* Something like that. *Did Rita miss my grubby little snout? It's lonely in the burrow without Rita, even though she's a flighty little bird.* I mean they were childish, affectionate, silly, sentimental — all those things — and I was mortified to hear them read out loud, but I felt a lot of other things too. 'Those are mine,' I said. 'Where did you get them?' He told me he found the first one on the floor, which I doubt — I was extremely careful with them — and then he found the others in my desk drawer. 'I won't apologize for reading them,' he said, 'I read them because I've been worried about you lately. You've been moody and standoffish in a way that isn't like you. You had one day last week, if you remember, where you cried the entire day.'

"Well, the reason for that was because I'd had my monthly … female problem … and it just played hell with my mood. But he had barely noticed at the time, and I certainly didn't wail to him about it; I would have been ashamed to even mention it. I just curled up on my bed the way one does with these female concerns and prayed for death. No, he was just making excuses for snooping, and when I told him he had no right he whirled around and took a glass from the cupboard — it was one of the Calico Lane glasses — and smashed it in the sink with such force it just exploded. Shards flying *everywhere*. And now he was roaring at me.

"'You take this innocent little story, these innocent little characters, and you twist them into this disgusting ...' Words failed him. He didn't know what to call the terrible thing I'd done, but he reached into the cupboard again and smashed another of the glasses. I don't know how many there were but he smashed them all, one after another. *Who is he!* It wasn't a question, it was a demand, and he delivered it in this subterranean growl I'd never heard from him before.

"I told him David's name, and right away he said, 'You're having sexual relations with him. Don't deny it. I can tell from those notes. I can read between the lines.' I honestly would have laughed if I wasn't so frightened. I told him we hold *hands*. That's *it*. We hold *hands*. I told him David was an intelligent, sensitive boy — one he would like if he ever met him — but of course, he didn't want to hear that. 'If it's all so innocent, why haven't you ever brought him home? You're hiding him because you know what you're doing is wrong. You're giving yourself to him and you're hiding it because you're ashamed of it — as you should be.' I couldn't say anything to persuade him otherwise. He just kept saying I was lying and I was a disgrace and he couldn't bear to look at me."

It's hard to convey, now some forty years on, what an experience like that would have cost a girl of fifteen in 1911. If I have written rather breezily about sex in the earlier chapters of this memoir, it was partly to convey my ungentlemanly attitude toward the matter when I was still in the throes of Emily's "cruelty," and partly a reflection of Saranac's unique sexual dynamics occasioned by its youthful population, isolated and facing a possible, even likely, early death. But one's sex life was simply not spoken of in those times, not in mixed company, and the damage to a girl's reputation of even a rumour, let alone an outright accusation such as Redmond levelled against his daughter, would be severe and permanent.

Aside from Dr. Tissot, neither I nor anyone in my circle knew anything of Freud's astounding applications of the Oedipus and Electra stories. So Sarah's tale of her father's transformation struck me as a disturbing scene from one of the darker fairy tales, even an instance of demonic possession.

"My God, Sarah," I said, when I had read her pages. "To have such innocent affections painted so black — it must have been devastating."

Sarah herself seemed strangely unmoved by the memory.

"Oh, it's all right. I don't mean to make it more that it was. It was just a strange and upsetting experience, and it happened a long time ago, so ... not worth worrying about."

"But it's so bizarre," I said. "It sounds like he was *jealous* — like the rage of a husband who catches his wife with another man — but you were just a girl."

"Of course he wasn't jealous. It just suddenly hit home to him that I was becoming a young woman and I had no mother to steer me through the shoals of ... men. So he was frightened. But you know, I was hesitant to write about it, because I wouldn't want you or anybody else to think this is the way I remember my father. A single unhappy experience like this only points up how lucky I was all the rest of the time."

Well, that was true enough; nothing makes happiness more vivid than a dose of real anguish.

"Did you ever tell Jasper this story?" I asked her. "Or show him any of your writing?"

She shook her head. "I don't talk to him about my past anymore. Jasper is entirely present tense."

I think I know what Sarah meant by that remark, but I must
tell you now about Saranac Lake's winter carnivals, which were
inaugurated in the pluperfect before the turn of the century. At
any given time, the town had a population of some fifteen hundred patients living a half-life of enforced idleness. Spending
endless hours seated in a cure chair, often in solitude and silence, could be taxing to even the sturdiest of souls. In the long
dark hours of an Adirondack winter, boredom and depression
became serious concerns. Consequently, both the sanitarium
and the town itself went to enormous lengths to keep the invalid populace entertained.

The winter carnivals quickly proved such a success that they
have remained a thriving institution to this day. The second
week of February was chosen because it was virtually certain
to be the gloomiest week of the year — brutally cold, dismal-
ly dark. They pulled out all the stops to brighten it. World-
famous entertainers such as Charlie Chaplin and Al Jolson were
brought in. The two theatres lit up with musicals, comedies,
concerts, or vaudeville. Pavlova might dance, Caruso might
sing, Harry Houdini might perform a superhuman escape. But
the thing that lent the enterprise its fairy-tale character, that
made it truly magical, was the ice palace.

Weeks in advance, teams of men and horses toiled on the
surface of Lake Flower, sawing enormous blocks of ice which
were then dragged to the site atop Slater Hill. Over the course of
those weeks, under the supervision of architect William Distin,
they constructed a castle entirely of ice. As it rose block by block
it would catch the evening sun and glow so vividly it seemed to

throb. Even half-built it was an imposing structure, but when Carnival Week arrived and it was bathed in coloured klieg lights it was a thing of splendour. You couldn't look at it and not be cheered. It soon spawned imitators from Quebec to Sweden and no doubt to Russia, and it was easy to see why, but part of the enthusiasm may have been generated by the local bartenders who came up with inspired variations on the rum toddy.

In that second week of February, Jasper and Sarah invited me to spend the last night of the carnival with them. We ate a marvellous dinner at Cane's Restaurant that Jasper paid for, and the conversation fizzed as pertly as the wine. We had come through our several stresses and *contretemps* and had now reached that stage where friendship truly begins to feel like love — easy, secure, and dependable — and I basked in their company like a seal. There were many toasts.

"Second draft finished," Jasper told us, and we held our glasses high.

"Chapter fourteen done," I announced, and the glasses clinked again.

We toasted Sarah, who had been commissioned to paint a portrait of Dr. Tissot in addition to one of his wife, and this was a signal honour in Saranac society, because the sanitarium doctors were the top gods of our local pantheon. (Indeed, the monument to sanitarium founder Dr. Edward Livingston Trudeau had been sculpted by Gutzon Borglum, the master of Mount Rushmore himself.) We finished off with a hot chocolate and rum concoction called a Black Bear, and that may partly account — but only partly — for the giddy pleasure we shared that night.

Supper finished, we wrapped ourselves in scarves, coats, boots, and gloves and walked out into the fairy story. We had dined early, so that now the streets were filled with revellers heading into the hotels and restaurants to eat, while we wove our way through them toward Slater Hill. Bathed in its colours, the castle now looked as if it had been constructed by the same firm that does the aurora borealis. Flags flapped on the battlements, and an arctic breeze nipped at our ears. Sarah raised her fur-trimmed hood, and with that simple act of snow-white witchcraft transformed herself into the family czarina.

Brightly lit booths lined streets that had been closed to other traffic. Vendors sold pretzels, hot chestnuts, cotton candy, hot cider, mulled wine, scarves, mittens, knit caps, fur caps, and Adirondack souvenirs from postcards to maple syrup to flannel pyjamas in regulation black-and-red check. Carved black bears were everywhere and in every size from a few inches to a few feet. The usual midway tests of skill caught Jasper's attention and he challenged me to try the high striker contraption that rang a bell if you swung the mallet hard enough. Any prize would go to our czarina. I sent the dinger about seven-tenths of the way up, but Jasper actually managed to hit the bell, which neatly summed up my relationship to this dark prince — as writer, swain, and human being. He called upon Sarah to choose the prize, and she selected a simple necklace with three stones of amethyst for February. "And because it will always remind me of the three of us on this wonderful night."

We strolled farther along, arm in arm, Sarah in the middle.

Madame Lupu, the local fortune teller, sat in a booth before a gigantic Tarot card that showed a boatman poling a hidden passenger along a river through a forest of swords. It was a haunting image, and I wouldn't even have noticed yet another booth selling hats and scarves had not the woman behind the counter called out: "*Chapeaux! Chapeaux! Messieurs-dames, voici les plus beaux chapeaux pour homme et pour femme.*" French was often heard in Saranac Lake, and the winter carnival attracted many visitors from Montreal, the closest big city. Jasper fell in love with the hats, some of which were distinctly theatrical. It turned out that Hélène, the cheerful proprietor, did occasional work as a costumer for a Montreal playhouse.

"*Et voilà,*" she said, pointing to a cavalier hat such as d'Artagnan must have worn, "it's perfect, no?"

"Oh, ye-e-s," Jasper purred. "Oh, yes, *Madame.* I must have it."

He pulled off his wool cap and shoved it into a pocket. Hélène gave him the hat, pointing out that it was already cocked on one side, and that the plume was a genuine ostrich feather. Sarah was ecstatic, and I will admit right now that Jasper Keene in a cavalier hat was as dashing as any Barrymore or Fairbanks you care to name. The proprietor practically dissolved when he leaned an elbow on the counter and inquired *sotto voce* if she might not have an *epée* to go with it.

"Alas, no," she said. "But I have two more hats, if your friends would care to try them."

Clearly, we were enjoying one of those *ordained* moments Sarah had talked about, because both hats fit. Here she was transformed from czarina to *gamine*, and even I looked passably roguish, at least to my own eyes.

Jasper/d'Artagnan reached for his wallet but I refused to let him pay yet again. He gave me a quizzical look. "Very well, my boy," he said. "I can recognize the poet's pride."

What the bill came to I do not now remember, but I do remember that it hurt.

The transaction finished, I spun around and the three of us clasped hands in time-honoured fashion and shouted *all for one and one for all!* and fell about laughing. All three of us were in love that night, and I believe that — for one fleeting moment at least — we even loved ourselves.

"And now," Jasper said, draping his arms around our shoulders, "we take the castle."

"Oh, I don't know about that," I said. "That might be a little too much for …"

"Nonsense. The girl's in the peak of health, aren't you, my dear?"

"The peak of happiness, maybe," Sarah said. "But I still have to be careful. Dr. Conway says I have a new rattle in the upper lobe and I don't want to make it worse."

"There," I said. "Discussion over."

"Make it worse? A little exercise in this magnificent air? It's the very cure! Never mind tuberculin, the Adirondack air is the Grail itself. Nothing like it to clear the chest. I call upon the ghost of Edward Livingston Trudeau as my witness."

"First and foremost," I pointed out, "he prescribed rest."

"You two musketeers go ahead," Sarah said. "I'll wait by the fire."

"I'll not have it, you laggards! To the battlements!"

Jasper took both our hands and towed us behind him at a speed that made us stagger on the hardpacked snow. Other carnival-goers pointed at our hats and laughed.

He slowed when we reached the grand entrance.

"I'll go first. Sarah, you stick behind me. And young Porthos, you bring up the rear."

"Porthos!"

"Pathos, then — young Pathos, you bring up the rear. Quick, now — we'll take in the highlights on the way down." He was referring to remarkable aspects of the ice castle. The ice stairs themselves, which were of necessity carpeted with boot-friendly sisal, the carved arches, and within the icy rooms we could just glimpse ice tables, ice chairs, ice thrones, and even ice fireplaces, and the whole aglow with shifting reds and greens. But Jasper was relentless. We were not allowed to linger at any passing hall or doorway, and by the third flight, my joyful mood was disturbed by the first stirrings of anger. I did not want to be angry, and I determined to squelch it, but my neck began to sweat beneath my scarf. I asked Sarah if she was all right, but she didn't answer.

And then we were at the battlements, some sixty feet up. Mounts Pisgah and Baker, often reduced on winter nights to masses of black on black, were silvered by a bright crescent moon that rendered the shadowy hulks benign. Below us, revellers walked the streets and rode the sleighs and threw their snowballs in high criss-crossing arcs. Knots of people huddled around the ashcan fires, their faces deep orange, and somewhere — from where, I couldn't see — a brass quintet was playing Bach or Corelli, the horns echoing amid ice and snow with serene power, as if celestial trumpeter Gabriel himself had put together a band for a brief engagement in upstate New York.

"Oh my, yes," Sarah said, unconsciously picking up Jasper's favourite phrase as she took in the scene.

"I agree," I said. "This will do very nicely."

Jasper just stood there, gloved hands resting on the battlements with a satisfied smile on his face as if he had conjured up the whole vista, which in a way he had. Many other revellers trooped through the castle, and yet I felt as if we had it all to ourselves. I can't say I have ever shed tears of joy myself, but Sarah shed them now, and they glistened in the festive lights.

"It's impossible to be happier than this," she said. "I *cannot* be happier than this. No one can."

She turned and Jasper took her in his arms, smiling at me over her shoulder.

"Well, d'Artagnan," I said. "I'd say we've taken this castle, wouldn't you?"

"Oh my, yes." He nodded, so that his plume fluttered in the frigid air. "Yes, young Pathos, I'd say we have taken the castle."

The tips of my ears were on fire with the cold, and I demanded an emergency transfusion of another Black Bear lest I perish right there on the battlements.

We headed back down the icy staircase in reverse order: me first, followed by Sarah, followed by Jasper. Perhaps I was feeling the cold more than they were, because I didn't linger on the middle landing or in any of the icy Romanesque doorways until I was nearly at ground level. I paused halfway down the bottom flight of stairs and waited, visions of hot chocolate growing ever more vivid in my mind. Tipsy merrymakers pushed by me, and I was about to beeline for the nearest fire when Sarah appeared at the top of the stairs, Jasper close behind.

Sarah smiled when she saw me and raised a hand to wave. Then that same hand clamped itself over her mouth but could not hold back the torrent of blood that burst between her fingers, raining out over her coat and reddening the stairs. It was as if a demonic hand had reached in and ripped from her chest mortality's crimson flag. She clutched at the handrail and, had Jasper not caught her by the shoulders, would have fallen all the way down.

CHAPTER 17

Sarah was taken first to the hospital, where she received round-the-clock care for three days and was allowed no visitors, after which she was moved to St. Mary's — Sisters Hospital, as it was known — a three-story, multi-porched house, with several additions tacked on the back. Each of its many windows and porches was shaded by a brightly striped awning that, despite the snowy weather, gave it the look of a seaside resort.

I cannot deny a certain fascination with nuns. The idea of shutting yourself away from the world is one that appeals to most writers, and the ability to do so implies a certain strength of character. To deny yourself any possibility of love and marriage, I thought, must mean either you were capable of suppressing the desire to hold, kiss, and cherish another human being (unthinkable to me) or that you felt no such desire in the first place — a state that any human heart, once broken, will envy. And although I was lusting to be rid of my own, the state of virginity, elective and untroubled, held in my imagination a magisterial, mythic glow. These elusive, untouchable creatures were caring for the woman I loved, and I could not have been more grateful.

White-habited sisters flitted in and out of the hallway as I waited to speak to Sister Mary Magdalene. She was a tall, sharp-featured woman who rose when I entered her office and, ignoring my proffered handshake, greeted me with a minimal bow, really just a slight incline of her head. She did not invite me to sit, so we stood there face to face as she informed me that Sarah's condition was grave.

"By that you mean she's dying?"

"It is not for me to say." Seeing the effect her words had on me, she softened a little. "I have seen patients in worse condition survive for many years. Others in much better health succumb. What I can tell you, and Dr. Duckworth will tell you, is that she must lie utterly still. Even the slightest excitement at this point could do enormous damage."

"I have no intention of exciting her. I only want to see her, to comfort her. To be company."

"But you're not a family member."

"Sarah has no family. Her mother died years ago and her father died on the *Lusitania*."

"Yes. We're aware."

"Suppose I told you I'm her cousin."

"Mr. Gascoyne, we know very well who you are, and I'm glad you have not tried to deceive me in that way."

"Has her cousin Jasper been in to see her?" I had neither seen nor heard from him myself since the carnival nor, at that point, did I want to.

"No one has been to see her. The sisters are doing all they can, and Dr. Duckworth will be checking on her twice a day. *He* will decide when she can have visitors."

"Very well, then, I'll speak to Dr. Duckworth. Thank you, Sister."

"Mr. Gascoyne." She said my name just as I was about to close the door behind me. The light now caught her spectacles in a way that made her features even more inscrutable. "What exactly *is* your relationship to Miss Redmond?"

"I love her." The words were out before I had time to consider them.

"Yes, I thought so. Thank you."

I had other patients to visit, but found I could not enjoy them. I resented them for not being as sick as Sarah, for still having some semblance of a life to live, even if only as an invalid. Worry for Sarah was my dominant emotion, but beneath this I felt tremendous guilt — really anger at myself — for being part of our reckless "assault" on the castle. I should have been firm, I should have refused to be a part of it; I had *known* Sarah was not feeling well, and yet I had failed her in the worst way. And I was furious with Jasper for his pig-headed insistence on the whole damn enterprise.

I nursed this anger for another few days before forcing myself to look him up at the Berkeley. According to the desk clerk, he hadn't been seen since the carnival, did I care to leave a message? I did not.

When I got back, Mrs. Pryce informed me that Dr. Tissot was waiting for me in the den. This was the first time he had ever sought me out and I approached that den with the dread of an errant student summoned to the vice-principal's office.

"You nearly killed her." This was his greeting. He was seated in an armchair near the front window, his features in shadow. "I hope you're satisfied. Now sit down and tell me exactly what happened and don't you dare leave anything out. Because I don't mind telling you, I'm hearing from several fronts that you should be summarily dismissed from your position, if not horse-whipped out of town."

My voice dulled by shame, I laid out the events of our carnival night more or less exactly as I have related them here.

When I was finished, he shook his bulldog head from side to side. "What the deuce were you thinking? Good God, man, the woman was bedridden just weeks ago. By now you're as aware of the protocols for recovery as I am — as we all must be. And here you go drinking, and capering about in silly hats — in temperatures that would frighten an Eskimo — and then you haul her up Slater Hill and march her up to the top of the castle. I'm deeply, deeply shocked, Paul, I truly am."

"I knew it was reckless. I thought it was a bad idea and I told them so. Sarah herself said she shouldn't do it. I was all for calling it quits right there, but you don't know Jasper: when he wants to do something it *will* be done and no argument."

"So in your view you were merely aiding and abetting. The woman is on the verge of *death*."

It took me a moment to collect myself.

"Look, I'm ashamed of my part in it. I wish I had behaved differently. When I couldn't stop them, I should have stomped off home; I know that. But I didn't. I was caught up in the moment. In the excitement. We weren't drunk — not on alcohol, anyway — we were simply having a fabulous time, gloriously happy to be alive. Sarah said more than once that she had never been as happy as at that moment on the battlements, that one *couldn't* be happier than that, it wasn't humanly possible. The three of us were sharing a moment of tremendous joy. And yes — it came at a terrible price."

"Indeed. Unfortunately, Miss Redmond is the one paying it."

I pressed on with my tutorial rounds, but anguish over Sarah never left me. A patient might be talking to me about their memoir of skating in Central Park, or a favourite (always eccentric) uncle, and my mind's eye could see nothing but Sarah's face. My imagination could travel nowhere but to her bedside. My students would have to repeat themselves, and even then I would have trouble taking in what they were saying. Mrs. Pryce was having none of it.

"Cheer up, Mr. Gascoyne. All troubles are temporary."

"Thank you, Mrs. P. Kind of you to remind me."

"Why, this town is full of people facing far more troubles than yourself, and yet they soldier on and even manage to smile."

"Thank you, Mrs. P. You're already cheering me right up."

"The sisters will not hold Miss Redmond's previous deceptions against her. They will give her excellent care, bless their hearts, and there's every chance she'll pull through. Now you set your mind on that thought and don't let your worries spoil your daily work. A smile is nature's most excellent remedy, and call me Scottish but it costs nothing."

I trudged upstairs and sat on the edge of my bed. Mrs. Pryce's pharmacy of clichés did nothing to elevate my mood, but in taking an audit of my emotions, I rediscovered — somewhat dusty and in a rarely opened cupboard — a sense of responsibility toward my students. They were paying me, after all, to enhance for them the pleasures of reading and writing. And so I resolved to become an actor — not for the stage, but for private performance with my patients, colleagues, and Mrs.

Ursula Damn Pryce herself. I could not *be* happy, given Sarah's current peril, but I decided to *play* the role of a man who could.

And so for the next few weeks, I went about my daily routine as if nothing were troubling me. Somehow I managed to stand apart from myself, and treat my physical being as a puppeteer treats his marionette. It worked before my students, and before my housemates at breakfast and supper. I believe I even cheered them up. It was a tremendous relief when Dr. Tissot allowed his anger to dissipate and generously invited me back for our Tuesday evenings. I did not have to hide my feelings from him, at least not totally. But alone in my room, nothing had changed. I did not attempt to write. I did not even sit at my desk. A heart blackened and broken is not in the least conducive to composing fiction or poetry. For that, I would have to await that famous Wordsworthian tranquility, but there was no hint of it on the horizon.

I stopped by Dr. Duckworth's office several times for a report on Sarah's progress, but he refused to see me. I had to ask Dr. Tissot to intervene, to explain that, Jasper having vanished, I was Sarah's only conduit to the outside world. He was none too happy with the request but he complied. Dr. Duckworth still refused to see me personally, but allowed Sister Mary Magdalene to keep me informed. I stopped by every day just before lunch, and she would tell me little more than that Sarah was stable, by which she meant no great progress but no worsening, either. She still had a fever, most days, and was crushed that "that Keene person" had not come by.

One Thursday or Friday I was alarmed when, less than an hour after I'd seen her, Sister Mary Magdalene showed up at the Pryce cottage.

"Is it another hemorrhage?"

"No, but it may soon be, if she doesn't calm down."

As we hurried back to the hospital, she told me that although Sarah was no more feverish than usual, she was "highly excited and irrational." The condition of her lungs precluded the administration of too much sedation, but she desperately needed to calm down.

"Please leave your coat and overshoes in the front hall. We don't want to give her the idea that she's going anywhere."

"Isn't that a bit harsh?" I said, sitting on a bench to remove my galoshes. "She's a patient, not a prisoner."

"Call her what you like, Mr. Gascoyne, we prefer to keep our patients alive."

I could hear Sarah's voice before we were halfway down the hall.

"No, I will not! I will not! I want my clothes!"

"She's been like this before," Sister Mary said, "but we've always managed to calm her down. I know she's fond of you. Now see what you can do."

When I entered her room, Sarah was in the far corner, glaring at the young nun who stood between her and the door. She was in nightclothes — her beautiful black hair damp and tangled, her eyes wild. She caught sight of me over the nun's shoulder and stopped in mid-tirade.

"Paul."

"Yes, I've come to see you."

"Oh, Paul." She leaned over and gripped the metal bedstead.

Neither I nor the young nun said anything as she wept; the tears were plainly a great relief. Her bed, clearly an earlier battlefield, was in a terrible mess and I asked the nun — Sister Veronica was her name — if there was a private porch where Sarah and I could talk.

She spoke to Sarah. "Come on now, Miss Redmond. I'll set you up nice and comfortable in your cure chair and you can have a visit with the gentleman." She turned to me and said, "Down the hall on the left."

I found the porch, which was sunny with windows wide open to a biting wind. I was glad I had not taken off my coat. Sarah was wheeled in, sealed into her cure chair, pale hands resting on the blanket. The bones of her face were prominent, her skin stretched taut and luminous with fever. Her voice was raspy.

"Paul. It's so kind of you to come."

"I've been trying to visit since the night of the carnival."

"Have you seen Jasper? The nuns can't locate him — at least they say they can't." She took a small tin of pastilles from the pocket of her robe and put one in her mouth.

"I've been to his hotel several times. They don't know where he is, and I've heard nothing from him at all. It's frankly — well, never mind. How are you feeling?"

"Physically? Well, I get these damn fevers, obviously. My throat is raw. But my chest — it feels as if a mouse is crawling around inside my lung, taking a nibble whenever he feels like it. Could you adjust my chair back? She's left it too low."

She leaned forward, and I re-slotted the frame into position, giving her a better view of the pine forest. Some of the smaller trees were bent at the top under their weight of snow; it gave them the look of penitents.

"Sarah, I want to apologize for my behaviour at the carnival. It was unforgivable. Please let me make it up to you; I'll help in any way I can."

"You have nothing to apologize for. We were having *fun*."

A gust of wind blew a scattering of snow through the open windows.

"I should have made every effort to talk sense into — well, first of all myself, but also Jasper."

She waved this away before I was finished. "No one can tell Jasper anything. And you'd think I'd be intelligent enough to look after my own health. But I've never been smart about anything."

"I disagree," I said lightly. "I consider it extremely clever of you to study literature with me. And even more important, to be my friend."

"Dear Paul. Who wouldn't want to be your friend?"

Her smile creased the new hollows of her face and quite undid me.

"You must know I love you, Sarah. That I'm *in* love with you."

"You poor thing." A pale hand raised itself to touch my arm, then withdrew. "You mustn't be."

"No must. I just am."

"You wouldn't be, if you knew me better. I don't deserve your love."

"Don't be silly. Who better?"

"But if you love me, you're just going to be unhappy. I'm with Jasper, and that isn't ever going to change."

"You don't know that."

"I do, Paul. I do. And losing your friendship … I couldn't bear it."

"Friendship is not an issue — you have my friendship always — I'm talking about love."

"You just wait. You're going to find someone beautiful, someone perfect, some ghostly poetess, some wispy ballerina, who will absolutely adore you and make you happier than you can imagine. You don't want me."

"Why, Sarah? You're low now, but you're going to get better."

"I'm not sure that's the general opinion around here — though of course everyone is relentlessly cheerful. In any case, that isn't what I meant. You are a good man, Paul. You are rock-solid. You're like one of those immense rocks we saw on Baker Mountain. What are they called?"

"Erratics. Oddly enough."

"Well, you're not erratic at all. You're that rare thing: a writer — an artist — of immense talent who is also capable in the real world, that impossible terrain that drives others to madness or an early death. You must see that Jasper and I are not of your kind. No doubt we are both defective human beings, but he and I are clearly meant to be together. I think I knew this before I even met him."

"But Jasper's not here," I needlessly pointed out. "He must secretly be Houdini, because he's certainly got the vanishing act down."

She looked away from me, and out to the lawn where patches of snow steamed in the sunlight.

"Despite Jasper's bravado," she said, "you must see that he is sometimes shocked by his own behaviour. Remorseful too. I recognize it because I am the same. I pretend to know why I am so desperately attracted to him but I don't, Paul. Not really. I just … am. When I'm with him, the world is a perfect place, not a flaw in it. Is that a quality in him or a quality in me? I don't know. And because I don't know, there's nothing I could do about it even if I wanted to. Which I don't. Why doesn't he come, Paul? I *ache* for him — every minute of every day."

"I'll keep checking for him at the hotel. Oh, and I suppose I could look up Charlie Sands. If anyone knows where he is, he would."

"I truly don't deserve your kindness."

"Of course you do."

She lapsed into silence, once more contemplating the lawn, the snow, the graceful sway of the pines.

"Paul," she said finally. "Do you feel that anyone knows you — I mean really *knows* you, all the good and bad?"

"I hope not. Not the bad, anyway."

"I'm serious."

"I think *you* know me pretty well."

"Nobody knows me," she said. "I never walk into a room, whether it's full of strangers or friends, and think, *yes, so-and-so knows me.* Never."

"But you were just saying about Jasper."

"Jasper *connects* with me — in a way I can't explain. But he doesn't know me. Not really. No one does."

"In that case, Miss Redmond," I said in my schoolmaster voice, "we must get you writing your memoir again. Your assignment? Write something — an incident, a passage of time, an event — that reveals something no one knows about you. If you're really brave, perhaps it could be something you'd prefer people *didn't* know."

"I could never do that."

"Well, if you refuse to reveal anything about yourself, you can hardly complain that no one knows you."

"I couldn't. In any case, they won't let me write anything for now. I'm not even allowed to sketch yet."

My visit with Sarah must have had a calming effect, because Sister Mary Magdalene informed me that I was allowed to come again, provided I did not intrude on her "curing" hours, when she was obliged to remain absolutely still. Some of that Saranac optimism must have rubbed off on me, because I took this to mean Sarah was getting better. But when I came back the next day, she had developed laryngitis. Laryngitis was not uncommon in severe cases of tuberculosis, and if left untreated a patient's coughing could tear the lining of the throat. Sarah was now on a regime of medicinal drops, lozenges, and inhalants, and strictly confined to communicating by whisper.

"I had a story," she whispered, but stopped. She closed her eyes a moment and touched her throat before beginning again. "I had a story all prepared for you — in my head. But then I got worse and, despite their sweet optimism, I know I'm going to die."

I tried to argue, but she raised a thin sculpted hand to stop me.

"In a funny way," she whispered, "it frees me to tell you something 'true,' as you put it. Something I never wanted anyone to know. But now ... I don't want to die with no one having known me. Who I really was. But ..."

The fever-bright eyes closed again.

"But what, Sarah?"

"It will disgust you."

I laughed at the impossibility of such a thing, and she gave me a puzzled look.

"You're the only friend I have, Paul. Promise me I won't lose you over this."

"You won't lose me, Sarah. Honestly, there's nothing you could tell me that would change my feelings for you."

"Promise me," she whispered. Her hot fingers gripped my wrist. "Word of honour."

"Word of honour," I said. "You won't lose me."

"I can't talk any more now — I'll have to write it out. They don't give me enough paper here, not for more than a note or two."

I reached into my satchel and handed her a thin sheaf of paper and a couple of pencils. She immediately hid the paper under her blankets, saying, "I don't need the pencils. I have plenty in my portfolio."

"Aha. You've been sneaking out of bed."

Sarah reached once more under the covers, this time pulling out her own small sheaf, which was covered in minute handwriting. I reached for it but again the hot fingers squeezed my wrist.

"You must burn it."

"Really?"

"You must, Paul."

"Then I will. If that's what you want."

"Swear to me. You'll burn it the moment you've read it. Swear, Paul."

No one could have resisted the intensity in those eyes, the fierce whisper.

"I swear, Sarah. Of course I swear."

Not wanting to associate my desk with anyone's writing other than my own, it had become my habit to read and annotate my pupils' writings in the library. But in keeping with Sarah's demand for absolute secrecy, I read what follows on my own private cure porch; it no longer bothered me to sit in coat and hat on a porch with the windows wide open for a couple of hours at a stretch even when the temperature hovered around freezing. I had my editorial pencil at hand, but I made not a single mark on these pages, which were written in a tiny, more concentrated version of her script. She picked up where she had left off with the episode concerning her father's strange fit of anger, and I give it here not word for word, but as closely as I can, because I later burned the manuscript as Sarah wanted.

"When I told David about my father's fury, he did not understand it at all.

"'This is peculiar behaviour on your father's part.' (David always spoke in tones more rational than your average fourteen-year-old.) 'I see why he might be worried for you — especially as you have no mother. But what you are describing is rage, as if you have wronged him *personally*, and he has no call for that.'

"'But he's my father.'

"'And whatever he may say, Russell still wants to hold paws with Rita,' David said, taking my hand.

"'We mustn't call each other those names. We can't be together anymore.'

"'Sarah, no — don't let him spoil it for you.'

"'It's not a matter of letting him. He's my father.'

"We crossed through a grassy field and an orchard that no one seemed to look after. We had often walked home this way. The air was thick with the smell of windfall apples, and a privacy so deep it felt like stepping into a magic spell. And it was there I told David I could not see him anymore. His eyes were wet with tears as he turned and fled, and I can no longer bear the smell of windfall apples.

"Since the Calico Lane affair, my father had taken to asking me pointed questions about boys in my class, especially David. So when I was able to tell him that we were no longer speaking to each other, he was mollified. He even comforted me. 'Not to worry, my pippin. You'll never want for the admiration of the human male — just not too soon, eh? There'll come a proper time for it, and the right man for it, and no one will stand in your way. Least of all me.'

"My father and I resumed our lives as if nothing had happened. I hated myself for hurting David. Ours may not have been a real romance, but when one spring day I saw him holding hands with another girl, there was nothing unreal about the heartbreak. My pillow was soaked with tears.

"As to other boys my own age, every now and again one might show interest in me, but I was immune to their charm (not that they were overburdened with charm). And eventually, much later, there was Thomas.

"My hand is trembling as I write this, and I must ask you once more to destroy these pages as soon as you have read them. I only pray that you will not hate me after you have done so.

"Father sensed my grief, despite my resolution to hide it, and perhaps even felt some guilt about the pain he had caused. He was solicitous of me, bought me little gifts (which somehow made me feel worse), and allowed me more time to work on my own drawings and paintings. I managed to lose myself in these pursuits and did not even think of having another 'beau,' if that's what David had been, for the next couple of years.

"Angelique, where we lived, is barely a village, but the surrounding countryside was being bought up by a handful of wealthy men — people for whom 'country house' means 'magnificent mansion.' Father used to say, 'Just you wait. They're happy to live on it now, but soon as they can make money on it they'll break that land into lots and sell it and it'll be goodbye fields and farms.' I've no idea if he was right, but all these rich

families owned horses — magnificent horses for proper riding
— and I had lately developed a passion for drawing them. I
would set my easel up across the road from their fields and do a
watercolour of whatever animals were at hand. I ended up doing
a lot of donkeys because, unlike the horses, they were curious
and would come right up to the fence and flick their ears at me.

"I became a curiosity for the landowners as well. Wobbling
along on my bicycle, easel and portfolio strapped across my
back, I'm sure I cut an eccentric figure. One day a man in
a rather splendid automobile — with a uniformed *chauffeur*
no less — pulled up and asked to see what I was working on.
Maxwell Burridge, his name was. Apparently, Mr. Burridge
was impressed, because he asked if I did houses as well (a lot
of these people are inordinately proud of their houses and like
nothing better than to have an architectural portrait done).
One thing followed another and soon I was drawing and painting houses, barns, horses, and eventually wives and husbands.
It was quite remarkable, really, because they could have easily
afforded painters with real reputations, but it's a thing I've noticed about the rich — the Ballards being generous exceptions
— they don't like to spend money. So between my price and my
novelty value I was soon turning down commissions because I
still spent much of my time assisting Father.

"I was nineteen. I was out of school and lonely. My father
was good to me but I had no friends. Or rather, I had *one*
friend — Betsy Lynde — but she got married and moved to
Pittsburgh. Father was in no rush for me to meet young men.
My life began to look like endless days in his developing room
or designing little sets. No glimmer of a social life.

"With all the painting and drawing I was doing, I learned
that it was not just words and pictures that tell stories but also

physical objects. I was drawn to old barns. Barns in various stages of ruin. One day I was sketching a decayed old structure with half its roof gone and the door hanging off its hinges. Traces of red paint remained here and there like old wounds. At the same time, it had a heroic look — beaten, but still standing, surrounded by vast fields in every shade of white and brown and grey. (I forgot to mention that it was winter — end of January 1915 — but relatively mild. Still, I managed to ride my bicycle most days.)

"I was so engrossed in my decrepit barn and getting the texture of weathered wood just so that I failed to take note of the dark clouds in the distance. That is, I *noticed* them, but only as an interesting background for my barn. The temperature dropped. The day darkened. I scrambled to pack my portfolio. A sudden wind blew my easel over. The first drops of rain stung my face. Before a minute had passed, the barn had vanished in swirls of rain and snow.

"A man came out of the side door of the house and came pounding up the drive with his coat flapping around him. By the time he got to me, his beard and eyebrows were white with snow. 'Clearly, you're a madwoman,' he said, 'but come inside — if you'll promise not to harm me — and we'll sit you by the fire.'

"He was a big man. He tucked my easel under his arm, and I followed in his wake up to the house. We went in the side door, which led to the biggest kitchen I've ever seen. He took my coat, put a kettle on the stove, and invited me to sit in the library — yes, a house with an actual library! — where a warm fire crackled.

"'You have a beautiful home,' I said, which made him laugh.

"'Not much chance I'll ever own a property like this one. But I'm grateful for the opportunity to work here. Thomas Cross is my name.'

"I told him my name and we shook hands. His was massive. The way my fingers disappeared in his grip made me feel a child, though not unpleasantly. Now that the snow had melted from his beard I saw that he was much younger than I had supposed. Out in the storm, I had mistaken him for a man of forty, but now I took him to be about twenty-four, which proved to be correct.

"He went back to the kitchen and poured tea. He told me that the house was owned by a man named Lathrop, who had designed all the other large houses in the area. Lathrop was away in Chicago for a month. Thomas's job was to finish building bookshelves he had designed to fill the designated spaces. A worktable on one side was covered with boards and saws and hammers, and the room smelled of sawdust. Thomas had hopes of becoming an architect, and was soon to be apprenticed to the prosperous Coolidge and Hodgson firm in Boston. He had only to finish up in the Lathrop house and then he would be on his way.

"The best thing about this current job, he told me, was that Mr. Lathrop had welcomed him to borrow the books that were stacked in crates all around the room, so long as he returned them.

"'It's the art books I'm loving,' he said. 'There's one over there that — well, I'll show you.'

"He got up and retrieved a book that had been, and still was, important to me. *European Masterpieces* by C.J. Carswell. Carswell is a brilliant art critic, but this was just a glorious picture book — one I'd spent hours poring over. Thomas sat down on the sofa beside me and opened the book on his lap and began leafing through it to his favourites, pointing them out to me. Most of the pictures were of Renaissance works

— lots of bare-breasted women and glistening men — including photographs of Bernini's *The Abduction of Proserpina*. Even though I've seen his sculpture only in photographs, it is a work with special resonance to me. Every detail moves me: the dimpled flesh of her thighs where Pluto clutches her (marble made flesh!), her outstretched hand pushing his face away, the tears of stone on her cheek. But Thomas's eye seemed more attuned to works that showed an interior. 'Look at the woodwork in that,' he'd say. 'Look at that cabinet!'

"Mostly, we sat there without speaking, the only sounds the turning of a page, the odd snap from the fire, the wind and sleet at the windows. Perhaps it was the relief and gratitude at having been rescued from the storm, perhaps it was the heat of the fire, perhaps the shared love of art, which generated an intimacy not common between two people who have only just met — no doubt it was all those things — but it was also the physical proximity. Here we were, side by side, on a sofa before the fire, turning the pages of a book that was open on my lap. I became aware that I could feel Thomas's body heat, all along my right side. It was almost as hot as the heat of the fire on my face and knees, and a sudden realization made me blush from my shoulders to the top of my head. It dawned on me that what I was feeling, sitting next to a man I had never seen until half an hour previous, was desire. Thomas's hand brushed mine, turning a page, and the sensation was so thrilling I almost cried out. Had he made the slightest move toward me, had he touched my arm or a strand of my hair, I would have begged him to remove my clothes at once. I know that this is not the normal reaction for a woman, I knew there was something wrong with me, but I wanted this man to take me right there and then.

"Paul, you have no idea how difficult it is for me to write this, to not rip this page to fragments. I'm bracing myself for your disdain. Were this mouse not devouring my lung, were I not certain I was dying, I could never tell you these things. What woman could? We are not supposed to experience lust — there, I've used the word — lust. Women are taught from such an early age — through instructions both spoken and unspoken, written or implied — that they do not in fact experience desire until they are married. If then. But even married women are neither expected nor encouraged to enjoy physical intimacy; it's supposed to be a service they provide their husbands, a duty to be endured — willingly perhaps — but not enjoyed, not sought out.

"My mother died too early to ensure my proper 'finishing.' I was trained by happenstance as an amanuensis, an artist's assistant, and perhaps on occasion a muse. I was not brought up to be a lady. Nor to be a working man's wife. In short, there is no *place* for me, no common and comfortable niche into which I might fit. And these realities have combined to create something less than a lady but not quite — at least I *hope* not quite — a whore. I've read *Madame Bovary*, for that matter I had read Thomas Hardy. I knew that *some* women could experience desire, though they always pay a terrible price. I was molded by these circumstances so that I lack a lady's reticence — restraint, modesty, self-control, call it what you will — and I am capable of lust. The word sounds ugly to my inner ear as I write it. You must think me a changeling, some hideous creature of a species yet to be identified, nor would I disagree.

"Thomas Cross did not make a single amorous advance that day. He was perfectly proper, polite, and blithely unaware of the effect he was having on me. The storm moved off, I collected my things, and thanked him, and we made our goodbyes. In the doorway, he asked if I was happy with 'my barn,' as he called it. No, no, the rain and sleet had thoroughly destroyed it; I would have to do it over again. 'Well,' he said. 'Perhaps we'll meet again then,' and I told him I hoped so.

"I came back three days in a row, and each day he invited me in for a cup of tea. By the third day, I was sketching him with his shirt off as he worked — he looked beautiful in the light from the fire from one side, and the soft winter light from outside. And then — once again, I must beg you not to despise me; it's a thing you hear of in relation to artists and their models, though the artists are always men — we became lovers. I know you will have trouble believing this. I can scarcely believe it myself, but it's the truth. Even as I write this, the whole experience — the winter weather, the fire, the smell of wood and sawdust, seems like something I must have dreamed. God knows I wish it were.

"Perhaps you will accept that it might happen one time. One time, and then I would come to my senses. Or he would. But neither of us did. We continued in parentheses for a time, as if this house, this drawing room, had been snipped out of real life and given to us for an interlude in some other plane of existence where ennui is transformed into passion. We exchanged no declarations of love, even though I yearned to hear one. No promises were made although I so much wanted to make one. Almost without my willing it, one of the sketches began to transform itself into an oil painting. I believed then — and still believe — that it was probably the best painting I've ever done. It was hard to part from it at the end of each day, and every morning when I woke up I couldn't wait to be with Thomas and to be working on it again.

"I make it sound as though this was a period of months. I felt as if I had known Thomas for years, but it was only a matter of days — ten days, to be exact. The bookshelves were soon ready to be painted. I watched him with bucket and brush, sometimes on a ladder, sometimes reaching up with a muscular arm, other times crouched low on the floor. My eyes just couldn't get enough of him.

"One day he put his materials aside and came and sat near me on the sofa — I was working on my painting.

"'Come and sit beside me,' he said. He had been unusually quiet that afternoon, and I began to sense that something momentous was about to happen.

"I put aside my brush and sat beside him.

"'Sarah,' he said, 'there's something I want to tell you. I should have told you the very first day we met but we got talking so ... so much that I somehow didn't. And now, even though it's too late to do any good, I feel I must tell you. Because I sense that you want something from me — from us — that I cannot give. I'm so afraid you're going to hate me, Sarah. I'm engaged.'

"I suppose I must have sat there with a stunned expression on my face. It was as if I'd been hurled out of my happy life — the one I was meant to live — and thrown into someone else's unbearably tragic tale. I don't pride myself on my intellect or my education but I've never thought of myself as a stupid person. I had never anticipated being a complete fool, and I couldn't take in this new reality. In any case, my shock must have been evident, because Thomas started filling up the silence by telling me all about his betrothed, going on about lovely she was, how accomplished on the piano, and I don't know what else — oh, and that she was the daughter of the architect to whom he was about to be apprenticed.

"I sat there dumbfounded, my life collapsing on top of me like a circus tent.

"Thomas moved closer. Touched my arm.

"'Sarah, are you all right?'

"He stroked my shoulder.

"'Sarah. Sarah, I know I never promised you anything. I know I didn't set out to seduce you. But I also know, I've come to know, these last few days that you are expecting — or at least hoping for — something more. But it isn't mine to give. I'm so sorry if I've hurt you, I never meant to.'

"He was speaking in the softest voice, barely audible, as if — never mind the words — as if his voice itself would shatter me. He kept talking in this soothing voice, but I don't remember anything else he said.

"Certain things are so implacable in life, don't you find? Certain facts. So … adamantine. Death is the obvious one, but others too. A moment comes, an event transpires, a truth is revealed, and it's as if you have been sentenced. The judge may ask have you anything to say but you don't, there is nothing, there is no word, no statement, that will relieve you of this new knowledge, the changed existence you've been handed. Which is a long way of saying I had no response to what Thomas had told me, neither question nor answer. I knew that nothing I could say would make any difference. So when eventually I did manage to speak it was only to say, 'Would it be all right if I come back to finish the painting?'

"'Oh, my dear,' he said. 'Of course. I think that would be an excellent idea. I need at least another two days to finish the shelves.'

"'I'll do that then,' I said, and got up to put on my coat.

"If I am strictly honest — and I'm trying to be — the reason for my devastation was not that I had been dreaming of marrying Thomas. I had not been fantasizing about spending the rest of my days with him, not in the traditional sense at least. But the two of us in this beautiful room together — somehow *that* had had the dreamlike feel of something that had always been and would always be. I know it sounds ridiculous, like the very inverse of how one is meant to think of love and marriage, but I believe it is the truth. It did nothing to lessen the impact of what he had told me. There was now a third person in the room, and one of us was never meant to be there. I was nothing — nothing that had been transformed by erotic alchemy into something — and had now been returned to my nothingness.

"Luckily, my father was away — far away; he had several portrait commissions in California. I would not have been able to hide my emotions for long, and I could not have borne another fit of jealousy. You'll remember his reaction to my holding hands with David. I think my dread here needs no further explanation. At home I tried my best to continue as if all was well, made dinner for myself, attempted to read in the evening, but sleep evaded me."

I would have my own difficulties with sleep after reading all this. I said before that Sarah's memories as presented here are a mixture of things she wrote and things she said. That's true, but in this case the discussions came *after* my reading about the entire episode. It's difficult to convey, now, what this kind of revelation would mean to a young man in love in 1917. It was just assumed that one's beloved had never before lain with another man, no matter how many beaux or suitors she may have had. I do not defend it. Like anyone else of my now great age, I am a time traveller, a visitor from another era. I have travelled into the future and regularly find myself bewildered or appalled by how things are done here. So it's only to be expected that a young reader of today will find the attitudes and responses of 1917 equally strange. To be plain, I was in agony. Once again, Sarah was revealing herself to be another woman entirely. Her own suffering was clearly far greater than anything I was experiencing, but I was shocked — and shock prevented me from imagining any point of view other than my own. And there were yet more pages. Dear God, how could there be more?

"I went back the next day," she continued. "Thomas greeted me cheerily, a little warily, but I could tell he was relieved I was not screaming at him, not on my knees begging. His life was going to continue along its ordained path: he would go to his waiting job, and marry his waiting fiancé, and this blissful little idyll of ours would fade into memory — a happy one, for him.

"I was cool, polite. I wanted only to finish my painting. You may tell me that sounds foolish, or that it rings false; there's nothing I can do about that except to tell you that it's true. I was still in shock, if it's possible to go about your affairs as if nothing has changed when in fact everything has changed. I wanted to treat the physical aspects of our relationship as if they had never happened, couldn't have happened. I told myself we were two craftsmen working on our individual prospects. We would finish our work and never see each other again.

"Thomas understood my coming back as something entirely different. When we had worked for a couple of hours, I left my easel and went to stand at the window to rest my eyes. I heard Thomas come up behind me. He put his hands on my shoulders.

"'Don't,' I said.

"'Come now, Sarah. Let me comfort you. I know you're in pain.'

"'You know nothing about me.'

"'Come sit beside me on the sofa.'

"'No.'

"I went back to my easel. Thomas once again came up be-hind me and gripped my arms, tighter this time so that I could not paint.

"'Let me go,' I said. 'I want to finish this.'

"He squeezed my arms tighter. 'Come to the sofa, Sarah.'

"I refused. Told him again to let me go. Instead, he pulled me over to the sofa and sat me down and put his arms around me and tried to kiss me. I tried to push him away but he was too strong. He clutched my hair and forced my face around and pressed his kisses on me. It's a remarkable thing, how in a single instant something once precious can turn irredeemably ugly. I struggled and struggled and somehow managed to pull away but he came after me again.

"'Don't touch me,' I told him. 'Touch me again and I swear I will inform your father-in-law-to-be exactly what kind of man his daughter is going to marry.'

"I could not recognize the man who glared at me now. It was as if the mask had been ripped from his face, and in place of the manly, gentle visage I had come to know there was now the snarling features of someone I didn't recognize. I'm speak-ing of a matter of an instant, because it was only a mere fraction of an instant before he swung a fist at me — backhand, so that the knuckles caught my cheekbone and I fell.

"How long I was unconscious I don't know. Perhaps I was just momentarily stunned, but the next thing I was aware of we were on the floor and he was inside me, rutting like some beast in a sty. The pain was astonishing. I begged him to stop, over and over. I would have struck him had I been able to move, but he had my wrists pinned to the floor. The tears poured from my eyes, utterly useless, a currency he did not honour; it may be they further enflamed him. Paul, I ask you to try — please try — to gauge my shame, my nausea, as I tell you this horrible story, which I have told to only one other person (not Jasper).

"When it was over, we lay beside each other, not saying anything. I couldn't fathom why I was still alive; it was as if I had been killed but had not died. *You should have killed me.* The words rang in my skull but I did not say them aloud. He should have killed me, not because I would write to his fiancé's father and destroy the life he had planned for himself. No, he should have killed me for the sake of completion, to finish the project he had started with such ferocity and which is still, years later, ongoing. Why stop halfway?

"'Don't sit on the sofa,' he said. He was towering over me now, like some Greek warrior over a bleeding Trojan wife. 'I'll bring you a towel.'

"He must have been frightened by the blood because he addressed me more gently now. He brought me a glass of water that I did not want. He brought me the towel, and when I asked him to leave so I could see to myself he did so. I placed the towel where it needed to go and I rearranged my clothing as best I could. My dress was torn at the shoulder, another victim of the struggle. I asked him to bring me a safety pin and somehow he found one and gave it me.

"Everything from the moment I sat up was absurd. His consideration — *let me help you with that, can you manage the painting as well as the easel? Perhaps you should come back tomorrow* — was absurd. My speaking to him as if he was just a workman there to do a job was also absurd.

"'I don't want the painting,' I told him. 'You'll have to burn it.'

"'That seems a shame. Why not come back tomorrow and take it then?'

"'No, Thomas. I won't be coming back.'

"He wanted to carry my materials out to the porch but I wouldn't let him. I didn't want him to touch anything of mine.

"'Sarah,' he said, as I was getting on my bicycle. 'You didn't mean that, did you? What you said about writing Coolidge and Hobson?'

"'Of course not.'

"'Good. Because if you did, it would perfectly destroy my life.'

"'And mine,' I said.

The pain of mounting the bicycle, even with the towel in place, was excruciating, but I rode that bicycle down the road toward Angelique and away from Thomas Cross.

I decided none of it could be true. I had told Sarah that memoirs need not be strictly factual, and clearly she had decided to turn hers into pure fiction — and melodrama at that. The thought carried with it some relief: disbelieving in the rape made it easy to disbelieve in the illicit affair that preceded it. I stowed the pages in my desk drawer and went downstairs for supper, a scene of the usual banter. When Mrs. Pryce was in the room, my housemates would try to outdo each other with optimistic platitudes; when she was out, they would share their weights and temperatures and gossip about other patients. I found it harder on my nerves than usual.

"Oscar Stein threw a hemorrhage yesterday," Broadway Ben confided. Then added, as Mrs. Pryce entered with another jug of milk, "but there's nothing like a course of illness to teach you what things are truly important. Isn't that right, Mrs. P?"

"Is that sarcasm I detect in your tone, Mr. Ladner?"

Sarcasm, in Ursula Pryce's world, was more to be feared than a new shadow on the lung, but she and Ben had been engaging in a stagey sparring match since the day of his arrival. He managed to annoy her at least once every mealtime, I think because he saw how much she enjoyed reprimanding him. He missed his friends in Tin Pan Alley, and suffered much from boredom.

Mrs. Pryce had recently bought a piano, claiming she had long been intending to do so, but everyone knew she had done it for Ben and his mood improved tremendously. He noodled on it, outside of rest hours, working on Broadway tunes, but once a week he would play a Mozart or Haydn sonata for our entertainment. Over time I had come to enjoy my housemates' company, but I sat through supper silent and leaden as an actor who has wandered into the wrong play. *It's all fiction.*

Back in my room, I retrieved the pages and sat in my armchair beside the fire; the pages trembled in my hand as I read on.

"I've told you about some of the stranger peregrinations my father's business took us on. One of the strangest was our visit to Dr. Boyard. This was long before Thomas Cross; I would have been about fifteen at the time. All my father told me was that Dr. Boyard offered 'health services' to young women.

"Well, you couldn't read a newspaper without coming across advertisements for such services. They consisted mainly of mail orders for unguents and powders for which I saw no need; I lumped them in with snake-oil salesmen. Dr. Boyard had recently been prosecuted for performing 'illegal operations,' and though she had been found not guilty, I had a sense that this woman and her business were, frankly, sinister.

"So I was surprised when we arrived at the address on Yorkville Avenue to meet this diminutive woman who looked no more sinister than a stage pixie. She was tiny, with an impish cast to her features, brisk yet warmly welcoming. 'Come in, come in. Please, hang your coats up and let me give you the Cook's tour.' She raised a warning finger. 'One stipulation: in the unlikely event that you should recognize anyone here, you do not acknowledge such, you just walk on by.'

"And that is how I came to know Dr. Boyard. Perhaps spurred by having recently cleared her name, she had hired my father to do portraits of her and her husband. I think it was a way of certifying her respectability. She was certainly eager to show us she was not a monster before sitting for her portrait. I will tell you one thing: until I found myself in Saranac Lake, Dr. Boyard's clinic was the *cleanest* place I'd ever seen. Every surface except the floors was white, and sunlight poured in through every window.

"She showed us through her dispensary, where several women were waiting for medications or advice. Most of them appeared to be in their forties or older. Next, we were led upstairs to the floor for patients who required a short-term stay following a surgical procedure; Dr. Boyard had a cheerful greeting for any nurse or patient we passed. Up another flight of stairs was the area for women who were bringing their illegitimate babies to term before giving them up for adoption. They could stay for as long as seven months. They must have been frightened about what the future held for them, but they spoke to the doctor with respect and even affection. I did see one girl in tears, but she was being attended to by a matronly nurse, and Dr. Boyard promised to stop by later.

"Following our little tour, the three of us piled into a taxi along with the photographic equipment for the short trip to the townhouse on Fifth Avenue, where she lived with her husband. Another surprise. It would never have occurred to me that such a dark, shadowy creature would be married. Frankly, I wouldn't have been surprised if she smoked cigars and wore a tuxedo. But here was her husband, a smiling man dressed like a banker and wearing the thickest spectacles I have ever seen. They gave him the look of a gopher, and the two of them — so differing and yet so affectionate — brought to mind certain characters out of Calico Lane.

"The house was decorated with many mirrors and much bevelled glass so that everything glittered and shone. We set up the equipment and photographed Dr. Boyard in the drawing room (lilies were involved), but her husband, who was a lawyer, wanted to be photographed in the library, which was chock full of history volumes and biographies (Napoleon heavily represented). The work took not much longer than had the tour, but while my father was talking with Mr. Boyard in the library, the doctor handed me a *carte de visite* and said, 'Should you ever feel the need.' I tried to give it back but she put her hands behind her back and shook her head. As my father came out of the library, I stuffed the card up my sleeve.

"But to get back to February 1915. Two days went by and although the bleeding had slowed it did not stop. My father was due home in two days. I didn't have a doctor in Angelique — I don't think there was one — but I had been seeing the same physician in Hoboken ever since I was a child. He was a kindly old man who always smelled of peppermint but I was not about to go to him with this particular problem. Unmarried women are not supposed to have such difficulties, and even a married woman would have had to endure some difficult questions. I dug out the *carte de visite* I had kept all this time and took myself back to Dr. Boyard's clinic.

"She remembered me, and spoke to me in the direct, professional tones I imagine a male doctor employs with his male patients. It was only as she did so that I realized my Hoboken doctor had always taken a paternal tone with me, although to be fair he had of course been seeing me since I was a baby.

"When we were in the examination room, Dr. Boyard began with an admonishment.

"'Miss Redmond, I'm going to ask you a question or two and it's very important that you not make up a story. Please just tell me the facts. Nothing you say will shock or upset me, I'm only here to help, but I can't help you properly unless I know what has happened.'

"'I was on my bicycle, and—'

"'No, no. There's no point making up a story — you have a real story, and that's the one I need to hear. Now, let's start again. Tell me about the man. Was this someone you were in a romantic relationship with? Someone you're seeing regularly?'

"She now had to watch me cry for ten minutes. You know, Paul, I'm tempted to tell you she said, *Now, now, my dear. There, there,* the comforting things you say to a baby but she did not. She just sat and waited as if waiting for the rain to stop. Somehow this was more comforting than being mothered. When I could speak again, I told her about Thomas Cross, without naming him, and that we had been lovers, and that in our latest encounter he had become overexcited and had inadvertently injured me.

"She left the room briefly while I put on a hospital gown, and when she came back she had me lie down and examined me thoroughly.

"'I'm fine,' I said, 'except for the bleeding.'

"She said nothing, just poked and prodded and peered closely — all this before she examined me in the most intimate way. It was all I could do not to cry again. Then she put aside her instruments and gave me a stern look.

"'You are not fine. You have a bruise on your right cheek despite your efforts to cover it up, and a darker one on your throat that was undoubtedly made by the man's thumb. You have marks on your wrists and a bruise on your inner thigh. The bleeding is from a tear in your _____.'

"'It was my fault, I shouldn't have refused him. I had never refused him before. In fact ...'

"'In fact, you were raped.'

"She said this terrible thing to me, this little pixie of a woman, but she said it calmly, stating a fact. Her directness silenced me.

"'There's no point calling it anything else, Miss Redmond. Now, I can fix this tear, but you must decide whether you want to seek legal recourse.'

"I told her that under no circumstances would I be pursuing the matter in court or anywhere else. I wanted to put it behind me quickly and forever. Dr. Boyard warned me that it isn't always that simple, that unforeseen circumstances might force me to change my mind. Her questions on this point caused me such panic — I believe I may even have screamed — that she eventually dropped them. A nurse was brought in, some sort of cocaine drops were applied, and I was duly — physically, at least — put back together.

"I was never more lonely than in the days that followed, alone in the house with nothing but heartbreak and fear to keep me company. Luckily, my father decided to extend his

California sojourn. He had been there for already three weeks, but the movie people were paying him double his customary fee for a portrait, and the commissions kept rolling in. He sent me a letter saying he was considering an additional trip to San Francisco before coming home. Despite the loneliness I was thankful for his absence; I did not relish the thought of lying to him.

"I started letters to my father, to Betsy, and tore them up. I wanted so much to tell someone — someone I loved — what had happened to me, and at the same time wanted no one to know, ever. Writing this now I realize this was the beginning of my career as an actor (or liar, if you prefer) playing a version of myself that did not exist. So I wrote perfectly anodyne little notes, missives from a character I did not recognize, and sent those.

"My inner being was a chaos of emotions, but the overarching one at this time was dread — dread that the stars would align themselves into the worst possible pattern. And so they did. Two months after my last encounter with Thomas Cross it became certain that I was *enceinte* with his child.

"I was fortunate in one thing: the money from my commissions. With this I was able to make the necessary arrangements. I left a note for my father explaining that I was going to visit Betsy in Pittsburgh — she was about to have a baby — and I would be staying with her for at least a week, possibly two. And then once more I found myself in Dr. Boyard's office.

"We went over the details of my predicament — I mean the social details — and she outlined the various 'remedies' available: from carrying to term to adoption to various noxious and unreliable medications and, yes, to the surgical procedure. I want to emphasize that neither Dr. Boyard nor anyone else pressed me to choose any particular course of action. My choice was my own, and I told her that my drastic situation required the most drastic solution.

"To ease my horror, Dr. Boyard introduced me to two young women who had had the operation within the past few days. They told me separately, albeit tearfully, that it had been necessary, and that it was painless except for a few sharp twinges that were rapidly fading. Both of them claimed it was a tremendous relief to know it was over.

"And that was how I became, in the eyes of the world and before my own conscience, an officially certified whore."

CHAPTER 18

The day after reading these pages, I sat down facing Sarah on her cure porch. She looked gaunt, even a little hollow-eyed, but I spent no time on preliminaries.

"This is fiction," I said, rattling the pages in front of her. "This did not happen."

Her condition forced her to whisper, but though her speech was hushed and breathy, her anguish was clear. "Paul. You didn't burn them."

"There's no need, Sarah. It's fiction — compelling fiction — though I wouldn't recommend trying to publish it."

Her slim fingers, icy cold, gripped my arm.

"Paul, you promised. It's *not* fiction. These are secrets I've told no one but you. Can't you understand that it's torture to have them out in the world? You must burn them as soon as you leave."

"You're asking me to believe that you met repeatedly with this man, this carpenter person — in a stranger's house — alone and unchaperoned."

"I knew it was wrong, I knew it was a mistake — a terrible one."

"And you did it anyway."

"Have you never made such a mistake? Willfully? In a fit of passion? Maybe you haven't, but I notice you don't ask about rape. I suppose you don't believe me."

"How can I, Sarah? First you were the widowed Mrs. Ballard — with a fully embroidered shipboard romance. That turned out to be false — why would I believe rape? Or even the adulterous affair?"

I turned away from her. Beyond the edge of town, two ravens cawed and wheeled over Ampersand Bay. When I turned again, Sarah raised a hand to her forehead, shielding her eyes. I had to lean forward to hear her whisper.

"I'm sorry. I should never have burdened you with such a confession. I hope you can forgive me — one day, if not now — and forget that you ever read it."

"I don't know what to say, Sarah. I don't know what to think. I'm just — it's not as if you're a stranger, some third party I know nothing about and have no feelings for. You were …"

"I was somebody else. Some figure in your imagination. I know that feeling — Thomas Cross was such a figure for me, until he raped me. What I may have been to you I don't know — a Madonna? A Juliet attached to the wrong Romeo? I make a bad Juliet. But for some reason — some reason that has nothing to do with who or what I actually am — you've chosen to idealize me. And I will admit to taking pleasure in your admiration; even though undeserved it was balm to me — me, the last person anyone should idealize. And now that you know the truth your admiration will cease."

She shook her head, amazed by her own folly. "Why did I expect anything else? How could anyone ever imagine truth was beauty? Clearly, telling you the truth was a mistake. I wanted at least one person to have known who I was. I thought that you were the right person, but I was wrong. Because it isn't just that you don't know me, Paul, it's that you have constructed in your mind a completely false version of me, not just untrue but the *opposite* of the truth, a version I could never live up to even if I were not ... what you now know I am."

Her face had the ashen look of a castaway waking to find herself marooned, a distant ship sinking below the horizon. She slumped in her chair.

"You need your rest," I said, rising.

Her voice broke through in a ragged croak. "Burn them, Paul! If you have any feeling for me at all, burn all of them — right from the beginning."

I wanted to be anywhere but on that sunlit porch facing those imploring grey eyes. Anywhere but this convent-hospital. I had a vision of an ocean liner in my head — never mind the *Lusitania*, never mind war and Germans and U-boats — I wanted to sail away to some exotic land where *I* was unknown, in some version of myself that had never encountered the shattered woman I had just left. But I was not allowed the fantasy for even five minutes, because on my way out Sister Mary Magdalene called me into her office.

"A short visit today, Mr. Gascoyne."

"Yes. Some rather pressing business I have to attend to."

"I don't know if you had time to notice Miss Redmond's condition is in serious decline. She is wakeful at night, when not experiencing nightmares. Her appetite is greatly diminished, no matter what we try to entice her with. Of the three essentials

— rest, good food, and fresh air — she is now existing almost entirely on air. Her chances of recovery diminish by the day."

"I didn't realize. I — we had other matters to discuss."

Sister Mary nodded. "Unfortunately, Sarah has no religion to sustain her. I think you are not a believer, but you can understand how faith might be a comfort in her present distress. With faith there is always hope. Without it, one must rely on mere humans, who may or may not give comfort, may or may not be reliable — may or may not be there at all."

Then in a change of tone from the philosophical to the inquisitorial, she opened a file, uncapped a pen, and said, "What can you tell me of this Jasper Keene?"

"I assumed you knew — he's a very successful playwright."

"Yes, yes. And?"

"And Sarah is in love with him. I thought you knew that too."

"Well, she *calls* it love. She certainly expresses an ardent *need* for him. Do you have any idea where this person might be found?"

"None. I've made inquiries at his hotel. Apparently, he has not checked out, but they have no forwarding address. Most likely he's in New York."

"He seems remarkably elusive for a show-business person. One expects such people to be always visible. Even gaudily so."

"Oh, Jasper can be gaudy when he wants to be. Elusive too."

"So you know him well? You're good friends?"

I hesitated. She looked up at me, pen poised.

"You're not sure."

"It's complicated. But yes, I consider him a friend."

"The two of you are rivals for Miss Redmond's affections."

"Sister, you're wearing a nun's habit but you're speaking to me like a police inspector."

"Piffle. The two of you are rivals?"

"It's not much of a contest. Jasper is her man and that's that."

"But you're the one who could make her happy."

"That is doubtful in the extreme."

"To the extent *anyone* could make her happy, put it that way. Of course no one *makes* anybody else happy — even I understand that much about emotional relations. But Miss Redmond is saying, not in so many words, that she will die if she does not see this man. Literally *die*. She is an artistic soul, and we have to allow for artistic exaggeration, but such creatures do have a great, if mercurial, capacity for ardour. I suspect this has little to do with Mr. Keene's actual character, and everything to do with whatever role he is playing in her inner drama. The man's a playwright and an actor; he will have a talent for creating starring roles for himself."

"Oh, I can vouch for that."

"None of which diminishes Sarah's anguish. And that anguish — at least in her own view if not in Dr. Duckworth's — may very well kill her."

"I wouldn't have thought tuberculosis needed the help."

"Needed or not, in this case it has it. If we were to ask you to track down Mr. Keene, would you be willing to do that?"

"It would not be my first choice."

"No. But would you consider it?"

No, I did not want to consider it. I hurried back to my room and locked the door and tried to recover my bearings. As a young man properly raised in the ethos and mores of my time, it had never occurred to me that I would fall in love with anyone who was not a virgin, let alone a woman who had terminated the spawn of a rapist, or claimed to.

I reread her account, and part of me — a big part — was revolted, but my chest ached with a deep, deep wound that brought me to tears. I admit these tears flowed for myself, not Sarah. The blackest self-pity inked over all my other feelings — Look what *I've* lost! — and though I dimly realized it as unworthy of the heroic, stoic, generous, kind, and rational figure I had once hoped to be I was in no way prepared to disown it.

I read again how Dr. Boyard took her in.

"We were in her office, a cramped little space with room for her desk and a couple of chairs and not much more. The doctor had her hair pulled back tight, and with her tiny spectacles balanced on the tip of her nose she looked rather schoolmarmish. She sat patiently as I wept, saying only, 'You cry as much as you want, and we'll talk when you're able.'

"She asked an assistant to bring us tea, and when I had collected myself she began to question me.

"'Sarah, my guess is that you're not here for *Madame Renaud's Monthly Tonic*, am I right?'

"She had to wait for a second torrent of tears to subside. Her use of my first name pierced me. I heard in it the voice of my mother. I felt the need to curl up in her arms, and rest my head in her lap until all my tears dried up.

"'I take it your mother is unable to help.'

"I told her my mother was dead.

"'Do you have any brothers or sisters?'

"'No.' It seemed an odd question, but nothing about the situation was normal. 'Normal' was a train station I'd departed long ago.

"'You live alone with your father?'

"'Yes.'

"'What about other relations — aunts? Cousins? Anyone who might be of help if you decided to keep the child?'

"'No. Well, I have one aunt — Aunt Isabel — she's lovely. Very much like my mother. But she lives in England. I've written to her, and I'm going to stay with her after — after all this is over.'

"'Could she help you raise the child? Perhaps raise it as her own?'

"'I haven't told her about it. We haven't been in contact for some time. And I know that if I were to become a mother — even for a day, for an hour — I could never give up my child.'

"'That is a natural feeling, but many young women overcome it — not because they want to but because they have to.'

"'I could not. I would not.'

"'Then perhaps you should bear the child. No matter how frightening that may seem to you now.'

"I told her it was impossible. Absolutely impossible.

"'When a young woman is feeling so desperate, it can distort her view of things. She is likely to underestimate the care and resourcefulness of other family members, however distant.'

"'I don't understand why you're questioning me like this,' I cried. 'I've thought long about my situation and already made my decision.' Her questions were racking my nerves to the limit.

"'If we terminate your pregnancy, I want you to be absolutely sure it was the right decision, the right thing to do.'

"'The *right* thing? No, I don't think it's the *right* thing. It's the necessary thing. I have no choice in this matter.'

"'But you do, Sarah. You're in the process of making it.'

"'I'm not. It's made. It's done. Can we please go forward? Can we please get on with it?'

"She urged me to drink some tea. To take a few deep breaths.

"After some moments she said, 'You may think you're dealing with the worst right now, but you're not. The worst — for you *and* me — is if you come back three months later and accuse me of talking you into it. I can't have that. I can't ever have that. Believe it or not, Sarah, I do *not* want to go to jail. I'm going to have you sign a paper recognizing that the decision is yours alone, and that you are aware of the risks — they aren't common, but you have to acknowledge them. Now, you say you're nineteen. I'm going to need proof of that.'

"'I've brought it with me.'

"'Very good. We'll get to the papers in due time. Would you care for more tea?'

She poured herself another cup, and then she broached the question I had been dreading most of all. Somehow, before coming to her office, I had not anticipated interrogation.

"'I need to know who is the father. Because if you are in fact *married*, and you're carrying the result of relations with your lawful *husband* …'

"'You already know who it is.'

"She consulted her notes. 'Is it the man who raped you? You never did tell me his name. Is there any possibility it could be someone else?'

"'You know who it is,' I said again. 'Why do you keep asking?'

"'Because if there *were* a lawful husband in the picture, I could be booking myself an uncomfortable cell in Sing Sing.'

"Her tone was gentle through all this, but it was torture all the same.

"'Is the father married? You can tell me in complete confidence. I would not be in business long if I betrayed the trust of my patients.'

"'I already told you he has a fiancé. I don't want to destroy his future, and I have no reason to hurt his bride. No one would believe me, anyway — I was willingly alone with a man not my husband day after day for more than a week. And I went back to him even *after* knowing he was engaged to someone else. My word would be worth nothing against his. I've poisoned everything. Everything.'

"'Don't be so quick to condemn yourself, Sarah. Just provide me with the information I need and you have every reason to expect a long and happy life.'

"I couldn't raise my eyes to her. I stared at the tips of my shoes, the gleaming floor, the feet of her desk, which were capped with brass in the shape of claws.

"'Does your father know you're here?'

"'No. And he never will. He's away right now. Please don't ask me any more questions. If you force me to say more, I will leave this place and I — I don't know what I will do.'

"'But perhaps, if he knew, your father would agree to raise the baby with you. You could remain here until the child was born and then raise it at home.'

"The memory of my father's rage over my holding *hands* with a boy was enough to preclude that idea. And what kind of life would it be? I would never be free to be *out* in the world, and the idea of my father raising an infant at this stage of his career (which he would never have done anyway) was preposterous. He was barely home, for one thing. No, I was never going to tell him, and that meant I could not spend seven months in the clinic, give birth to a baby, and then give it up for adoption either. No. I would have the operation, recover for a few days, and then flee the country.

"Dr. Boyard went through all the alternative remedies. You will have guessed by now that I declined them all. No, I would not risk drinking tansy and ergot. I would accept no procedure except the most drastic, the most certain, and final. When Dr. Boyard suggested I take another week to think about it, I showed her my ticket for the *Cameronia*, departing at 10 a.m. on May 1.

"'Brave girl,' she said. 'I wouldn't face German U-boats for all the money in the world.' But Germans were the least of my fears. I signed every piece of paper she put in my way and was shown to a tiny room with a bed, an armchair, and a dresser on which someone had set a spray of violets.

"My window looked out on a courtyard full of chestnut trees, but I sat on the edge of my bed and stared at the wall, seeing nothing but the *Cameronia* cutting across the Atlantic. I conjured imaginary storms — pelting rain, colossal waves crashing over the bow, jagged spears of lightning exposing the night like flash powder. I saw the periscopes of U-boats finning after us but always outmanoeuvred, left diminishing in our wake. I saw them with untouchable equanimity. I had resolved to trust Dr. Boyard, as I am now trusting you, Paul. I'm clinging to you the way I clung to that floating doghouse that saved my life.

"On Tuesday I was not allowed to eat anything after breakfast for the entire day, and the next morning I was led to the procedure room. I was nervous, but Dr. Boyard stood beside the table and held my hand as an assistant administered ether. Ether is not something you want to inhale if you have any choice in the matter. My stomach was turning even as I lost consciousness. Then there was nothing. I woke in my own room, where I was promptly sick in a basin. A cramp throbbed in my abdomen, but the nausea and headache caused by the ether were worse. Dr. Boyard came in and placed a cold compress on my forehead, and gave me a handkerchief scented with lavender and other aromatics that eased the nausea. I will never forget the tenderness of her touch.

"By the next day, the cramp had dulled, the nausea had receded, and my appetite returned. I *looked* almost normal. In the mirror my face could have been the face of any other young woman. No signs of debauchery. Had it been the face of a stranger, someone I was commissioned to paint, I might have thought, 'How sweet she looks. How good-natured.' Neither ink nor graphite nor oils could have hinted at my true nature. 'No one will know,' I thought. 'No one will ever know what I really am.'

"On Friday morning I ventured out and bought clothes that I could not have packed at home without raising suspicion. Also a trunk to pack them in. Afterward, I sat on a bench in Washington Square. The people that came and went through the park seemed bright and unnaturally vivid, as if lit from the inside. They seemed intricately real to me the way strangers never do. I saw each passerby as an individual with a history as detailed and painful as my own — perhaps as secret — though not as guilty. I could not believe any had done the things I had. I watched the strollers walking their dogs, and twirling their parasols, and considered every one of them as innocent as a child, while I had just committed one crime in order to erase another. It could not be erased — neither could. Still, encouraged by Dr. Boyard's faith in me, I forced myself to believe I might yet live a life as bright and clear as these shadowless strangers.

"On Saturday I was up and packed before sunrise. An attendant brought me breakfast on a tray. I was touched to find

Dr. Boyard had travelled down from Fifth Avenue much earlier than usual just to see me off. She beckoned me into her office and gave me some pills to help with any nausea I might experience crossing the Atlantic.

"Then she looked at me sternly and said, 'I want you to promise me two things.'

"'Anything,' I said.

"'Promise me that you will allow yourself to be happy.'

"'Well, yes,' I said. 'Of course I shall try to be happy.'

"'No, Sarah. There's no *of course* about it. When you lie awake castigating yourself, remember my words: *allow yourself to be happy.*'

"I promised her I would. She made me hold a hand over my heart as I did so.

"'And the second thing?'

"'Promise me you'll come right back to me should you ever need help again.'

"And so I promised. A motor-taxi arrived to take me to the Anchor Line wharf, and that concluded my sojourn with the woman the press had called 'the witch of Yorkville Ave.'"

---

* Contemporary readers may be skeptical of Sarah's rather rosy portrait of Dr. Boyard. Perhaps this is as good a place as any to point out that anti-abortion sentiments had risen and fallen at various times over the previous fifty or sixty years, but by the time of which I write they were becoming increasingly frenetic. Male physicians had been providing such services for decades, but now there were enough female graduates of medical school that treatment for "women's problems" could be provided by women. Unsurprisingly, female patients flocked to these new practitioners, who thus became highly successful, outraging the old (male) guard. Consequently, the all-male American Medical Association became relentless in promulgating scare stories of incompetence and outright evil. The actual atrocities were the result of desperate women, usually poor, turning (usually too late) to mail-order potions, folk remedies, or untrained people wielding sharp objects, and had nothing to do with the services of physicians such as Dr. Boyard. I understood nothing of this at the time, and the disparity between Sarah's account and my tabloid sense of "reality" was all the more reason to doubt her.

"The pier was already crowded, and I had to wait in a long line. I didn't mind. The sun was climbing into a sky of piercing blue, the river sparkled, and gulls carved noisy arcs overhead. The ship, modest by Cunard standards, looked to me enormous, powerful, a conveyance of the gods. My anticipation, already keen, mounted by the minute. I longed to see nothing before me but sky and sea, and nothing behind but the V of the *Cameronia*'s wake. The river breeze reeked of creosote, coal smoke, and seaweed, but to me it smelled of optimism, of *future*. I would stay with Aunt Isabel, I would try to find work, I would write to my father and tell him I had run away to mend a broken heart. As I inched closer to the gangway, I began to feel less a criminal and more an adventurer. I had made it through, engineered a harrowing escape. I would live in England — my mother's homeland — and I would be *new*. I would be a *good* person, and live a life, if not virtuous, at least not poisonous. It was the first day of May.

"When I reached the gangway, an Anchor Line man stamped my ticket and tore something from it and handed it back.

"'Up you go, Miss. The man in blue will direct you.'

"My trunk labelled 'Not Wanted' was trundled off in one direction, my 'Wanted' suitcase in another, and I walked up the gangway clutching the railing. The slop of water below brought on a touch of vertigo. The man in blue — a startlingly handsome officer — took my ticket and compared it with entries in a ledger.

"'Your cabin's been changed.'

"I must have looked dismayed because he smiled and said, 'Not to worry. You're on the main deck now — and you'll have a porthole.'

"He gave me directions and it was all I could do to restrain myself from running up to that upper deck and my cabin. I was so excited I misread the number as fourteen, when it was sixteen, and couldn't fathom why my important-looking key wouldn't open it. I took a deep breath, looked at my boarding pass once more, looked at the number on the cabin, and stepped smartly up to the next door. The key turned with a pleasing *clack*, and in I stepped.

"A man was silhouetted against the bright circle of the porthole, looking out. He turned to me and said, 'So, Sarah. I can assume you've dealt with it?'

"My suitcase dropped from my hand.

"My father took a few steps closer. I could not fathom how he could come to be there. It was like something out of the nastiest kind of folk tale. There was a quavering in his voice, but he did not speak harshly. His voice was neutral, soft. Somehow that made it all the more frightening.

"I stammered something unintelligible. What was he doing here? How had he known where I was?

"'I was concerned about you. Your so-called commission that was taking so long. You were behaving out of character — secretive, stealthy. It made me uneasy, so I hired a man to keep a protective eye over you while I was away.'

"'You hired someone? To follow me?'

"'A good man. Reliable. Discreet. Such people are hired all the time.'

"'By loving fathers? I hadn't heard.'

"'You were venturing out too often. Staying out too long. There was a strange excitement in your manner. Something furtive. I was worried.'

"'Jealous, you mean.'

"'Of course I wasn't jealous — you're my daughter. I was concerned about your reputation. What kind of father would I be otherwise? I needed some reassurance while I was away.'

"'But you had me followed — to the Lathrop house? To the ticket agent's? Even to Dr. Boyard's?'

"I was feeling faint, and sat myself down on the edge of one of the beds. All that bright optimism on the pier was gone, drained out of me.

"'Obviously, I had reason. Eventually, my man sent a telegram: REGRET TO INFORM YOU WORRIES WELL-FOUNDED. WORST IS TRUE. And upon my return, I found photographs he had sent. How could you, Sarah? How could you do this? And with a man who was engaged.'

"I told him I had not known that — or had not known it until it was too late. But that made no difference to my father. I did not tell him I had been raped; he would not have believed me.

"'Again and again you went back to this fellow. To be alone with him in that house. How could you do this to me? Have I not given you a good home? Have we not been happy together? I have done nothing but love you, care for you. Why have you shoved this knife in my back? Why twist it so? What have I done to deserve it? Have I not loved you as a father should?'

"Self-pity brought him to tears. In a way, it was a relief, because the rage I had feared was subsiding. He had no questions about Thomas Cross — had he forced me? Did he not think to wear a sheath? He asked not a single question about what I had gone through with Dr. Boyard — Did it hurt? Were you frightened? There was no rage, but neither was there any tenderness, not that I deserved any. He stood over me, impossibly tall, his hat a black halo.

"His suitcase lay open on the other bed. He was on board neither to see me off nor to drag me home. He would be crossing the Atlantic at my side, we would not be staying with Aunt Isabel, we would simply have a quiet holiday in Scotland so that he could 'get over things.' I curled up right there in my coat. I hadn't the energy even to take off my shoes. Father sat beside me on the bed and undid the laces and pulled them from my feet."

Of the eight to ten residents who might be dining at Ursula Pryce's table at any given time, one or two were sure to be in a state of dark melancholy. They had every reason to be. Even those whose families supported their cure financially might well avoid their invalid for fear of their own health; husbands, wives, and intendeds, faced with the changed condition of their loved one, were known to stray; careers, employment opportunities, futures that had once seemed certain vanished; and the threat of death hovered around them in the form of thermometer readings and weight loss. Sustained melancholy, being of no benefit to the patient or to fellow sufferers, was anathema in Saranac. Mrs. Pryce was by no means alone in her crushing optimism. The doctors, whose word was law, saw sorrow as an enemy second only to dirt and dust, and their most reliable weapon against it was good cheer.

After an initial period of resistance, I, too, had done my best to cheer those who were in an emotional slump. I even imagined I was good at it. Somehow, I had forgotten how bitter it can be to have one's pain, however implicitly, accused of being unhealthy or unwarranted. Well, it came back to me now, as I sat miserably at breakfast while others chattered around and at me with lethal bonhomie.

Mrs. Pryce: "Cheer up, Mr. Gascoyne — it can't be so bad as all that."

"Thank you, Mrs. Pryce. I'm sure you're right."

"Spring's coming early," somebody said. "Woke up to hear my first robin."

Broadway Ben had been keeping a low profile lately, having got himself into trouble with Mrs. Pryce by playing the piano in the middle of the night. None of the patients complained but Mrs. P had threatened to throw him out. He spoke now in tones more modulated than his usual Brooklyn squawk.

"Say, Professor, I know you're working on a novel just now. But you ever think about writing a play?"

"Wouldn't know how."

"Or even an idea for a play. You come up with a good notion for a musical I got friends'll whip it into shape toot sweet. And don't forget — if you can write poems, you can write song lyrics. Think about it."

"If I had Mr. Gascoyne's talent, I would never be sad — not for long, anyway." This from Janet Linney, a retired teacher in her sixties who was expert at pleasing Mrs. Pryce. "I would just write poems all day long. Maybe even poems about being sad. And then I wouldn't be."

Mrs. Pryce: "You know, it's often well to consider how much worse off others are than oneself."

Miss Linney: "That's true. Health is wealth, they say. So if you're not sick, you're rich!"

Mrs. Pryce: "The world will open up for you — it's just a matter of time — and then you'll leave us all behind. You're a good writer and a good teacher — all your pupils say so."

Miss Linney: "And handsome. And young. You're quite a catch, Mr. Gascoyne, if only you knew it."

Retorts lined themselves up in my head. *I'm not a poet. I'm not a good writer. I'm not handsome. And not a single woman I've ever cared about thought I was worth a dime.* But that is the untenable position such merry assaults force one into. Either you attack yourself in a ridiculous attempt to justify your melancholy, or you choose meek acquiescence. I chose silence, but it was astonishing to me that they could not hear my suppressed screams.

I excused myself and headed out for my appointed rounds, but my feet carried me back toward Sisters Hospital and Sarah's porch. My mood was fluctuating wildly. Angry one minute: Was *anything* Sarah Redmond ever told me true? Maybe the whole thing, maybe her entire history was made up. Had she really survived the *Lusitania?* Calm the next minute: If some of her stories were not true, it could be that there was no Thomas Cross, no pregnancy, no operation. And that was to be celebrated, or would be.

I tried to settle my erratic mind by enumerating exactly what part of Sarah's story I believed. Yes, the affair was probably true. She could easily have alleged pure seduction on Cross's part, but she indicted herself for wanting it to happen, even encouraging it. The pregnancy? I was beginning to believe that as well. Sarah had nothing to gain and a good deal to lose by revealing this. And having accepted the pregnancy, I had little trouble believing the abortion. But the rape ... Why would Cross rape her when she had already been his willing lover — not once but many times? And she had portrayed him as such a congenial figure up to that point, a kind, thoughtful man who gave no sign of a violent nature; it didn't ring true. No, I began to sense that she had invented this as a way to assuage the desperate shame she had expressed so clearly. She needed someone to blame other than herself, or at least in addition to herself, and I couldn't entirely blame anybody for that. Certainly not the wraithlike creature who looked up at me from her cure chair.

"Paul," she whispered. "You've come back. I'm sure you didn't want to."

The hollowed cheeks and taut, fine skin made her eyes enormous, and while she may have intended only gratitude, their expression could have been mistaken for love. For my own protection, I took a distinct coolness of tone.

"I burnt your pages," I said. "You can set your mind at rest on that score."

"Thank you. Have you heard from Jasper?"

"No. Neither has his hotel." I had not in fact looked into it again.

"But he's still not checked out?"

"Not as far as I know. Sarah, listen. Have you told Jasper any of what you told me? Any of what you wrote?"

"Jasper. No, I would never tell Jasper. And you mustn't either."

"But I don't understand. Why in God's name would you tell *me* your story and not Jasper? He's the man you love. If you intend to marry, I don't see how you can keep this from him."

"I can't defend it on moral grounds. I can't defend it at all. But I know what I would see in his eyes, if I told him — I see it in yours. He wouldn't believe me, and I could not bear it."

"I don't disbelieve everything you wrote."

"Only most of it. Oh, dear God, I can't stand this. Paul, why would you come back here if you believe nothing I say or write?"

"I — well — I am coming to believe a lot of it. I believe you had the ... liaison with Mr. Cross. I suppose I can believe in the, uh, need for Dr. Boyard. But I can't see how to make sense of the violence you describe."

"Of course not. Why would you? It's not as if men have ever taken women against their will."

"You said yourself you *were* willing. He had no need to force you to do anything. You made quite a point of it."

"That was before I knew of his bride-in-waiting."

"But you went back to him. After that. You went back."

She looked away from me and was silent for a long time. I could think of nothing to say that would make anything better.

Still keeping her gaze averted, she said, "Can't you see, your reaction is exactly the reason it has never even occurred to me to accuse Thomas publicly. Why would any man respond any differently than you? It's a fact never stated yet universally known: Women lie and they do wrong and then they lie to cover up the wrong and the previous lie. And that is why I couldn't tell Jasper. Ever. I couldn't bear his thinking me a liar. I could not ... live. Although it seems ever more likely I won't have any say in that matter."

"Jasper loves you. It's true he has a jealous nature, but he's also passionately in love, and I can't see him throwing you over for something that happened in the past. Not for long, anyway. If nothing else, it would be too conventional."

"Like you, Jasper *thinks* he loves me. But it's not the *real* me, and it never can be unless I tell him everything and risk losing that love forever, however misplaced it may be. Jasper is many things, but he is not ... solid. And clearly no paragon of rationality. Why should he want me, after such knowledge?"

"If you hold him so low, why love him?"

"*Why* is not involved. What is the *why* about gravity? It's just a fact, it's the way things are — or at least how *I* am. Dear Paul. You probably don't even remember. That day when you and Jasper had your disagreement about *Romeo and Juliet*? That night at the Riverside Inn. Jasper said Shakespeare was clearly on the side of youth, of passion, of defying all obstacles."

"And I said Shakespeare called it a *tragedy*. Two very young people are dead because heedless passion bound them to a runaway train."

"Yes. And I told you I'd make a bad Juliet because I would never want to be caught up in such a maelstrom of emotion. Well, I now know myself well enough to know that that is exactly where I am; that it's exactly the kind of love I feel for Jasper. If it's not real love, there's nothing I can do about that. I've never experienced any other kind. I *ache* for him, Paul. I *yearn* for him, weep for him, pray to whatever it is that controls our fates to bring him back to me. Without him, what's all this struggle worth? Why try to get well? I lie awake in the dark and all I see is his face. What does it matter if this is not what your emotional dictionary — or Shakespeare's — defines as real love? It's my world and God knows I wish I could but I can't step out of it."

"But if it brings you such pain ..." Astounding that I could make a comment like this, given my own inner maelstrom.

"The only way I could be without pain would be to never love at all — or to be dead."

We sat in silence for a time and her words hung in the air. Through the wide open window, the sounds of wheels on pavement and calling voices taunted me. For some people at least, life continued on its normal, more or less comfortable, plane. I knew what Sarah would say next. And I knew what I would answer.

CHAPTER 19

I was on the train for several hours before my gloom began to lift. The Hudson rippled and shimmered through the surrounding hills, and as we rolled farther south the landscape turned deeper green and blossoms flowered. Sarah needed me. Even if it was only to track down the man she preferred over me, she needed me. And, despite my anguish over her past, I sensed that Sarah's confession would slowly make me love her even more. I still did not — could not — believe she had been raped. But I understood why she might say so, what would drive her to believe it. I would get over the rest of it, I knew that now, and my feelings would be all the more tender. Such is the erotic power of damaged perfection: the strand of hair falling out of place, the crack in the masterpiece, the maculate Madonna.

Train travel has always had the effect of inducing in me a certain tranquility, and as we clattered past the boats plying the river, and rumbled through cloud-shadowed Catskills, the bits and pieces of my burgeoning novel began rearranging themselves in my mind. As mentioned, I had originally intended it to be a fictionalized yet acerbic recounting of my "tragedy" at the hands of Dread Emily. But I was coming to see the events almost entirely from Emily's point of view. Imagining the difficulty of her position was giving me much more pleasure than simply dramatizing my own self-pity could have done.

While considering the kind of effect I wanted my story to have, the works of two very different novelists came to mind. Thomas Hardy was still more important to me than more-current sensations such as Edith Wharton or Willa Cather, and I vowed right then to read *Tess* once more. But Theodore Dreiser had enjoyed a massive success with his *American Tragedy* (set, coincidentally, in the Adirondacks), and his women who come to grief against America's social realities. And Dreiser, I considered loftily, was not even a good writer.

Those books were now illuminated by Sarah's memoir and, even more vividly, by my reaction to it. In my efforts to weave various personal elements into my novel (my doomed academic career and a Jasper-inspired rival among them), I became sensible of implausibilities in Sarah's account of her flight from New York. No, I did not really doubt that she had been on the *Lusitania*, but how did it happen that she and her father were *both* booked on the *Cameronia* a mere day after her treatment at Dr. Boyard's clinic? Her chief motivation for abortion and secrecy had been fear of her father's rage, yet suddenly they were crossing the Atlantic together.

I spent a restless night in a cheap hotel on 34th Street. For the past eighteen months, I had been missing New York and imagining how much I would enjoy a few days in Manhattan, but Herald Square was an aggravated attack on the senses. The sidewalks swarmed with shoppers, and the intersection was a tumult of motor cars honking at horses and drivers yelling at each other. Away, I had remembered the smells of pretzels and bratwurst, but back in the psychotic centre of the metropolis all I could smell were concrete, horse dung, and urine, and if there is a hell, I'm sure the musical motif will be the *roogah, roogah* of stymied flivvers.

I threaded and dodged and bumped my way up Sixth Avenue past the Flower District and then the Fashion District, where burly men pushed wheeled racks of clothes and yelled, "make way, make way." By the time I reached Times Square, I was thoroughly nostalgic for my room and desk in the North Country.

There was only one J. Keene listed in the city directory, at an address on 57th Street, but when I got there the building turned out to be Carnegie Hall. I thought this had to be wrong, that the correct address would turn out to be the building next door, or on the street behind it. But no. The doorman informed me that Jasper had indeed lived in one of a half dozen apartments upstairs, but had moved out over a year ago, forwarding address care of the William Morris agency.

Agents and impresarios were unknown territory to me. Whenever I attended a play, I succumbed totally to the staged reality conjured out of nowhere. While my study of novels and poetry meant that my mind was distracted from any book I might be reading by considerations of form and technique, my complete ignorance of dramaturgy allowed a stage show to take me over as if it were my own personal dream. I neither knew nor cared what was involved in putting plays together. Few readers will be surprised, therefore, that I went up to the Broadhurst

Theatre's box office window fully expecting to have an informa-
tive conversation on the whereabouts of Jasper Keene.

Of course the place was closed. The curtains inside the
box office were drawn, and a laconic sign informed me that it
would open at one o'clock. The theatre doors were locked tight.
I stood under the marquee, a hapless tourist at a loss. A truck
pulled up and a man got out and opened the rear doors. He
slammed a ramp down out of the back, and unloaded a clothing trolley just like the ones I had dodged on Sixth Avenue,
except the materials included feathers and sequins. The driver
slammed the ramp back up, locked the rear doors, and steered
the trolley into a narrow alley beside the theatre. I followed a
few steps behind.

He banged his fist on a grubby blue door, and a man came
out chewing a very wet-looking cigar. The delivery man went
over each item, while the other checked things off on a clip-
board. A form was duly signed, and the trolley trundled inside.

"Excuse me," I called before the door could close. "Excuse
me, I wonder if you can help me."

"Doubt it," the stage manager said. "Unless you've got the
six pirate swords I'm waiting on."

"No, no — I just, I'm looking for Jasper Keene. The
playwright?"

"Yeah?"

"I'm a friend of his."

"That so. Wait here."

He and the costume trolley went inside and the door
banged shut behind them.

Five minutes went by. Ten. I raised my fist to pound on the
door when it opened again. The man stuck his head out and
looked at my fist, then at me.

"How you know Keene again?"

"I'm a friend."

"And where do you know him from? You don't exactly scream Broadway."

"I'm a friend of Jasper's from upstate — Saranac Lake. We have a mutual friend who is gravely ill and I'm here to tell him."

"That so. Well, he's not here."

"Wait!" I stuck my foot in the door before he managed to close it. "Do you know where I might find him? I don't have a city address, only his hotel up north, and the directory's out of date."

"I have no idea where he is."

"But you must. He has a play opening here — in September."

"Not unless he changed his name to George Bernard Shaw he doesn't."

"What do you mean? He told me his new one opens here in September."

"Jasper Keene is not here and we're not expecting him any time soon. There's plenty of people'd like to know where he is."

"But this — I told you. There's a woman. She may be dying."

"Try his agent."

Few writers had agents in those days, and I had only the vaguest notion of what they did for a living. I don't think I had even heard of William Morris until I moved to Saranac Lake. It hadn't occurred to me that this representative of movie stars and vaudevillians might also represent playwrights. The office was just a short walk from the theatre at 40th and Broadway above a bank.

The receptionist was a thirtyish woman who was typing furiously on a massive Underwood. Around her the walls were decorated with posters from various movies and plays the Morris company had been involved with, including one of Jasper's first play, *The Lady's Man.*

"I wish I could type that fast," I said, when she finally looked up.

"Who are you here for?"

"I'm trying to get in touch with Jasper Keene. Is there someone here who would know where I can find him?"

"Sir, you can't just drop in. You'll have to make an appointment with his agent."

"Very well, let me make one now."

A man emerged from one of the offices and pulled papers from a wall of boxes and began sorting them on a table.

"Jasper Keene is represented by Mr. Abrams," the secretary said, consulting a diary. "I can get you in on Tuesday."

"No, no, this is urgent and I'm only here until tomorrow. And come to think of it, I've actually met Mr. Abrams."

"Well, are you a producer? A booker? What is your business with Mr. Keene?"

"I'm here on behalf of a mutual friend — in Saranac Lake. She's gravely ill, and may even be dying. He'll want to know."

The man turned from his mail and looked at me. It was Abrams. "Saranac Lake, right? You're the poet."

"That's right — it's urgent, I'm afraid. He needs to come now. Can you give me an address? I tried the 57th Street one. Maybe you have somewhere I can send a telegram? Or *you* could send him a telegram. Please."

"Berkeley Hotel. If he's not there, your guess is as good as mine."

"I don't understand. He has a play opening in September."

Abrams tossed some of his mail into a wastebasket and tucked the rest under his arm. His tone cooled. "Unless you have a contract with my client, I'm not at liberty to discuss his business arrangements."

When Abrams left I had a sudden brainwave.

"Miss, I'm wondering if you have any extra playbills from *Married or Not.* I've seen the Saranac Lake production — twice in fact — but I'd love to know more about the Broadway run."

She got up from her desk and went to a filing cabinet. She reached in and, without a word, came back to me holding out the playbill.

I ate a roast beef sandwich at a Schrafft's lunch counter and read the names of the cast over and over. Almost all of them were the same as the production I had seen upstate. Then I read a *Tribune* someone had left behind. Ninety percent of it was taken up with war news from Europe, and the editorial was urging Wilson to throw the United States into that inferno. I didn't want to think about the war, and I certainly didn't want to think about being called up in the event of a draft. I stirred the dregs of my coffee and tried to determine whether I still considered Jasper a friend. I tried to tell myself there must be a good reason for his abandoning Sarah. He must be deathly ill somewhere, or in some other kind of trouble. What possible excuse could he have?

The newspaper had an advertisement for Dr. Boyard's "Health Services for Women" and, now having time to kill, I wandered down Fifth Avenue all the way to Washington Square and Yorkville Avenue. The building was a modest red brick townhouse but well kept up with freshly painted shutters, ornate oak doors, and sparkling windows. The plaque that announced Dr. Boyard's services was no different from any other medical practice. From the exterior, at least, it perfectly fit Sarah's glowing description. A pang of sorrow shot through me at the thought of Sarah, her terror and shame, as those handsome oak doors closed behind her. And then I wondered if it was sorrow at something entirely made up.

I walked back through Washington Square. The trees and flowers were much further along here than in the North Country, but they struck me as a poor imitation. I had an idea I would stop into Simon Crawford's office on 4th Street, but the closer I got the greater the weight on my heart. My thoughts were too much with Sarah and Jasper to enjoy the academic conversation in which I used to revel, and I still felt that I had failed Simon, and disappointed him. My lectures on Keats and Coleridge seemed a lifetime ago. Someone else's life. I walked over to Broadway and hired a taxi to take me back to my hotel.

I made a nuisance of myself with the hotel switchboard. First, I called the two other Keenes in the directory but neither of them had heard of Jasper. Then I proceeded to ring every name on the playbill that had a listing. The stars did not answer, but I put through calls to seven other people. All were picked up by answering services with whom I dutifully left a plea for these people I'd never met to call the Sisters Hospital if they knew where Jasper Keene could be found. It was not an undertaking likely to succeed, but at this point I had no other ideas.

CHAPTER 20

When I got off the train in Saranac the next morning, the sky seemed even more vast and of a richer, deeper blue than when I had left. A fresh coverlet of snow had set spring back a couple of weeks, but it scattered soft white light that lent the morning a cheerful cast. This geography-induced cheer did not extend to Mrs. Pryce, however, who not only failed to emit her usual "beautiful morning" but only glanced up from her bookkeeping to greet me with silence.

"Everything all right, Mrs. P?"

"Everything is glorious, Mr. Gascoyne. How could it be otherwise?"

As I removed my coat and hat, Miss Linney beckoned me into the den, where she was writing Lake Placid postcards.

"Best to tiptoe around Mrs. P for a few days. She had to throw him out."

"Throw who out — Ben?"

She nodded. "Silly man played his midnight serenade one too many times."

"What a shame," I said, and added, as if I were a well-known sage on matters of the heart, "They're clearly made for each other."

Two young nuns were working in the garden as I walked up the front path to the Sisters Hospital. They waved to me cheerily — several of the sisters had come to know me by name — and put aside their spades for a moment. We chatted about the weather, agreeing that, yes, it was exceedingly warm for April.

"Dr. Duckworth is making his rounds," the older one told me, "but he asks that you speak to him, first, before you visit Miss Redmond."

"Speak to me about what?"

"He didn't say. But he was ..."

"Emphatic," the younger one said.

"Yes. Emphatic."

I didn't have far to look for Dr. Duckworth. He was coming out of the elevator, as I was about to get on.

"Mr. Gascoyne, I believe."

Although I'd been hearing his name constantly, this was the first time we'd met. Duckworth was one of those fortyish men, common at the time, who feel it important to look sixty. He had the doughy, self-satisfied look of a bank president, right down to the walrus moustache.

"The sisters tell me you wished to see me."

His look told me he didn't *wish* to see me at all, he simply had instructions to impart.

"Miss Redmond is not doing nearly as well as she should be. Her throat is improved, and while the cavitation has not advanced, it hasn't receded either. The sisters tell me she is following her bedrest orders, but I frankly have my doubts. She is still losing weight, which is not what I would have expected at this juncture. I believe the reason is emotional turmoil. You are a cousin, I believe?"

"Is that what she called me?"

"Yes. In the course of naming you as the closest thing she has to next of kin — which is why I can discuss this with you. The major obstacle to her improvement at this point is her emotional state. She is very worked up over this Jasper Keene person. From the little I've heard, he sounds like the *last* sort of man she needs."

"Jasper has many good qualities."

"Whoever or whatever he may be, Miss Redmond is desperate to see him. And all this fretting and anguish are roiling the hormones and getting her heart rate up and undoing any good the bedrest may be doing her. Do you know Mr. Keene's whereabouts? Are you in contact with him?"

I answered no to both questions. "His hotel seems to think he's in New York, but he isn't. I went there specifically to find him."

"And you have no other leads?"

"None that I haven't tried. I've put a few calls out, but they're long shots."

"It's important. Whether or not the man is sound, I believe his presence is the only thing likely to calm Miss Redmond. If there's any assistance you can give in finding him, I hope that we can count on you. That *she* can count on you."

"I'll do anything I can."

"Then you'll let me know the minute you hear from Mr. Keene?"

"I will."

I pressed the buzzer for the elevator.

"One more thing, if you don't mind. Do you know about artificial pneumothorax?"

"Dr. Tissot told me a little, but that was some time ago."

Dr. Duckworth gave me a summary explanation. Human lungs are lined with double-layered membranes called the pleura. The outer layer is attached to the inside of the chest wall; the inner layer is attached to the lung. Thus, when the respiratory muscles expand the chest, the lung also expands, and when they contract, the lung collapses inward. Normally, the two layers of the pleura have no space between them, but in the AP procedure, a needle is inserted between the ribs and nitrogen gas injected. This causes the lung to collapse in on itself and prevents it from expanding. In a sense this was the microcosmic application of the sanitarium's macrocosmic prescription for total rest. With the lung immobilized, the tubercles would die from lack of oxygen. And without the push and pull of normal respiration, lesions and cavities would have a chance to heal and scar tissue to form.

"But it has to be repeated, doesn't it? Two of my pupils have had it multiple times."

"The gas slowly leaks out and has to be recharged every six weeks. For Miss Redmond I am recommending the permanent version. Strongly recommending."

"Doesn't that involve removing ribs?"

"I would start with two, and see how things progress."

"I thought that procedure was for patients in much worse physical condition."

"Miss Redmond is an excellent candidate because the right lung is still entirely clear. She could soon live a quite normal life. Any encouragement you could give her to consent would be useful."

As I rode up in the elevator, I grew increasingly nervous. I had prepared a few careful thoughts and questions regarding Sarah's "memoir," but there was simply no precedent — certainly not in my life — for conversing with a woman who presented an appalling history of adultery and rape, fictional or not, and was now facing a frightening surgery. I was countless fathoms out of my depth.

I paused at the open doorway of Sarah's room. She was seated in her chaise on the porch with a book open on her lap, but she was looking out over the grounds at the waving trees, the shifting castles of cloud, with a rapt expression. The windows were wide open, the breeze lifting strands of her hair. Add a wimple and she would have made a convincing postulant. Once again, I wished for the painter's talent.

The floorboard creaked as I entered her room, and the change in her expression was dramatic: the reverie gone, the mild gaze replaced by urgency.

"Paul! Have you heard anything? Has he written at least?"

"Nothing, I'm afraid."

I picked up the wooden chair from her room and set it down on the porch.

"You have your voice back," I said. "It's so good to hear. You have a beautiful voice."

"Ha," she said, as if I had insulted her.

"What a lovely view."

Apparently, I was determined to behave as if nothing had changed. I could not be sure exactly what had. I referred to her history just now as "fictional," but that assessment was far from fixed. The uncertainty had the disorienting effect of an optical illusion — one minute it resembles two faces, the next minute it's a chalice — but the implication was far more profound. Either Sarah was possessed of a frightening imagination, or she was the victim of a heinous assault.

"I would have thought Jasper would have stayed in touch with *you*, at least — he admires you so much."

"Apparently not — and why should he? He was just being kind."

"Jasper isn't kind. I love him but I would not describe him as kind."

"Still, you must admit he's *capable* of kindness. He gave me a very fine typewriter."

"Gestures, yes. He wields a good gesture now and again." She looked at me, grey eyes full of pain. "He's killing me, Paul. And the worst thing is, he *knows* he's killing me."

"Sarah, really. Try to calm yourself. What would you say to me, if I were suffering this way over a woman?"

"'Forget her. She's not worth it. Clearly, she hates you.'"

"Maybe. But the truth is we don't know what Jasper is thinking. We don't know much about him at all."

"I know Jasper very well. Too well."

"Do you? You can't have known him very long."

"Some things are instantaneous, I'm sure you understand that much."

I considered that for a moment. I wanted to speak of anything except her memoir.

"I bumped into Dr. Duckworth. He tells me he's recommending pneumothorax."

"Yes. 'We'd like to remove a few ribs and disfigure you for life.' Just what every woman wants to hear."

"It does sound extreme. But he makes a good case for it. What will you do?"

"I don't know. But I suppose if Jasper were around I would do it. Well, I know I would. But he's not here, is he?"

"Perhaps we could hire a private detective," I said brightly, as if this were an original thought.

"My experience with private detectives has not been happy."

"Of course. Sorry." *Stupid*, I thought. How can I be so damn *stupid*?

A few minutes went by while neither of us spoke. As the clouds nosed their way among the mountains and the awning snapped and flapped overhead, the porch once again took on the feel of an ocean liner. The irrepressible breeze and the cry of gulls over Ampersand Bay heightened the illusion, and for a moment it seemed as though Sarah and I were conversing on the *Lusitania*. Her skin was now drawn taut across her forehead and cheekbones and, ever fair, was now translucent, tiny lilac veins visible at her temple and wrist. It was difficult to reconcile the ethereal vision before me with the carnal entanglement she had described. I imagined her in the great ship's mortal agony, and pictured that moment on the Queenstown wharf when the fisherman saw her come back to life. A wave of tenderness passed through me, and I wished myself in his place, to be the one to conjure tea and blankets, to hear her first confused words.

"I love you, Sarah." This was the last thing I had expected to hear myself saying, and yet I knew it was true.

She turned, frowning, to me. Such was my state at that moment that even her frown was beautiful.

"How is that possible? You're very sweet to say it, especially after all I've told you. But it's not possible. Not if you believe what I wrote."

"But I *did* read it, so apparently it *is* possible."

She scanned my face before turning away again.

"You think I made it up."

"That's not true, Sarah. Well, it's sometimes true. I veer between taking every word for fact and every word for fiction. And then I think you've developed a story that's *partly* true. And partly ... exaggerated. Oh, hell, Sarah, I don't know what to think. I have no maps for this, no precedent — not within my own life at least — to make it seem possible."

"I had no precedent for shipwreck either."

"But there's nothing about *you* that makes these horrible events seem possible."

"Then I wrote it badly. I was trying only to lay out the reality — the truth about myself — but clearly I didn't succeed."

"The writing itself is fine."

"How can it be fine if it's not credible?"

"Well, the nature of the subject matter ..."

"... is disgusting. Yes, I know. It's disgusting that a German captain thought nothing of slaughtering twelve hundred civilians too. Do you have trouble believing that?"

"No. For obvious reasons."

"Because you trust newspapers. It's just me then. My lack of credibility."

"I just can't imagine a man such as this, this Thomas Cross, whom you describe as intelligent, kind — let alone with a fiancé waiting for him — inflicting such an atrocity on a lovely young woman whom he apparently admired."

"Yes, it is indeed hard to credit. Had anyone suggested the possibility to me even ten *minutes* before it happened, I would not have believed it either."

"Besides which, as you yourself tell it, he had no need to force himself on you."

"No. Not *before* I knew he was engaged. Will you punish me now for my honesty in this? It seems a cruel irony that people had no trouble believing I was married to Stephen Ballard but can't accept the flat-out truth when I present it."

She shook her head and began chewing on a nail — not a habit I'd observed in her before. Then she said, "Is it *because* of the Ballards? What I did to the Ballards? I deceived them, and so you assume I'm now deceiving you?"

"No. You did nothing wrong to the Ballards."

"But apparently I'm capable of slandering Thomas Cross — a man you don't even know — by inventing this disgusting story, and wronging you by telling unspeakable lies."

"Sarah, that's not what I'm saying."

A long silence ensued. My words, rather than Sarah's writings, had darkened the day. Finally, she said, "Did you burn them at least?"

"Yes. Yes, of course."

She nodded without looking at me.

"Sarah, you must realize that the last thing I want to do is cause you any pain. The *last* thing."

"And yet you do such a good job of it."

"I'm sorry. Truly. But you don't want me to lie about something this important. To pretend to believe you? To play along? It's not that I'm innately distrustful, after all. You *did* invent an entire shipboard romance, not just for the benefit of the Ballards, but for me. When there wasn't the slightest need."

"You were teaching me to write, Paul. You told me I could make things up, it didn't have to be true, and now you're shocked that some of it wasn't. In any case, I didn't invent the shipboard romance, it was invented by others — by a ring, by a fisherman's wife, by the Ballards themselves. I fell into it and, yes, for a time, made it my own. But there were reasons for that, which you very well know. So no, I do not want you to pretend to believe me, I want you to *know* me. Silly idea. How exquisite — you want *me* to think *you're* honest, but I'm not to be trusted. But then, how could I expect otherwise, given my history?"

"Oh, Sarah. I've just said I love you."

"Love a liar? I don't think so, Paul. I want to think you mean it kindly, but you must be imagining someone else."

After leaving Sarah I stopped in at the police station to file a missing person report. The duty sergeant's interest faded when I told him the missing person was male and thirty-five. He asked me a series of questions in a bored monotone. *Does he have means to support himself? Has he a secure place of abode? Is he a person of regular habits and duties? Is he generally reliable?*

I knew what the result would be well before the questions stopped.

Now, if a palm reader had said to me — or, no — if the angel Gabriel had appeared to me a year previously and announced, *You will soon seek help from a private detective*, I would have said, *Sorry, wrong address*. And yet I left the station and went straight to the postal telegraph office, where I consulted a city directory. If you needed a doctor, nurse, or boat livery, believe me, Saranac Lake was about the best place you could be, but not if you needed a private detective.

I walked over to the Berkeley Hotel and scanned the array of New York papers in their lobby. Among the classified ads, I found phone numbers for three private investigators. The concierge assisted me with the rigmarole of placing a long-distance phone call. I had to fork over a sizeable deposit before taking a seat in one of their booths. The switchboard operator connected me one by one to the investigators' offices. The rates they quoted me were out of the question. I went back to the desk to retrieve my change — it wasn't much — and headed downstairs for a solitary supper in the Grill.

I ordered roast trout and a half-bottle of Sylvaner, which I could ill afford, but it had been an unhappy day and I was attempting to cheer myself up. My meal over, I sat there toying with the salt and pepper shakers, and reflecting on how badly I had handled Sarah's emotional state. Regardless of how true or false any part of her story might be, she was facing a hideous operation, possible death, and the absence of the man she loved (or needed, or was obsessed with). If I could not *be* what she needed, why could I not simply bring her what she needed? Why did I insist on cross-examining her? What hole in my heart was I trying to fill at her expense? "God damn it," I said, not realizing the waiter was right behind me.

He asked if there was something wrong with the meal.

"No, no, not at all. Sorry. Just remembered something."

He cleared away the remains of my meal, and returned with a dessert menu, which I ignored. I sat there wondering how best to "handle" Sarah from now on, but my thoughts kept being forced out of my head by loud voices from another table. One man was holding forth, while his table mates murmured token agreement, as if they'd heard the stuff many times.

"Everybody up here knows that Adirondack air is the best medicine," he was saying. "Why else we got three major sanitariums and a city full of cure cottages? We got the freshest air in the world. But patients get here and they get parked on their porches and you never see 'em again. Suddenly, being out in the fresh air is *dangerous*, it's *against the rules*. I bet there's not one of 'em — except maybe the tragedies — couldn't benefit by a week in a guide boat and a lean-to. I've seen it myself a thousand times.

"Thing of it is, my business is down thirty percent from where it was ten years ago, and it ain't because the fish ain't bitin, it ain't because the stags ain't waitin. It's the fact that the entire place feels like a hospital. Which it *is*. I hear it from my sports all the time, *Charlie — I'd love to come, but I just don't like the idea of heading into a town full of disease*. Well, I mean, who does? I ask ya: who the hell does?"

His two friends, no doubt wearily familiar with this rant, made their excuses and left the restaurant, but the orator, whom I recognized as Charlie Sands, ordered himself another beer. I put down some cash for my own bill, and went over to his table.

"Mr. Sands, my name's Paul Gascoyne — we met a while back at this very table. Do you mind if I join you?"

"It's a free country."

I flagged the waiter and ordered another beer for myself. Sands and I were exchanging pleasantries when he snapped his fingers — loud as a pistol shot — and said, "You're the poet! You recited that poem that time!"

"Yes, well, I write other things now."

"Ha! Poet at my table — that's a first." He took a long swallow from his beer and set the glass down and wiped the foam from his moustache. "What can I do for you, Mr. Gascoyne?"

"I need to go hunting."

"You're gonna have to wait for the season, 'less you're thinkin rabbits."

"I'm thinking Jasper Keene."

"Did you try the front desk?"

"He's not in the hotel and he's not in New York. I think you know where he is."

Charlie's eyes smiled at me over the rim of his beer glass. He set it down and said, "Let me ask you this. Has it occurred to you that if Mr. Keene wanted you to know where he was then you would, in fact, know where he was?"

"It has. But it's not relevant — not under the present circumstances. I think you know where he is, and I want to hire you to take me to him."

"Hokey smoke," he said. "Listen to the man. If I did know — and I'm not saying I do — why the heck would I tell you?"

Charlie Sands was not a skilled prevaricator. He was trying for a poker face, but the slight upturn at the corners of his mouth, and a new vividness in the crow's feet, showed he was enjoying playing the old fox to my yappy beagle.

"I'll tell you why," I said. "Sarah Redmond, the woman Jasper loves, is currently in Sisters Hospital barely able to speak. She's facing permanent pneumothorax, and may not have long to live. She is desperate to see Jasper. Frantic. And Dr. Duckworth says her emotional state is preventing any chance of recovery. A visit from Jasper could make all the difference. At the very least, it could buy her some time."

I said more. I took my time about it. I wanted him to get the complete picture.

Charlie sat back from the table as I talked, arms folded across his chest, lifting the odd eyebrow or emitting a quiet *uh-huh.*

"That it?" he said, when I was done.

"The situation is dire, Mr. Sands. This is not a casual request."

"Jasper know her condition?"

"No. He would not stay away if he did."

"Only reason I'm giving you the time of day is I seen you with Jasper and I know he likes you. He's talked about you a couple of times. As to what he may or may not have said about Miss Redmond, that's his affair. In the course of a camp, a man might say things he would never say in the city or the courtroom or over the backyard fence. Guides don't go blabbin about who they guided where, or who shot what or caught what, or what a man may have said or not said. And you're putting me in a spot here, Professor. It's not my place to tell you where he might be or even if I *know* where he might be."

"You haven't."

"Aw, don't get slippery."

"Just tell me this — is he within a one-day trip there and back?"

"I suppose I can tell you that much. Yes."

"All right, look — I don't have a lot of money, but I'll pay you double your usual rate to take me to him and bring us back."

"Son, you're not doin this right ..."

I bristled at that *son* but took it.

"If you tell me there's a woman in distress and I decide to help you — by which I mean help *her* — that's one thing. I know who she is and I know Jasper loves the lady — he's crazy about her. So, if I *did* take you to him, I could still stand the sight o' my own face. But if I was to do it because of the *money*, that would make it somethin else. Make *me* somethin else. And not somethin I like."

"Your regular rate, then. Surely, there's nothing wrong with getting paid for doing what you do."

"*If* Jasper turns out to be okay with you showin up, and *if* he agrees to come back with us, *then* I will accept the usual rate. But if he don't, why, then I'll have done the man a disservice. And the last thing I'd want is to be paid for it."

CHAPTER 21

We were on Kiwassa Lake just south of Dewey Mountain when the storm broke. A sudden darkness, a damp gust, and then a few fat drops made targets in the water. A wall of wind blew in out of nowhere and smacked us full on. Charlie rowed us shoreward and under some overhanging trees and secured us to a fat branch. He unfurled a tarp and we each held it clasped over our head so that we looked like a couple of Carmelites. Even under the branches, the rain hit heavy on the tarp.

"First thunderstorm of the spring," Charlie shouted over the rain. "Won't last long."

"It's magnificent," I shouted back.

"Yup. She's pretty good."

Thunder rumbled distantly and then cracked right overhead. We both ducked, laughing.

My ears rang, and pressure waves hit me in the belly. A little while, and then the thunder was distant again and the rain stopped. The quiet was deep, the way it is after a storm, no sounds but the drips of leaves and a distant crow. Charlie took us out again and as he rowed us around a bend the forest closed in and all I heard was the rattle of oarlocks and the drip of water off the oars. After a while the sun came out and though it didn't hit the water it lit up the endless forest to the west.

Every few minutes Charlie would emit a single word — *cardinal, flicker, goldfinch* — always before I heard them. We did not encounter any other boats. We hit some white water and my stomach began to thrum with … I want to say anxiety but, in truth, it was fear. April or not, snow was still thick on the ground out here, and the woods when the sun went away were cave-dark. Every year, an adventurer or two lost their way and thus their lives by underestimating the indifference of nature. Get lost in the Adirondacks and you stand a good chance of dying.

We had a tranquil hour or so. Charlie said nothing the whole time, and I felt no pressure to speak either. The guide boat, shaped like a canoe but wider and flatter, was comfortable enough that I was thinking a nap might be nice, when Charlie dug in with his left oar and swung us around so that we were now making straight for rocks and shadow.

"Is this really where we need to go?"

"You might wanna duck down a little."

I leaned over to avoid getting brained by low branches. A long minute of darkness, and then the water widened into a black pond. A rampart of rock rose up on one side, and on the opposite shore a deer and two fawns dipped their heads to drink and then raised them again and blinked at us, onyx-eyed.

"How do you even find this place?" I said.

Charlie shrugged. "Same as anything."

After a while I ventured, "Are you always this subdued with clients?"

"Pretty much — 'less they have a lotta questions, which some of 'em do."

"About fish and so on."

"Bears mostly."

I had no questions about fish and I refused to vocalize my anxieties about bears. For the next two hours, we travelled in silence. I thought about Sarah and her story and tried not to. I thought about the things I could believe and the things I could not. I thought about what I would say to Jasper and how he might respond. I thought about how different my life might have been had I not quit my university job, or even further back, if Emily had not jilted me. It must have been at least two hours I travelled in such useless surmise. We passed a rocky spit and Charlie made another sudden and — to me — unprovoked dogleg into the mouth of a stream entirely concealed by rock and tree cover.

"You brought Jasper this way?" I said.

"Only way there is," Charlie said. "'Less you wanna climb clear over and around Pisgah to get here."

"I'm extremely hungry. Surely, you must be too?"

"I could eat."

We broke out into another pond, smaller than the last. Trees, rocks, a lip of sand. An intermittent clicking sound made me prick up my ears. I sat up straighter and looked around. Nothing in or about the boat could account for the clicks. But as Charlie arrowed us toward that strip of sand, I realized with a profound sense of unreality that I was hearing the sound of a typewriter.

"Hang on." Charlie leaned forward and rowed harder until the boat scraped bottom. He jumped out in his waders and hauled boat, oars, and me up onto the sand. I climbed out and helped him pull the thing farther up, not that he needed help. He led me around an outcropping of rock and up a small incline to a clearing where Jasper was seated in a lean-to, typing. I was half-expecting him to look like a castaway, with an enormous beard and ragged clothes, but he was as neat and trim as ever. He hit a carriage return and looked up.

"Brung a friend," Charlie said.

"So you did." Jasper's face and manner retained nothing of his characteristic gusto. His eyes were dimmed, his voice dull, as if he had taken a beating in some private war.

"Sorry," I said. "We're interrupting your work."

"So you are."

"Professor's got somethin of an urgent message for you, Jasper. I'll just go stretch my legs while you sort that out."

"You do that, Charlie. Thank you," Jasper said, and resumed typing.

If you are not familiar with the Adirondack version of the lean-to, you may have in mind the thrown-together huddle of sticks and boughs beloved of the Boy Scouts. But the structure Jasper had been living in for the past few weeks was a small log cabin, minus a front wall. In addition to the built-in bench and table where he was writing, there was a set of shelves holding a few tins and jars and several books. A narrow bed clung to the back wall.

All around us forest smells drifted in the sodden air — balsam, rain, loam — softening the acrid smell of wet campfire.

"This is where you've been hiding?" I said. "For *weeks*?"

"Why don't you just state your business?" Jasper said, still typing.

"Sarah may be dying."

Jasper stopped typing, and sat paused over his machine for a moment before turning to face me.

"*Really* dying? Or are you just ..."

"She's in rough shape. Duckworth thinks pneumothorax is her best chance. Permanent pneumothorax."

"Doctors will always tell you their services are essential. They'll even forget their own first principles — in this case, the curative power of the air we're breathing. The girl needs to be out in the woods, simple as that. It was Dr. Charlie Sands cured me, not Dr. Tissot. Not Taylor. Not Duckworth. Why, with summer coming, you get Sarah out into the woods and she'll do fine. The girl is stronger than she thinks she is and stronger than she looks. She survived the *Lusitania*. Get her out into the woods. You'll see."

"Is that true? It doesn't appear to be doing you any good."

To this he gave no hint of a response, dull eyes waiting.

"The doctors are concerned about Sarah's emotional state," I told him. "She's in misery because you've abandoned her. See, I don't know about *you*, Jasper, but Sarah really meant it when she said she couldn't live without you. She doesn't want to. And what the hell is wrong with you, anyway? You tell her you love her, you tell the entire world you love her, you clout me on the head to prevent *me* from loving her, and then the minute she needs you — *needs* in a life-and-death sense — you just vanish. I don't understand how you can be so cruel."

Jasper pulled the paper from his typewriter and set it in a small wooden box. He took another sheet and rolled it into the machine.

"My boy," he said without looking at me, "the only responsibility of the artist is to do the work. The pages must be filled, the work must be finished. No matter what else may be going on. That's the true test."

"For Chrissake, Jasper. No one's asking you to sacrifice your career. Come back with us now."

He stood up, knocking his chair over backward.

"You still don't get it, do you. What possible good would my rushing to her bedside do? The reason she's *in* the hospital is because of me. *My* stupidity, *my* blindness. I dragged the two of you up that damn ice castle. I drew *blood*, Gascoyne, I drew *blood*. What possible good can come of putting us together when *I'm* the one who keeps breaking her heart?"

"This is your chance to stop doing that. Maybe your last chance."

"Which is exactly why I've stayed away — that, and my guilt for having been so reckless of her safety. Do you think I *want* to hurt her?"

"You do a good imitation of it."

"What I want or don't want has nothing to do with it. The picture is clear. It's a matter of who I am and who Sarah is."

"Believe me, Jasper — you have no idea who Sarah is."

"My boy, you're speaking gibberish."

"Her words, not mine."

"I don't believe that."

"All right, not her exact words. But it's what she conveyed."

"Sarah and I knew each other instantly. We don't even need to speak. And yet — here is the colossal irony — the fact remains that I only bring her misery. Ultimately. Whatever excitement, whatever deceptive bliss may lead up to it is just the fever before the hemorrhage. Do you need new spectacles? Do I need to draw you a map? What more explanation do you require? I want to be with Sarah every minute of every day.

I'm drawn to her with such — I have no words for it — with such power. She is opium to me. When I'm with her, I cannot get enough, not if there were a hundred hours in a day. I'm ravenous for her, but her being within reach makes it worse. It's torture to be apart from her, but I hope I am man enough — from this distance at least — to resist temptation. I say over and over how Sarah and I are meant for each other, *made* for each other, and it's true. But so are fire and powder, Paul, so are fire and powder, and we don't need Friar Lawrence to tell us. Surely, it must have occurred to you, no matter what I might say or what Sarah might say, that the girl would be far better off with you."

"Many times. If only because I love her more."

"Oh, I doubt that, my boy. I doubt that very much."

"All right," I conceded, "maybe that's not true. But right now it's you she wants, it's you she needs — doctor's orders — and I promised her I would do everything I could to find you."

"Oh, my. Aren't you the noble little knight."

"Hardly. It's the least I can do."

"And now you've honoured your vow."

"Come back with me, Jasper."

Well, he didn't come back with me. When Charlie returned from his ramble, he read the tension between us immediately.

"I'll wait in the boat," he said, and I followed him down to the water a minute later.

He steered us to a sunny spot in the wide pond we had crossed earlier and we ate the lunch of bacon sandwiches and raisin pudding his wife had prepared.

"You're a very discreet man," I said, leaning back against a tree. "It must be an asset with your clientele."

He thought about that for a minute.

"Men come out here for all kinds of reasons. Some think it's about fish or about guns, but it's never just about fish or guns. Sometimes it's a trip down memory lane — Poppa took 'em huntin when they was young, say, or they climbed Whiteface when they was handsome and strong and had no responsibilities. Some men have to prove somethin to their friends or their womenfolk. Some want to prove somethin to themselves. Some want to forget somethin about themselves. And, I don't know why, exactly — maybe it's the heaven-blessed quiet of the forest, or the magic of the air in these mountains — but a lot of 'em feel the need to talk. Talk in a way they don't talk anywhere else. *Think* in a way they don't think anywhere else. I don't know what kind of man I'd be if I made amusing little stories out of that stuff."

"It's funny, you know. I think the day after I first moved to Saranac I made a note that the doctors here form a kind of priesthood, but I'm beginning to realize you guides are another."

Charlie tossed the last of his coffee into the bushes.

"Is it just you," he said, "or are all poets so full of it?"

When I stopped by the Sisters Hospital the next day, the two young nuns were painting the new gazebo. They waved to me and one of them called out, "She's doing much better today!"

"Oh, Paul, I'm so glad you've come," Sarah said when I appeared in her porch doorway. "I was just about to send you a message."

"Well, now you can deliver it in person."

"Come out here and sit down."

The nuns were right. Sarah seemed to have thrown off the sense of oppression that had threatened to suffocate her; the spark was back, the graceful hand gestures.

"What was the message?" I said, setting my chair down.

"The message was: Please forget what I said about finding Jasper. I had no right to ask you." She raised a pale hand to stop me before I could demur. "I just realized that you're right. I have to accept that he's gone, that he doesn't want to be with me, no matter the reason, and I have to face forward instead of constantly looking over my shoulder to see if Jasper's coming. He's not, and that's fine. I'm going to live without him. I don't know why it suddenly seemed so simple. It's as if I've been clenching my fist tight, tight, and wondering why it hurts so much."

Again her slender arm rose, the delicate fingers clenched to demonstrate.

"But then I open it — slowly, reluctantly — and find I've been squeezing with all my might on a shard of glass." She opened her empty hand. "And I've decided to stop doing that. I'm just not going to do that anymore."

"That's a pretty dramatic change," I said. "What made you —"

"Oh, it was no great insight. Just — after you were gone — I realized how unreasonable I'd become. Asking you *again* to do something that must be terribly painful for you. And I was thinking is this who I've become? Is this what I'll be for the rest of my life? Selfish, self-absorbed, self-pitying? Self, self, self — who can live with so much self? It's unbearable. You've been so good to me and all I do is cause you pain."

"That's not true," I said. "You were upset with me."

"But I shouldn't have been. Of *course* you couldn't believe my story — who could? We'll just forget it, shall we? I think I got carried away with my own pen. I'm sorry, and I plan to be a proper friend once I get out of this damn cure chair. And that's the other thing I have to tell you: I've decided to go ahead with the pneumothorax."

"It's probably the right decision," I said. "And a brave one."

"Not really. When I look at the choices open to me, it seems like the *least* frightening one."

"Dr. Duckworth managed to persuade you."

She shook her head. "Dr. Tissot. Dr. Tissot himself came round — did you send him? I know he's a friend of yours."

"Nothing to do with me," I said, wondering if that was strictly true.

"Well you know what he's like. So soft-spoken, but very persuasive. He just reassured me about the hundreds of procedures they'd done. It's helped so many people. And if it works, it's relatively quick. So. I guess he appeared at just the right moment. I'd just decided to stop stabbing myself with Jasper, and then I was saying to myself, 'All right, Miss Resolute, now what?' And then Dr. Tissot appeared. He's like a character in a play: the rational man surrounded by silly excitable people. And those *slippers*."

"Ah, yes. Hard to distrust those slippers."

A few minutes later, I rose to leave; I had pupils to catch up with. As I carried my chair back inside she said, "You didn't go to any more trouble, did you?"

"Trouble?"

"About finding Jasper."

"Well, I did look into hiring a private investigator."

"Oh, Paul. You didn't hire one, I hope."

Was it wrong of me to keep from her that I had, in fact, found Jasper? Possibly. But Sarah's new resolution to forget him seemed a healthy one, and I couldn't bring myself to undermine it. You may accuse me of becoming a dispenser of false cheer on the level of Mrs. Pryce, but I'm not sure I would have told Sarah anyway, for what was to be gained by her knowing that the man she pined for was determined to never see her again? Nor was I blind to the advantage for me if Sarah succeeded in forgetting him. In that respect, I was love's mercenary.

One of the more pleasant developments at this time was that the severe Dr. Duckworth was replaced by a younger man named Dr. Slade who took a broader view of what constituted a rest cure.

I spied him one crisp day as he was taking his lunch *al fresco* in the sisters' new gazebo and asked if I might speak with him. In contrast to Dr. Duckworth, he had an open, sunny demeanour and seemed content to look his age, which was about thirty.

"Miss Redmond has told me all about you," he said when I introduced myself. "And so have the sisters."

Two of them were coming up the path as he spoke. In their white habits, they resembled a pair of swans.

"I hear an accent," I said. "Are you from Scotland?"

He laughed. "I grew up in Michigan, but I took my medical degree in Edinburgh."

"I imagine the training is pretty much the same, isn't it?"

He nodded. "Much the same. Certainly, about the basics, and the problems peculiar to tuberculosis. Although I will say our attitudes differ as to what constitutes a rest cure — and what constitutes exercise, come to that."

He told me how in the British Isles they preferred a system of graduated exercise, that people who are able to walk *should* walk, and not be confined to bed for endless hours a day.

"To be sure, you don't want patients climbing mountains or even going shopping the day after a hemorrhage. The key is to start short and slow and then gradually build up — emphasis on *gradually*. But there's no point letting the entire body atrophy in order to coddle lungs that don't require it."

"You'll have your work cut out for you persuading Dr. Tissot on that score."

"Dr. Tissot is a remarkable physician. He was skeptical at first, but he's also open-minded — which is rare among the older medical men. I showed him the records we've been keeping in Edinburgh, as well as the records they use over there to justify the regimen, and he quickly came round. At least to the extent of letting me work this way with my own patients. Then there'll be a comparison of results and we'll see."

I told him I was mightily glad to hear it. "And what about pneumothorax patients?"

"Miss Redmond, you mean."

"Well, yes."

"It's all right. I can discuss her case with you — she's designated you as her next of kin."

I had almost forgotten. His words kindled a glow in my heart.

"I find much reason for optimism. Such is the margin of safety we're all born with, we can lose up to five-sixths of the lung tissue and still live. In Miss Redmond's case, the right lung is perfectly clear. And the left has stabilized enough — for the moment at least — that we can safely collapse it, immobilize it, and that should render the disease inactive."

"And exercise?"

"Assuming all goes well, she'll be ready for very short walks within a few days, I'd say. And then slowly work up to longer walks. Emphasis on *slowly*."

He packed up his little lunch basket and stood up and shook my hand.

"It was a pleasure to make your acquaintance, Mr. Gascoyne. I understand you're a poet and professor all rolled into one."

"I can't claim either of those titles at the moment, I'm afraid."

"Well, next time we'll let you do the talking. Otherwise, I'm liable to recite you reams of Robbie Burns. The Scots are quite mad about him."

"Well, in Saranac we're quite mad about Robert Louis Stevenson. So you'll feel right at home."

Meeting Dr. Slade was for me one of those moments where one's outlook takes a sudden shift from gloom to sunlight. I began to feel, for the first time since that terrible night on the ice palace steps, that things might turn out tolerably well. Jasper would find the peace of mind to finish his play-in-progress, and would be back to Broadway — the real Broadway — and renewed acclaim. Sarah's pneumothorax would be a success and she would be out of bed in a matter of days. With any luck the European war would be over and I wouldn't even get called up. Well, I realized even then that it was a *mood* I was revelling in, not the future, but my optimism would not be smothered.

Sarah's operation took place the next morning, and I was able to visit in the afternoon. She was lying in bed, peacefully dozing, so I opened a book and sat reading. Every so often a nursing sister would come in and check her pulse, nod at me silently, and disappear.

"How are you feeling?" I said, when Sarah finally stirred.

"I don't know." Her eyes darted this way and that, taking in the room. "Seasick."

"That'll be the ether," I said sagely, remembering her earlier description of its effects.

"And a terrible headache."

"Do you have any idea how happy I am to see you?"

She smiled and beckoned me to hold her hand. Hers was cold.

"I feel lighter," she said. "But awfully lopsided. They took three ribs."

"Three! I thought it was to be two."

She held up three fingers in silent contradiction.

"Well, Slade says it all went swimmingly," I told her. "You have every reason to expect a quick recovery."

"I love Dr. Slade, don't you? He's so ... reasonable. He lets me draw as much as I want, read as much as I want, write whenever I want. None of this absolute immobility nonsense."

The next couple of weeks were remarkable for what we did *not* discuss. Sarah never mentioned Jasper, and I certainly wasn't going to bring him up. I wondered how he was faring, if he was still out in his wilderness or perhaps back in New York. I imagined vaguely how he and I might meet up again in the future — perhaps on his opening night, but I didn't mention this.

Nor did we talk of Sarah's ghastly "history." When I accompanied her on her first tentative strolls, I found I didn't want to discuss it. Sarah seemed happier by the day, and I was not about to darken her outlook by bringing it up. But I was certainly thinking about it. Although I had come to believe most everything about the abortion and Cross's deception, I still had my doubts about the rape — for the reasons I have already mentioned, but also because it occurred to me that remembering the event as rape was the perfect way for a wayward girl to blunt the cutting edge of self-blame. This way, she could bear a large measure of condemnation without having to bear all.

Did I manage to persuade myself? Not thoroughly. But I decided I could live within the cloud of uncertainty. Something would change, I thought, and one day I would know for sure. No matter what she had written or told me about her past, there was nothing about her in her current state that said *liar* — she was sincerity incarnate. I could accept that terrible emotional turmoil had pushed her into believing things that were distortions of the truth, if only to protect herself from terrible self-knowledge. It would not stop me loving her. I am not trying to defend my reactions, only to explain them — to myself as much as to anyone else.

Sarah's program of graduated exercise began with short circuits around the first floor of the hospital. Every few steps she had to stop to catch her breath.

"They told me that having one useable lung wouldn't differ all that much from having two," she said, leaning on my arm, "but I feel like an engine that needs stoking."

"Don't worry," I said, with more assurance than I felt, "you'll get better by the day."

"Or die trying."

"Nobody wants that. Time for another break."

The "big day" came when she was allowed to go outside and walk around the grounds.

Dr. Slade accompanied us to the front door.

"Slowly," he said, holding the door open. "Very slowly. You promise?"

"I promise," Sarah said, and made a little cross over her heart. The girlish gesture and the look on her face — obedient and yet impish — evoked the adolescent of the earlier part of her memoir. For a brief second, I saw her as Iphigenia dancing for the Achilles who would never come. Then we were outside, and the cold spring breeze blew such thoughts away.

The hospital grounds were steeply sloped, so once again Sarah took my arm. I was honoured, because in 1917 men and women did not walk arm in arm unless they were married, closely related, or engaged. Sister Veronica smiled at us as we passed, and I thought I detected a certain knowingness in her smile; she was seeing marriage in our future.

Sarah's strength was well up, and the grounds gave her no trouble.

"I think I can manage," she said, and took her arm from me.

After two circuits around the hospital, we sat in the gazebo. Sarah was wearing a white dress with a choker of blue ribbon, and chimed perfectly with the Adirondack sky and clouds.

"It's so extraordinary," she said, looking back toward the Sisters.

"What is?"

"Dr. Slade — the operation. It's just so extraordinary to me. That man reached inside me and sawed off three ribs and sewed me back up. I can't get over it. It's as if I was a broken doll, and he put me back together."

"I suppose that's what surgeons do."

"Extraordinary."

"Don't tell me you're developing a crush on the doctor. I'll hang myself from the nearest tree."

"Oh, don't say that." The light went out of her face.

"Not to worry — just joking."

"Paul, don't ever say that."

We walked on and I tried to make amends by reciting as many silly rhymes as I could remember, starting with Blake's "Mr. Cromek," managing most of "The Owl and the Pussycat," and ending with "The Walrus and the Carpenter," which — luckily — Sarah also knew by heart. She completed each verse by reciting the last line and by the time we'd circled the hospital for a fourth time she was smiling once more.

Over the following weeks, we took an afternoon trek around Moody Pond, and one cloudy morning I was at Sarah's side as she went step by step up Helen Hill. The most memorable day was a picnic in Pine Ridge Cemetery. We sat on a stone bench beside a mossy wall and ate cold chicken and salad and drank hot tea from a Thermos. After our meal I sat on the bench smoking a cigarette while Sarah wandered among the graves. The day being damp and windy, she was wearing a dark blue cape rather like a nurse's cape but with a hood. Every once in a while, she would turn and the light would catch her face within the shadow of the hood and the first filaments of a story drifted into my head. A ghost story. Saranac Lake, being built on a foundation of deadly disease is an easy place to imagine ghosts. But a ghost story — that is, the story of a haunting — requires a story *behind* the story, events in the life or surrounding the death of the deceased. What tale could I invent for this pale, comely spectre?

Sarah joined me on the bench, perversely animated by her stroll among the dead — her colleagues, as she had called them when we first became tutor and pupil.

"It's good to see them again," she said, "but I feel a bit guilty that I'm up and around while they're stuck in permanent bedrest. I feel as if I've deserted them."

The day came when Sister Mary Magdelene was actively considering releasing Sarah from the Sisters Hospital. Dr. Slade pronounced her case "arrested," and thought she might soon be able to take up her teaching activities. I visited her in a porch of the hospital that had a view of Mount Pisgah. Sarah had never looked so healthy.

"I start teaching week after next," she told me. "Dr. Tissot has got me into the san's workshop. Have you seen it? It's a wonderful studio. I'll be able to build up a client list from there. I can't *wait* to be painting again — I mean *really* painting. Isn't it wonderful?"

"Indeed it is." I had been prodding Dr. Tissot to make an arrangement with the sanitarium, but I didn't mention it to Sarah; the joy on her face was recompense enough.

"Now there's one thing I have to take care of before I settle into my new regimen. And it's a big thing, I'm afraid. In fact, it frightens me."

"You don't look frightened."

"Nervous, then. Agitated. I have to decide what to do with the house in Angelique. I have to decide whether to sell it outright and find something here, or perhaps hang on to it and just rent it out to people, if that's even possible. In either case I would have to empty it out. The Gartners have been so kind about keeping an eye on it, but I can't ask them to do that forever — not without paying them, and they are getting on in age."

She took a deep breath before continuing.

"And there's all the artwork to deal with — mostly my father's. Negatives and glass plates will have to go to Campbell Clark Gallery. And there are one or two paintings of my own I'd like to keep. Anyway, I want to take care of it as soon as possible so that I can forget about it and have my mind free for pleasanter subjects. But — here's the difficult part — I don't know a thing about houses and real estate, or any kind of business really, so I was hoping you would accompany me."

"We can't very well travel together, Sarah. People will talk."

"We wouldn't have to *say* we're travelling together. And we certainly don't have to share accommodations. Oh, Paul, you've put up with so much from me — *done* so much for me — I promise never to ask you for anything ever again."

"You can ask me for anything. Any time."

The fact that I knew no more about house selling than Sarah did nothing to dampen her enthusiasm.

"You truly are a knight in shining armour," she said, echoing Jasper, minus the sarcasm. "I hope you know I adore you."

"I'm not sure I know it, Sarah. But I sure enjoy hearing you say it."

Gascoyne, I said to myself as I headed back along Main Street, she's happy and healthy and looking forward to life again. Not to mention that she adores you. *Says* she adores you. My boy, I added, imitating Jasper's paternalism at its most benevolent, this is your moment and if you don't seize it you're a contemptible fool. Oh my, yes.

CHAPTER 22

The night train was due to depart at eleven-fifteen. In my excitement I found myself at the station far too early. Having only a small suitcase, I didn't have to deal with baggage check-in. It had been an unusually warm day but the waiting room was still heated for mid-winter, so rather than swelter I spent half an hour pacing the platform. When the train finally arrived, only a few people disembarked; it was a Wednesday, and most patients chose to arrive at the beginning or end of the week. Sarah and I had arranged to meet "accidentally" on the train, so I didn't waste any more time hanging around outside.

I boarded, stowed my suitcase in the rack, and took my seat by the window. Sarah was not yet on the platform. I was staring at the scattered individuals outside, some waving goodbye to unseen others, when a familiar voice said, "Well, if it isn't Mr. Gascoyne."

Nurse Troy was there with her handsome friend beside her.

"Hello, Nurse Troy," I said, picking up on her formality.

"Mr. Gascoyne teaches patients about great books and they all adore him. This is my fiancé, Dr. Nordstrom."

I stood awkwardly to shake his hand. He didn't look any more eager to linger than I was but Nurse Troy went on.

"I'm dragging him to Poughkeepsie to meet my parents."

"Congratulations," I said to him. "You'll be a medical dynasty in no time."

"And where are you off to?" she asked me.

"New York," I said, having prepared a response in advance. "Visiting friends in Manhattan for a couple of days."

"Long journey for a couple of days."

"They're good friends."

"Well, enjoy your trip," she said, and the two of them moved on up the car.

Only a month or two earlier, the discovery that a woman I had pursued was engaged, even though I had since abandoned the pursuit, might have ignited a nasty little flame of envy. But loving Sarah seemed to cloak my heart in a mantle of benevolence. I was genuinely happy for Nurse Troy in all her pink and blond and strapping Nordicness; I even regretted my erstwhile campaign against her virtue. I sat back down and resumed my watch on the platform. No one else appeared to be boarding. The station clock said eleven-ten. I got up and walked to the end of the car and went down one step.

A railroad employee standing below me said, "Best not get off now, sir."

"I know. Just looking for someone." I leaned out to check one end of the train and then the other. Fortune's dark vehicle was parked near the baggage car, where three pine coffins were being trundled aboard.

I picked up a newspaper on the way back to my seat and made a pretense of reading it. My nerves were beginning to rattle and buzz, but I focused my mind on the pleasures awaiting me: the long ride with Sarah, perhaps a meal in a swanky Manhattan restaurant, and then a trip across the Hudson to the New Jersey house where she grew up. That visit was bound to be a sad occasion for Sarah, and I felt honoured to be sharing it. There might be a tearful moment or two, and some difficult questions about her father's estate and legacy, but I would be once more by her side at a moment of high emotion. Long ago she had said she wanted at least one person to know her — know her truly — before she died, and she had chosen me. It might even be a propitious time to propose marriage. That thought took me by surprise. To go from those heavy seas of doubt and turmoil to the sudden calm of imagining a life together? And yet it arrived in my mind with an air of sedate rationality. Sarah had not given me the slightest indication that she would accept, but one of the thrills of love is surely the mad confidence that one's feelings must be reciprocated — soon, if not instantaneously. Every dark, dramatic episode she had related faded into the background, leaving me to picture a life overflowing with love and art and children; mere facts could do nothing to squelch my optimism.

"Mr. Gascoyne?"

A man in Western Union livery was standing in the aisle with an envelope in his hand.

"A telegram?"

"Just a message, sir. Urgent."

The departure bell was clanging. Conductors were calling all aboard along the length of the train.

My Dearest, Dearest Paul,

I hope this reaches you in time.

If I had a shred of common sense, I would do everything in my power to deserve your love and spend the rest of my life with you. But Jasper has returned! And you know, where Jasper is concerned, I have no common sense at all. I am thrilled and overjoyed — and possibly doomed? — but my heart gives me no choice. Please forgive me for yet again abusing your faithful and generous nature. I know that you will find love and happiness with a woman far more worthy than I.

With tenderest affection,
Sarah

I wish I could say I decided to stay on the train, that I weighed up the pros and cons of getting off or staying on and made a rational choice to remain on board. But in this, as in all my experiences with Sarah and Jasper, I made no decision at all. I simply sat there, stunned and unmoving, as the night train left the station and carried me away.

After a miserable night in my sleeping berth, I disembarked at Grand Central Station at nine a.m. *What in God's name am I doing here?* I asked myself as the IRT hurtled me to the Upper West Side and my old friends, Simon and Caroline Crawford.

They rapidly discerned that I was in pain and served up great quantities of tea and sympathy as only one's old friends can. They made no demands on me whatsoever, bore my silences with equanimity, invited me to take in art galleries and museums with them. The three of us attended a revival of *Lady Windermere's Fan* that managed the difficult feat of making me laugh. Later, they updated me on university politics, which confirmed in me a resolution never to return to academe, but of course we also talked about books. Simon was currently enthused about a Melville seminar he was running.

"We got into an interminable discussion of why the whale is white," he told me. "One student decided it was a reference to the communion wafer, which provoked animated disagreement. Another said Melville was being courageous and original by deploying the colour white as a symbol of evil."

"I don't think I have the patience for discussions like that anymore," I said. "The reason the whale is white is so that they can find the damn thing again — and recognize him when they do."

"You don't think there's anything more going on than that?"

"Well, it has to remain plausible as well as recognizable. Many species throw up albino versions, but he couldn't very well make it tomato red. Or paisley."

"Spoken like a true practitioner," Simon said. "Nuts and bolts."

"I'm not much of a scholar anymore — that's for sure. Or much of a practitioner, either."

Caroline asked me, gently, how my writing was going and I had to tell them, honestly, that I had no idea. I had had high hopes for my novel-in-progress, but the chance of my ever making a living by my pen seemed ever more slim.

"Well, don't wait too long to test the academic waters again," Simon said. "There are more English departments forming all the time, but that won't last forever."

The next morning I took the subway up to Penn Station, and from there an autobus to the ferry and across to Hoboken and another bus to the village of Angelique. I had promised Sarah my help, and could not so soon forsake my shining armour. I sensed that if I continued behaving as if Jasper were not in the picture, it could only work to my benefit. The Hudson River glittered in the morning sun.

Angelique turned out to be little more than a crossroads and a few shops. Indeed, if you were to look for Angelique today you would not find it, for the village was long ago absorbed into West Hoboken. I asked for directions in the general store, and had no trouble finding Sarah's house, or the neighbour she had mentioned, Mr. Gartner, who was seated on the porch steps. He must have been eighty, or thereabouts, but he was a wiry, bright-eyed man, who sprang up from the steps where he sat.

We shook hands and introduced ourselves.

"Where's Sarah? She wrote that she was coming too."

"Last-minute change of plans," I said.

"Not ailing again, I hope."

"No, no. A friend of hers has taken a turn for the worse, so …"

"I see." He rubbed a hand through thick white hair. "Well, the missus will be mighty disappointed. Can't tell you how much we were looking forward to seeing that girl again — maybe even having her back here. Especially after what she's been through."

"If you're not comfortable handing me the keys, I completely understand."

"No hesitation at all. Sarah spoke mighty highly of you in her letter."

He showed the keys to me one by one on their ring.

"Round key's for the front and back doors. Square one's for the side, silver one's for the studio. House shouldn't be too stuffy. I always air it out at least once a week, and I opened it up this morning, too, when I knew you were coming."

"You've been looking after the place since ... since the *Lusitania*?"

"Doesn't take a lot of looking after. She's a solidly built little place. Wasn't all that much to do once I put the sheets over the furniture."

"Still, it's very good of you."

He waved this away.

"Sarah was special to us. I only wish we could have gone up to see her in Saranac Lake but Martha — my wife — she's bedridden and I pretty much have to stick close to home. We sure loved looking after that girl when she was little and her dad was away."

He smiled, remembering, fine white wrinkles fanning out from his eyes and mouth.

"They were always such a happy family, I never knew why he took off like that. Wanderlust, I guess. Artistic type, for sure. Tell you the truth, we'd have been overjoyed to take Sarah in for good when her mother died, but Redmond did the right thing coming back. The two of them had a good life before the *Lusitania*. They were like a married couple, in some ways — I guess because he'd been away so long, and they were both always painting or drawing or taking photographs together."

Mr. Gartner clearly enjoyed talking about Sarah, the funny things she'd done as a little girl, the school plays, the schoolyard "tragedies," the high marks. I let him talk on. It was a profound pleasure to hear him speak of her with love — especially this kindly, undemanding love. His memories were a striking counterbalance to the stories Sarah had written. The house before me was a cheerful bungalow of red brick, white trim, and mullioned windows. Despite his modesty Mr. Gartner had plainly given time and care to the plantings — laurel, honeysuckle, and juniper — that lined the front walk and framed the house itself.

"Well," he said, "you'll have a lot of things to think about in there, so I'll leave you to it. If you need anything, I'm right next door. Don't hesitate."

I thanked him, and entered through the side door, which opened onto a vestibule full of boots and overshoes and other rain gear. The kitchen was not much bigger than a galley but had a wide window overlooking the backyard. The yard was surrounded by a high wooden fence, and the ungainly wooden structure of their studio lent a discordant note to an otherwise attractive view. Beside it lay the famous "pond," empty now, where Sarah had been cast as Ophelia, mermaid, and anonymous drowned girl. My eye was drawn below the window to the kitchen sink, and the memory sprang, unbidden, of her father smashing the Calico Lane glasses in a rage.

Mr. Gartner had removed the protective sheets from the furnishings. Framed photographs were everywhere, and I was surprised that most were not professional portraits but ordinary snapshots: Sarah at the beach, Sarah on her mother's lap, five-year-old Sarah absorbed in an oversize picture book. Of course, it was Sarah I was hungry for, not the house, not the past, so I didn't take in details that didn't directly speak of her. A closet full of her dresses certainly held my gaze, but I shut the door again before it could drown me in reverie.

I gave a quick glance to the master bedroom, noting only the large brass bed. The room, the house generally, looked surprisingly well cared-for for an uninhabited place, but the floors did creak terribly underfoot, and I remembered Sarah had mentioned this detail in her writing.

A handsome den at the front of the house was filled with overflowing bookshelves, and books lay everywhere in small stacks or precarious towers. Most were art books, but there were also a great many works of Classical literature and history. I found Carswell's *European Masterpieces*, which Sarah had spoken of with such reverence. The binding was cracked and many of the plates were loose — including Bernini's *The Abduction of Proserpina*, which I gazed at for some time. Although I remembered Sarah's description ("marble made flesh!"), I had never seen it before and sat there amazed that so indirect a rendering — a photograph of a sculpture of a myth — could wield such power.

I went back through the kitchen and used the silver key to open the studio. It smelled mightily of photographic chemicals. I fumbled around in near-perfect darkness until I found a row of light switches. The space was much larger than it had appeared from outside. The far end was empty except for the fireplace before which Sarah had danced as Iphigenia. In the foreground a large camera stood sentry in a black hood. A door to my left led to a darkroom crammed with sinks and trays and jugs of chemicals. Ungainly photographic equipment loomed like machinery out of Jules Verne.

One wall was covered by three sets of wide, shallow drawers such as you might find in a map library. I opened one at random and found prints of portraits separated from each other by filmy paper; I didn't recognize the subjects but it was easy

to see why Redmond had been in demand. They had the customary formality, but also managed to find the spark of character that made each subject unique. Another drawer contained
photographs of ruins that Redmond must have taken during
his European wanderings; I recognized Tintern Abbey.

In other drawers I found photographs of Sarah as Puck, as
Ariel, as a woodland sprite or elf. The costumes were charming, and it moved me to see Sarah's gamine beauty captured
in such cheerful scenes. As she had noted, she was indeed
"skinny as a boy" and the upturned nose and undiluted glee
of her smile were perfect for these roles. The Iphigenia, taken
when she was older, stopped me — just that — stopped me.
The gown, as Sarah had written, was indeed diaphanous, and
Sarah, as she had *not* written, was beautiful, but the image as
a whole was clearly designed to appeal to male lust. Sarah had
said Redmond had been aiming to capture innocence betrayed and in this he succeeded — but the innocence was not just
Iphigenia's, and the unseen betrayer was not Agamemnon. I
wanted to throw my coat over the girl, and had Redmond been
there in person I believe I would have struck him.

It's possible, but only *just* possible, that my reaction
stemmed not from a discriminating eye or strict morality
(readers will know that I was no paragon on that score), but
solely from my love for the woman that fifteen-year-old dan-
cer would become. It's conceivable, but only *just* conceivable,
that a photography connoisseur might have found the image
merely risky rather than unconscionable. The same might
be said for Redmond's photograph of "Ophelia," the nubile
adolescent plainly revealed amid a ghostly penumbra of pei-
gnoir that clings to her wetly as she dies. I admit it made vivid
the sad poetry of youth and death, but it also exposed young

Sarah to the eyes of any man in the room. Even the "Drowned
Daughter," which raised my outrage high into the red zone,
might just possibly have been assessed by a jaded art lover as
a legitimate rendering of tragedy. I was no more sophisticated
in matters of visual art than I was in the fine points of theatre,
but one of the most remarkable things — to me — about these
images was that they were not hidden. No lock, no secret com-
partment. They were stacked and stored in exactly the manner
of the portraits, the narratives, the pictures of ruins. Redmond
had apparently seen nothing wrong with them, but Sarah had
not mentioned if they were ever exhibited, and I was sure that
any public showing would have caused a scandal, perhaps even
a police raid.

Now somewhat shaken, I went back into the house to see
what papers I could find that would be relevant to a possible
sale. It seemed likely that the papers of such an artistic household would be in hopeless disarray, but whatever else he was,
Lionel Redmond had apparently liked to keep his business
affairs in order. The drawers of his oak desk contained files
of contracts, invoices, and receipts, as well as business letters
filed according to date and correspondent. The fattest file contained letters and statements from the Campbell Clark Gallery.
Another was devoted to the Manhattan law firm of Pearson,
Park, and Randall. A statement from Union Square Bank
showed that the mortgage on the house had been paid off long
ago, and I found papers from Fyfe Real Estate and Insurance,
who had facilitated the original purchase, including the deed.
Redmond's will was less than three pages long. I had never read
a will before, but this one was straightforward, leaving everything, without exception, to Sarah. I collected all the relevant
papers and stuffed them into my satchel.

On top of the desk, aslant across a wooden inbox, lay a plain grey envelope of legal size addressed to Lionel Redmond, stamped *personal and confidential*. The return address was a Post Office box number. It was unopened, and postmarked May 4, 1915 — three days before the sinking. Beneath it was a second, identical envelope, but this one had been opened. I lifted the flap and found yet more photographs, but these were of a very different kind. I pulled them out and spread them on the desk. Each had a caption area at the bottom filled in with date, time, and location. One photo showed a Jersey Power & Light truck parked beside a utility pole; the caption read *Observation Post*. Several showed Sarah on her bike, overburdened as she had described with easel and other equipment, arriving at the Lathrop house on different days in February 1915. The pictures had clearly been taken through the van's windows. Low ridges of snow lined the sides of the road, and the grounds of the house were blanketed, but the road itself was clear. Other pictures showed Sarah entering the house on different days, the door being held open by Thomas Cross. He was tall and broad, so that Sarah looked almost a child beside him. Most of the pictures were of Sarah's bike, showing it unmoved for one, two, three, or four hours. Courts, of course, did not require images of the delinquent couple actually in bed together in order to prove an illicit affair; the shared time and location was enough. That alone was good reason for a woman to avoid being alone with a man for any length of time. The worst was assumed, the reputation — and in many cases the life — ruined.

I had already come round to believing most of what these photographs implied. They shed no light on the question of rape — they were too distant to show the bruise Sarah said Cross had inflicted on her cheekbone — but the sight of her pedalling along to her fate unaware that she was being watched brought tears to my eyes. And this time my tears were not for myself; these men had hurt someone who deserved nothing but affection and respect. Yes, the detective's photos were forensic, not artistic, but they began to strike me as all part of a bigger collection, for in all of them Sarah — her youth, her body, her will even — had been appropriated to her father's purposes. I knew that the fifteen-year-old girl had consented to and been an eager participant in the "artistic" project but that hardly amounted to a free and mature decision, and in no way had the nineteen-year-old agreed to surveillance. Iphigenia was one thing, but the girl photographed on her wobbly bike could not have looked a less likely subject for the gossip pages. I wanted to step into the images — into the past — and warn her, protect her, not just from the photos, but from the reach of men, for it seemed to me there was a direct line from Thomas Cross "rescuing" her from the storm all the way to her near-drowning in the Irish Sea.

Yet more photos were taken in the West Village: Sarah entering Dr. Boyard's clinic in late February, Sarah entering and leaving the Boyard clinic in late April, Sarah on the steps of Henderson Brothers Ticket Agency at Broadway and 19th for her *Cameronia* passage. An invoice from Kennedy-Kirk Investigations billed Redmond for a considerable sum. Presumably, their report was either mailed separately or given over the phone, or perhaps Redmond had taken it with him to thrust in his daughter's face.

I picked up the first envelope. Its being unopened stopped me for a moment, but it was addressed to a dead man — one whose personal effects I had been ransacking with Sarah's permission for the past hour — and I opened it. The three photos were stamped with "Boyard Clinic" and a patient number. The first was a head-and-shoulders shot of Sarah, and a cry escaped me as I first laid eyes on it. She was wearing a hospital gown or some other minimal garment, rather than her customary high-necked dresses, that revealed the pale column of her throat. At first I thought the dark band across it was a shadow, or a photographic irregularity, but then I realized it was, in fact, the mark of a hand. To the right, slightly higher up, was the bruise-like blotch of a thumbprint. And that was not even what had made me cry out. Her left cheekbone was bruised and swollen, and she had the beginnings of a black eye.

"Sarah," I whispered, and lay a finger gently on the mark.

The remaining two photographs were of a medical nature and I won't describe them. How the Kennedy-Kirk investigator got hold of the photos I can only imagine, but I suspect theft or bribery. They perfectly matched Sarah's account of her treatment at the Boyard clinic — and at the hands of Thomas Cross.

On my trip back, I lay in my dark little berth, listening to the clack of the wheels and fantasizing about Thomas Cross, how I would travel to Boston and seek him out and knock on the door of his architectural firm and march right up to his desk and tap him on the shoulder and punch him so hard it would spin him around in his chair. I imagined an alternative: I would make copies of those pitiless photographs and mail them to his employer, or perhaps to his wife. I even pictured Lionel Redmond, discovered half-dead on a rock somewhere in the Atlantic and hauled back to New York City to face a withering cross-examination by Paul Gascoyne Esq. as to his motives in creating with his daughter his personal photo-graphic seraglio.

Well, the *Lusitania* had taken that out of my hands, and Sarah had emphasized that she in no way wished to damage Cross's life despite what he had done to hers.

As the train rumbled on, the lightning flashes of outrage were dimmed by thunderclouds of guilt. Sarah had told me in hard cold English what had been done to her, and I, the so-called professor of English, instead of responding with con-cerned inquiry, had misread her to suit my innate preference for comfortable ignorance. *I would like to be known by at least one other human being in the world — truly known for who and what I am — before I die.* Sarah had given me the chance to be that person, and I had failed her — failed her as surely as if I had encountered a suffering creature with its leg in a trap and blithely walked by.

Long before first light, I climbed out of my berth and pulled on my clothes and went back to my window seat. I willed the train to go faster, positively ached when it slowed for curves, and thought I would go mad when we were mysteriously de-layed at Lake Clear. I was desperate to beg Sarah's forgiveness, to tell her that *yes, someone knows you! At least one person in this world knows you!* And loves you. When we finally arrived I was first off the train and ran the length of the platform to a waiting taxi.

"Mr. Gascoyne!"

Sister Mary Magdalene called out to me from her office be-fore the front door had even closed behind me.

"Mr. Gascoyne, where have you been? We've been trying to reach you."

"Why? What's the matter?"

"Miss Redmond has gone missing. She went out yesterday morning before lunch, supposedly to go to the post office, but we haven't seen her since."

"She didn't come back to the hospital?"

"No. And she doesn't appear to have taken any of her things with her. There's no note, and we've heard nothing — absolutely nothing. I've had to alert the police."

"Isn't that a bit extreme? Perhaps she made a day trip to Lake Placid and got delayed."

"Possibly. But there's another element to consider. Jasper Keene has made an appearance."

"That's a surprise."

"And not a happy one. The man has been coming around here and spouting the most irresponsible madness. Telling everyone how there's no cure like the natural world, he's living proof of it, how staying in bed is far more of a strain than walking in the woods and contemplating the mountains or a good old Adirondack storm. Sarah's been coming back in the evenings absolutely exhausted. We've begged him to stay away. We've warned her that she cannot keep flouting doctors' orders or we'll have to discharge her. She seems to think she's *following* Dr. Slade's orders for graduated exercise, but he's appalled at this development."

I looked at my watch; it was nearly ten o'clock. I couldn't believe Jasper would keep her out all night, or that Sarah would stay out without letting the hospital know she was all right.

"What are the police saying?"

"I've given them a photograph and they're organizing a search. They're in front of the town hall if you'd like to help."

"Yes, of course."

"You know her better than anyone, Mr. Gascoyne. If you know where Sarah might be, you must tell us at once."

"I don't. I have no idea. She could be anywhere. Have you checked with Mr. Keene's hotel? He's usually at the Berkeley."

"They don't know where he is. Surely, she must have favourite walks, favourite places?"

"I can think of two. I'll check those and then I'll head over to the town hall."

I left my suitcase with Sister Mary Magdalene and hurried over to Pine Crest Cemetery — the afternoon we had shared amid its moss and stone and elms was one of the happiest Sarah had spent, at least with me. I made a quick circuit around the graves, and stood for a moment on the stone bench where we had enjoyed our picnic overlooking the dead she had referred to as her colleagues. But Sarah was not there; there was no one there at all.

I went down Front Street to the river, almost stumbling down the grassy slope. The path was not easily walkable north of this area, but to my left lay the very spot where Sarah had first entered my life, as drenched and exhausted as if she had just that moment washed ashore from the *Lusitania*. I strode along the river walk, looking to my left into the trees and to the right at the river rushing along its high spring watermarks. It was dark under the trees, and suddenly cold.

I emerged, blinking, beside the Five & Dime and turned toward Main Street aiming for the town hall but then had another idea. I stopped into the Arlington Hotel and borrowed a city directory. Charles Sands, guide, was listed at an address nearby. I had a distinct memory of his loyalty to Jasper, and wasn't sure he would tell me where he was, if he knew.

I found the house on Terrace Street. I ran up the steps and knocked on the door, but there was no answer. I pounded again. Nothing. I peered through the lace curtain on the other side of the door, but there was no sign of activity. The scent of wet pine was taken over by a strong smell of paint. I went round to the back where Charlie Sands was painting a canoe fire-engine red.

"It's the professor," he said. "You looking to bag a bear?"

"Do you know where Jasper is?"

"Not a clue, sir. Not a clue. Brung him in a few days ago."

"Miss Redmond is missing. She's been gone all night."

Sands stood there holding his scarlet dripping brush.

"That's not good."

"She's been seeing Jasper every day, so if you know where they are, you have to tell me. The police are mounting a search. Has he gone back to that lean-to?"

"If he did, I didn't take him."

"Well, would he be able to get there himself?"

Charlie answered with a simple, definite no.

"Could another guide have taken him?"

"Not without talking to me. Guides don't poach."

I didn't have to ask him to join the search. He set aside his paintbrush and wiped his hands on a rag.

We passed the bookstore, the photography shop, the bank, and as we were passing the postal telegraph office we met uniformed police constables heading off in different directions. Police Chief Ruggles was directing search teams in front of the town hall.

"I understand you're her next of kin," he said when I introduced myself.

"I'm her cousin. Her parents are deceased."

"Well, I hope you've got some leads for us. Otherwise we just have to follow the usual routines."

I told him about the river walk.

"We've got men heading there now. Anywhere else?"

"Well, I already checked the cemetery."

He scowled at me.

"It's one of her favourite places. But I've just come from there. Maybe Moody Pond?"

"We've got people on the way. She's not likely to go into the woods on her own, is she?"

"Not on her own. But if she's with Jasper Keene, she might."

"All right. If we don't catch a trace of her through canvassing local businesses, that's going to mean calling out the fire department, the guides, the whole damn world." He looked at Sands.

"Charlie? Any ideas?"

"I just brung Mr. Keene back from out Kiwassa way four days ago. Doubt he'd be back there now."

"It's a lead. Take three men and head out there now."

Charlie moved off to round up some help, and the chief turned to me.

"Anywhere else you know of?"

I shook my head. "Sorry. Tell me how I can help."

"Seeing as you're the closest thing she has to family, you'd best head back to where she'd be likely to get in touch with you. Say she wakes up in Old Forge or wherever and wants to telephone or send a telegram, we need you to be there to receive it. I've got the photo over at the *Enterprise*. If the initial search turns up empty, we'll be printing up missing posters and a story in the paper."

The chief signalled to three uniformed men on the town hall steps. "All right, then. Let's get going."

They clambered aboard a flatbed truck, and I watched them drive away.

My legs were heavy as I went back along Main Street and I had to sit down on a bench outside the telegraph office. I tried to calm myself by taking rational stock of the possibilities. The most likely scenario, if I ruled out actual catastrophe, was that Sarah and Jasper had on a whim decided to head off somewhere else, whether by automobile, boat, or train. They might be as close as Lake Placid or as far as Montreal or New York. There was nothing for me to do about that — the police would cover the station, the marina, and the car rental places.

Across the street a couple of policemen came out of the bank and went into Munn's Groceries. Next to the Humidor, Madame Lupu was setting out her sandwich board sign with a huge tarot card, big enough to be easily legible across the street. This time it was The Fool, carrying a tiny bundle on a stick over one shoulder, and capering on the edge of a cliff. It reminded me of Jasper, the memory of a brilliant winter's day.

I got up and walked quickly to the Riverside Hotel where I hired a taxi to take me to Baker Mountain. He dropped me at the side of the road beside a sign that said *Lookout*, with an arrow pointing straight up. The last time I had been here, with Jasper and Sarah, it had been deep winter. The trail looked radically different now; it was wet from runoff, and in some places was little more than mud. My shoes soon felt like buckets of ice water. The lower part of the trail was not steep and, luckily for me and my nonexistent reckoning skills, free of branching paths that would have soon had me the subject of a second search party.

If Jasper had taken Sarah for an overnight stay in the woods, it would be at his personal dugout, where Charlie Sands would

soon find them. There was no compelling reason to believe the
two of them had come up Baker Mountain, but the police chief
had asked about Sarah's favourite places, not Jasper's. As the
climb got steeper and my breathing more laboured, I began to
worry that now *I* was the reckless one, that I should have gone
back to my room to await any message that might come. Still,
the going was much easier — and quicker — than I remembered. I recalled how hard it had been on Sarah, and how she'd
had to beg Jasper to slow down. And how he had resolutely
ignored the Danger sign — it was still there, still stern — with
the two of us in tow.

And then I saw the erratic — the massive glacial rock
that marked the spot. It loomed twenty yards above and to
the right, an improbable chunk of prehistory. I leaned my
back against it, catching my breath. All right, I told myself, I
would screw up my courage, take a quick look, and then head
back down. Trailing one hand against the rock, I made my
way around it to the ledge. Here was the magnificent view
Jasper had insisted we see, and yes, it was and would for all
eternity remain, to use his word, sublime. Shadows of clouds
flowed across the face of Mount Pisgah and the sanitarium.
The three of us had needed sunglasses in the winter, but the
sun was higher now and I could survey the entire landscape
without having to shade my eyes. I was six feet from the edge
of the cliff, but the sheer depth of the valley below was already
giving me vertigo.

To my right was the leaning birch Jasper and Sarah had
clung to. I took a few deep breaths and reached for it, edging
my way to the precipice. I knelt, and let go so that I could lie
flat, then forced myself to inch right up to the edge and look
over. Far below, Sarah lay supine, her face just visible above

Jasper's left shoulder, her pale hands thrown out, as if in ecstasy, to either side. Jasper's body, cloaked in his trademark
duster, covered the rest of her body. Above them and to one side
lay the full black moon of his hat.

CHAPTER 23

By the time the rescue crew could reach them, Sarah had been dead many hours. Her body had cushioned the impact for Jasper, and he was taken, gravely injured, to the General Hospital. When they had done all they could for him, I was allowed to sit beside his bed. Most of his face and head were wrapped in bandages, his breathing barely perceptible. A nurse came in every ten minutes to check his pulse and the various fluid bottles surrounding him.

"He's not going to make it, is he?" I said.

"That's for the doctor to say."

The doctor, not one I had met, appeared half an hour later, going through the same routine as the nurse.

"He's not going to make it, is he?" I said again.

The doctor glanced at me, a quick scan head to toe. "You're Gascoyne? The one who found them?"

"Right. How long do you think he's got?"

"Maybe an hour," the doctor said, noting something in the chart. "Maybe less."

A few minutes after the doctor left, Jasper stopped breathing.

Even though I hadn't seen them fall, I was the principal witness at the inquest, which was held at Fortune Undertakers just two days later. The room held forty people, but there were others crowded around outside and across the street. The district attorney explained to the jurors that, should the evidence warrant, they could find death by misadventure, death by suicide, or even murder-suicide. In answer to the DA's questions, I told them how I first met Sarah, when she had just climbed out of the Saranac River. Dr. Taylor, who had been her physician at the time, testified that in his opinion this had not been a suicide attempt. As I was not an expert, my own opinion was not sought on the matter. He was more interested in my experience with Jasper and Sarah on the mountain, how Jasper on one manic winter's day had held Sarah in his belt over the precipice. In the present case, the belt had been found firmly in the loops of his coat.

Given the circumstances, I expected the jury would decide on death by misadventure, or perhaps suicide *and* misadventure — Sarah prepares to leap, Jasper dies reaching to save — though I did not think that was what happened. But the jurors found, on a balance of probabilities, for double suicide. I had and have no X-ray to see into their hearts — perhaps they simply preferred the idea of overwrought lovers. Certainly, the entire town was transfixed by what the papers were calling a romantic tragedy. My own view, which I cannot prove, is that Jasper once more performed his dancing-on-the-cliff routine and Sarah tried to stop him. The two of them tumbled, clinging together, and Jasper landed on top, which was why he survived, even if only for a few hours.

Two letters came for me at the Pryce cottage. The first was from Sarah's erstwhile "mother-in-law," Mrs. Ballard.

> *Dear Mr. Gascoyne,*
>
> *It was such a pleasure to make your acquaintance at Mrs. Pryce's Cottage, and I'm so sorry that the evening turned out so unhappily. Perhaps it will surprise you, but after I recovered from my initial shock, I came to understand how Sarah could have come to feel trapped in her assumed identity — an identity that I, as well as others, assumed for her. Mr. Ballard, slowly but surely, is also coming round to this view. We both have missed her terribly. Perhaps you think it strange that we should care so for a young woman to whom we are no relation and who arrived in our lives through accident and misunderstanding, but you must remember that we had just lost our son in the very atrocity that Sarah survived, and her own trusting and kind nature did the rest. I'm writing you now to ask if you think she might accept a visit from me. She and I shared many happy and affectionate days together and I find myself yearning to be with her again. And so I burden you with this request: that you would be so good as to "test the waters" and let me know Sarah's feelings on the matter. If, for some reason, you are unable*

or unwilling to do this, please let me know as
soon as possible, and enclose her present address
so that I might risk a more direct approach.

With every wish that we may soon meet again,
Mrs. Cyrus Ballard

The letter was postmarked the day before Sarah had gone missing, but the Ballards would have read the news by now. Nevertheless, I had to inform her that Sarah had died. This I did by telegram, but I also took pains over a letter and mailed it the same day. Like me, Mrs. Ballard had come around too late — more understandably in her case — and I tried to be as gentle as possible. I told her that Sarah had missed both her and her husband, felt deep affection toward them, and always spoke of them with wonder and gratitude. I tried to make the circumstances of Sarah's death as unsensational as possible, expressing firm disagreement with the inquest jury.

I became somewhat obsessed with the idea that if Sarah had not gotten on the *Lusitania*, she would never have met Jasper, and wouldn't have died. It didn't make sense, of course, but I did wonder why, having survived the traumas of betrayal, rape, and abortion, Sarah climbed aboard the doomed ship with her father. He presumably had the first investigative report with him, but not the second. So even if she had blamed her crisis on rape, he would not have believed her. And his jealous attachment to her had already been made plain. Why did she not quit the *Cameronia* and head right back to Dr. Boyard's? I have no definitive answer, but it seems likely that by that point she was just so beaten down that she surrendered to what must have felt like fate. What more could the gods possibly throw at her? Well, the gods had answered.

The second letter was from one Alistair Pearson, attorney-at-law, inviting me to a reading of the last will and testament of Miss Sarah Redmond, in which I had been named as a beneficiary. When, two months later, I sat down in the boardroom of Pearson, Park, and Randall, the elderly and all-but-blind Mr. Pearson informed me that I was not just a beneficiary but the *sole* beneficiary. I must have looked incredulous, because his scribbling secretary nodded vigorously at me in the affirmative.

The will was dated back in March, before Sarah had even asked me if I would accompany her to New Jersey to straighten out her real estate concerns. She was leaving the house and all its contents to me to dispose of as I might see fit but in the hope that I might one day use it as a place "to live happily and write many books." I looked to the secretary, who again — silently but vigorously — vouched for Pearson's accuracy. The old man then read a proviso that, should I decline the offer or die before being able to take advantage of it, the house and contents were to be sold and all proceeds were to go to the Sisters Hospital.

It was around this time that Charlie Sands came to see me, bearing the wooden box that contained Jasper's manuscript. There was nothing in it resembling a finished play, a second draft, or even a first draft of a play. Disparate scenes that featured Jasper's characteristic "jousting" style bore no connection to other, equally promising, scenes. They appeared to be from several different plays, none of them completed beyond act 1. For the first time since Jasper's death, I felt sorry for him. He was buried without fanfare in his hometown of Hartford, Connecticut, a place I had never heard him mention. The lack of attention to the death of a prominent playwright puzzled me, and it was only later that I learned what was behind it.

Investors in Jasper's projected third play discovered that his accounting practices were "unreliable." In his attempt to show the Shuberts and the Frohmans that there was still room for the actor-manager, he had made fatal errors. The full-page ads for his second play (which had gone a long way toward making his name) had come at an enormous cost — paid for out of the investors' funding for the third, unwritten play. He paid his actors almost double the accepted theatrical rate, and kept his second play in production long after it was losing money, including his own. The *Herald* termed his claims of huge profits "overenthusiastic"; investors called them fraud. It may be no defence, but one can see behind Jasper's vice of malfeasance the virtues that had made his plays and acting so popular — exuberance, plenitude, and his hell-or-high water willingness to take risks. Whatever else it was, his choice to cross a line and risk what didn't belong to him was completely in character. I can only guess that, despite his stellar performance as Broadway's hottest playwright, it was his guilty knowledge of what he had done, and dread of the consequences, that thwarted his attempt to write a third play.

Sister Mary Magdalene saw to the arrangements for Sarah's burial.

"There is no chance that young woman committed suicide," she told me. "She was getting better. She would have seen through that charlatan, she would have regained her health, and she would have married you."

Her certainty made me smile. "I doubt that she said that."

"*Oof.* It's just obvious. Completely obvious."

The sisters turned out in force, their white habits vivid against the cemetery greens and browns and blacks. A sizeable crowd formed around them, drawn by the breathless local coverage: "Accident or Lovers' Leap?" Despite the headline the *Enterprise* article was respectful of Sarah, mentioning her artistry, her father's "beloved" photographs, and her survival of the *Lusitania*. There was no mention of the earlier scandal concerning the Ballards.

Dr. Tissot asked me if I wanted to say a few words, but I told him I was not in any shape to speak. He gave a surprisingly good eulogy, and a minister from the United Church said the usual prayers. I broke down at "ashes to ashes," and did not regain my composure until people were filing out of the cemetery.

Dr. Tissot placed a hand on my shoulder. "Come and lunch with us. The wife has concocted a batch of her apple crumble."

"That's very kind," I said. "But I think I need a little longer before I'm fit company."

"Of course. One o'clock, if you change your mind."

Off in a corner of the cemetery, a smaller ceremony was wrapping up. The priest shook hands with a large man beside the grave and made his way toward St. Bernard's, missal in hand.

I walked over and introduced myself to Benny Barstowe.

"I remember you, Professor." He tapped his right temple. "I got a good memory for faces."

He put down the small suitcase he was holding to shake my hand.

"I'm sorry I couldn't be here for Ronnie," I said. "I had my own ..."

"You don't got to explain nothin."

"Ronnie was one of my favourites — even when he decided that radio and astronomy were more interesting than novels and poetry."

"Kid was interested in everything. Everything." The big man's voice caught a little. I don't know who started the idea that men don't cry; let this be my vote for banishing it.

"His enthusiasm always cheered me up."

"Yeah, Ronnie did that. Listen, that's a tough break about your lady. Miss Redmond. I never met her, but I seen you with her one day and I thought hey, that's one lucky professor. Some women — don't mean to be impolite or nothin — some women, you just see their face, it calls to you. You know what I mean?"

"I do. But she wasn't my lady, unfortunately."

"Don't sell yourself short, Professor. I seen youse two together and I know what's what." He picked up his suitcase.

"Sorry I don't got longer to talk, Professor. Train to catch. Thanks for teachin my kid brother."

"You're welcome. It was a complete pleasure."

"Oh, hey. You ever need help some way, you get in touch."

He reached into his coat pocket and pulled out a business card. It was blank, except for a post office box number.

A cemetery worker was filling in Sarah's grave. I walked the footpath past stone crosses and urns and weeping angels, past the headstones of the Catholics and of the Hebrews, past the section reserved for doctors and the shady plot of the Moodys, founding family of this city-sized sanitarium, the place where I had come to declare myself emancipated from the unwholesome coils of Romanticism, a modern twentieth-century man. It seemed unlikely I would ever become the writer Sarah and even Jasper thought I might.

Columns of sunlight angled through the trees. I remembered Sarah's comment about how walking in a graveyard made her an inverse ghost. My bad Juliet was inverse no longer.

I took a seat on the stone bench where we had enjoyed our picnic. I intended to remain for an hour or two, but all the emotions of the past few days, indeed of the entire year, had merged into absolute exhaustion. I wanted nothing more than my room and a nap. I got up and made my way across the cemetery and through the gate, leaving Sarah to lie at last with her colleagues.

AFTERWORD

Shortly after the events I have described I was called up, like so many young men, to serve in the U.S. Army. I survived basic training — but so barely that I was judged to be of less use on a battlefield than in the rapidly burgeoning art of counter-espionage. I'll save the details of that endeavour for another book. After the war I took up residence, briefly, in Sarah's New Jersey house but I could not bear the spectral presence of the girl who had lived there, and quickly sold the place. I never did write the kind of novel I had set out to. My wartime experience gave me a wealth of material that I mined for use in a series of spy novels that, to everyone's surprise including my own, became quite successful.

I didn't lose touch with Saranac Lake entirely. When Dr. Tissot died in 1922, I went back to attend his funeral and, partly as a result, became lifelong friends with his son, Daniel, who had become a physician and a lung specialist like his father. In addition to Daniel's many fine qualities, I think the friendship is based on my preference for the company of non-writers and his for the company of non-doctors.

The advent of antibiotics in the forties dealt a blow to the Adirondack Sanitarium, as it did to other TB centres and also to Saranac Lake. I have just come from the sanitarium's official closing, where I witnessed the departure of their last patient, former New York Giant second baseman Larry Doyle. *Life* magazine was there to cover the event. Many of the sanitarium's buildings are in disrepair, and the last of them will now be boarded up. The town itself is much diminished, with many empty houses bulky and oversized with their disused cure porches.

The Pryce cottage is still called the Pryce cottage, though it is now a private residence and Mrs. Pryce herself dead and buried in Queens alongside her husband, Broadway Ben Ladner. That they were meant for each other may have been the single correct observation I made in my entire sojourn in Saranac. It may not be a crucial lesson for an author, especially one as callow, pompous, and self-involved as I was, that he may misjudge people and get things wrong even when — especially when — he is most confident he is right, and yet I'm sure it must be a useful one. But then I would think that, wouldn't I.

New York City, 1954

ACKNOWLEDGEMENTS

My delineations of tuberculosis and its treatment in the early part of the last century are the result of extensive research and accurate to the best of my knowledge. The same is true of scenes involving the *Lusitania*. Amateur historians of Saranac Lake, an enthusiastic and knowledgeable bunch, may notice minor adjustments of geography and timeline. Any such adjustments are solely for the purposes of drama.

I had the assistance of several people in the writing of this book. Jane Warren, Dick Logan, Ann Logan, Janna Eggebeen, Heather Wright, and Jen Hale all read early versions of the manuscript and made helpful suggestions. I'm grateful to them all.

I owe a debt of thanks to Michelle Tucker at the Saranac Lake Free Library who found archival materials I would never have come across on my own. Sandra J. Hildreth gave me guidance on the realities of hiking the local mountains, and Chessie Monks-Kelly of Historic Saranac Lake was very helpful in my search for documents relating to the patients' emotional — as opposed to medical — experiences. And here's my special thanks to Chris Houston and Randall Perry for their invaluable support and encouragement.

I had the benefit of many books on Saranac Lake, and on the treatment of tuberculosis, but the one that first sparked my interest, and that I turned to again and again, was *Cure Cottages of Saranac Lake* by Philip L. Gallos. Readers who wish to know more about the reality behind my fiction could not do better than to start there.

G.B.

Toronto, 2025

ABOUT THE AUTHOR

GILES BLUNT was born in Windsor, Ontario, but spent his teenage years in North Bay, where he attended Scollard Hall. After studying English literature at the University of Toronto, he moved to England to write his first novel (never published). Following a stint as a social worker in Toronto, he moved to New York, where he lived for the next twenty years, working variously as a copy editor for *BusinessWeek* and a screenwriter for *Law and Order* and other TV shows. Eventually the success of the John Cardinal crime stories allowed him to write novels full time. The books won Britain's Crime Writers' Association's Silver Dagger award and the Crime Writers of Canada Award of Excellence (twice), and were twice nominated for the IMPAC award. They were eventually adapted into the *Cardinal* TV series, which aired to large audiences in more than one hundred countries. In recent years, Blunt has turned to literary fiction. In addition to *Bad Juliet*, he has written four other highly regarded standalone novels, including *Breaking Lorca*, which the *Globe and Mail* called "a tour de force ... an unforgettable window into the human capacity for cruelty and courage." He lives in Toronto with his wife and two cats.